HUNTER SHEA

SLASH

This is a FLAME TREE PRESS book

FLAME TREE PRESS
6 Melbray Mews, London, SW6 3NS, UK
flametreepress.com

Distribution and warehouse:
Baker & Taylor Publisher Services (BTPS)
30 Amberwood Parkway, Ashland, OH 44805
btpubservices.com

Publisher's Note: This is a work of fiction. Names, characters, places, and
incidents are a product of the author's imagination. Locales and public names
are sometimes used for atmospheric purposes. Any resemblance to actual
people, living or dead, or to businesses, companies, events, institutions, or
locales is completely coincidental.

Thanks to the Flame Tree Press team, including:
Taylor Bentley, Frances Bodiam, Federica Ciaravella, Don D'Auria,
Chris Herbert, Josie Karani, Molly Rosevear, Will Rough, Mike Spender,
Cat Taylor, Maria Tissot, Nick Wells, Gillian Whitaker.

The cover is created by Flame Tree Studio with
thanks to Nik Keevil and Shutterstock.com.
The font families used are Avenir and Bembo.

Flame Tree Press is an imprint of Flame Tree Publishing Ltd
flametreepublishing.com

A copy of the CIP data for this book is available from the British Library
and the Library of Congress.

HB ISBN: 978-1-78758-180-7
PB ISBN: 978-1-78758-178-4
ebook ISBN: 978-1-78758-181-4
Also available in FLAME TREE AUDIO

Printed and bound in Great Britain by Clays Ltd, Elcograf S.p.A.

HUNTER SHEA

SLASH

FLAME TREE PRESS
London & New York

"You're going to Camp Blood, ain't ya? You'll never come
back again. It's got a death curse!"
Crazy Ralph, *Friday the 13th*

"Was that the boogeyman?"
"As a matter of fact, it was."
Halloween

"Oh, I wish they hadn't let the place fall apart."
"Now it looks like the birthplace of Bela Lugosi."
The Texas Chainsaw Massacre

For the man who loves slasher movies
as much as me, Jason Kwap.

CHAPTER ONE

Ashley King powered down her laptop and wept.

The house was bright, the notes of birdsong drifting through the open windows. The twins next door, Ryder and Ronin, giggled as they ran between the houses, the slap of their tiny sneakered feet echoing in the narrow alley. Ash took a deep breath, savoring the aroma of the riot of flowers Todd had planted for her outside the living room and kitchen windows. The cross breeze worked better than any expensive air freshener she could buy.

Elvira leaped onto the dining room table. She swished her long black tail across Ashley's face.

"No walking on the table," she lightly scolded the cat, sniffing back her tears. She gently lifted Elvira off the table and walked her to the couch where she sat, petting her until the rescue cat purred loud enough to be heard on the other side of the house. It didn't take long for the old cat to fall asleep on her lap. There was so much to be done, but Ashley didn't want to disturb Elvira.

She looked over at the stack of crossword books on the end table and plucked the one she'd been working on from the top of the pile. Using her mouth to pull the cap off her pen, she dove back into the puzzle she'd almost finished last night. It wasn't easy, going to sleep when she knew there was an incomplete puzzle, but the sleeping pill had grabbed ahold of her and it didn't care how she felt about leaving things undone. Ashley had slipped into the darkness, dreaming of puzzles, the white and black squares leaping off the page, her body spinning through their intricacies, each answer spoken and then magically appearing within the empty boxes.

Elvira awoke just as she was writing down the last answer.

To leave a social engagement, missing out on the last bit.

She scribbled P-A-R-T in forty-six down and scratched Elvira between her pointy ears. The cat twisted her pointy ears, stared at

Ashley with wide orange eyes and yawned, showing her sharp canines and long pink tongue. Elvira had tiny bald patches behind her ears. The shelter had no idea exactly how old she was, but best guess she was hovering around fifteen. By the looks of her, it had been a rough fifteen years. Elvira had sat in the shelter for two years before Ashley brought her home. The cat was no looker, but she was a fighter.

"Todd is right. You really do look like a bat."

Elvira made a sound like a cooing pigeon that made Ashley start to cry all over again. Not wanting any part of the emotional turmoil, the cat plopped onto the floor and made her way to the kitchen, presumably to munch on the dry food in her bowl.

Ashley put the puzzle book back, got up and brushed the fur from her pants as best she could.

A heavy thump made her jump and cry out before she clamped her hand over her mouth. Her heart tripped over itself. Her throat went dry. She waited for a full minute, holding her breath, ears seeking out the source of the sound.

It came again and she instantly exhaled. Through the open blinds, she saw Mrs. Connover closing the doors to her car, her hands laden with shopping bags.

Rubbing her upper arms to quell the goose bumps, Ashley padded into the bedroom. The hallway light was on despite it being the middle of the day. She didn't like dark spaces, even if they were only seven feet long with nowhere for someone or something to hide. Which was why she had to take the sleeping pills at night. She couldn't leave all of the lights on when Todd was trying to sleep. Besides, their energy bill would be more than they could bear if she had her way when the dark of night crept in like an intruder.

She made the bed, Todd's side rumpled from his tossing and turning, the sheet by hers barely creased from the drug-induced coma that held her in place like a corpse in a coffin. The hamper was empty, the last load in the dryer. Ash emptied the pink-and-purple wastebasket into the kitchen garbage, came back to the bedroom and stripped. She lay on the comforter, the chill wind hardening her nipples. Fall would be here soon. October would bring the changing colors, crunch of leaves underfoot, pumpkins on doorsteps and longer nights.

Shivering, Ash refused to grab a blanket. It was best to let the cold wash over her – the cold and the light and the soft ticking of the grandfather clock that had been in her family for four generations. Her mother had insisted she take it when she moved in with Todd in the home he'd bought for them. "You're never alone when that clock is in your house," she'd said, tears shimmering in her eyes as she saw Ash off to her new life.

Ash had never been exactly sure what her mother had meant, and always forgot to ask her when they spoke. Did she mean the spirits of her grandparents were attached to the clock, making the move with her from Nyack to Yorktown? The family story went that Ashley's great-grandparents had taken the clock with them when they emigrated from Kenya. It was the only possession besides their clothes that made the long, oceanic journey. It might have been the only thing they truly owned, their clothes ragged hand-me-downs. The grandfather clock (or in Ashley's case, great-grandfather clock) had a place of prominence in their home until they died. Ashley's Grandpa Charles had once told her that he saw the reflection of his parents in the clock face glass many years after they had passed. Instead of being afraid, a young Ashley, who grew up on a steady diet of ghost shows and videos, had been entranced. She couldn't count the number of hours she'd sat at the foot of that old clock, hoping to catch a glimpse of her great grandparents, and then of Grandpa Charles and Grams Iris when they'd passed away within weeks of each other.

No one had ever stared back at her and she grew up and grew tired of seeking the ghosts of her family tree.

Or did her mother mean that the steady, assuring ticking of the clock would be her companion through the long nights and empty days? What she had never grasped was how Ashley preferred the silence, for within the soundless void, she would be able to hear... things, if they came near.

Things like the closing of a car door that nearly give you a heart attack, she thought. She put her hand between her breasts and felt the more assured beat of her heart, practically falling in rhythm with the ticking of the clock. Ash lifted her head and looked at her tawny skin. There were plenty of scars, but she did her best to never linger on them. Todd always marveled at what he called her perfect skin, especially when he was atop her, or she atop him, pausing to tell her how beautiful she was and how lucky he was for having her, all of her, in that moment. Her skin was far from perfect, though he loved her, warts – or scars – and all.

But he'd never really had all of her and deep down, she knew he knew it too, and that would make her sad. She'd bury her sadness down deep, lest she spoil the moment. There were very few *moments*, and Todd deserved to enjoy them as much as was possible, all things considered.

More tears came. Ash let them roll down her face, the comforter absorbing the wet droplets of her DNA. She wondered, as her mind found it hard not to wonder, even in times of great sorrow, if the day would come soon when science could clone a new Ashley from the dried-up tears in her comforter. Would Ashley 2.0 have the same emotions and memories? God, she hoped not. A clone should be a better, brighter you.

"Sheri!"

Her best friend, the friend she hadn't been able to find for the past terrifying hour, stopped before entering the darkened bungalow. Ash's chest ached and her thighs and calves burned. She'd heard Jamal's screams and come out of her hiding place amidst the rubble of the burned-out theater.

Sheri's jacket was torn down the front, white stuffing puffing out. The moment she saw Ash, she started crying.

"Oh my God, Ashley!"

Ash started running. The bungalow seemed like a much better place to hide and she would be with Sheri.

Sheri waved her on, swiveling her head back and forth, wary, afraid.

Moonlight glinted off the polished surface of the glass as it sliced out of the gloom. Ash didn't have time to warn her friend. The glass, appearing to hover in the air by itself, slashed at the back of Sheri's lower leg. There was a cry of sheer agony. Sheri collapsed, hands flailing for her leg. The glass struck again, and this time Ash was close enough to hear the rending of fabric, the awful piercing of flesh and muscle. Blood spattered the ground and doorway.

"Help me! Ash, please help me!"

Almost there. Ash's legs pumped as hard and fast as they would go. Sheri scrabbled at the dirt, trying to pull herself away.

The glass came again, slicing deeper into the same awful gash.

Sheri wailed, rolling onto her back.

He stepped out of the shadows.

Ash hesitated. Her overriding fear refused to pump more blood and adrenaline to her legs.

Sheri raised her hands defensively and screamed.

A heavy foot crashed down on her chest.

The breaking of her bones echoed throughout the ruins.

Sheri's screaming devolved into desperate gasps, then choking.

The glass came down again.

Ash closed her eyes. She couldn't make herself watch.

"Sheeeeerrrrriiiiiii!"

Ash woke up gasping. She was covered in sweat. For a moment, she couldn't move her body. Animation returned in a flash and she jumped from the bed, trying to catch her breath.

In an instant, the nightmare was gone. But the feelings of dread and guilt and loss remained.

"Jesus."

She looked down at her legs, touched her chest and face. Sleep often came like that – suddenly, unexpected. Just as it often ended with her dazed, bewildered and empty.

Ash ripped the comforter from the bed. Still naked, she strode past the open windows into the laundry room, stuffing it, along with two capfuls of detergent, into the washer. Elvira watched her from her perch on the windowsill.

Her phone rang. She dashed to the living room where she'd left it. It was an unknown number. She swiped the call away.

The grandfather clock chimed three o'clock.

A floorboard creaked. She whirled around, hands raised in a mix of self-defense and awkward offense. Elvira stopped to look up at her jumpy master, licking her lips.

"I can't take this." Ash put her hand on her stomach, practically feeling the knot of dread that was always there, a new, unwanted organ, more useless than an appendix. It took her a few moments to settle down, her mouth watering as she fought the urge to puke.

Once she felt her legs were steady enough, she went to her closet and found the clear plastic laundry bag she'd stuffed at the very end of her clothes rack. She laid it on the bed and pulled the zipper. Her fingers brushed against the torn shirt, the stains on her jeans having faded with time into varying shades of brown blotches and splashes. The ragged tears in her jeans looked like attempts to be hip and fashionable, though they were anything but that. Scissors had not been carefully applied to make those rents in the fabric.

At the bottom of the closet were the boots that had also been relegated to its darkest corner. Mud and blood still clung to them, had become one with them.

Reaching into the bottom of the bag, she found the framed picture of her and her best friend, Sheri Viola. They were wearing their cheerleader uniforms, smiling, arm in arm outside the football field, their dark skin in beautiful contrast to the white and gold uniforms. The picture had been snapped in their senior year just before the last game of the season. Everyone said Sheri looked like a young Halle Berry and they were right. Her short hair, sharp cheekbones and penetrating eyes made guys weak in the knees. Ash let her fingers linger on Sheri's face. She would give anything to touch her now, to hear her voice one more time, to listen to her laughter.

After slipping into fresh panties, she put on her comfy bra, and searched for a pair of thick socks and well-worn jeans. They were very loose at the waist, so she had to rummage around her dresser drawer for a belt. The shirt came on last. She thought she could smell the place and everything that went on that night, all of it caught in the amber of the cotton shirt.

She looked in the mirror hung on the inside of the closet door.

"Hello, Lara," she said to her reflection.

There was a time her body had filled her 'Tomb Raider' outfit quite nicely. Now she looked like a little kid wearing her big sister's ratty old clothes. Her collarbone peeked out from the open V of her shirt, a prominent ridge that alarmed everyone who knew her. She buttoned up the shirt so she couldn't see it.

The boots were stiff as wood, one of the laces breaking off in her hand when she tried to tie them. Wriggling her foot, she figured the boot was on tight enough. At least her feet hadn't shrunk.

Fighting back the urge to cry yet again, she walked out of the bedroom, making a tour of each room in the house from top to bottom, stopping to make adjustments here and there. When Elvira went to follow her into the basement, she picked her up and put her on a chair. "No basement for you, E." She kissed the cat on the nose and closed the door behind her.

Todd had plans to build a man cave down here after they were married. Until then, the quasi-finished basement was a place to store all of their boxes and plastic bins. They'd been in the house for almost a year now, but still had a ton to go through. Her mother had bequeathed them enough Christmas ornaments to decorate two trees. Those bins were stacked in a corner, going all the way to the ceiling. Her mother loved Christmas so much, Ash often joked that she'd been born in the North Pole and raised by elves. Ash was tempted to open one of the boxes, but knew if she did, she'd fall through the rabbit hole of Christmas memories.

Picking up what she needed from Todd's workbench, she leaned against a table sagging under the weight of tiles that were one day destined to go in the bathroom down there. She took out her phone and went to the page she'd bookmarked, starting the video and turning up the sound.

How many times had she watched it? Twenty? Fifty? She knew it by heart. Every word. Every movement. But for some reason, at this moment, her memory was failing her.

Ash watched it once from start to finish, and then hit replay.

It was time to get to work.

CHAPTER TWO

"You guys still on for this weekend?"

Todd Matthews slipped into the left lane, eager to get out from behind the big car carrier. The Honda in the back bounced dangerously every time there was the slightest dip in the road. He could just see it breaking loose and heading right for his windshield.

"So far so good," he said through the Bluetooth system in his car. "But you know how it is."

"Yeah, I know," his friend Vince Embry replied. Todd could hear a TV on in the background.

"Aren't you supposed to be at work?" he asked.

Vince chuckled. "I am at work. Today's office just happens to be a sports bar. I get more done here in an hour than a full day at corporate. No one around to bug me and beer keeps me motivated."

"I wish I could pull that off."

"You can if you let me give your resume to my boss. He really liked you when you met him at that office picnic."

Spotting his exit coming up, Todd put on his signal and drifted into the right lane. He'd stopped to pick up a bottle of wine and was running late. He was about to call Ash to let her know when Vince rang. His buddy was a world-class talker and would probably still be yapping when Todd pulled into the driveway.

"I can't see myself spending all day staring at spreadsheets and sitting in meetings," Todd said. "I'd lose my mind within a week."

"You get used to it."

"No thanks."

"The money's decent and the benefits are great."

"And I'd have to wear khakis and polo shirts with loafers. No thanks, bro. I'm too young to look like my father and his friends."

"So, looking professional makes me an old dork?" Vince said. He took a loud sip from his beer, the sound filling the car's interior. Todd winced.

"Actually, yes. Yes it does."

There was a slight pause, then Vince said, "You're right. But I have a great 401K and dental."

"I'd never live long enough to cash out that 401K if I had to be stuck in an office," Todd said. His house was just two blocks away. He had to wait for a group of pre-teens to cross the street. They took their sweet-ass time. Todd wanted to rev the engine and shake them up, but he remembered being just like them when he was a kid. There was nothing quite like the narcissistic worldview of a twelve-year-old. People Todd's age barely existed and were to be ignored.

"You know, most construction guys end up with all kinds of physical issues by the time they're fifty. You want to be a bent, broken old man before your time?"

The kids finally passed and Todd hit the gas.

"Yep," he said.

"You should be here right now. The new shift just came in and there's a girl here who's so hot, she might set the bar on fire."

"Look but don't touch," Todd said.

"Not even just a little?"

Todd gripped the wheel. "Window-shopping only. Heather would cut off your dick and feed it to the dogs."

"Dude, I was only joking. But we're talking exceptional here. Like Zoe Saldana with Pam Grier's body. Right up your alley. I'll take a picture and send it to you."

"You do that and I'll kill you. Last thing I need is Ash seeing pictures of other women on my phone." He realized then that Vince had had one beer too many. "Go back to your spreadsheet, settle up your tab and go to your hotel room to beat off."

"You're a wise man. Think I'll keep my black dress socks on while I do it." When Todd's disgust couldn't be contained, Vince chuckled and said, "Just wanted to leave you with that image."

Todd hung up on Vince's laughter, cutting off the engine as he parked in his driveway. All of the blinds were open as usual so Ashley could allow the maximum amount of sunlight in. He grabbed his lunch pail and wine and locked the car.

"Guess who's home?" he called out, making sure to kick off his steel-toed boots in the vestibule. Elvira came trotting over, gave him a look and meowed before moving on. "Nice to see you too."

Todd was more a dog than a cat person, but Ash had taken to Elvira immediately, so he'd had to suck it up. The cat was never going to be his best friend, but they had maintained a peaceful respect for one another. Plus, Elvira was downright ugly. He'd woken up several times to that battered, balding face and thought he'd fallen into a fresh nightmare.

"Hey Ash, I got that cabernet you wanted to try. It was cheap too. At least it doesn't have a screw top."

He went right to the kitchen, found the wine opener in the junk drawer and popped the cork. He didn't know if ten-dollar wines needed to breathe, but he was determined not to be a heathen.

"Ash?"

Unbuttoning his stained work shirt, he tromped to the bedroom. Sometimes, when her anxiety really hit hard, she would pop a couple of Ativan and zonk out. She slept much better, much sounder, in the daytime, and the pills helped give her a reset when she needed it. He wished to hell he could make her fear of the dark go away, but he was smart enough to know it was out of his control. What he could do was provide a safe place for her and be there when she needed him. Any higher aspirations would just lead to frustration.

He did a double take when he saw the bed was empty.

It wasn't like her to not be home. Her car was still in the driveway.

Maybe she's with Claire, he thought. Claire Pozzo was recently divorced and had started a love affair with wine and younger men. She loved to regale Ash with her latest exploits. When Todd asked Ash why she liked Claire so much, she'd said, "I think it's because she's, well, light and airy. There's no darkness or sadness there. Her marriage sucked, she got out with no reservations, and she's happy. I like visiting her glow."

Visiting her glow. That was such an Ashley thing to say.

Or it had been, before everything went to hell. The fact that Claire resurrected that small part of his fiancée made him like her too.

He checked his phone. No text.

Heading back to the kitchen and dining room, he looked around to see if he'd missed a note.

Ash never left to go anywhere without leaving a trail.

Where the hell was she?

Todd's chest grew tight.

"Ashley?"

He was about to run outside and check the backyard when he saw the basement door was open a crack.

Of course.

The basement was so full of boxes and junk it was practically a soundproofed room. Ash had been threatening to bring order to the chaos down there for months. The second he opened the door all the way, Elvira dashed ahead of him, nearly causing him to fall headlong down the stairs.

"Your cat tried to kill me...again," he said as he descended the creaky wood steps. "I may have to get a restraining order against her."

Something smelled strange. It was a pungent combination of ammonia and shit. Just great. Now the cat was using the basement as a litter box. It was bad enough she liked to pee in the tub.

Sniffing, Todd made the turn into the main room. "I swear, Ash, this cat—"

Ashley's blue face and bulging eyes turned lazily several feet off the basement floor.

"No!"

Todd sprinted across the room and grabbed her around her waist, shouldering her weight.

Her dead weight.

Blinded by tears, he struggled to extricate her from the noose. He reached up to feel her chest, to hope for signs of a beating heart. Her pungent excrement that had dripped down her legs stained his arms and shirt. He cried her name over and over until his throat was raw. He didn't want to let her go. If there was any chance she was still alive, he had to prop her up, allow her to breathe. But he had to find a way to cut her down. She couldn't remain trapped in the noose forever.

Todd held on tight, draining his tears into her cold, lifeless body.

CHAPTER THREE

"Do you want something to eat?"

Heather Embry looked at Todd with the same pitying look every single person had given him over the past three days. They had left Ashley's coffin at the cemetery four hours ago. He sat at the kitchen table, away from the crush of mourners that had flocked to his house – his and Ash's home – after the funeral. He wondered if the coffin was still there, or if it had been lowered into the oblong grave?

Had they piled dirt onto it yet? Was she now truly gone? For some reason, as long as she was above the ground, he felt she was still here, still a part of his life. The moment his love was buried beneath clods of soft, heavy earth, she would be lost to him forever.

There was no rationality to the way he felt but he didn't give a solitary shit. He stared into space, desperately seeking some kind of tether to Ash. Would he feel it in his heart, in his soul, the moment she was sealed away from him? Could anything penetrate the throbbing sorrow that was making him more and more numb by the second?

"Todd, honey, you should eat something."

Heather wore a black dress with a white scarf. She'd taken it upon herself to handle the post-funeral dinner. Aluminum serving trays were scattered all throughout the kitchen and dining room. There was enough food to feed a football team and more.

For the first time, Todd noticed the house was quiet.

"Where is everyone?" he asked, his mouth so dry it hurt to talk.

"They left about a half an hour ago. Vince and I saw them all out. Everybody understands." She squeezed his shoulder.

He had barely registered a word that had been said to him all day, so it was no surprise he didn't even mark their leaving.

Heather held an empty plate. The thought of eating made him nauseous.

"I'm not hungry," he said.

Heather sighed. "I can't force you, but you haven't had a bite in days."

She was right. The last thing he'd put in his stomach had been his lunch the day he'd found Ash hanging in the basement. Two ham and cheese sandwiches, a pear and a bag of chips. His painfully empty stomach should have growled at the thought, but it was as dull and dead as the rest of him.

He was grateful Heather didn't press him. Instead, she went about cleaning the kitchen. He heard Vince in the living room straightening things.

"Where's my mother?" he asked. He was finding it hard to concentrate. Even his vision was blurred. Whether it was from tears or exhaustion he didn't know or care.

"Henry drove her to the hotel. You don't remember?"

He rubbed his eyes. His mother had said something to him, but was that today or yesterday? She hadn't looked well. Ashley's death had devastated her. It had wrecked them all.

To have survived what she had gone through only to go out at the end of a rope.

Why was that rope even there? He didn't need it. It wasn't as if he was one to tie things up or save people from the bottom of a well. Why in the fuck did he buy it? If it hadn't been there....

"I'm going to call and check on her in a little bit," Heather said, blissfully unaware of how much he hated himself. "Today was...too much for her." Tears rolled down her cheeks. "She needed to lie down. If I don't keep busy, I'll be just the same."

She wiped her eyes with the back of her hand and went back to spooning leftovers into plastic containers. Her stifled sob barely reached Todd's ears. He knew he should get up and console her. She was Ash's best friend – or had been since Sheri had been killed. He willed his legs to stand, but they wouldn't obey.

Vince came in with a stack of plates. Todd caught his eye, and then turned away.

"I want to see Ash," he said.

The plates rattled when Vince put them in the sink.

"What was that?"

Todd turned to stare at him. "I need you to take me to see Ash."

Vince leaned against the counter. Heather put an arm around her husband, almost the same way Todd had wrapped his arms around Ash's body as it dangled from the noose.

"You know you can't do that, buddy," Vince said. His eyes, like everyone's the past couple of days, were red and raw.

The chair scraped against the floor when Todd stood, and banged against the wall. "I'm going."

Vince grabbed his arm as he went for the car keys on the hook attached to the cabinet. "No. You're in no shape to drive. I'll take you."

The sudden urge to go to Ash felt like the unleashing of a captured bolt of electricity in Todd's core. He'd been sleepwalking without the benefit of sleep for the past few days. Now he had energy to burn. His finger thrummed against his thigh as he waited for Vince to part from Heather, the couple exchanging words that might as well have been spoken in a foreign language.

"Okay, let's go, bud," Vince said, his hand pressed to Todd's back as they walked to the car.

Vince tried to help him into the car, but Todd shrugged free from his grasp. He wanted to get to the cemetery as quickly as possible. Before….

Before.

"It should be raining," Todd said dreamily. Sunlight sprayed over the changing leaves. Ash loved the fall. Since her suicide – a stabbing pain creased his stomach every time he even thought of the word – the nights had been hit with an early frost. The leaves were morphing into their fall palette more and more each morning.

Vince took the entrance to the highway. "Why do you say that?"

"It always rains in the movies, doesn't it? When you bury someone you love."

Vince's mouth retracted into a thin, almost imperceptible line. "Yeah, I guess it does."

Heaven's Passage Cemetery was only ten minutes away but it felt to Todd as if they were on a cross-country trip. He didn't even wait for the car to stop before opening his door and clambering out.

"Todd, wait!"

She was still here!

Ashley's coffin sat upon the contraption that would eventually lower her into the cold and hungry ground. Several men milled about, all heads snapping his way as he ran.

I knew you were still here!

"I can still feel you!" he shouted. Vince's hurried footsteps ghosted him.

The men backed away as Todd draped his body over the coffin. Days of tears suddenly burst from the dam of his grief.

"I can still feel you."

The wood was cold and slick. He pressed his face against the coffin, muttering her name over and over. When Vince went to touch him he lashed out. "Leave me alone!"

He knew, he knew, he knew. All along, he knew she hadn't been buried yet. Her absence hadn't felt…complete. Now that these men were here to take her good and fully away from him, the impending emptiness was too much to bear.

He didn't know how long he stood there, his arms hugging her coffin, racking sobs making his ribs and spine sore.

"Come on," Vince whispered close to his ear. "We have to go."

Todd ignored him.

How could Vince be so eager to leave Ash? She was his friend too. Didn't he love her? Didn't he miss her?

Now his friend's hands were on him, trying to gently tug him away. Todd's muscles bunched, his feet digging into the upturned earth around the coffin.

"Ashley."

They were going to take him away from her. Vince and these strangers would intervene, sooner rather than later. He knew it.

Your face. I need to see your beautiful face one more time.

He ignored the fact that the mortician couldn't erase what death by slow strangulation had done to her. At the wake, Todd had found it near impossible to look inside the coffin. The few glimpses he did take showed him someone who looked like a plastic, distant relative to his fiancée. But it wasn't her.

Would she be different, this close to leaving him forever? He had to see. He had to see and touch her one last time.

Todd struggled with the lid.

Men shouted around him.

The coffin lid wouldn't budge. Why was it locked? Did they think she was alive and would try to get out? Were they conspiring to keep her from him?

Todd grunted and his fingers sought the seam, several nails breaking off as he tried to pry it open.

And then multiple hands and arms were on him, dragging him away. He was locked in their evil embrace as surely as Ash was locked in the coffin.

Todd shouted her name until black spots jittered and whooshed in his vision. Her coffin, his fiancée, grew smaller and smaller as he was pulled farther and farther from her, the inexorable tug of a black hole sucking him in until there was nothing but an icy, indifferent darkness.

CHAPTER FOUR

The flowers on his doorstep confused Todd when he went out to get the paper. His brain was still wrapped in a dull fog, the sleeping pill he'd taken the night before making him groggy. He hadn't wanted to take the pill, but his mother had insisted. She'd even slept over to make sure he did.

It had been two weeks since the funeral. So many flowers had been sent to the funeral parlor and the house that first week, he thought he could open a florist shop. That was the way it was when someone young passed on. In Ashley's case, there were ten times the typical allotment of sympathy bouquets because of her so-called celebrity status.

He stooped down to pluck the card from the little plastic holder sticking out amidst the pink carnations.

REST IN PEACE, FINAL GIRL. MAY GOD GIVE YOU STRENGTH AND COMFORT.

Todd crumpled the note and stuffed it in his robe pocket. He grabbed the flowers, walked purposefully to the side of the house and dropped them in the trash. He leaned on the lid for a few moments, blinded by his anger, waiting for the swell of sudden rage to be swept away.

"Hi Mr. Todd."

It was Ronin, the boy next door, whose hair was a perpetual ragged mop. The kid was a bundle of energy, always on the move. Todd and Ash had once watched him do somersaults on his lawn for over an hour. They eventually had to turn away, feeling exhausted, and they hadn't even moved a muscle.

Todd took a breath and put on a fake smile. "Hey Ronin. Where's your sister?"

The twins were inseparable. At least his sister Ryder could sit still for periods of time.

Ronin shrugged his bony shoulders. "She's sick or something. Mom said she can't come outside today."

"I'm sorry to hear that."

Todd was setting off to go back inside when Ronin said, "I miss Miss Ashley."

The pure sincerity in the kid's voice nearly stopped Todd's heart. He fought against the beast that was his sorrow and said, "Yeah. Me too."

"She was the only big person who liked to play with us." There might have been an accusation there, but Todd couldn't register it. He could only nod and hurry into the house so the boy didn't see the tears that had sprung from his eyes.

He leaned against the door, using his sleeve to sop up the tears.

First anger. Now sadness. It was too early for this.

"They forget to deliver the paper?" his mother asked from the kitchen. He heard the scrape of the whisk in a plastic bowl, which meant she was whipping up her maple pancakes. She could see him through the mirror in the living room.

Todd looked at his empty hands. He'd forgotten the paper. He slipped outside, found it between the potted mums to the right of the porch, and dropped it on the dining room table. "I almost forgot."

She came out carrying a bowl of lumpy batter. "Something wrong?"

There was no point trying to hide anything from her. She knew all his tells and was relentless.

"More flowers," he said.

"Oh."

"Another final girl weirdo. I threw them away."

She leaned into him and put her arm across his shoulders. "Whoever it was, they meant well."

He extracted the paper from the plastic bag and unfolded it. The headlines meant nothing to him. He'd fallen completely out of touch the past two weeks and no longer cared about politics or murders or the latest insipid celebrity gossip.

"All those well-meaning, anonymous assholes killed her," he said, his strong hands crushing the edges of the newspaper.

His mother kept silent, kissing the top of his head and going back into the kitchen to put the pancakes on the griddle. She turned on the radio, and hit the seek button until she found the classic rock station. The sizzle of pancakes played under the thunderous beat of Cheap Trick.

Todd's gaze drifted to the window looking out the side of the house. The trash cans were under that window.

Final girl.

The last thing Ashley ever wanted to be was a final girl. Who would? It was bad enough that she had to live with the memory of that night. To have to be reminded of it constantly was more than she, or anyone, could bear. How the hell was she supposed to ever heal and find some semblance of recovery when the world seemed bent on making her relive the horror day in and day out?

She could have lived in peace if it wasn't for you freaks, he thought.

The post-traumatic stress that Ash suffered from was some of the worst her doctors had ever seen. And these were men and women who had treated hundreds of people straight from the throes of combat in theaters all around the world. Todd and her parents had accompanied her on countless trips to Manhattan for therapy, sometimes six days a week. They went to the top recommended therapists and psychiatrists in the country, spending more money than they cared to watch fly out of their savings accounts. Todd often wondered if it was possible to ever put Ash back together again. He vowed that no matter what happened, as long as she would allow him, he would never leave her side. He'd already lost her once. He was determined not to lose her again.

He did, anyway.

Those final girl vultures did what a psycho killer couldn't.

"Here you go." His mother placed a plate of pancakes in front of him. She'd warmed up the syrup, steam rising from the small creamer glass Ash had giddily found at a tag sale last year. For all of the darkness that hovered over Ash, one of the things that lit her up was collecting all kinds of unique glassware. The cabinets were filled with singular glasses and service bowls. No two things matched, as she preferred finding lone, misfit items at garage sales and flea markets. "Now, eat up and get changed. I don't want to miss my plane."

Todd poured a few drops of syrup on his pancakes. He was

suddenly far from hungry, but it was better to choke at least one pancake down than suffer his mother telling him to eat until he did. He was grateful that she had stayed with him throughout this ordeal, but also looking forward to being alone.

"Your plane takes off in five hours," he replied. "You couldn't be late if we walked to the airport."

She patted his shoulder. "Those security lines take forever."

He nearly choked on the dry wedge of pancake. Forever was exactly how long Ash was gone.

His mother pulled out a chair and sat beside him. "And you can't let the people who followed Ash get to you. In their own way, they're in mourning too."

Todd dropped his fork. "They didn't even know her. They don't have the right."

Her somber, pale eyes softened. "You can't control how they feel. Or what they feel. They didn't kill Ashley. She was such a strong girl. But I don't know anyone who was strong enough to... to..."

He took a deep, hitching breath and held her hand. "I know, Ma. I know. I just can't make myself believe they didn't play their part. At least the man who did what he did to her is gone. These final girl cultists never go away." Todd had wanted Ash to change her name and move away with him to another state, maybe New Hampshire, and simply disappear. She'd refused, saying the killer had taken so much from her, she wasn't going to let him take her identity too.

"But they will. Let them grieve. They'll fade away before you know it. You'll see."

She got up to clean the kitchen while Todd forced himself to finish the top pancake. He tossed the rest in the garbage when her back was to him.

He was heading to the bedroom when she said, "You know you can call me anytime."

"I know."

"Even if it's just to talk about nothing."

"Yeah." He was surprisingly anxious to get in the shower. He'd been cooped up in the house for weeks and the thought of going to the airport was oddly refreshing.

"Do you have any plans for next week?" she said.

His foreman had bumped his bereavement leave from one week to three once he'd seen him at the wake. Everyone told Todd that work would help take his mind off things, help with the healing process.

But he had other work in mind.

"Not really. I have a dinner invitation from Vince and Heather and I need to take the car in for an inspection and oil change. Nothing exciting."

"Try to keep busy. If I hadn't when your father died, I don't know what would have happened to me."

Before he closed his bedroom door – it used to be *their* bedroom door – he muttered, "Oh, I will."

He had plans.

He just didn't think his mother would approve.

CHAPTER FIVE

The Killer Podcast had been one of Ash's favorites, though Todd could never understand why she wanted to subject herself to two idiots who probably never left their basements babbling about serial killers and their victims. When pressed, she would say that if she could understand why a person would do what that man had done to her and her friends, she might find a way to put it all behind her.

Poor Ash and her puzzles. She couldn't leave one unsolved. She would have made a great detective, so long as she was allowed to work on one mystery at a time until the culprit was apprehended or the mystery laid to rest.

Todd didn't see the appeal of podcasts. He preferred music to amateurs with microphones. But Ash loved them, downloading new episodes of dozens of podcasts every week. She never missed an episode of *The Killer Podcast*. He always knew when she'd listened to it because she would get quiet and introspective, answering him in monosyllables. He saw her mind desperately trying to unravel her own personal mystery, and hell, taking her to a place and a night he could not follow.

The hosts, Jay and John, at least did their homework, tackling each crime with tons of research. Their devotion to such a twisted subject sickened him. What kind of people would choose to wade in this kind of muck and madness and sorrow?

Rubbernecking freaks. That's what they and all the final girl followers were.

The Killer Podcast had interviewed the older brother of Jamal Banks two years ago. Todd and Jamal had played together on the bowling team in their junior year of high school. They were friendly but never friends. Ash had met Jamal through him and they had hit if off in a completely platonic way. Jamal had been with Ash on just about every one of her urban exploration jaunts. His brother blamed her for Jamal's death. Not the Wraith, who he and many others were convinced was a passing, homeless lunatic either high on drugs or criminally insane. There would have been no Wraith if they hadn't been there at the wrong time.

Jamal's brother (why couldn't Todd remember his name?) went on an unedited diatribe against Ash and the cult of final girl followers who gave her fame.

"Ashley King should be the one in the fucking ground, not my brother!"

When Ash had heard that episode, it had nearly broken her all over again. She hadn't slept or eaten for days. She just cried. She didn't want to be touched or consoled. Todd listened to the podcast and wanted to hop in a plane to New Mexico where Jamal's brother was living and beat the living daylights out of him.

All that week, Ash wept and Todd fumed. She was the first to regain her composure.

"Leave him be. Pray for him," she'd said out of the blue one night. He'd been watching TV but not watching and she came out of the bedroom, her eyes red but clear for the first time since the podcast aired.

"Fuck him."

"No. He's processing a tragedy. Or not processing it. And in some ways, he's right. But not entirely. No matter, he's entitled to feel any way he wants."

Jamal's body had been found in two parts. A jagged stone had been used to cut through his abdomen and spine. From what police could tell, the killer had jammed his fingers into Jamal's eye sockets so he could carry his top half like a bowling ball. His legs had been stomped post mortem until the bones were merely pebbles wrapped in sinew.

"I can't pray for him," Todd had said.

"Then I'll pray for both of us."

Ash had prayed often.

Todd had willfully forgotten how to make the sign of the cross.

He tapped the sides of his head with his palms to chase the memories away, and opened his laptop and found the email from *The Killer Podcast*. They had an assistant, Hilary, who had been communicating with him. She'd rearranged their schedule the moment Todd reached out to her. The name Ashley King held a lot of power in their sick world. The fact that her grieving fiancé wanted to be on the show called for all hands on deck. They normally recorded at eight pm every Tuesday, but Todd insisted he would only do the show on Monday morning. It was a lame attempt at jerking them around, but they didn't hesitate to alter their schedule. He hoped they were missing a day of work at Walmart for this.

He had to have a very early morning beer to temper his nerves before he connected with them on Skype. He wasn't worried about being on a podcast, so much as wanting to keep his cool, at least in the beginning.

Headphones on and sitting back in his chair, Todd found their name on Skype and connected the video call. It took a few moments before he heard one of them say, "Hey, Todd, thanks for being on time. We can't say that about most guests." It was followed by brief, nervous laughter.

It took several more seconds until the black screen was replaced by live video of John and Jay.

"I thought this was only audio," Todd said, already bristling.

The one with the red hipster beard and black-rimmed glasses smiled and reassured him. "We only use the audio for the podcast, but we think it's important to be able to see the person we're talking to. You can lose nuances without the video."

We wouldn't want to lose any nuances, Todd thought.

"Hi, I'm Jay," the other one, a thin guy with sunken cheeks and the pallor of a corpse, said, giving a small wave. He looked like he was in desperate need of an IV and feeding tube. "I apologize for not mentioning this in our email. I'm so used to it, I just don't think about it. Is it okay with you? If not, we can always drop the call and do straight audio."

"No, it's fine," Todd replied. He wondered if they'd caught on to his skipping any pleasantries. He was sure they could read his face and tell instantly he was not a fan.

All part of the nuance.

John scratched his beard and said, "Let me just start by saying Ashley and you and your families are in our prayers. When the news broke, it was devastating. She meant a lot to a ton of people and it's horrible it ended the way it did."

I'm sure the news wasn't near as devastating as finding her body hanging in the basement, Todd thought. His expression must have given him away because Jay gave a worried look and jumped in. "I know this is a hard time for you. You don't know how much we appreciate your reaching out to us. If at any moment you want to stop, just say the word."

Todd had the feeling Jay would try to convince him to go on if he were to throw up the white flag. He could see it in his cadaverous eyes. These guys were hungry for Ash's story, no matter how tragic. They were beyond vultures. They were demonic.

Swallowing back a ball of bile, Todd said, "Thank you. It was…a shock." Though when he was tired and couldn't hold his emotions in check, he flitted upon the realization that her suicide was no surprise at all. Maybe he should have been more astounded that she'd lasted as long as she had. He hoped he'd at least given her some moments of normalcy in the five years they'd been together since the massacre.

John said, "We're not big on pre-show preamble. It robs the spontaneity from the interview. So we'll just do a ten-second countdown and start the show."

"You don't have to hold back on language," Jay intoned. "There are no restrictions here."

Other than good taste.

They were silent for a moment, then John said, "Welcome to *The Killer Podcast,* your exploration into the dark soul of man. I'm John Jackson, joined as always by my co-host on this journey into mystery and madness, Jay Anselm. Today, we have a very special episode. As you all know, Ashley King was the country's, if not the world's, most beloved final girl. Having endured the horror of the Resort Massacre, life was never going to be the same. She quickly rose to fame as the embodiment of feminine empowerment and survival. Five years ago, she went into the abandoned Hayden Resort to do some urban exploration with four of her closest friends. By the first light of day, she was the only one of their group to leave the fallow grounds."

Now it was Jay's turn, his baritone adding a level of gravitas to the broadcast. "Sadly, Ashley passed away several weeks ago. Fans have been left wondering why, their hearts broken. Maybe tonight we'll be able to provide some answers. Our guest this week is Todd Matthews. He was Ashley's fiancé, her former high school boyfriend who reconnected with her immediately after the Resort Massacre and never left her side. Thank you for coming on with us."

At first, there was silence. Todd wasn't aware they were waiting for him to say something. Just hearing the words *Resort Massacre* sent him into a dull fugue. Jay and John stared back at him. "Uh, you're welcome."

"I think I speak for all our listeners when I say you have our deepest sympathies. I'm sure you've seen the outpouring of love these past few weeks," John said.

"There were certainly a lot of flowers," Todd said.

The funeral parlor had received so many flowers, they had to commandeer the next viewing room to fit them all. Bouquets and arrangements from every corner of the globe had been sent to her funeral. Todd and her family had made it a point not to publicize it, but somehow word had gotten out. The overwhelming aroma of flowers had been almost too much to bear. It was what prompted Todd to dig up all of the flowers he'd planted for Ash around the house several days ago.

"The big question," Jay said, "is how are you?"

There was no point sugarcoating things. Todd replied, "I'm not good. I'm not good at all."

His honesty set them back for a bit.

John bent closer to the microphone and said, "We understand that you were the one that found her. I can't imagine what that must have been like."

Todd bristled. "Where did you hear that?"

"I've read it from several sources," John said.

That information had never been revealed to the press. Which meant someone on the local PD had leaked it, probably for a price. Shit!

"I'm really not here to discuss that." Todd moved closer to his screen. "And to be honest, it's nobody's business."

John looked nervous that he was going to lose Todd's co-operation. "I understand and I apologize for bringing up an unsubstantiated rumor."

It was bad enough all of the news outlets had let the world know Ash had hanged herself. Todd recalled the throng of photographers that had swarmed the house when the men from the medical examiner had wheeled her body from the front door and had to push their way through to the open doors of the black van. The flash of cameras had been like watching fireworks going off right in front of his face. They'd not just wanted to photograph the sealed bag strapped to the gurney. Todd knew that deep in their dead hearts, they'd hoped the zipper would come undone and they would capture the very last photo of Ashley's face. Or even a pale, lifeless arm.

Jay said, "What was it like for Ashley, these past five years?"

Oh, the things Todd wanted to say. The beer fizzed up his throat, hot and full of needles. "It was as tough as you'd think," he replied after swallowing hard. "She was never the same after that night, as you would imagine. I did the best I could for her. We all did. But it was impossible to escape that night. She was the strongest person I ever met, but honestly, I don't think anyone could ever recover from what she'd been through." He stared into the pinhole-sized camera in his laptop. "No one."

He could tell Jay wanted more details, but was afraid to press after the way the interview had started.

"The world hadn't seen or heard from Ashley for going on four years now. I understand her desire to move on, to reclaim her privacy," Jay said.

Yes, she had made a conscious effort to remove herself from the spotlight. She'd always been shy and was uncomfortable in the slew of interviews that had followed that first year for many reasons. This was all at a time when the last thing she needed was more stress. But she felt compelled to tell her story, the parts that she could remember, as a warning, for the killer had never been caught, and also a giant F-you to the psycho.

Now here Todd was, dragging her back into the spotlight. He felt sick to his stomach.

Jay continued, "Was she ever able to recall any details of the Wraith?"

"No. She only remembered that he was a man. But she was never able to tell us what he looked like."

"There was always the hope that with the passage of time, her memories would come back to her and possibly lead to the Wraith's capture."

"Ash wanted nothing more than to see that sick bastard arrested and sent to the electric chair. She tried, but nothing ever came."

John said, "Do you think her memory loss was from the head trauma she suffered or was it her mind's way of blocking out that night to preserve itself? Or both?"

Todd bristled. Yes, Ash had gotten a concussion when she'd been struck on the side of her head with what they believed to be the handle of a shovel. But she'd been through a battery of tests and there had been no damage to her brain. Her wounds ran far deeper and were more difficult, if not impossible, to heal.

"I think, no, I *know* she simply blocked it out," Todd answered. "She might have remembered it all or parts of that night next month, next year, on her seventieth birthday or never. It would come back when she was ready to receive it."

And now it never would. He eyed the refrigerator, wondering if he should pause the interview to grab another beer. Then again, he didn't want these schmucks telling the world Todd was a broken drunk. In fact, the beer he'd had before the show was the first drop of alcohol he'd had since Ash's death. He didn't want anything to stand in the way between him and his grief.

"Did she ever worry that the Wraith would try to find her?"

Here's where Todd had to lie. Ash's all-consuming fear of that madman coming back to finish what he'd started had plagued her until the very end. Terror of the man the world had dubbed the Wraith because he was a faceless, nameless killer, had denied her peace, especially at night. Ash had stashed knives everywhere throughout the house, as well as aluminum baseball bats and cans of pepper spray. Todd had found many of them as he stumbled through the house these past few weeks, but he knew there were more tucked away in corners.

"Her main concern was that he was still at large and could cross another innocent person's path. The Wraith, like all killers, was...is a coward. I think he knew that we would be prepared should he dare to come around. It's not so easy to murder someone when they're not unarmed and unsuspecting. So, no, she didn't think he would come for her again."

He didn't add that deep down, he wished the Wraith would. Todd would be there, waiting, and the story would turn out very different the second time around.

John raised an eyebrow. "Wow. That's actually encouraging to hear. It makes her even more of an inspiration for all women who have been abused or worse."

That's exactly what Todd wanted. He needed to erase the idea that the Wraith had won, that Ash had never truly gotten away. Like it or not, a legend had formed around Ash, and Todd needed to make sure it wasn't tarnished by her suicide.

Jay said, "Even though she wasn't able to give a description of the Wraith, was she able to remember exactly how the night unfolded? I mean, from the point of her friend, Sheri Viola, being attacked."

By attacked, he meant having her Achilles tendon severed as she was stepping into one of the abandoned luxury bungalows.

Todd shook his head. "No."

Another lie.

"Do you think it's almost a good thing the details had been unreachable for her?" Jay asked.

"Yes. Would you want to remember every graphic moment of the night your friends were slaughtered and you spent six hours running for your life?"

Both hosts blanched.

"I'm sure no one would," Jay said.

"Exactly. Our subconscious knows what's best for us and it acts accordingly," Todd said. *At least until the nightmares are left to roam free*, he thought.

"Todd, I have a question and I'm not sure if it's been asked before," John said. Todd prepared himself. "You were with Ashley and her friends that day. There are numerous reports from people in Topperville that took note of all of you because, well, it's a small town and people in small towns are wary of outsiders."

Where was he going with this? Todd had a plan today and thought he knew the questions because he'd heard them all before.

"The theory is that the Wraith was a drifter who had been hiding out in the old Hayden Resort and Ashley and her friends had the misfortune of stumbling into him. Now, I don't want to sound insensitive, but do you think maybe the Wraith was in town, saw you and followed them to the Hayden?"

A little confused, Todd said, "Sure, that was always a possibility."

"Because you were, well...." John ran his hand through his beard before finishing. "Maybe the fact that you were an interracial couple set him off. I've been to Topperville several times and I don't think I saw a single African American. Ashley and Sheri and Jamal would have stood out."

Ash always stood out because she was beautiful and bright and full of life.

Jay said, "I get the feeling that there's an element there, and in many places around the country, that would still object to an interracial couple. It's disheartening to think in this day and age that's still the case, but we can't put our blinders on just because it makes us uncomfortable. Racism exists. Evil exists. Sometimes, the two intersect and horrible things happen."

Todd sat back in the creaking chair. "Wait, are you saying those good people were murdered because Ash was black?"

"It is something to consider," John said. "Or that she was black and with a white man."

"So, she's to fucking blame for all of this happening?"

Jay was quick to say, "No, we don't blame Ashley at all. We're just trying to evaluate everything and come up with a motive. Killing in the name of racism isn't something new."

"If that's the case, why did he kill Fred and Addie? They were white."

Todd wondered if the microphone could pick up the sound of his teeth grinding.

"They were also witnesses," John said. "Or maybe it was bloodlust that couldn't be stopped once it started."

Todd glowered at the smug sons of bitches. "Essentially, according to your half-assed theory, Ashley and I brought this on them."

"That's not what we mean," Jay said.

Todd raised his palm and cut him off. "You can sit around and speculate all day and night instead of being productive members of society. That's your prerogative. The truth is, none of us will ever know. Even if you caught the Wraith, I doubt he'd ever tell. Because even he wouldn't know. What drives a man to slaughter four people he's never met and have never done a thing to him? You'd have to dissect their brain and find the rot to know. But to say it was racism is fucking laughable. I know exactly who to blame."

He didn't speak, letting his words hang in the air and distance between them. He might have been thrown by their asinine hate-crime conjecture, but he'd gotten to exactly where he'd wanted to go nonetheless.

"Please," Jay said, "tell us. If anyone would know, it's you, the person closest to Ashley."

Todd wanted to smack the inquisitive, anticipatory looks off their faces.

Finally, he said, "You."

John pulled away from the camera. "Me?"

"Yes. And him." He pointed at Jay. "And all of you listening to this. Anyone who idolizes serial killers and mass murderers, who wants to romanticize a so-called final girl, you are all responsible for Ash's death. Because you couldn't fucking let it go. You gave a sick, twisted murderer infamy. You pinned your horror movie fantasies on a poor woman who just needed to be left alone. She refused to just disappear because she wasn't going to let you take her name, her home, away from her. The Wraith had already robbed her of just about everything. So she took a stand, and you never once let her move on. For five years, all of you have been reopening the wound over and over again. You did it so goddamned much, you made her bleed to death. Who was the Wraith? The Wraith is you! Except he killed quickly, where you tortured Ash slowly, day by day, taking pieces of her ounce by ounce until she had nothing left inside her. Ashley King was not your final girl. You could never have her, just like the Wraith couldn't have her. So what did you do? You finished what he started."

Jay and John were pummeled into silence.

Todd continued. "You want to do something good for once?

Then you do this. You spread the word. Let the Wraith know that I'm right here at 1980 Lake Avenue. He still has unfinished business, and I'm happy to be the one to end it."

CHAPTER SIX

Vince brought a twelve-pack of some IPA strong enough to use his palate as a punching bag. Todd politely finished one bottle, then switched to regular Budweiser. They sat on the back patio, warming by the fire pit on a chilly October night. It had been a little over a week since Todd's now-viral appearance on *The Killer Podcast*. He'd asked his boss for an extension on his leave and it had been granted, though Todd sensed he couldn't push things much further.

"Look what else I brought," Vince said. He reached into his jacket and pulled out a clear plastic bag filled with cigars.

"I haven't smoked a cigar in years," Todd said, his breath curling in the glow of the porch light.

Vince opened the bag, unwrapped a Nat Sherman cigar and handed it to him along with a butane lighter. "Well, I figured a condemned man should get the good stuff."

Todd bit the end off, spit it into the grass and lit up. "If that's the case, you could have brought a bottle of Johnnie Walker Blue instead of that crazy super hops concoction."

Vince lit his cigar, inhaled and blew out a long funnel of smoke. "If Heather saw the bill, I'd be condemned right along with you."

Not for the first time, Todd patted his jacket pocket just to feel the unyielding reassurance of the knife he kept on him at all times.

With the windows closed in all the houses around them and no one about because of the chill, the yard was completely silent. Todd, channeling Ash, was grateful for it. If someone were to try to creep up alongside the house, they'd hear them without any trouble.

As if on cue, a bright shaft of light swept past the alley between the houses, flicking across the lawn. Todd got up and ran down the alley with his hand in his pocket. A pair of teen girls sat in a blue Honda, staring at the house. One of them got out and placed a supermarket bouquet of flowers on the curb alongside all of the others that had been piling up.

Sighing, Todd traipsed back to the yard and slumped into the Adirondack chair. Vince had his head back, puffing away while looking at the stars. "More groupies?" he asked.

"Yeah. Don't forget to bring some flowers home for Heather. Another bunch was just added to the chuckle patch."

"Maybe giving out your address wasn't such a good thing," Vince said. "We thought it was bad before when people really had to search to find it. Now, you can't get a moment's peace. You look like you haven't slept for days."

There was no denying it. Todd had mirrors. He could see the swelling dark bags under his glassy eyes. Lately, there'd been more hair in the drain and his color was off. He seemed to be turning gray, from his hair to his flesh.

"I wasn't thinking things through in the moment," Todd said. "I was so focused on the Wraith and letting the final girl cultists know what I thought of them, I forgot that they'd be on this place like white on rice. I caught four of them taking pictures of the basement on their hands and knees at two in the morning."

Vince eyed the bulge in Todd's jacket pocket. "If you don't learn to ignore them and get some sleep, you're going to accidentally hurt someone…or worse. Exhaustion does not make for sound decision-making."

Todd grinned. "Now you're starting to sound like Detective Chavez. He was pretty pissed when he first got word. Something about I'm not making things any easier by presenting myself as a target. They have a patrol car swinging by all the time now."

The bottle of IPA clinked against the leg of the chair when Vince placed it on the ground between them. "He's right. This Wraith guy, even if he's still alive, I doubt he's plugged in and checking the news. You only opened yourself up for more of the very thing that you hate the most."

"But as long as there's even a slight chance he'd go for the bait, I had to take it."

Officially, there was no question that the Wraith had survived the night. Extensive DNA testing of the blood that had splashed all about the resort had linked it to the victims. There wasn't a drop unaccounted for. There was hope that perhaps he'd suffered a wound that led to internal bleeding and he'd curled up and died in a hole somewhere.

Todd never thought it had ended so simply. Neither had Ash.

"How about this?" Vince said, the wood of his chair creaking as if it might break at any moment. "It's not a school night for me. Why don't I stay here and keep watch while you get some shuteye? You can finish the cigar, have a couple more beers and pass out. I did guard duty in the army, so you know I'm trained and qualified."

"You keep drinking those and you'll be asleep before me." In the darkness, just beyond the cone of light, were six lawn bags filled with final girl flowers, gifts and food, including trays of lasagna and homemade pies. The garbage men would not be happy with him when they came on Monday.

Vince upended the bottle and poured the rest of his beer out. "Consider me cut off."

"Look, you don't have to do this. I'm okay."

His friend grabbed his arm. "I do and you're not. I'm not gonna be the one to push you toward therapy, because I tried it and it was just a big waste of time and money. Plus, I know how stubborn you are. The whole thing will have failed in your mind before you ever stepped in a shrink's office."

Ash's lack of progress despite the constant psychiatric intervention had cemented Todd's belief that the whole thing was a crock. No, there was no way he'd ever go to a shrink.

"And tomorrow, we can think of a way to get you out of this funk. And maybe clean the place up a bit. You, my friend, are no housekeeper."

Todd gave a pained, brief laugh. "Yeah, that was Ash's domain. Everything had to be in its place. Funny, I can't remember if she was like that when we were dating in high school. That seems like something I shouldn't forget. There's a lot of shit that's just, I don't know, foggy."

Vince gave him the butane lighter to reignite his cigar.

"And that's why it's bedtime at the Alamo tonight. Seriously, before you hurt someone, and not the someone you really wanna hurt. If The Wraith comes by, I promise I'll wake you up."

Todd drank his beer, his chest feeling as if it were caving in on itself. His body had taken the offer of uninterrupted sleep before his mind. His eyes felt warm and his vision wavered. He let the silent tears snake down his cheeks.

"I just want that motherfucker to pay for what he did, man." He sniffled and took a puff of his cigar. "She came back to me, but he took her away for good at the same time. Jesus, Vince, is it too much to ask to set things right?"

His friend didn't answer for what felt like eons. Todd didn't look at him, because he thought he heard Vince sniff back a tear too. "In this fucked-up world, yes, sometimes it is too much to ask."

★   ★   ★

Todd heard Vince knocking around the living room, the television on low.

Sleep.

It would be great to actually sleep through the night. That's if he even could. He felt exhausted enough to sleep for days, but his body was so used to jumping up at the slightest sound, he wasn't sure he could make three straight hours.

The bed was a rumpled mess. The comforter was mostly on the floor, the pillows scattered to all four corners of the bed. He sat for a moment, trying to calm his mind, when he finally took notice of the funk in the room. How long had it been since he'd changed the sheets? He hadn't. Ash had been the last to change them. That had been over a month ago.

Fresh, clean sheets. Whenever Ash went on a jag of insomnia, she'd tell Todd she needed fresh, clean sheets. Together, they'd tear off the old and make the bed and she was right. For that night, at least, she would sleep.

Todd picked the comforter off the floor and tossed it into a ball on the chaise longue Ash insisted he buy and set under the window. Next went the top sheet, and then he yanked the bottom sheet off, catching a face full of sweat and tears. Phew, it was bad. How had he not noticed it before?

Rummaging under the sink in the attached bathroom, he found the can of Febreze and sprayed it liberally on the mattress. He stripped the pillows and did the same with them, then sat back and let it settle in for a bit.

Maybe I should flip the mattress, he thought. If he was going for a fresh start, that would solidify it. He ran his fingers over Ash's side of the mattress. She'd gotten so skinny, her body hadn't even made a lasting impression. It was as firm and unblemished as the day they'd bought it, whereas his side had a marked indentation.

No, he wouldn't flip it. He would turn it around so Ash's side would be on his side. Despite having the whole bed to himself now, he still needed to sleep closest to the door. When she'd agreed to move in with him, he'd insisted on it. She'd first smiled, and then cried, holding him tight. He hadn't needed to tell her that even in their sleep, he would always put himself between her and her worst fears. If the Wraith were to find them in the dead of night, he'd have to go through Todd.

Todd slipped his hands under the mattress and lifted. It was heavy; his construction-honed muscles had weakened over the last month but not so much that he couldn't easily move it around. The corner of the mattress clipped his night table and sent his phone charger and magazines to the floor.

"Shit."

He adjusted his grip on the mattress, lifting it higher and shuffling along the edge of the bed frame.

"What the heck?"

The corner of an envelope poked out from between the mattress and box spring. He pulled the envelope free and let the mattress fall back.

"You okay in there, buddy?" Vince called out.

"Yeah. I'm cool."

Seeing his name printed on the envelope in Ash's looping cursive took his breath away. He lost all feeling in his legs and was suddenly sitting on the bare mattress. He turned the envelope over, his hands shaking. It hadn't been sealed. Todd had to take several deep breaths before he could gather up the courage to lift the flap.

Inside was a single folded sheet of paper. He gently laid the envelope down and unfolded the note.

The police, and even his mother after the funeral, had scoured the house, searching for a suicide note. Without one, the possibility that her death had been murder and not suicide was greater. In the end there had been no signs of foul play. Everyone but Todd had lamented over Ashley not leaving some parting words.

For Todd, no words were needed. He knew the fear she'd lived with.

Reading the note was difficult through the veil of tears. He rubbed his eyes and composed himself.

"Oh, Ash."

He read the note slowly and carefully, his chest heaving.

Todd, my love,

I hid this where I knew it would take you some time to find because I feel you'll need some distance between the terrible thing I've done to you and this moment. I can't tell you how many times I've tried to write this. It's the hardest thing I've ever done. Elvira has been in her glory swatting around all the crumpled balls of paper I've thrown on the floor.

I'm so sorry. I wish there was another way, but you and I both know I was beyond saving. You did more than any one person could ever do. You gave me your unconditional love, and for that, I thank you and will love you from this moment and into the next world. I have to believe there is a next world, a place of peace. Even if I and the billions of religious people are wrong and there's only an eternity of nothing, that is more comforting that the thought of facing one more day here. I can never repay you for what you've done for me, just like I can never give back what you need and deserve. I'm broken, Todd, and there's only one way to fix me.

I know people will say what I did was a selfish act, that I was careless with the love you and my family have given me. You know better. I'm tired of being afraid. It's an exhaustion that no amount of sleep or reassurance or even love can cure.

Something happened two weeks ago. Something I hadn't the heart or nerve to tell you or my parents.

I remember.

Well, not everything, but enough to scare me to death. Not just for myself. But for you and everyone who would ever have the misfortune of being around me. This thing I'm about to do, it's not just about ending my pain and fear. It's about saving you.

I can't tell you exactly what happened that night, though some images that are coming up are too brutal to bear. They're a trail of horrible breadcrumbs, but I can't make myself follow it to the end. I do remember what I did that night. It's what I did every time we did our urbex trips. I recorded myself. And then I left it there. It's one of my quirks and it never harmed anyone. I wanted to be a part of the history of the places we explored. Part of the mystery (and you know I can't resist mysteries). All throughout that night at the Hayden, I left clues of what had brought us there, and video. Yes, video. Again, I'm not sure what I captured, but I do remember hiding a memory card or two somewhere in the resort. I remember thinking, no, knowing, I wasn't going to make it out alive that night (and in many ways, I didn't). It was more important than ever to document the horror of that night and hope someone would find it.

But they never did. And I forgot all about it.

So why did I suddenly remember?

It doesn't take Sherlock Holmes to realize my memories were shaken free from a little news article I saw online one day. They're finally going to raze the Hayden Resort. It should have been burned to the ground long, long ago, and it almost had been. They say demolition begins next week. I know you, Todd. If I'm not around to change the sheets, put new towels on the racks and do the laundry, things will pile up until the smell finally forces you to clean. ☺

I don't have it in me to go back to the Hayden, even with you and an army, to recover those recordings. I'm kind of happy they will be destroyed along with the resort. Now, it's too late and that night is truly buried. I should have died at the Hayden that night. It's only fitting we go together. I knew that if I told you, you would go there, even without me, and do whatever you had to do to find them. Because you want answers. You want justice.

You don't want the answers to this, my love.

And I don't want to take a chance that I'll remember more.

I want to leave in our home, wrapped in the warmth of the love you gave me. I want you to remember our love, and try to forget this one thing I've done. If I had stayed any longer, and recalled any more, my end would have been far more tragic. You have to trust me on this. You always did trust me, even if I didn't always deserve it.

Please forgive me. I love you.

Your Ash

Todd read the note over and over again, his fingers tracing the words. He handled the note as if it were made of thin china, making sure his rough hands didn't so much as crease the paper. After each reading, he gingerly put it down on the unmade bed and cried. He didn't even realize the sun had come up as he read it for the last time, birdsong alerting him that he hadn't slept a wink.

He opened the blinds, and then slipped the note back into the envelope. Then he made the bed, showered for the first time in a couple of days and changed.

Vince, his sentry, was asleep on the couch, one leg hanging over the side, his mouth wide open, emitting ragged snores.

Todd tapped his friend's foot.

"Huh?" Vince put his arm over his eyes. "What time is it?"

"She told me," Todd said.

"Who told you?"

"Ash."

Vince put his arm down and sat up, suddenly wide-awake. He went from the dull haze of sleep to deeply concerned in a flash. "Ash? Todd, what are you talking about?"

"She *did* leave a note. I found it when I went to change the sheets. If I wasn't such a goddamn pig, I would have found it sooner."

Todd hurried to the dining room. He opened Ash's laptop and powered it up. Vince struggled to get up, complaining about his neck, and stood behind Todd's chair. "What are you doing? Where's the note?"

Todd held up a hand. "Hold on. I need to see something."

He typed in *Hayden Resort demolition* in the search bar. A slew of articles and related posts popped up. Most of them had to do with the murders. Too many had Ash's name, along with 'final girl'. But there was one, seven returns down, that gave notice about the demolition of the old resort. Todd chewed on the callus on his thumb. It gave a date of three weeks ago. There was no follow-up.

Todd pounded the table, making Vince jump.

"What?" Vince said.

"Maybe they're wrong," he said.

"Who's wrong? This is too much, too early for me. Where is the note?"

"In the bedroom," Todd said dismissively. "She said when she saw an article that the Hayden was being torn down, her memories started to come back."

"Holy shit."

"Yeah. Holy shit."

His stomach was twisted with unease. Ash had always tolerated the strange fixation people had with her being a final girl. She didn't engage them, but she never spoke bad about them. That was his territory. Ash had killed herself right after she'd started to remember, which meant he'd been wrong. The final girl cultists weren't to blame. It was so much easier to direct his anger toward them because they were a real, tangible thing. Because the truth was, he *was* mad as hell and needed someone to rail against. Anyone but Ash.

Vince gripped his shoulders. "You okay?"

How many times had he been asked that question since Ash's death? He answered it like he'd had every other time.

"No, I'm not okay." He scanned the too-brief post about the demolition of the Hayden. A paragraph had been dedicated to the night of the massacre. There was no specific mention of Ashley. "It could still be there."

"What? The Hayden?

Todd closed the laptop. "It happens all the time. Demo crews get delayed more often than you think. I have to see for myself." He pushed away from the table and rushed to the bedroom. Vince followed him.

"You're going there now?"

"Yep."

As Todd stepped into the bedroom, Elvira popped out of the bed, stopped and stared. She'd been hiding under the bed and couch most of the time since Ash took her life. Heather had said it was because the mangy cat was mourning Ash in her own way. Todd thought it was just because she didn't like to be around him. He found it odd that the cat chose this moment, when he'd had 'contact' with Ash, to come out and engage him. As he sat on the edge of the bed to put on his socks and boots, the cat, purring loudly for the first time in a month, rubbed against his calves. He scratched between her ragged ears. "You can feel her too, can't you?"

The note had brought Ash back to him, in a sense. There was a part of her at the Hayden, if the Hayden was still standing. He had to find her.

"You're really doing this," Vince said, holding the doorframe.

"She said she recorded that night and left it there."

"That's major evidence. What you need to do is pick up the phone and tell the police."

Todd laced his boots, opened the closet and took out his leather jacket. "Not a chance. And if you try, it won't be pretty."

Vince held his hands up, palms out. "Whoa, buddy, I'm on your side."

"If the cops get there before me and they find it, they'll throw it in some evidence locker and I'll never see it. I'll never see *her*."

"What if there's something on there you can't un-see?"

"Then it'll only bring me closer to Ash."

He wondered if Ash had managed to record any of the actual murders. Had she captured the face of the Wraith? All of that was secondary. What he wanted most of all were the final images of her.

Squaring his Jets cap on his head, he turned to Vince and said, "You coming?"

His friend sighed deeply. He could see the rush of conflicting thoughts running through his head. He tapped the doorframe and said, "Of course I'm coming. It's only what, an hour and a half from here?"

"We'll make it in less."

Vince trailed Todd as he hurried to get his car keys. "Try not to get us killed. Okay?"

Todd opened the front door and waited for Vince to get his jacket and shoes on. Elvira sauntered into the living room, sat on her haunches and cocked her head, her jack-o'-lantern eyes boring into him.

"One thing before we go," Todd said.

"What's that?"

"I gotta feed the cat."

He left her two cans of food and refilled her water. Before she tucked in to eat, she looked up at him as if to say, *Good luck. Find her.*

"I will," he said.

"You will what?" Vince said.

Todd headed out the door. "Never mind."

CHAPTER SEVEN

Vince made them stop at McDonald's so they could grab something for breakfast. They munched on sausage and egg biscuits as they barreled up I-87. The early Sunday morning traffic was nonexistent, the low slate clouds making it look and feel like winter. Todd's Mustang powered its way north. Vince adjusted his seat belt for the hundredth time, his eyes wavering on the digital speedometer. "You know this isn't a race, right? If the place is still standing, no one is coming on a Sunday to finish the job."

Todd squeezed the steering wheel. "I know. I feel like I'm going to jump out of my skin."

"That's fine. I just don't want us wrapped around the divider. Take a little lead out of your foot. If you kill me, Heather will be really pissed. Especially once she finds out I forgot to pay the premium on my life insurance policy."

He gave Vince a sideways look. "You serious?"

Vince nodded. "You know how disorganized I am. I just found the bill last week. It had been sitting under a pile of papers for months. So, for the moment, I'm worth more alive than dead."

Todd eased off the gas, but still kept the muscle car ten miles an hour over the speed limit. "Better?"

"Better."

"I don't want Heather mad at me."

"No. You do not."

They smiled for the first time that day.

After breakfast was done, they drove most of the way in silence. The exit sign for Topperville looked as if it had been shot by red paint balls. Todd turned left at the shuttered deli, its roof starting to sag. The last time he'd been here had been five years ago, not long after the massacre. The deli had had a hopeful for sale sign in the window then.

Driving down Route 33, Todd had to take it much slower. The one-lane road wound its way deeper into Topperville, the street lined with houses. Some of them were in terrible disrepair, with well-kept ranch homes right next door.

"I can't imagine what the property values are here," Vince said. It was his first visit to the old Catskills town. "How the hell do you sell your house when you have total wrecks on either side of you?"

Todd slowed to look at a blackened barn, half of it in a pile of charred, shattered sticks. The field around it was brown and barren. It looked like the whole place had been firebombed. To the left of it was a farmhouse washed out by the sun and wind and rain, many of the windows cracked or broken. The porch was littered with pebbles of glass that he thought would glitter like diamonds in the sun.

"You don't sell your house," Todd said. "In a place like this, you just ride it out until you're gone and it's not your problem anymore."

He stopped at an intersection, a blinking yellow light overhead.

"Is that an actual general store?" Vince said, rolling down his window. The cooler air instantly chilled the interior of the Mustang.

The aging store looked like it was still functioning, the front window display crammed with regular household items. There were signs for the New York Lottery and two brands of beer. A small brass bell had been mounted over the door.

"It's like going back in time," Todd said. "Except it's kind of sad instead of nostalgic."

Across the street was an American Legion that he bet served as the town bar, at least for the veterans and their families. A curtain had been drawn over the fogged window, the facade in desperate need of paint. Next to it was a narrow Laundromat that promoted only twenty-five cents for ten minutes at the dryer. There was a beauty salon that might or might not have been functional, along with a pizza parlor that boasted it had the best pizza in town.

"That's because you're the only pizza in town," Todd said softly.

"What?"

Vince was captivated by an enormous weeping willow, its sagging branches reaching all the way to the ground, the ropy tendrils woven together into a carpet.

"Nothing." Todd eased through the intersection. He had to jam on the brakes to avoid hitting a pair of black cats that popped out from behind a mailbox, chasing one another across the street.

"Great," Vince said. "Not just one, but two black cats cross our path. You believe in signs?"

"No."

Todd had only been here once before, but the way to the Hayden had been burned into his memory. There was no need for GPS.

Topperville had once been a bustling town in the Catskills Borscht Belt. The Hayden Resort had been the center of it all, a major vacation destination from its opening in the 1930s all the way until the early seventies. Legendary comedians like Henny Youngman, Pat Cooper, Jackie Mason, Joan Rivers and Sid Caesar had all performed there, drawing in thousands of predominantly Jewish patrons from New York, New Jersey and Connecticut. He'd gleaned this from the slew of stories that had flooded the news after Ashley's night of hell. Of all the comedians that had been named, he'd only known Joan Rivers, thanks to Ash's love of those shows where the comedian and her buddies ripped apart everyone's fashion sense. Todd had read that they used to call the mountainous Catskills the Jewish Alps. Driving through it now, it was almost impossible to imagine. Topperville looked more like an afterthought, an abandoned experiment left to the dust of time. When the Hayden closed, the town went on life support.

"My aunt and uncle almost went to the Hayden for their honeymoon," Vince said.

"You never told me that."

"You never talk about this place. I didn't think it was worth bringing up."

Vince was right. Ash and Todd would talk around the Hayden, but never mention it by name. It was too painful for her and Todd never wanted to add to her misery.

"They ended up in the Poconos instead. They had the champagne glass tub and everything. It sounds way corny, but they loved it. I wonder if the Poconos is as dead as this place."

"They have casinos now, so I'm sure they don't know what to do with all the money they're making."

A rotting painted billboard half devoured by trees and vegetation still alerted drivers that they were only a mile away from the Hayden Resort. The wood was badly splintered, so it actually read: W C ME! THE W LD FAM S HA N ES RT ON Y 1 MI !

"Sign's still there at least," Vince said.

"I need more than the sign."

There were no houses on the final stretch to the Hayden, so Todd opened up the Mustang. He'd become so jittery, he could have stopped the car and run the rest of the way. At least it would have burned off some of his nervous energy.

Hugging the curb around a tight bend, he saw a relatively new fence demarcating the edge of the resort's property. On the other side of the fence, there was nothing but tightly packed trees, obscuring his view into the resort.

It was nothing but trees until they came upon the entrance, ten-foot stone pillars on either side of the long driveway that took visitors to the main building's front door, where they would be met by a valet and escorted to the front desk to check in.

The Mustang rocked when Todd stomped on the brakes.

"It's still here," he said. His heart beat wildly, making it difficult to breathe. Somewhere beyond that fence was his Ashley, or at least the very last impressions of the Ash he dated and loved in high school, before she became the haunted Ash he loved even deeper and hoped to marry.

Metal no trespassing signs had been affixed every few feet on the fence that wrapped around the thousand acres of crumbling resort. Just like at Todd's house, there were wrapped bouquets of flowers, candles and teddy bears piled by the front gate.

"This place is huge," Vince said. "You could get lost in there."

That would have been hard to do in its heyday, but now, venturing off the weed-choked path would plunge a person into a primeval forest. Todd was able to see the top few floors of the Hayden's mini-rise hotel. There was no longer glass in any of the windows. He suspected it was now the world's largest birdhouse. Beyond it, hidden from view, would be over two hundred bungalows dotted all throughout the property.

Todd killed the engine and got out, his gaze locked on the hotel. He laced his fingers through the links in the fence, the metal so cold, it burned to the touch. The gate was locked by loops of heavy chains and a padlock the size of his fist. Razor-sharp concertina wire wound its way across the top of the fencing, discouraging anyone who had the bright idea of climbing over. He tugged on the gate, getting it to move a few inches, but not enough for him to wedge his body through.

He looked down at the deep tire treads of construction vehicles, the tracks going well beyond the fence into the heart of the resort.

"Looks like someone would need a blowtorch to get in there," Vince said.

He was right. Todd had done his share of demolition jobs. The fencing here was taller and sturdier than any he'd ever seen. They sure as hell didn't want anyone getting in.

Or were they also concerned about someone getting out?

Todd shivered. "There's always a way in," he said. "It's just a matter of finding the weak spot."

Vince grew concerned. "Wait, you're not thinking of going in there, are you?"

"You thought I drove all the way up here just to see if it was still standing?"

Vince huffed, his breath fogging the air between them. "Well, yeah. I figured if we found out it hadn't been torn down, you could reach out to the contractor and see if they could bring you on. That would give you free, and I might add, legal rein to go anywhere you want."

It was actually sound thinking, except Todd was pretty sure the foreman wouldn't hire him once he discovered his connection to the place. If word got out, the media circus would start up again. They wanted this place removed with zero fanfare. Why would anyone want to give it any more grisly publicity than it already had?

"I don't think it would be that simple," Todd said. He slipped his boots into the links and climbed partway up the ten-foot-high gate.

"Hey, at best, you're going to cut yourself to shreds if you try to get over," Vince said. His hands were thrust deep into his pockets.

"I just want to see," Todd said. He was able to afford himself a view of an extra floor of the main hotel, but that was it. He thought he caught a glimpse of the roof of the skating rink to his right, but there were too many trees to be sure. After that night, he had found a map of the grounds, trying to help Ash piece together the bits her mind held onto so they could trace her steps. At first, he'd thought it would help, but he quickly realized it only made her night terrors worse.

"I think…I think I'm better off not remembering," she'd said to him out of the blue one night when they were on the couch watching TV.

He'd held her while she cried, then went to the dining room where he'd left the map he'd printed and thrown it out. In the end, she was right. And there was no need to try to figure out where she'd gone and how she'd gotten away. The police saw enough by following the blood and bodies.

Todd jumped off the gate. The cold metal rattled.

Now he wished they had made some progress. It would help him retrace her steps and find what she'd left behind.

"We're going to have to do some recon," Todd said. "Find the weak link."

"I'm freezing my balls off, man. I'm not dressed for mountain breaking and entering. In fact, I'm going to warm my balls up right now. Thank God for seat warmers."

Vince got back in the car and motioned for Todd to join him.

It *was* cold. Far colder than back home. Todd had no intention of going inside the Hayden now. He hadn't come equipped with the necessary tools to make his way inside. They had locked it up good, much more secure than he'd thought.

But he would return.

With his back turned to the gate, he heard the snap of a thick dry branch. He whirled around, the nape of his neck prickling.

The air was still and heavy. His eyes darted all around, searching for where the sound had come from. He waited for more, the inevitable crunch of dry leaves as something approached. It would most likely turn out to be a deer. They multiplied like gremlins doused in water.

There were no follow-up sounds, no scuffling of critters great or small. Just the long, dead silence of a sprawling murder scene.

Todd knew it was his imagination, but he couldn't shake the

feeling of being watched. Why else would the hairs on his arms still be standing straight?

He stepped closer to the fence, peering into the dark spaces between the trees.

"Who's there?" he said, the volume of his voice not high enough to travel far.

A slight breeze rustled the brittle, colorful leaves, ushering the lullaby of autumn.

Something was there, just out of reach. He felt it in his marrow.

Or was it someone?

The sharp bleat of a siren nearly caused his heart to burst out of his chest. Todd jumped, and then went into a defensive crouch.

The glare of flashing red and blue lights hurt his eyes.

Next thing he knew, two officers were stepping out of their cruiser and approaching him with their hands hovering over their holsters.

CHAPTER EIGHT

"You look a little too old to be trespassing onto private property," the younger cop said.

Todd instinctively held up his hands. He'd had a few run-ins with the police when he was a wild teen, but he'd never been arrested.

"I was just taking a look around," he said. His initial shock over, he managed to keep his cool.

"Out of the car," the other cop, a burly guy still wearing a short-sleeve shirt, most likely to showcase the solid mass of tattoos on both arms, said to Vince. There were snakes and skulls and all sorts of nightmare visions. Todd bet the sinister body art worked on intimidating some of the people he confronted. He had a few of his own and wasn't impressed.

Vince stumbled out with his hands high in the air. He shot Todd an *I told you so* glance. "Look, we had no intention of going in there. Seriously, my friend was just looking."

"Uh-huh," the young cop said. He had a deep scar on the side of his right eye but it did little to harden his boyish looks. "We get a lot of people up here who tell us that, and then we find their buddies already inside."

Todd stepped forward and the cops tensed. He made it a point to stop. "We're telling the truth. There's no one up here but us."

"Let me see your license and registration."

When Todd and Vince went to get their wallets, the tattooed cop said, "Slowly."

Todd handed his over and said, "I have to get my registration. It's in the glove compartment."

Up close, he saw the young cop's last name was Cooper.

Cooper said, "That's fine."

Todd rummaged through the mound of junk that had accumulated in the glove compartment. Vince babbled something to the tattooed cop.

"Found it," Todd said. He backed out of the car and handed the slip of paper to Office Cooper.

"Stay right there," Cooper said.

Both cops got back into the car, entering their information in the computer to see if Todd and Vince had any warrants.

Vince jammed his hands under his armpits and leaned against the Mustang. "Now can we go home?"

"You have any unpaid tickets?" Todd joked.

Vince paled. "Shit. I can't remember."

"Relax. They're not going to throw you in jail." Todd watched the cops as they studied their computer screen.

"I know that. I'm just a little light on cash at the moment." Vince stamped his feet to keep warm. "I feel like we're seventeen again, the night we got busted for toilet-papering Ms. Roundtree's yard."

Todd suppressed his laughter. He didn't think the cops would appreciate it. "Dealing with the five-oh was the easy part. It was the punishment from our parents and Ms. Roundtree that really sucked. How many extra reports did we have to do that semester?"

"Too many."

Cooper and the tattooed cop, whose nametag declared him as Landers, emerged from their warm car, holding out Vince's license and Todd's license and registration.

"I'm real sorry," Cooper said to Todd.

Confused, Todd said, "No, we're sorry for causing a fuss. It won't happen again."

Office Cooper shook his head. "I mean, I'm sorry for your loss. And I understand. I thought I recognized you when we pulled up."

Of course. Todd had been linked to this place through the news almost as much as Ash. He hated that they dubbed him her white knight who dropped everything in his new life in Denver to come to her aid. He was no knight, and in the end, he hadn't been able to save her.

Office Landers added, "I'll bet you were hoping to see this place flattened."

Todd decided it was best to play along with what they were giving him. "To be honest, I'd hoped it was just going to be a big hole in the ground."

Cooper adjusted his belt. "There's been a delay. They started on the bungalows, but someone got hurt. Everything is suspended, but I hear they're coming back next week to finish the job. If you want, I can arrange it so you can have a front row seat the day they blast the hotel."

The mini-rise building was where the bodies had been stacked, though forensics sussed out they'd been murdered elsewhere around the property.

Todd gritted his teeth. "I'll just be happy to know it's all gone."

"I hear you," Landers said. "It must be hard."

Todd felt the best reply was stoic silence. The truth was, talking about it with strangers was difficult. But he had learned there was still one week left before it was all gone, and that was vital.

"We're sorry to bother you," Cooper said. "You wouldn't believe how many dumb kids and plain old ghouls we've had to chase away from here."

"Actually, I would."

"I bet it's been no picnic dealing with all those final girl lunatics," Landers said. "I can't tell you how many of them we've busted. As you can see, they've been here a lot lately." He looked at the flowers and other in memoriam gifts. "They tell us they get some weird kind of strength by being close to where your...."

He let the rest hang in the air.

"Some of them even have tattoos of the place...and Ashley," Cooper added. "I don't know why people would want to commemorate such a thing on their body forever."

Todd shrugged. "I gave up trying to understand them years ago. I had enough to worry about."

"Feel free to stay as long as you like. You've earned it," Landers said.

Todd wondered if he should press his luck and ask them if he could go inside. Knowing what the answer would be, he simply nodded and thanked them.

As they were getting back in their squad car, Cooper said, "The offer still stands." He handed Todd his card. "You call me if you want to see the place come down. Take care now."

Todd and Vince watched the car pull away, their breath curling over their faces.

"That was a close one," Vince said.

"That was better than I could have hoped for."

"Care to tell me why?"

Todd held up his fingers. "One – now I know I have a week to plan and get in. Two – we have all morning to look around the perimeter. And three – even if I get caught when I come back, it looks like the local cops will give me a break."

"Or four – you press your luck and end up with a mug shot anyway."

Todd stared at the hotel. A hawk circled overhead. "To be fair, I don't give a shit. I'm going in and I'm going to find it."

*   *   *

By the time Todd pulled into his driveway, he felt like the walking dead. Exhaustion and the excitement of the day had sapped every ounce of his energy. Vince had barely been able to say 'so long' when he'd dropped him off. His best friend had shuffled to his door where Heather waited. She cast a quick glance at Todd before ushering Vince inside. Todd had been too tired to try to read that glance.

He went straight to his refrigerator and gulped down a bottle of water. It was going on eight o'clock. He hadn't had anything to eat or drink since McDonald's almost twelve hours earlier. He felt something bump his leg and he jumped, spilling water.

Elvira gave him a passing look as she sauntered by.

That cat never nuzzled him.

"Good to see you too," Todd said. He squatted by her food bowls and ran his hand over her back while she munched on some dry food. She was still aesthetically an ugly cat, but he was seeing her in a new light. She'd been through hell and it showed. So had Ash, though most of her scars hadn't been visible. There had been a long gash on her leg and other nicks and welts on her body, plus the weight loss, but no one had been able to see the real damage the Wraith had inflicted on her.

"Bet you have some stories you could tell."

Elvira raised her head from the bowl and licked her lips. He scratched under her chin and was shocked to hear her purring.

Flecks of dirt fell off his jeans onto the linoleum. His clothes were a mess. A day spent crawling and climbing around the Hayden had left its mark. He should just strip down and toss it all in the washing machine, but now that he was on the floor next to a very content Elvira, he wasn't sure he had the strength.

Instead, he lay down on the cold, hard floor, petting the cat.

He had hoped to find one access point that would be easy to get through. In fact, he had found half a dozen where the soil under the fence was soft enough to dig under or the concertina wire was sparse. He and Vince had traversed the entire perimeter of the Hayden, Todd scribbling the best spots on an impromptu map he'd drawn on the inside of their McDonald's takeout bag. The map was tucked in his jacket pocket. He should study the map and get to planning.

But first, he'd wait until Elvira finished eating.

The cat crunched away while Todd's thoughts drifted.

He awoke with the sun on his face. His shoulders, hips and back ached. Groaning like an old man rising from his deathbed, Todd grabbed hold of a knob on one of the kitchen drawers and pulled himself up. The clock on the stove read 7:32. No wonder he hurt. Twelve hours on the floor had left him near-crippled. He limped to the bathroom, shucking his clothes along the way.

While he peed, he opened the medicine chest and found the bottle of ibuprofen. He popped three of the orange tablets and washed them down by drinking straight from the faucet.

"Shower."

It pained him to step over the lip of the tub. He cranked the hot water until it was just shy of scalding. Leaning his forehead on the wall, he let the hot spray beat against his aching muscles. He stayed that way until the water turned tepid, a warning that he better finish up before there was no hot water left.

As he dried off, his stomach grumbled with such force, it echoed in the tiny bathroom. He prayed there was food in the fridge, because he couldn't see himself getting ready and leaving the house. At least not until his bones didn't feel like they were made of rotted wood.

Todd cracked four eggs and scrambled them, adding a few splashes of hot sauce and sprinkling in some pepper jack cheese. He spooned the eggs over two slices of toast and winced when he sat down at the dining room table to eat. Elvira lounged on the other side of the table. Normally, Todd would yell at her to get off and she'd scatter, but not before flashing him a dirty look.

Today, he was grateful for the company.

By the time he finished eating in silence, he'd started to feel a little more human. He loaded the dishwasher and got Ash's final letter – he couldn't bear to think of it as her suicide note – and brought it into the living room, where he spread it on the coffee table. He had to move her puzzle books aside to make room. His mother had tried to gather them into a pile and put them in the closet, but he'd rather rudely told her not to touch them. He wanted them just where Ash had left them.

He took out a notepad, hoping to remember the things that Ash brought along with her when she went urban exploring. It was still hard for him to remember her as the school's wild child. Breaking into abandoned places had all started with her and her best friend, Sheri Viola. As she had explained it to him, they'd gotten baked in her bedroom while her parents were out for the night and fell down the YouTube rabbit hole. Once they came across a home video of some teens who had broken into a shuttered hospital, they were hooked. The interior of the hospital was covered in graffiti, as one would expect. Some rooms still contained beds and IV poles, as if waiting for a patient to return from X-ray or a walk down the hall.

It wasn't until the intrepid teens, filming in night vision, got to the morgue deep in the basement that Ash's fascination was cemented. She'd shown Todd the full video and it had given him the creeps.

The doors to the cold storage lockers had been thrown wide open. Within each were the bones of dead animals. There were obvious cats and dogs, and others that might have been raccoons and squirrels. All of the remains had been picked clean of flesh and posed with outstretched arms, as if awaiting crucifixion. One of the boys noted a dull hum in the room that wasn't captured by the camera. They were naturally very afraid, but too curious to just leave. They had to see more, find where the hum was coming from. So they left the morgue, the camera shaking as they hurried along down a long, litter-strewn corridor. As they went farther down the hall, the hum became audible on the recording. It was coming from behind a steel door.

Todd was sure the boys had had a few beers before slipping into the hospital. There had been a lot of tasteless jokes, giggling and macho grandstanding. They were too wound up to pussy out and not open the door. After a bit of idiotic teen cajoling, one of the boys opened the unlocked door. Inside was a solid wall of pitch black. Just as they were about to enter, a blurry shape ran across the doorway. The boys started screaming and running, the rest of the video too nauseating to watch as it bounced around, flashes of the floor and ceiling filling the frame.

When Todd watched it, he assumed the teens had disturbed a homeless person living in the basement. To Ash and Sheri, the boys had stumbled upon a ghost. They were hooked from that moment on. The very next week, they'd pried the boards off an abandoned house on Cedar Street and filmed themselves going from floor to floor. They found porno mags, dirty mattresses, beer cans and an old photo album left behind by the final tenants. There were no ghosts, other than the remnants of the lives that had left long ago.

As the years went on, Ash and Sheri's urban exploration crew would expand and contract as others, intrigued by their stories, came on to break into abandoned department stores, amusement parks, hotels, motels, asylums and residential homes. Ash's fascination grew into an obsession. When she wasn't traipsing through crumbling structures, she was studying from those who'd gone before her. She grew more safety-conscious, wary of rotting floorboards and asbestos. The kits she brought helped her account for just about every situation.

Everything but a crazed killer.

Todd wrote down the things he remembered Ash taking on that last trip. There were flashlights, of course, and rope, an air filtration mask for asbestos and mold, pocket knife, long-sleeved shirts and jeans, good boots, water, energy bars, video camera and so much more. The necessities were spread out amongst the team so the burden didn't make getting around cumbersome.

He wished now he'd gone with her at least once. When they were dating in high school, she picked up urbex just as they were breaking up. She had a very good reason to dive headlong into her new hobby, especially after what he'd done. They hadn't seen each other until a few days before she went to the Hayden.

That was one thing the news had wrong. They were not dating when he agreed to drive her and her friends to the Catskills and he had not come to save her. Todd had dared to comment on one of her pictures on Facebook, an old photo of their sophomore year squad hanging out at the mall. He figured she would ignore him at best, curse him out for daring to sneak around her Facebook page at worst. To his surprise, she sent him a private message, asking him how he'd been and what he was up to. They started talking, at least through direct messages, from there.

He had planned to come back to New York to see his mother, and Ash suggested they meet for coffee. When she saw the minivan he was driving – a loan from his mother – she asked if he would take her and her friends to the Hayden so they could do some exploring. He was mildly shocked that urbex was still a thing for her. Weren't they too old for that kind of stuff? At their age, trespassing meant jail, not a slap on the wrist for being an uninformed teen.

Still, he'd agreed, if only not to ruin the rebuilding of at least their friendship. Truth be told, he thought he'd have to suffer a far greater penance. When she'd held his hand as they walked down the fading main street in Topperville, he'd been shocked, his heart skipping more than a few beats. He realized then, standing outside a hardware store, that he still loved her. That love was only overshadowed by his shame.

Todd dropped his pencil, rubbing his eyes. He didn't want to think about that.

Instead, he reread the note.

He paused when he came to the lines: *I can't tell you exactly what happened that night, though some images that are coming up are too brutal to bear. They're a trail of horrible breadcrumbs, but I can't make myself follow it to the end.*

Breadcrumbs.

Was she trying to tell him something?

He practically leaped from the couch.

Of course she was!

Ash and her puzzles. He did his very best to indulge her, especially since working out a puzzle or mystery took her mind off that night. It would only make sense that as bits and pieces came back to her, she would leave her own trail of breadcrumbs, puzzle pieces for Todd to put together.

"Where did you put them, honey?"

He scanned the living room, his hands on his hips, searching for hiding places. Just like the note she left under the mattress, he was positive she'd secreted something else behind.

Now it was only a matter of finding it.

CHAPTER NINE

"What the hell happened in here?"

Heather paused in the doorway. Vince must have still been in the car, most likely juggling trays of food and bottles of wine. The couple always came ready to feed an army. Todd waved her inside. He hadn't changed his clothes in two days and he knew he stunk.

"I've been looking for breadcrumbs," he said sheepishly.

"I don't understand," she said, mild shock on her face. "It looks like vandals were set loose in here."

He couldn't deny that. All of the furniture had been upturned. He'd unzipped couch cushions, emptied drawers on the floor, uprooted potted plants and ransacked his way through every cabinet.

"I prefer to think it looks like an earthquake hit," he joked, but it fell flat. "I'm not crazy, Heather."

She took a tentative step inside, looking down to avoid stepping on something. "I don't think you're crazy."

"Yeah, you do."

"No. I think you're grieving. You haven't lost your mind."

"But I have lost my housekeeping senses." He used his foot to clear a path from the front door to the dining room. At least the table and chairs in there were still upright.

Heather grinned but he couldn't tell whether it was genuine or forced. "You never had much to begin with."

Vince came strolling inside, his hands full, and blurted, "Holy shit, were you robbed?"

It wasn't a stretch. They had all worried about the final girl followers breaking in to snatch a memento of Ashley. Girls and boys, men and women were still cruising by the house, dropping things off and peeking in the windows. Todd was sure a few of them had watched him ransack the place. He had no desire to scan the web for blog posts or images about Ash's insane fiancé ransacking their home.

"You don't like my feng shui?"

Vince's mouth dropped open. "To be honest? No." He put the food and wine on the table and slumped into a chair. "Care to tell me what you're up to now?"

Heather pulled Todd in for a hug. She smelled like lilacs. Ash loved lilac body wash. He held onto her a little longer than usual, fighting back a sudden swell of emotion. It was bad enough they had walked into his handiwork. He didn't want to break down in front of them too.

"He's looking for breadcrumbs," she said to her bewildered husband.

"Have a seat and I'll show you," he said. It took some time to get to the bedroom and find the note. He brought it back to Heather. "I found this the night Vince slept over. Please, read it."

Vince found the corkscrew at his feet. "I think I'll just drink straight from the bottle." While Heather read the note, Todd found three unmatched glasses in the dishwasher and Vince poured.

There was a sheen of tears in Heather's eyes when she was finished. "Poor Ash," she mumbled, wiping her eyes with her sleeve. "But Todd, I don't get it. What are you really looking for?"

He ran his hand through his greasy hair, wishing he'd known they were coming so he could have either said he'd meet them somewhere else or at least showered and changed. His balance was off too, thanks to lack of sleep. "I think she was telling me she'd left the parts she remembered behind. I...I need to find them."

Vince took a long sip of his wine and then said, "Buddy, I can understand your wanting to search the Hayden because of what she said. But I don't see the mystery here."

"That's because you didn't know her like I did!" Todd snapped and was instantly sorry. In a much softer tone, he added, "Everything to her was a kind of mystery. She liked them before, but after, especially when it was quiet in the house, it's what kept her sane. She always wanted me to help her figure these things out, and I tried, but you know me. I like beer and action flicks. I'm not big on problem-solving. Not that kind, anyway. I know how her mind worked, and this—" he pointed at the note, "—was both her goodbye and a clue."

They were distracted by the sound of a car pulling into the

driveway. Todd looked out the window and saw a twenty-something guy and two girls get out of a white Nissan. They took a couple of selfies with the house as a backdrop. Todd knocked hard on the window, startling the trio. They dove back into the car and peeled out of the driveway.

"Jerkoffs," Todd said.

Heather found the plates on the counter under a mound of knickknacks and spooned out a healthy portion of baked ziti and urged him to sit down. "I don't want to hear another word until you eat."

"I promise, I'll eat later. I have a few more things to check."

She put a firm hand on his shoulder, pushing him toward the chair. "Unfortunately, I don't believe you. So now you have to eat."

He looked at her and realized resistance was futile. "Fine."

"And after we eat, we're all going to put this place back together," she said.

Vince shook his head. "Why do I have to clean? He made the mess."

Heather shot him a look that made him throw up his hands and apologize. When Heather turned her back to fill two more plates, Vince said to Todd under his breath, "Thanks a lot, buddy."

"You heard Mom," Todd said, the small joke relieving some of the mounting pressure that had kept his head and body buzzing for days now. He didn't know he was hungry until the first forkful of ziti and sausage hit his tongue. It took all his will not to inhale everything on his plate.

There was no small talk while they ate. It seemed inappropriate when surrounded by the disaster of his fervor. Heather filled his plate a second time without his needing to ask. The food and wine helped to fill and relax him. He dropped his crumpled napkin on his plate and sat back. "Stick in the fork. I'm done. That was amazing, Heather. Thank you. For the food and for making me eat."

She leaned over and kissed his cheek. "You're welcome. I'll wrap up the rest and put it in the fridge."

Vince said, "You know, when we came here, I thought for sure you'd have all these plans laid out to rope us into breaking into the Hayden. I'm not sure which I prefer."

"Oh, that's coming. But first, I need to find where Ash left everything."

"Getting arrested is not in my future plans."

"You saw how the cops treated me once they knew who I was. We won't get arrested," Todd said. He got up and stared at the chaos of his living room.

"Maybe not you, but I don't have the same clout."

Heather closed the refrigerator door. "Sure we do. It's called clout by association."

Todd slowly turned to face her, not sure he heard her correctly. "What do you mean *we*?"

She smiled. "It means I'm going with you. Ever since Vince told me, I can't stop thinking about it. We can't let what she hid there get destroyed. We have to at least try."

"This is news to me," Vince said.

"Yeah, well, now it's out there and you're not going to change my mind."

"The place is a wreck. It'll be dangerous. You could get hurt," Todd said.

"If I do, you two will be there to take care of me." She finished her wine in one long gulp. "So, where should we start cleaning up this mess?"

"Not yet," Todd said. "I can't put everything back until I've found it. Whatever *it* is."

Heather sighed and said, "What haven't you checked yet?"

"I've gone through every room in the house, including the basement." He hated being in the basement. He couldn't stop furtively looking around down there, expecting to see Ash again, still hanging. The basement made him lightheaded and put a knot in his stomach.

A pile of rubble in the living room shifted and collapsed. Elvira popped out of the mess and picked her way to the kitchen.

"Did you check her grandfather clock?" Heather said.

"Of course I did. It was one of the first places I looked. There wasn't anything in the lower door. I even checked to see if she stuck something behind the pendulum."

"Did you check behind the clock face?"

"What do you mean?"

"Come on, I'll show you."

Todd and Vince followed Heather into the bedroom. Each nearly took a header when the clutter on the floor shifted under their feet. Todd kicked the rest out of the way to make a clear path for Heather.

She opened the glass door to the clock face. She then gave the face a gentle push, and there was a click. Using her fingernail, she swung the clock face out. Inside was a small compartment that was empty save for one item.

"She never told me about this," he said.

"All ladies need their secrets," Heather said.

There was a folded pink bandana inside. The fabric was stiff with age. Todd's fingers trembled as he removed it.

"What is it?" Vince said.

Todd felt weightless. "It was her bandana. She wore it the first day we met. I...I didn't know she saved it." He looked to Heather. "Did you know she held onto it?"

She nodded solemnly. "She showed it to me one day. Even after you broke up, that was a very special day for her. *You* were special."

"Jesus." Todd brought the bandana to his nose, hoping to inhale any remnant of her scent. Like her smile, it was gone. Their breakup right after graduation had been rough. As far as he knew, she'd thrown out everything that reminded her of him. When they got back together, she'd said many times that she'd never stopped loving him, but for some reason, this bandana spoke far more than words. He felt Heather's hand at his back.

His eyes burned with tears he refused to allow to come to fruition.

It was then he felt something inside the bandana. He rubbed the thin, tiny square between his thumb and finger and knew instantly what it was.

"I don't mean to be an asshole, but I think I just need some time to be alone now," he said.

"We understand," Heather said. She rested her cheek against the back of his shoulder and hugged him.

"You call us if you need anything," Vince said.

"Thanks."

He didn't move again until he heard the front door close.

Todd unfurled the bandana, catching the memory card in his palm.

He should have been angry with Ash for hiding this from him. But he couldn't stop thinking about her note and how she'd said she was trying to protect him. Right now, it wasn't making any sense.

Try as he could, it was impossible to maintain even a shred of anger at her. No, he was disappointed with himself. He couldn't unlock the mysteries within her when she was alive, her warm, comforting body beside him each night, listening to the ticking of her grandfather clock. He was more determined than ever now to follow the breadcrumbs she'd left and hoped that wherever she was, she could watch him and find peace.

Going back to the dining room, he found her video camera under a mound of haphazardly tossed clothes and powered it up. He slipped in the memory card, opened the video viewer and lost his ability to breathe when the screen was filled with her beautiful, haunted face.

CHAPTER TEN

Todd, you're only outside in the yard right now and already I miss you. I can hear you trimming the hedges and I feel horrible for doing this with you so near, but if I don't record this now, I don't know if I'll ever find the strength.

What I'm going to do — what I've done by the time you find this — wasn't an act of cowardice. I know people say that about suicides all the time, but they're wrong. At least in my case. I'm tired of living like a coward. So I have to be brave for the first time since that night and do what needs to be done.

Please don't hate me. That's always been my biggest fear. That we would grow old and you would look back and regret the life we spent together. I know you like to fix things. What if you looked at me when I'm eighty and still broken? Would you still love me then?

I know it's going to hurt, but the pain will fade. I miss Sheri and Addie and Jamal and Fred every single day. It feels weird to say that the pain isn't as sharp as it once was, but it's the truth. You have a whole long, wonderful life ahead of you. Mine was taken from me five years ago. You don't get to come back from the dead, despite all those horrible zombie films you made me watch.

But what I've learned is that memories you buried deep down inside can crawl back.

I was washing the dishes when the first images of that night came rushing back. I dropped a plate and when it smashed, it scared poor Elvira so much, she jumped about two feet. It was, it was like watching a movie reel where the editor just slapped random bits of the film together and sped up the playback. I don't know what shook it all free and why it hit me like that. It was as if it came from someplace outside of myself. You asked me that night if I was okay and I told you I was fine, just the usual.

It wasn't.

It was like a dam bursting. Suddenly, all these flashes of things that I had kept hidden from myself would hit me. They would come when I least expected it and each time it was like getting sideswiped by a tractor trailer. The only time I was free was when I was asleep, but you know how horrible a sleeper I've become. Basically, I've had nowhere to hide.

The worst part is, I know *he's* still out there. I don't know why. I'm sure that the answer lies in what I left behind at the Hayden. I can't access that part in my memories, but a part of me just screams that it's there. Maybe I'm better off in the dark.

Knowing he's alive and can come for me is too much. It was bad enough when I could convince myself that he crawled away like a wounded animal and found a dark place to die. You know how I still jump at noises and freak out in the dark. I used to think it was all part of the PTSD. Now I'm sure it's because I know we didn't do enough to kill him.

And if he comes for me, he'll get you too. I can't let that happen. I won't.

What's come back to me is just pieces.

I found something out about the Hayden. When I sit and try to concentrate on it, I get physically ill. It must have been real bad. But like most everything else, it's gone.

The longest fragment I have, and I don't know why, is when Fred was attacked.

It was cold that night, or at least it felt cold. The days were unseasonably hot, we hadn't been prepared for the early morning chill in the mountains. I think it was around three. That's the real witching hour. Not midnight like they show in movies and books. Anyway, something had happened to Addie. I wish I could remember what it was. I just know that we had to stop and rest for a while. Jamal wanted to make a fire but I told him he couldn't. It was too dark out there, any fire would be a beacon for the cops. I had a shock blanket in my first aid kit and I wrapped it around myself and Addie. I don't know where Sheri was. She could have been right with us. Or knowing her, she was probably off sketching one of the buildings. Fred was tending to Addie. Jesus, it's frustrating to be able to see almost everything.

I...I get the feeling we were thinking of calling it a night. We'd been so excited, we had climbed the fence to get inside earlier than usual, so we'd already had a couple of hours under our belts. With that place, we'd need a week of nights to take in everything. Our plan was to go back someday soon.

Someday.

You know me, I had the night all planned out. Our goal was to explore the main hotel, the attached indoor pool and the ice rink. The hotel was this mini rise with twelve floors. I guess thirteen if you counted the basement, which they didn't, for obvious reasons. It was in much worse shape than we imagined. I remember thinking that we shouldn't try to go up the stairs. At best, someone's leg would go through the rotted wood and get hurt. At worst, I've heard of people falling completely through the floor and dying. Maybe Addie got hurt in there. Man, this sucks.

I don't think we stayed in there for long. I'm not sure. My next memory is sitting with Addie with the shock blanket wrapped around us. There was a small lantern on the ground and we kept it on low. Jamal had picked a spot where we were surrounded by trees and stuff. Were we outside the rink? Maybe. I keep seeing the corner edge of some structure, but I just can't tell what it is.

When Fred was finished with Addie – doing what, I wish I knew – he went to his pack and took out a flask. I was mad at him. Hmmm. If I was mad, that must mean we were still going to do more exploring. I wouldn't care if he drank when we were leaving. But if we were still going to look around, we couldn't have him buzzed or drunk. His life and our lives depended on it. And that place was in real bad shape. What was still standing was rotted to the core.

We got in a fight, and now I see Sheri and she's mad at Fred too. He's telling us to back off and it was just a couple of sips. It was cold and maybe we should all have some to warm up a little. For people who enjoy breaking the rules, we had very strict rules of our own. No drinking was a big one.

Jamal tried to take the flask away from him and Fred pushed him into Sheri. He hit into her so hard, she fell and now I was really mad. We were all yelling at each other and making a lot of noise.

That's another rule broken, but this time we all did it. We might have been in the middle of nowhere, but sound travels, especially at night.

That has to be how *he* found us. Maybe, if we'd all just stuck to the rules, we could have gone in and out without him even knowing. The Hayden was huge. He could have been on the other side of the resort for all I know.

But we called him to us.

I think Jamal and Fred wrestled around for a bit, but they were best friends and it didn't escalate. In the end, Fred handed over the flask. Sheri got up and was okay, but Addie, I think she stayed sitting. Could she even get up? Why the hell can't I remember?

I do know that we weren't ready to go anywhere. Not yet. Everyone settled down and we decided to eat. Jamal handed out the energy bars and bottled water. Sheri shared a box of raisins. Doing that kind of stuff is hard work and you need carbs and sugar to get you through the night. It makes for a hell of a crash when you're done, though.

We got real quiet. I thought someone a mile away would be able to hear us chewing. We'd never fought like that before and I think we were all feeling kind of weird.

All of us heard something in the woods.

We were startled at first, but then Sheri said it was probably just a deer. We'd been seeing deer in the distance all night. In hindsight, we should have known that no deer would come that close to a bunch of loud-mouthed humans. They're smarter than that. Way smarter than us.

We ignored it. And then it came again. It was the sound of scrunching grass. The Hayden hadn't seen a landscaper in decades, and some of the grass went past our knees. It hadn't rained for a while and everything was starting to turn brown and brittle.

To me, it sounded like footsteps, like a person walking, not an animal. I grabbed the lantern and turned it off. What if it was a cop? The last thing I wanted was to get arrested again. I'd just finished paying the fines from when I got busted at that vacant hospital in Port Chester.

Nobody made a sound.

We should have run. At the time, we didn't want to give our position away. I know I hoped whoever it was would walk right past us in the dark.

I always carried pepper spray with me. You never knew who was squatting in these places. You needed protection, and not bringing a gun was another rule. No guns, since what we did was illegal and if we got caught, we didn't need a weapons charge thrown in.

This time, I left the pepper spray in my pack. I was convinced it was a cop and I didn't want to spray him or her in the face. I waited to see the beam from a flashlight or hear them tell us to come out.

Whoever it was, they didn't bother to mask the noise they made as they walked around us. That's why I thought it was a cop. We were the ones in hiding, not them.

It got real tense. It sounded like they were circling us. I was afraid to even take a breath. I think Jamal was to my left. In the dark, it was too hard to see. I know I was holding Addie's hand. She was squeezing it so hard, I thought she would break it.

The footsteps started to move away.

And then the worst possible thing happened.

You know how those first aid shock blankets are made of that loud, silver kind of paper? Addie started shivering. When she went to pull the blanket tighter around her, it made this god-awful noise. I tried to stop her but it was too late. Fred shushed her, but she'd already stopped moving, so that also gave us away.

The walking stopped.

We waited a long time. Whoever was out there waited right along with us. None of us wanted to be the first to make another sound. That's when Fred knew it wasn't a cop and probably some derelict. He shouted that we knew he was out there and to get going.

He didn't get a reply. There were no more footsteps.

"Maybe it was an animal," Sheri said. With the shock blanket crinkling, we could have easily missed a deer or fox taking off. They're real fast and can put a lot of distance between you in a hurry.

Jamal made a joke about us being afraid of a rabbit or something and Fred laughed. Fred asked if anyone wanted to come with him to check out the pool.

That's when he turned on his flashlight.

And that's when we saw him.

We didn't actually see *him*. It happened so fast. Suddenly, there was someone standing right in front of Fred who shouldn't have been there at all. I mean, how could he have possibly gotten that close without us hearing?

Fred didn't even have time to react.

I saw the man's torso, and his arm lash out at Fred. He hit Fred with something that looked like a pipe or piece of rebar. There was rebar everywhere you looked. The sound it made when it hit Fred's skull. Oh my God. I can still hear it as if he's standing right next to me. It was a thump, like if you kicked a car door, and then it just sounded...it sounded *wet*.

Fred's flashlight dropped to the ground and we lost the light.

We screamed.

Someone was grabbing me. Either Addie or Sheri were shouting Fred's name over and over and over.

In the dark, I heard another *thump*.

Next thing I remember, we were running. I can't see who was running with me. I get the impression that we somehow split up. I was crying and half out of my mind with fear. I kept thinking, if Fred calls out for help, I wouldn't have the guts to go back for him. And that filled me with so much shame. I was especially ashamed at the relief I felt when I didn't hear him.

Absolute terror makes your mind do funny things. You think you're a certain type of person. When the shit hits the fan, is that the real you that comes out? Or is it just the fear taking over? I don't know, Todd. I've lost myself to fear all these years.

And that's all I remember the first time we saw him, the Wraith, and how Fred died. You told me not to read the reports later, but I did. I know that there was almost nothing left of Fred's face when they found his body. I didn't see it, but I heard it and I don't know which would have been worse.

Whenever I close my eyes and think about running, I can see my video camera in my hand. I'd been practically attached to it all night. I'd film little bits and put them on a USB that I wrapped in a plastic bag and hid. It's a strange thing, I know, but it was my thing. I know me. I was in the Hayden for close to four more hours. I know I recorded whatever I could, not to leave a piece of myself, but to have some kind of proof. If he got me, I knew he'd destroy my camera as easily as he'd destroy me.

So I left a saved recording around the Hayden. If I lived, I assumed I'd remember where I put it and easily find it for the police. If I died, I hoped they'd come across it during their investigation.

But I was wrong. I didn't remember until now, when it's too late and I'm too afraid to go back there. And the police, I think they were too unprepared and horrified by what happened to tear the place apart looking for any more evidence than what was around the bodies of my friends.

The Wraith used the remains of the Hayden to murder them. He came out of the darkness and he returned to it. I know we hurt him. We just didn't kill him. I'm beginning to wonder if we could.

No matter. It's all gone now. We're all gone now. And you're safe.

That's all that matters to me anymore.

You're safe.

The Hayden and its dark past, the threat of the Wraith, we're all going to die together. I just thought you should know, my love. I'm sorry I kept it from you until now. I had to keep you safe, and I had to keep you away from that place.

I love you more than you could ever know. And I love you still, even while you're watching this.

Goodbye, Todd.

Please remember me. And always, always love me, too.

CHAPTER ELEVEN

Todd opened one bleary eye to check his ringing phone. It was his foreman, probably pissed, definitely wondering where he was. He swiped his thumb across the screen to send the call to voice mail.

His head was pounding and his stomach felt curdled. He had to go to the bathroom, but he couldn't will his body out of bed. He unscrewed the cap on the bottle of water he'd left on the bedside table – a bottle he didn't remember putting there – and drank greedily.

All of the sheets and blankets had been kicked to the floor. He was sweating, the funk of alcohol so thick he thought he could reach into the air and ball it up like snow, yet he was so, so cold. Muscles aching from dehydration, he reached down to snag the corner of a blanket and pulled it over himself.

The laptop was open on his side of the bed. For the past two days, he'd been sleeping – no, passing out – on Ash's side. It would be easy to turn it on and watch the video again, just as he'd done day in and day out since he'd found it.

As he rolled over to do just that, he felt a heavy pressure shift on the mattress. He was startled to see Elvira had jumped up onto the bed. She positioned herself between him and the laptop, flopping onto her side to show him her sagging, shabby belly.

Elvira never went on the bed. Under it, yes, but never on it.

Her orange eyes pierced into his throbbing skull.

"Are you trying, tying to tell me something?" he mumbled. His throat hurt. He must have been snoring loud enough to rattle the walls last night. Drunk snores. Ash hated his drunk snores. She'd tell him they made the house *too loud*.

Elvira's paw flicked to her face and she licked it…loudly. Todd had to turn away.

Of course Elvira wasn't capable of understanding the implications of his watching Ash's video again.

But Ash would have known.

Had she urged the cat to block his access to the laptop?

Todd didn't believe in ghosts. That was Ash's territory. But ever since he'd found her last recording, he sensed that some part of her was near.

He hadn't expected a video, though he should have if he'd just taken a moment and thought about it instead of tearing through the house like a madman. Ever since she'd gotten her first phone in high school, she'd been addicted to taking pictures and videos, just like all the girls and most of the boys in their class. Personally, Todd hated selfies. He couldn't have cared less about chronicling every single thing he did throughout the day and sharing it with the world.

Ashley King was a product of her generation. Their parents would have called it vain or narcissistic, this need to constantly preen and smile for the camera. For some of the kids he knew, that was a dead-on assessment. Especially someone like Elise Judge, a girl so vapid and self-obsessed, she would marry herself if it were possible.

Ash found using video to capture special moments easier than writing in a diary. She said it gave her a more complete, a more accurate snapshot of her past. She was always nostalgic like that, desperate to capture the moment for posterity. Watching old interview shows had become a nighttime comfort for her after the night of the massacre. Lying next to Todd in bed, she'd follow links and suggested videos on her phone until the dawn, the volume on low because she didn't want to put in headphones and be deaf to the world around her.

He'd woken up one morning to her arm draped over his back and her phone hovering in front of his face.

"Watch this," she'd said excitedly.

He couldn't match her giddiness at the moment, but he indulged her.

She started a clip of a talk show from the seventies. Director Orson Wells, graying hair slicked back, cigar smoldering in his chubby fingers, was explaining how he couldn't trust history. The proof could be found right here, at any time. Tell someone a story and see how distorted and inaccurate it became in just one retelling. History was always being rewritten, from the moment it passed hands.

"Finally, someone gets it," Ash had said. "It's how I've always felt. I just could never get the words right."

So yes, it was only natural she'd leave him a video instead of a note. She must have known how seeing her face again would have rocked him to his core. So much so that he was sure he no longer had a job.

Had she sent Elvira onto the bed to tell him enough was enough? He looked into the cat's eyes and could find no answers.

Sitting up, he saw himself in the mirror hanging over the dresser. He looked like death.

"There's your sign."

His phone rang again. He knew if he didn't answer, he was more than likely fired.

He ignored it and went to the bathroom. He had to wake the hell up and steam the toxins from his body. There were even empty beer cans on top of the toilet tank.

"Enough already."

It was time to stop feeling sorry for himself and save Ash's history. There was a lot of work to do and precious little time.

★   ★   ★

The Gridiron Sports Bar was crowded for a Thursday night. It was easy to see why. Thursday Night Football played on almost a dozen televisions. For once, there was actually a competitive game. The bar was packed two people deep. Every table in the restaurant had been taken. Todd and his friends had pulled two round pub tables together and sat in the corner of the bar area. It was the only place that wasn't directly under a blaring television.

The waitress, a pretty girl who didn't look old enough to work legally, brought them their platter of wings and another pitcher of beer. Jerry Mulcahy was telling them about a brawl he broke up at a diner the past weekend and how it had spilled into the middle of the road. Someone had sucker punched him square in the face. His eyes were still black and the left side of his nose was a little swollen.

"Did you find out who did it?" Vince asked, piling his plate with drumsticks and blue cheese dressing.

"It wasn't for lack of trying. I would have liked to introduce the schmuck to my baton. There were seven of them, juiced-up peacocks with too much booze and little peckers. Me and my partner had a hell of a time getting them in cuffs, but we were sober and had the upper hand. I didn't even realize my nose was broken until our backup arrived." Jerry's glasses sat high on the bridge of his nose. He had a blue, black and white tattoo of the American flag on his forearm that flashed out of his sleeve when he reached over to pour the beer. He was small in stature but could fight like a heavyweight. Todd had always said Jerry would end up on one side of prison bars. He was just glad he chose the side that held the keys.

"It looks like it hurts," Heather said.

Jerry waved it off. "Only when they had to set it. Now it just sucks that it feels like I have a stuffed nose all the time. They need to make weed legal and outlaw alcohol. Fucking potheads don't do shit like this."

Todd looked at the beer in Jerry's hand. "If you couldn't drink beer, you'd lose your mind. Not to mention, we tried to make alcohol illegal and it didn't exactly turn out so well."

"Just replace Budweiser with bud and my job will be a hell of a lot easier on the night shift. Trust me."

"You even bother busting anyone for weed anymore?" Bill Croft asked. He munched on a carrot stick, one eye on the game. Todd was sure his friend from high school had money on the Packers.

"Mostly just the dealers," Jerry said. "I really don't give two shits if someone wants to kick back with a joint. However, if they think they can smoke in their cars and drive around stoned, they're gonna see my lights in their rearview."

Todd sipped at his warm beer. He hadn't been able to drink much. His liver had thrown up the white flag that morning. That was a good thing, because from here on out, he needed a clear head.

Face smeared with Buffalo sauce, Vince said to him, "Okay buddy, why did you assemble the Avengers in the loudest joint in town? If you're going to tell us that you decided to sell the house, we totally understand. You know you can crash with Heather and me if and when you're between places."

"Um, no, I'm not selling the house." Several people had suggested it, not blaming him if he wanted to distance himself from the place the love of his life had killed herself. As much as he dreaded going in the basement now, there was no way he was going to distance himself from Ashley.

Heather backhanded Vince on the arm. "You're so dense." She fixed her gaze on Todd. "It's about going to the Hayden, isn't it?"

"Yeah. I made some calls and the place is going down for good on Monday. Which means I have to go there tomorrow and give myself a couple of days to search for anything Ash left behind."

Vince said, "That place is freaking huge. It could take weeks, not days."

Todd shook his head. "Actually, no. Ash had planned to visit certain parts of the property that night. Plus I have the police report that mapped out where everything occurred. That narrows it down a lot. There's a bunch of bungalows, but only two were entered that night. The main hotel was in ruins, so they didn't stay in there long. Stuff like that."

"So you want us to help you look?" Bill asked. "They letting you in before they take it down?"

"Not exactly."

Jerry rolled his eyes. "Of course not. Which is why he's asking his cop buddy to come along so he can B&E and not end up getting fingerprinted."

Todd bit into a wing. "Actually, that's only partly true."

"What's the other part?" Jerry said.

"You have a gun."

"You expecting a shoot-out?"

"Just planning for anything to happen."

Was there even a ghost of a chance that the Wraith was still lingering around the Hayden? Probably not. He might have been a psycho killer, but even they were smart enough not to stick around a crime scene, even one that was five years old.

No matter, Todd would feel better if they had someone who not only had a gun, but was trained and responsible enough to know how to use it. Something in Ash was very afraid of his going back to the Hayden. There had to be a reason for it.

Jerry dropped his bones onto his plate. "So, you want me to help you break into this place and be your security guard?"

Smiling, Todd said, "That's one way to look at it." He held his breath, seeking an answer in Jerry's stony expression.

"I'm in."

Jerry tore into another wing and washed it down with a healthy swig of beer.

"You know Vince and I aren't letting you go without us," Heather said. Todd didn't fail to notice the quick, worried look Vince flashed his wife.

"What about you, Billy boy?" Todd said.

Bill held up a hand, waited for the play to end, and said, "Heck yeah. You know I can't pass up something like that."

Todd felt himself unclench. Ash would have been proud that he wasn't going to recklessly go to the Hayden alone. Then he thought that she would be upset that he was going at all. She only left that message and did what she did because she thought the Hayden was going to be destroyed. Guilt threatened to overwhelm his good mood.

"I'll email you guys all the things we'll need to bring along. We'd have to leave early, like one in the morning."

Vince groaned. "Why so early? It'll be dark as hell out."

"One thing Ash taught me was that the safest time to do urbex is on cold days and early in the morning. Fewer police patrols."

"I can take care of the local guys," Jerry said.

"Ash was there in the dark. I'll have a better idea of where she could have hidden her recordings if I'm in the dark too. I'll see what she saw. Does that make sense?"

Heather dabbed the corners of her mouth with a napkin. "Actually, it does. Should we all meet at your house?"

"That works. I'll have a midnight feast prepared so we can load up before we hit the road. Sound good?"

"I'm on a low carb diet," Jerry said. "Just throw some meat and cheese at me."

"Duly noted," Todd said, wondering why his friend who didn't have an ounce of fat on him was on any kind of diet.

They stayed until halftime, talking about anything but what

they were about to do. None o

experience. They were all going to

some closure, and he was more grate

just hoped he didn't come away from

What if he couldn't find it? Would his f

his life? Would this whole endeavor only

As they walked into the chill night air of

pulled him aside. "I think there's one more p

"Who?"

Jerry, Vince and Bill formed a circle around th

"I don't think it's a good idea," Vince said.

"She needs this too," Heather replied. "She's h

as Todd."

Perplexed, Todd asked, "Who are you talking about

He noticed Heather had a hard time looking him in th

was suddenly very interested in the blacktop at their feet.

"Sharon."

"No," Todd blurted. "No way."

"I had a feeling you would be going up there and I may

mentioned it to her yesterday."

"Jesus Christ! You know how irresponsible that is?" He couldn'

believe Heather, the most grounded of them all, had done such a

thing.

"As irresponsible as five people breaking into a construction zone

in the dead of night?" she shot back.

Todd stormed off, ignoring her as he got in his car and drove out

of the lot with a knot in his stomach as big as a dinosaur egg.

them had any urban exploring
support Todd and help him get
ful than he could express. He
the Hayden empty-handed.
...ilure haunt him the rest of
...ake things worse?
...he parking lot, Heather
...rson we should ask."
...em.
...rting as much
...e eye. She
...ave

...ne
...Sharon
mean older
...terests. Sharon's
...out of trouble when

...ne massacre, and it seemed had
...ietime along the way. Todd lay on
...ow. He was too angry to sleep.
...pened her mouth?
...y had already endured enough tragedy. He wanted
...entially visiting more upon them.

...t Heather been paying attention? Just a few weeks ago,
...sent a very public message to the Wraith, daring the killer
to come find him. Now they were going back to the scene of the
worst massacre in Catskills history. What if the Wraith was alive and
had been watching Todd all along, waiting for the right moment
to strike? Wouldn't their expedition be the perfect opportunity to
emerge from the shadows?

"I should just call it all off," he said to Elvira. The cat dozed on
the cushion next to him. Her ears twitched at the sound of his voice.

What had he been thinking?

He'd almost willingly endangered all of their lives, not just
Sharon's. Sure, Jerry was armed, but would that be enough?

Maybe.

Ash and her friends had been ambushed and they hadn't been
prepared. That wouldn't be the case this time.

But maybe not.

And that sliver of doubt made him decide that he would go it alone.

He had to tell them he wasn't going. Maybe say he had a moment of clarity and realized the odds of his finding anything Ash left behind – and the police hadn't already found – were slim to none. No matter, it wouldn't bring her back. Which was all maddeningly true. He just wasn't ready to let it go. Not until the Hayden was absolute rubble.

He grabbed his phone and was about to text them but stopped himself. It was three in the morning. They all had jobs to go to in just a few hours. It was best to wait.

Todd closed his eyes.

Get some sleep. Text them later. I'll leave in the afternoon and get an early start. Gotta find a place to hide the car. Remember to buy bolt cutters. Have to pack. Maybe I should get a new flashlight while I'm at it.

His brain buzzed with to-do lists until the sun's first rays bled through the gaps in the blinds and he finally fell fast asleep.

"Todd, this is Addie."

He shook the hand of the pale, wispy girl, her eyes so big and blue, they didn't seem real.

"Is this the *Todd?" she said, smiling.*

"The one and only," Ash said. She had her hand on his back. It felt right. Comfortable. Familiar, even when he had no right for it to be that way.

"Are you coming with us?" Addie asked. The sunlight streamed through her honey hair and Todd was sure most men got tongue-tied in her presence. She was undoubtedly beautiful – just not his type. He flicked his eyes away from her, back on Ash looking stellar in a simple white T-shirt and jeans, several holes placed strategically by her knees and thighs.

"I'm just the driver," he said. "I'd only get in the way. You guys are the experts." If there were such a thing for breaking and entering into abandoned resorts.

"We'll have to ease him in slowly," Ash said. The bridge of her nose crinkled when she laughed.

"You sure you don't wanna come?"

"If I got caught, I'd lose my job. I'm better off being the bail man."

Addie patted his chest. "Hope you've got a good line of credit."

Ash and Addie looked at one another and broke into fresh laughter.

"You won't need to bail us out," Ash reassured him. He must have looked worried to them. "We're good at this. Besides, the Hayden is so big, escape won't be an issue if it comes to it."

"We're fast, like gazelles," Addie said. "Well, except for Jamal. But he's real good at hiding."

That got them laughing again.

Now they were in the van with everyone and Addie was popping her head up front between Todd and Ash every few minutes, joking around, once panting like a dog, her tongue lolling out of her mouth, making moon eyes at Todd. Anything for a laugh. She asked him one last time to tag along but he'd refused, dropping them off along the resort's fenced perimeter.

Todd wasn't the most perceptive guy in the world, but even he knew she'd been flirting with him. Ash had taken it well, though she did seem a little peeved just before he pulled up to the Hayden. He and Ash had just reconnected and he didn't dare even dream that they could get back together. It was nice just being friends at the moment. But he didn't want to give the impression that he welcomed Addie's advances. Not if there was even a scintilla of a chance that Ash would let him back in.

Now the news was reporting how Addie Lawrence had been cracked apart like a wishbone. Both of her legs had been pulled violently from their hip sockets, rather than cut off with a sharp or blunt instrument. The medical examiner determined that she had still been alive, though hopefully not conscious, as the flesh was removed from her body, the sharpened edge of a vinyl record used as a cutting tool. A leak in the police department months later revealed that the record-cum-weapon was Somewhere There's a Someone *by Dean Martin.*

*   *   *

Todd woke at eleven, shivering under the sheet, his comforter having been tossed to the floor while he slept. He sat up in bed, massaging the bridge of his nose.

Poor Addie.

She'd been an only child. Her mother had been struck down with breast cancer six months after Addie's funeral. She joined her daughter in the family plot three months later. Donald Lawrence drank himself to death the following year. The Wraith had killed the entire Lawrence family.

Todd got up, grabbed his phone and sent a group text telling his friends the search was off. For the better part of an hour, he typed away furiously on his phone, responding to their replies. Heather was the most supportive of his decision. He couldn't hear Vince's relief in his texts but he knew it was there. Jerry pushed him a bit at first, hinting that he was psyched for the adventure. Heather, Vince and Bill basically got him to stand down and leave Todd alone.

Todd's eyes were bleary by the time every one of the texts petered out.

Tossing his phone on the couch, he said to Elvira, "Time to go. Try not to miss me."

The cat yawned, flashing her oversized canines.

Hating shopping of any kind, Todd hustled through his to-do list. He bought snacks and bottled water at the deli. A quick trip to Shad's Hardware got him the rope, bolt cutters, air filtration mask and a heavy-duty flashlight. He had to swing by a sporting goods place to find a headlamp and small first aid kit. On the way back home, he dipped into the pet store to buy one of those cat feeders so Elvira would have a steady supply of food over the weekend. While waiting on line to check out, he made an impulse buy and got her a toy mouse that had catnip inside and a bell on its tail.

Back home, he realized he was going to have to go down into the basement. That's where Ash's backpack had been stashed away. He wanted a piece of her with him on this trip.

His hand lingered on the doorknob to the basement. His heart raced every time he went down there, which wasn't often. A wave of sadness threatened to drown him in tears. He squeezed his eyes and thumped his forehead against the door, pushing back the swell. Once he was sure he could keep it together, he opened the door.

The box where they'd stored her old urbex stuff was right where she'd hanged herself. He didn't know he was holding his breath until his lungs began to burn. Todd was dizzy with the conflict of wanting to still feel her presence, and terrified that he would see her hanging again. His right eye blurred with tears as he crept across the basement. He refused to look up at the rafter where she'd secured the noose. He knew that if he did, he wouldn't be able to take one step farther.

When the furnace kicked on with a click and a whoosh, his heart nearly stopped. Cursing himself, he gritted his teeth and focused on the stack of cardboard boxes. Ash's neat handwriting had marked her belongings with a thick black marker. The top box was filled with carefully folded clothes that she'd meant to bring to the Goodwill drop box.

After setting it aside without bothering to close the flaps back because he wasn't sure how much longer he could stay here, he ripped the packing tape off the top of the next.

Sighing with relief, he saw Ash's dull green backpack tucked under well-worn jeans and shirts. He pulled it out and hurried back upstairs, the hairs on the back of his neck prickling, the ghost of Ash's final moment of suffering bearing down on him.

Slamming the door closed, he held the backpack to his chest.

She'd called it her lucky backpack and the fact that she hadn't brought it to the Hayden gave proof to it. Would things have been different if she'd had this with her?

No, that was ridiculous.

This time, he let himself cry. Ash's backpack absorbed his tears.

He sat on the floor with his back against the cellar door until he emptied his tears. When it was done, he felt lighter, almost invigorated. He packed everything he needed quickly, then he filled Elvira's new feeder and gave her two bowls of fresh water. She was nowhere to be seen. She'd come out when she was hungry.

"Be good, Elvira. I'll be back in a couple of days."

He slipped the backpack over his shoulder and stepped outside.

Ash was waiting for him. It was time to find her.

CHAPTER THIRTEEN

"Mr. Matthews, I'm so sorry about Ashley."

The girl looked to be high school age. She clutched a teddy bear to her heart. Her two friends, both redheads wearing black T-shirts with Ouija board designs, stared at him with surprise and sadness. They all had on too much makeup, their jet-black eyeliner drawn on too thick, ears, noses and lips pierced like pincushions.

Behind them were ten other final girl devotees. Had school been let out early so the loonies could visit their shrine? Only two of them were boys, their goth getup silly enough to make Todd chuckle on any other day.

"Look, I really have somewhere to go," Todd said, angling between the trio of girls at his doorstep.

One of the girls pointed at his backpack. Ash's backpack.

"Are you going to the Hayden?" she asked.

Her fiery hair had a Bettie Page cut, her severe bangs inches from her penciled eyebrows.

Todd froze. "What?"

"Oh, maybe you didn't know."

The one with the teddy bear chimed in, "They're tearing down the Hayden Resort on Monday. We just thought maybe you were going there one last time."

Jesus. The lunatic final girls knew. Of course they did. The demolition was a matter of public record. And even if it was going to be done in secret, he was sure these people would find out anyway.

"Good for them," Todd replied tersely. The last thing he wanted to do was give them any hint that he cared.

"I understand. I'm sure it's painful to even think of that place," the redhead with the bangs said. He wanted to wipe that look of condolence off her face.

"They can do whatever the fuck they want with it."

The rest of the worshipers parted and let him get to his Mustang. He saw fresh flowers lined up against the garage door.

With twenty-six eyes staring at him, Todd slammed the door and gunned the engine, hitting the gas so the beast of a muscle car roared. Several of the girls jumped back.

He shifted the car in reverse and tore out of the driveway, his tires screeching. It was a dumb move. With his mind buzzing, he didn't bother to check his rearview mirror. Speeding into the middle of the street, he cut the wheel hard to the left and straightened out, mercifully not running anyone over in the process.

The temptation to open the window and give them all the finger as he drove away was rough, but he didn't give in.

He wasn't stopping until he got to Topperville.

*　　*　　*

Driving through the dying Catskills town, he hoped the final girl cultists hadn't made their way to the Hayden.

Hope, as usual, was a sucker's bet.

Passing by the dilapidated billboard for the resort, he spotted two cars parked underneath it, a group of people taking pictures at its base.

He punched the dashboard, avoiding eye contact with the murder tourists. His phone chimed. There was a text from Vince. It would have to wait.

His worst fears were realized when he got to the gated front entrance. Two police cars were parked nose to nose. They were surrounded by people, everyone holding a cell phone to take pictures and video. He recognized the two cops that had come upon him and Vince a week earlier. It looked like they had their hands full.

Todd pressed down on the gas a little harder. He didn't want them noticing his distinctive car.

"Okay, it's not like you were going in through the front door anyway. These assholes can't be everywhere."

Ash had once told him that before she and her friends ever entered a place, they would spend days, if not weeks, doing recon. They had to find the best places to enter, the prime time to do so, spot any potential dangers, track when the police cruised by and keep an eye out for people – crazy and otherwise – who had decided to make the derelict building or property their home.

All he had was the one day with Vince, searching for the easiest way to get inside the perimeter fence. It would have to do.

But first things first. He had to stash the car somewhere.

Parking it on the street outside a residential home was out. People would get suspicious of an unfamiliar car. He thought of tucking it behind an old repair garage that had last fixed an engine around the time the first Bush was president. Unfortunately, it didn't provide enough cover. The bay doors were long gone and part of the back wall had crumbled, giving a perfect line of sight to his car. He drove and drove, careful not to go too far because he had to walk to the resort.

The empty, sagging house on Sycamore Avenue fit the bill. The neighboring houses were also vacant. It had a separate two-car garage in the back. The hinges were stubborn with rust, but he was able to get the door open. Inside, it smelled of long-dead critters, ancient oil and must. A bird flew out of a hole in the roof, startled by the intrusion.

Todd parked the car and closed the door. Confident no one saw him, he shouldered his pack and consulted the crude map he'd drawn. It was a two-mile walk to the spot in the fence he thought would offer the least resistance. Squaring his Jets baseball cap on his head, he tightened the laces of his boots and set off.

*   *   *

There was still an hour until dusk, but the temperature was already plummeting. Todd was glad he'd put on thermals, even though he'd been sweating on the ride up to Topperville. His black North Face Thermoball jacket was formfitting but warm. It was perfect for this weekend, as he didn't want to be wearing anything too bulky because he'd be doing a lot of climbing around.

He walked between the trees on the west side of the resort, skirting the fence. He'd spotted only two other people on the south-western edge. They were taking pictures and picking up rocks, probably as mementos. Thankfully, it appeared that none of the other final girl fanatics were bothering to make their way up here in the wilder, more overgrown slope.

Through the links in the fence, he saw what he assumed was one of the holes for the Hayden's once-touted golf course. The grass had long turned to weeds, but he could tell where the greens had once been. Just a little more to go.

Taking a quick break to drink some water, he let the pack slide off his shoulders. It was heavy as hell. The bolt cutters were clipped to the outside of the backpack and had been thumping into the side of his leg with every step. It would have been easier to divide everything up between his friends, but he'd made the right decision to go it alone.

Looking down the hill he'd had to climb to get here, he couldn't see the streets at all. It was if they'd finally faded into the ether. Nor could he see the crowd of people at the front entrance. He assumed, possibly erroneously, that once it got cold and dark, the ghouls would head on back to their parents' basements and share their pictures on Instagram and Snapchat for the rest of the night. He hoped to hell that's what they would do, because he didn't need the cops lingering around.

Figuring it was best to wait until he got inside to munch on an energy bar, he trudged farther along the back end of the Hayden. It only took five more minutes until he found the part where the fence wasn't flush with the ground. With just a few snips of the bolt cutters, he was able to make a space between the bottom of the fence and the earth to crawl through. Sure, he could have cut a gap wide enough to simply walk through, but he didn't want to alert anyone who might be patrolling the area that someone had gotten inside.

Todd dropped to the ground at the sound of something rustling to his left. Momentarily winded, he looked up to see a crow bursting from a tree.

"Fucking moron."

He wasn't sure if he meant the crow or himself.

He found himself in the part where the golf course meandered and it provided very little cover. He had to do a crouch-scoot until he got to the outer edge of a strip of bungalows. His back and knees were already sore by the time he made it to the back end of the first bungalow.

Those damn final girl maniacs just couldn't get out of his way. He'd wanted to see more of the Hayden in the daytime, but now he'd have to keep hidden until they left. Peering through the open space where windows used to be, he could see clear through the bungalow to the entrance, which was far enough away for him to not be seen. The shadows were growing longer, the flickering red and white lights telling him the police were still stationed out front. There was no sense taking any chances. It was best to sit and wait.

A rotund rat trundled across the main living area of the bungalow. There went any chance of him going inside to wait things out for a bit. He ate half an energy bar and sat against the bungalow's back door.

Now that Todd was alone and inside the Hayden Resort, the gravity of the moment and the place finally weighed down on him.

Five years ago, Ash and her friends were here in a place that had been forgotten by the world. When had the screaming started? The police figured the killing had begun sometime between three and four a.m. Unfortunately, there was no way for Ash to give them a timeline. She'd escaped, and her mind had wiped it all clean to preserve her sanity.

Nature was devouring the Hayden and its nightmares. Weeds had pushed through the cracks and crept up every bit of manmade structures like a blanket of thick fog.

Breathing in the fresh mountain air, Todd smelled the pollution of the resort. It had been forever tainted by the night of the massacre. It might have been fouled even before then. Ash had hinted at just as much. What else had happened here?

Todd felt uneasy. It was almost as if he could feel the Hayden pushing him out, making him feel unwanted. He closed his eyes, searching for some remnant of Ash. If he sat still long enough, would he hear her carefully traipsing through the rubble or catch a whiff of her favorite perfume?

Or would he go rigid at the sound of her peals of terror?

Steadying his heart, he crossed his arms over his knees and rested his head against them.

"Are you here, Ash?"

Quieting his mind, he relaxed and let the Hayden come to him.

They found her on Route 33 at daybreak. She was covered from head to toe in blood. Long streaks had been carved down her cheeks, her tears slicing through the gore. Her clothes were torn. Dirt and grit filled a nasty, gaping wound in her arm. When asked what had happened, she'd been unable to speak. She shivered uncontrollably, even when they covered her in two blankets and turned the heat on high in the squad car.

It would be two whole days before she spoke a single word, and even then, it was only Mommy. By then, Ashley King had become a media sensation.

The horrors of the Hayden slipped into Todd's fitful dreams, twisting them into nightmare.

Ash was running inside the Hayden, before she'd climbed the gates and wandered down the street. Ash threw worried glances behind her, her flashlight long gone, the moon hidden behind invisible clouds. There was a foul taste in her mouth that demanded to be expelled. She didn't dare stop. If she paused for even a moment, he would get her. The hospital would later find that the source of the offending taste was a part of Sheri Viola's brain that had somehow lodged itself between her back molar and her cheek.

Hyperventilating, choking back vomit, the juices of Sheri's gray matter dripping down her throat, Ash ran, lifting her feet as high as her exhausted legs would allow, wary that she could easily be tripped up by roots and debris.

Heavy, frantic footfalls were close behind.

Thump-thump, thump-thump, thump-thump, thump-thump.

Her energy was flagging. Only fear kept her going now.

Todd watched her wend her way down the winding drive. She hopped over a chunk of concrete, her ankles just missing a sharp end of rebar poking from the slab.

He wanted to run to her, but he was paralyzed. He opened his mouth to scream, to gain the attention of the Wraith, but nothing came out. Todd could only watch in stony silence as Ash ran for her life.

She hit the padlocked entrance gates hard. They rattled on their rusted hinges. Two vertical bruises would later bloom on her forehead from smacking it against the unforgiving bars.

Ashley cried out, begging for help, her voice echoing in the stillness.

He was close.

She turned around. Todd saw the shadow rushing toward her.

Weeping now, Ash gripped the bars and climbed. The blood on her hands made it almost impossible to maintain her grasp. The rubber soles of her boots propelled her upward. She was almost at the top when the Wraith lunged for her. He swiped at her legs. A crimson line spread on the back of her calf like a child's smile.

Ash reared her head to the sky and wailed in agony. Hands fumbled for her kicking feet. Gravity swooped in to save her, pulling her over the top of the gate and drawing her to the hard ground on the other side.

The Wraith, his face as dark and unreadable as the pitch-black sky, glared at her from the ruined confines of the Hayden.

He did not follow her.

Ash stumbled down the center of the road, half-mad and losing blood. She would run a full mile before someone saw her from their window and called the police.

As Ash disappeared around the bend of Route 33, Todd watched the Wraith push away from the gate. The sun crested on the horizon. The Wraith slipped away like a vampire, sated on blood and carnage. The only evidence of his presence was the shattered bodies and lives he left behind.

Todd awoke unable to draw a breath. For a terrifying moment, he thought the nightmare had stopped his heart.

But then his heart gave a hard thump against his chest, as if to reassure him it was still there, still working. Hands and feet nervously fumbling, he drew in a long, croaking breath.

He panicked, unsure of his surroundings, cloaked in total darkness.

He froze at the sound of breaking twigs.

Someone was coming, and he didn't know where he was.

CHAPTER FOURTEEN

It was full dark and cold as hell.

Todd jumped to his feet. Standing swiped the cobwebs from his brain. His back to the decaying bungalow, he unzipped the backpack, careful not to make a sound. His hand found the butcher's knife he'd packed, just in case.

Whoever was coming crunched through the leaf litter, obviously unaware of Todd's presence.

Or maybe they did know he was there and wanted him uneasy and afraid.

He swallowed hard, his heart beating in his throat.

Fuck this, he thought, grabbing the flashlight from the pack's side pocket. He snapped the light on, the knife held high in his other hand. The blinding shaft of light fell on brown grass and leaves. The footsteps stopped. He swept the light to the left.

A pair of glowing eyes glared back at him.

The raccoon was bigger than any he'd ever seen. It scampered away, kicking up leaves in its wake.

Todd exhaled the great breath he'd been holding. A cone of fog flowed into the night.

The goddamn wildlife is going to give me a heart attack.

After waiting a few moments for his heartbeat to settle down, he checked to see if the police and final girl fanatics were still there.

All gone.

Perfect. It was time to get to work.

No one knew where Ash and her friends made their entry, but the forensics team and Ash's taped message to him corroborated that they spent most of their time at the hotel, the attached indoor pool and ice rink. The hotel had been in a dangerous state of disrepair, but it was also the centerpiece of the resort. He knew that if she had left a recording or note behind, it would be in there, in the heart of the Hayden.

Just in case there were any police lingering about, he took out Ash's video camera and turned on the night vision. He used it to keep an eye on the ground and avoid falling over or into any hazards.

None of the bungalow windows retained their glass. A majority were boarded up, but time had rotted and split the wood. There were no pebbles or shards to be wary of since they had been absorbed into the ground long ago.

He couldn't believe how dark it was. Just like the night of the massacre, the moon was obscured by clouds. It would be the entire weekend, according to the weather service. There was a threat of freezing rain or snow, depending on how low the temperature dipped. It sure felt cold enough for snow.

The gloom had weight here. It was like walking through miles of muck. It sat on his shoulders like a leering gargoyle.

He wasn't prone to fantasy or ghost stories, but walking down the boulevard of dead, empty bungalows made him uncomfortable. He tried to think what it must have been like in its heyday. Big band music from the theater and lounge would bleed into the night. The bungalows would glow from warm fires. Couples would be walking where he was now, hand in hand, enjoying the night air and perhaps a stolen kiss, or more, in the dark.

It was hard to imagine the Hayden filled with light and life. Every time he conjured up an image of happy travelers, it dissolved like paper dipped in acid.

What he saw instead was the Wraith stalking and murdering Ash's friends. Several times he had to pause, thinking he heard screaming, until he realized it was all in his head.

The hotel loomed in the distance.

It had been too dangerous to really explore five years ago. It would only be worse now. Of all the places in the resort, that was the one where safety in numbers came into play. He studied it through the camera. It looked perfectly fine, save the broken and boarded-up windows and graffiti that had been spray-painted from the ground to several floors up.

He picked up his pace, as if he were being physically drawn to the doomed edifice.

"Ash is in there. I know it."

The sound of his hushed voice brought comfort in the stillness.

Most of the portico was on the ground in big, chunky blocks. When the Hayden had closed, the entrance, with its revolving door and swinging doors on the wings, had been boarded up. The wood, underlying glass and steel were long gone now. It resembled a toothless, open mouth, the decay emanating from the old hotel like fetid breath.

Todd stowed the camera away, confident that he could use his flashlight wisely without being spotted. He kept it low to the ground, angling it inside.

The lobby looked as if it had barely survived a blitzkrieg. Some of the plush chairs and love seats that he'd seen in old pictures had been left behind. In the ensuing years, they had been ravaged by nature, animals, humans and time. Springs sprouted from shredded, moldy cushions. Legs and arms had been torn off and flung about the great room. The floor was a minefield of plaster, bricks, cans, bottles and reams of paper. Most of the paper came from discarded magazines and old files. Todd's light settled upon a pair of bare breasts, a man's hands cupping them from behind. He bent down to flip the magazine closed, saw it was only a few months old. The thought that people came here to get off made him sick.

He kicked a bottle out of the way. It spun a couple of feet until it clinked against a slab of stone. Wires hung from the ceiling, many years removed from carrying the current that supplied light to the grand hotel.

Just like it was on the exterior, graffiti was everywhere. And not the good stuff. Poorly construed tags, illegible to him because he didn't speak graffiti, had been painted on the walls, floor, rubble and shards of furniture. He even saw a big, block letter *BRITNEY LOVES COCK* sprayed onto the ceiling.

"How in the hell did they get up there?"

Video images from the news five years earlier superimposed themselves over the surroundings. Todd was standing in the center of the Wraith's masterwork. After he had murdered Ash's friend's, desecrating their bodies in unspeakable ways, he'd brought them all here, scattering their pieces large and small the way an old man would scatter stale bits of bread for the pigeons. So much of that footage had to be blurred because the blood at the time was still fresh.

Todd turned to his left and the broken pile of couches. That's where Jamal Banks's head and hands had been found, his index fingers jammed in his ears.

On the wall to his right was where Addie Lawrence had been pinned to the wall like a crucified Jesus, her severed legs forming an X over her head.

Pieces of a male body had littered the floor in wet, ropy dollops. By process of elimination, they knew it had been Fred Mass, his pale flesh in stark contrast to Jamal's. His head, what was left of it, had been stuffed under a board, only found when a cop had stepped on it and heard a loud squelch.

Sheri, her body bathed in blood, had been broken in so many ways, the Wraith had simply balled her up, leaving her in the middle of the lobby, her head pushed into her crotch, arms wrapped around her body and wrists wrapped with wire to keep everything in place.

Todd knew he was walking on their blood, but it was impossible to discern bloodstains from mold. He wished he didn't know the details of the police report, but at the time, he demanded that information from the police. The censored story in the news wasn't enough. How could he help Ash if he didn't know the true horror she'd experienced?

He let a savage shiver run up his spine, took a breath and moved on.

The walls by the east wing of the hotel were still black with soot, the remnants of the big fire that closed the Hayden for good. As he got closer to the wall, he could make out the faint, lingering odor of the fire. Amazing. It was as if the fabric of the Hayden refused to let go of the memory of the night that had killed it.

Recalling those news stories, he was amazed by how much worse the Hayden had gotten. Instead of keeping people out, it looked like the massacre had attracted even more, and they had left their mark by dismantling what was already in disarray.

One thing that hadn't been destroyed was the check-in desk. It dominated the room. Once long enough to accommodate ten guests at a time, the mahogany counter was nicked and scarred and laden with detritus. He saw a rusty bell amidst the debris.

"Well, why not?"

He tapped the bell. The responding, warped ding reverberated through the bones of the Hayden. The unsettling echo made Todd shiver.

"Not going to do that again."

He snapped off his flashlight and waited for a moment, wondering if the noise had woken any strange denizens that had chosen to live within the tomb-like wreck. There was nothing but the susurration of the wind through the shattered windows and cracks.

Todd couldn't help feeling watched.

A thought occurred to him that he immediately tried to dismiss, but this place had him unmoored and unable to retain his pragmatic core.

What if the ghosts of Ash's friends were here? Could Jamal, Fred, Sheri and Addie still linger here, restless spirits trapped by the sticky despair of their final moments?

If ghosts did exist, he was sure he would find them here.

But they didn't, so it was pointless to even think about.

"Where did you hide it, Ash?" he said, getting his mind back on the task at hand.

The elevator doors had been welded shut. Only one of them had been pried open by determined vandals. He tested the floor by the elevator, approaching it cautiously. When he felt it would hold him, he poked his head and flashlight inside. The elevator car was nowhere to be seen, the cables taut as piano wire. He looked up, unable to see to the top. Someone had even spray-painted the shaft.

He backed out, sweeping the light around the room. To the right of the check-in desk was a noble staircase, the kind he could imagine royalty, or those who wished to be royalty, would descend to make a stately entrance.

The banisters had held true, but most of the steps themselves were missing. He looked through one of the gaps and saw what would be a debilitating fall. Were they this bad when Ash had been here? She did say they hadn't gone to the other floors, so there was no need to risk going up them. If he fell through and managed to survive, at best he'd break both his legs and end up buried under the rubble when they razed the hotel.

He could picture Ash's excitement at being here. It was impossible not to be overcome by the shades of the past and the cold certainty of the future, where nothing was able to escape rot and ruin.

Todd wandered to the coat check. The racks were there, holding a dozen or so wire hangers. Someone had dragged a mattress into the room. There were so many condom wrappers in the tiny room, they had practically formed a carpet. The mattress was solid brown. The stench of mold and musk and spent fluids was overpowering. He had to walk away, breathing into his sleeve to filter the air.

He'd been young and horny too, but he couldn't imagine ever being that hard up to use such a place. And what kind of girl would have let him? Certainly not Ash.

Back in the day, massive mirrors that went from the floor to the ceiling had been on the far wall, making the lobby look twice its already considerable size. It was no shock to see they'd been smashed, the shards resembling deadly sabers. One of those shards had been used to slice Addie to ribbons, according to the coroner. Cartoonish faces had been spray-painted where the glass once hung, gaping mouths and exaggerated eyes staring back at him. He put the knife down on a dented and rusted file cabinet.

The bottoms of the gilt frames were still attached to the wall. Making sure he didn't impale his lower legs on the glass, he felt within the frame for a memory card or even a rare written note. His finger grazed a triangle of glass.

"Shit."

He jerked his hand out, flicking off the spot of blood that bubbled up. Wiping it on his jeans, he went back to searching, being more careful this time. Four frames later, he came away with two more cuts on his fingers and nothing more.

The concierge desk had been hammered into two pieces. Empty bags of junk food had been speared on the splinters. Ash wouldn't have left anything there.

Because the lobby was in shambles, there were thousands of places Ash could have hidden a recording. He'd need floodlights and a team of a hundred people to properly go over the place.

Feeling defeat when he'd just begun, he angrily kicked a shard of wood. It sailed to the corner of the lobby. When he looked to see where it had landed, he came upon a vase filled with fresh flowers.

Seeing something so vibrant and alive felt wrong in this place of atrophy.

A small placard leaned against the vase. It read: *We will always remember. RIP Sheri, Addie, Jamal and Fred.*

Beside it was another vase crammed with beautiful red roses. A handwritten index card had been taped to the vase. That one read: *Ash Lives!*

In a flash, Todd grabbed the vase and launched it into the wall, shattering the glass and destroying the roses. His instant, near-blackout anger surprised even him.

Ash did not live. Not here. Not anywhere. At best, he would recover a memory, but nothing more.

But where? Why did he think this would have been less than impossible?

He leaned against an overturned chair, or what was left of it, and massaged the bridge of his nose.

"Just take a second and think. You know Ash. Where in this whole disaster would she hide it?"

Todd drew in a sharp breath at the sound of someone approaching the hotel. He snapped off his light, worried that if he tried to open his backpack and take out his camera with night vision he would give himself away.

There was nowhere to hide in the lobby.

He held his breath and waited.

CHAPTER FIFTEEN

The best he could do was crouch behind the remains of the chair. The ground was littered with so much glass, plaster and rocks, it would be impossible to even take a step without making a sound.

Twin flashlight beams shined into the lobby, jerkily bobbing and weaving as whoever held them walked closer to the hotel's entrance.

They came silently.

Must be the cops on patrol, he thought. He hoped it was one of the ones who had rolled up on him a week ago. He was pretty sure he could talk his way out of handcuffs with them. But that would also mean his search for what Ash left and the real story of that tragic night was over.

What if it wasn't the cops?

What if it's the Wraith?

Shit, the knife!

He'd left it on the file cabinet over by the mirrors.

It's not the Wraith. There were clearly at least two people heading his way. He was pretty sure a maniac like that didn't have an accomplice. But that wasn't true. Though rare, there had been serial killers who didn't work alone. He recalled that Dean Arnold Corll and the Freeway Killer had both been assisted by weak, twisted teens. After what had happened to Ash, Todd had taken a deep dive for the following year into studying the origin stories and twisted lives of serial killers and mass murderers. He'd done it all in secret, not wanting to upset Ash. He'd had many a nightmare that year, but he'd kept them from Ash, who was dealing with her own intense night terrors.

Whoever was coming, they were not raccoons.

If it was the police, it would be better if he didn't have the knife. It would be one less thing to explain.

Pulling his knees to his chest, he drew into himself to hopefully disappear behind the remnants of the chair.

He pulled his jacket up over his mouth to hide his frozen breath.
The crunch of glass announced their arrival.

Footsteps echoed in the demolished lobby. He strained to differentiate the steps. There could have been two people, if not more. Circles of light swept the walls.

"Man, what a dump."

Todd froze.

"Is it even safe to walk around?"

Rising from his haunches, Todd said, "What the hell are you doing here?"

Heather made a high yelping sound that would have been more at home coming from a Chihuahua. Multiple shafts of light blinded Todd. He had to put his hands over his face to quell the pain.

"Hey buddy, you didn't think we'd believe you called the whole thing off, now did you?" Jerry Mulcahy said.

"I'd hoped," Todd said. "And please stop blinding me."

They moved their lights away.

Vince, Heather, Jerry, Bill and, to Todd's horror, Sharon Viola, stood in the center of the lobby. She'd certainly grown into a woman since the last time he'd seen her. Sharon's nut-brown skin, prominent cheekbones and hawk's eyes imbued her with both beauty and a hard edge that belied her years.

Todd went to them to show them the floor would hold.

"We would have been here sooner," Vince said, shaking his hand. "But when we came, there were all these crazies and police around. We found a diner the next town over and had a bite to eat before heading back."

"I hope there's someplace to take a dump, because I can already tell those fries and gravy are going to be trouble," Bill Croft said. He had a hand on his belly.

Jerry laughed. "Look at this place. Where *can't* you take a dump?"

"I didn't bring toilet paper."

"That's what leaves are for," Jerry said.

"Or you can use pages from the porno mags I found," Todd said. He had to admit, a part of him was relieved to see them. He hadn't realized how heavy and eerie it was going to be on the Hayden grounds.

Heather stared guiltily at him. "Hi, Todd."

"Hey."

"You remember Sharon?"

Sheri's kid sister wasn't a kid anymore. She'd filled out since he'd last seen her. Had she been in high school then, or had she just started college? Even under her layers, he could see she had curves that would drive men wild. Her chest seemed exaggerated for such a small frame.

"I do," he said. "I hope you don't take offense, but I was really hoping you wouldn't be here."

She narrowed her eyes. "Well, none of us owns the market on pain." Turning away from him, she wandered around the lobby.

"You couldn't have ditched her?" he whispered to Heather.

"She was waiting outside my house when I got off work. There was nothing I could have done."

Except not tell her the plan, but that cat was already out of the bag and Todd wouldn't beat her up about it.

"We'll just have to deal with it," he said. "We have to make sure nothing happens to her. I don't even want her getting a splinter. Her parents have been through enough."

Jerry tapped his chest with his flashlight. "Already on it, bud. I'll keep a very close eye on her." His eyes were locked onto her ass as she leaned over the check-in desk.

"I'm sure you will," Todd said. He wasn't crazy about Jerry's leering, but at least she'd have his full attention all night.

Vince sidled up to him. "Heather tells me that Sharon has kind of separated from the family. Or what's left of it."

Todd watched Jerry and Bill head over to the elevators. "Be careful over there."

"Did you know that Sharon's also a stripper? I mean, an exotic dancer. Or is it just a dancer? I keep forgetting, no matter how many times Heather tells me."

"You serious?"

"Yep. Heather's been trying to talk her into quitting. She was on her way to an Ivy League school. Did you know she wanted to be a molecular biologist? But then it all went to shit and now she's just out to make money. It's sad how one tragedy can make a whole family unravel."

Ash's parents had gone the opposite way, seeming to grow stronger as a couple, but Todd always saw the hurt in their eyes. He was sure they saw it in his too.

Vince rubbed his hands together to warm them. "So, you find anything?"

Todd shook his head. Heather rejoined them after looking at the mirror frames. "It's a lot bigger, and much more run-down, than I expected."

"I was trying to think where Ash would have hidden something when you guys came in."

There was a loud thump as something crashed to the floor just behind Sharon. All of the flashlights whipped to the ceiling over her head. Dust rained down where a chunk of the ceiling had crumbled off.

"You all right?" Jerry asked Sharon.

She dusted her sleeves off with a glove. "Yeah. This place isn't going to get rid of me that easily."

Todd was pretty sure he'd just had a coronary event. Of all the people....

"We should probably go to the ice rink," he said. "It might be safer."

He desperately wanted to stay here and search some more, but now his major concern was their safety.

"Now that's a big dick," Bill said. He'd separated from everyone else, migrating to the other end of the lobby that had at one time led to the buffet dining area.

"What are you talking about?" Heather said.

He shined his light on a ten-foot mural of an erect penis. "Am I right?"

That's when Todd saw the clock. It was still on the wall, just underneath the crudely drawn testicles. "That has to be it."

"The cock?" Jerry said.

"No, the *clock*."

Todd ran across the lobby, nearly upending himself when he barked his shin on a table that had been stacked with empty beer cans. They clattered onto the floor, making Heather yelp again.

"Keep your flashlight on the clock," he said to Bill.

"Sure thing."

Todd didn't have to reach far to grab it. Ash had been tall, nearly five ten, so it wouldn't have been difficult for her to get it down. Or maybe, knowing her, it had been amidst the junk on the floor and she'd put it back where it had once proudly hung, letting guests know when it was time to head in for meals. It was a miracle it was still there, five years (or forty-plus for that matter) and not smashed on the ground. The hands had stopped at 5:07. He wondered if that had been in the morning or night. Had it ticked on well after the doors had been shuttered for good? If a clock ticked and no one was in the resort to bide its time, did it exist?

"Good catch, Bill," Vince said.

Bill scratched his head.

Everyone had gathered around Todd.

"What's the big deal about a clock?" Jerry asked.

"Ashley hid a recording in her grandfather clock," Heather said. "It was her last message for Todd."

"Damn."

Todd turned the golden clock over. The back was smooth and solid. He ran his wounded fingers around the edges. "There has to be a way to get inside it. It needed batteries or had to be wound somehow."

"Here, let me try," Jerry said. He savagely tore the back off the clock. Patience and precision had never been his strong suits. He handed the broken clock back to Todd.

And there it was. Nestled within the gears was an SD card.

Todd felt like crying.

He extracted it carefully, holding it as if it would disintegrate at any second. "I need Ash's video camera."

"Where is it?" Vince asked.

"My backpack."

"I'll get it." Bill hustled to get the pack.

Everyone stared at the tiny SD card as if it were a holy relic. Everyone but Sharon.

Bill unzipped the bag and held the camera out to Todd. He handed the SD card to Heather. "Hold this, please. Don't drop it."

"I promise, I won't."

It was better off in her hands, because his were shaking too much, he had a difficult time turning the camera on and finding the port to insert the SD card.

"Why would she hide a memory card in a clock in the first place?" Sharon asked.

Todd couldn't respond. Not now.

He turned the viewing screen around so they all could see, took a deep, tremulous breath, and hit Play.

CHAPTER SIXTEEN

Sharon Viola gasped behind Todd. "Oh my God, it's Sheri."

Ash must have balanced the camera on some bricks, the sharp camera light making her appear ghostly, smudging the finer features of her face. She was carefully sitting on the arm of a chair, stuffing poking out from torn fabric.

Behind her, Sheri was talking to Jamal but the microphone didn't capture what they were saying. They looked excited.

Ash tucked her hair behind her ears and squinted at something beyond the camera.

Todd couldn't breathe.

Just hours from this moment, her friends would be dead and she would escape wounded and mute, her brain burying the events to follow into the depths.

Ash turned to her friends and said, "That has to be it."

Sheri replied, "It does. Right?"

"What else could it be?"

"I'm not going any deeper," Jamal said. His belly hung a bit over his belt and his jeans were covered in dirt.

"No, don't. I think that's enough. We'll put it back after this." She held out her hand and Jamal passed something to her. Ash tucked it in her pocket before anyone could see.

Addie's head popped onto the screen. She waved at the camera, the light glinting off her perfectly white teeth. "Hi future person."

Ash laughed and nudged her friend out of the frame. "You guys go hit the pool. I'll do my thing and join you in a few."

"You sure?" Fred said, off camera. "This place gives me the creeps. I can stay with you."

"I'll be perfectly fine. Go." She shooed him away, smiling.

No, you won't be perfectly fine, Todd thought. She would fare better than her friends but she would never, ever again be fine.

Sheri twirled a lock of Ash's hair between her fingers and said, "Don't be long."

"I won't."

Sheri and Jamal shuffled out of view. Ash seemed to wait until they were gone before speaking again.

"Okay. My name is Ashley King and I'm at the abandoned Hayden Resort. I can't be sure where you found this, if you found it. I might just be talking to myself, which I've been known to do in places like this. But maybe there's a chance this recording survived and you came across it in a big open field filled with wild flowers and tall grass. Or maybe you bought the clock I'm going to hide this in at a flea market miles and miles from Topperville and you're wondering why I'm recording in the middle of what looks like a bombed-out building in the dead of night."

Heather sniffled. Todd saw Vince draw her closer to him. Bill chewed on a fingernail while Jerry watched with his hands on his hips, studying the video as if he were trying to evaluate a crime scene. Sharon's demeanor had softened considerably. She leaned forward with her hands on her knees, bringing her face close to the screen.

"What did you find, Ash?" Todd said, barely above a whisper.

Ash continued. "My friends and I do this thing called urban exploring. Not sure if it's still a thing by the time you come across this. If not, I'll bet Google is around and you can look it up. In a nutshell, we like to poke around abandoned places and try to absorb some of the past. I'm a little different in that I like to add my present to the past, kind of become a part of the location. I know it sounds weird, but I'm weird. Urban exploring is dangerous and most times, illegal. Not sure if that makes me a criminal or not. Anyway, we came to the Hayden Resort because it was once a very popular getaway in the Catskills. It's been left to rot for over thirty years now and it's in real bad shape. You can see that nature is winning the battle. If no one ever touched it again, this place would disappear in another twenty or more years.

"What makes this place interesting is how it all ended. By the 1970s, the Catskills was losing its shine. Bigger, better vacation spots were popping up everywhere. Air travel was getting more accessible and island destinations were becoming a thing. The Hayden would have died a slow death as fewer and fewer people came. Instead, it all ended early because of a huge fire that wiped out a good chunk of the resort. The fire took out the main restaurant and theater, along with a separate lounge and some bungalows. Ten people died in the fire, the flames spreading too quickly for everyone to escape. It must have been awful."

Ash paused. It looked like she was either picturing the night of the fire, or finding the right words to continue. Todd remembered tying her bootlaces when he dropped her off that night. He tried to latch onto the image of her beautiful face, but his memory kept inserting how he'd seen her that final time – her flesh almost purple, swollen tongue pushed from her mouth like a pregnant snake, eyes bulging from their sockets and her neck at an impossible angle. He looked away and blinked back tears, cursing his brain for ruining the moment.

"You okay, buddy?" Vince asked.

"Yeah. I'm fine."

Just like Ash had thought she was.

Sharon was almost on his shoulder, radiating scents of coconut and sweet perfume. It was at odds with their task and just jarring enough to get his attention back to Ash.

"I do a lot of research before we ever step foot in a location. The Hayden Resort was no exception. Since I don't live far, I made five trips up here to talk to the locals about the history. There was something about this place that touched me. It's hard to explain. I wanted to know more about it when it was thriving, just as much as the night of the fire that made it close its doors forever."

Todd couldn't help noticing how her delivery had been influenced by the types of shows and videos she voraciously consumed. She was sincere, of that there was no doubt. But she was also trying to be a professional narrator, and all for possibly nobody to see, the recording lost to the wrecking ball and/or time. He thought about how the final girl followers out there would clamor to see this, and vowed they'd never even know it existed.

Ash paused for a moment and looked around, as if she could hear something the microphone couldn't. Her eyes flicked to the side one last time before she returned to her story.

"I'm not a big believer in fate, but that may change after I literally ran into someone who flipped the entire story of the Hayden on its ass. I stopped at the Gulf station to get some gas a couple of weeks ago. It was so run-down, I wasn't sure it would even be open, but I was running on fumes. A very old man came out of the station to fill it up and he even washed my windows, like in the old days. He was dressed in the dirtiest overalls you'd ever seen, like a mechanic, except there was no place to work on cars at this Gulf. When he was done, I paid him in cash because he said he couldn't take cards. When I went to back up a little to make the turn, I kind of clipped him. He was standing in my blind spot and I didn't see him. I was so freaked out. I ran out to make sure he was all right. He kept telling me to, in his words, 'stop all my fussing', but I really thought I was gonna have a heart attack. I helped him inside, sat him down and stayed with him to make sure I didn't need to rush him to a hospital.

"Once he realized I wasn't going anywhere, he offered me coffee. The pot was so black I nearly gagged, but I sipped my coffee to be polite. He asked me what I was doing here, since it was obvious I was an interloper. He actually called me an interloper, but in a playful way. The second I mentioned the Hayden Resort, he got kind of stiff and quiet. I won't go into how I got him to talk again, but it wasn't easy. His name was Phil Merritt and it turns out he was the undersheriff when the Hayden fire took place. Not sure what an undersheriff does, but he was there when it happened and part of the investigation afterward. He even knew some of the workers that had died there. He said he played cards with two of the cooks, Paul Chess and Sydney Thomas, on a regular basis. He got a little teary eyed when he talked about them, but I learned he wasn't upset so much over their death as the death of his career."

"What the hell is she talking about?" Sharon said irritably.

"That's what we're here to find out," Heather said, her tone sharp enough to get Sharon to stand down.

Ash leaned closer to the camera, as if she didn't want the resort itself to listen in on her. "He saw the bodies when they were pulled out of the fire. What he saw rocked him. They weren't just burned up. In his opinion, they'd been mutilated before they'd been burned. He just assumed everyone would come to the same conclusion, from the sheriff to the coroner. They didn't. In fact, he was told that if he wanted to keep insisting they had, he'd be out of a job. He knew they were covering something up, but what? That's when he got to digging."

She took a moment to flip through the pages of a small notebook. "He said Sydney Thomas was old before his time. He'd been incarcerated in a Nazi death camp when he was a teen along with his family. He was the only one to make it out alive. Sydney came to America alone and scarred for life. Since this was the time before PTSD and the cultural acceptance of therapy, he was urged to simply move on with his life. I can't imagine how horrible that must have been. Being Jewish from Poland, he found his way to Brooklyn, and then was offered a job as a waiter for the summer season in the Catskills. He worked at the Granit, Grossinger's and the Nevele before landing a job as a line cook at the Hayden. Sydney never married and had no family or real close friends in America.

"When Phil realized something weird was going on with the fire investigation, he went to Sydney's apartment to see if his card buddy had been involved in something that would cause a huge cover-up. What he did was illegal, but at that point, he said it felt like his transgression paled in comparison to his boss's. Plus, he did it to find the truth, and that can't be wrong. Well, he found it."

Worry lines etched across Ash's forehead. Todd wanted to reach through the screen and touch her.

"Now, this is the part I didn't believe. I'm not sure I believe it now, but we found something that has me shook. Phil said Sydney's apartment was the neatest he'd ever seen. Nothing was out of place or dirty. One of his dresser drawers was used to store things like envelopes, stamps and neatly arranged folders. In one of those folders, Phil found a sealed envelope that had *Forgive Me* written across it. He tore it open and found a five-page letter. Basically, it was a written confession."

Jerry exhaled loudly. "Christ, here it comes."

"Here what comes?" Bill said.

"The part that makes you realize this place is on bad ground."

"Like an Indian burial ground?" Vince said.

"No. Like the kind of place that invites trouble. If this dude who survived a concentration camp had to write a confession, it's bad."

"Shh," Todd snapped. He'd paused the video but wanted to get back to it. The answers to what had ultimately killed her could be seconds away.

"Sydney worked for a head cook named Otto Knoop. Otto was a burly, quiet man who said he'd been a German prisoner of war during World War II. His family had immigrated to Italy at the start of the war and he fought for the Italian army. He was a pretty serious guy who mostly kept to himself, but Sydney didn't mind. In a subtle way, they'd bonded over their mistreatment at the hands of the Germans. It had been a busy summer and although Sydney would never call Otto a great friend, they did work well together.

"That all changed on the last night of the season. To celebrate the final service, champagne had been broken out. Someone brought a bottle of homemade grappa to the party and people got pretty drunk. For the first time that summer, Otto smiled and got along with everyone. He, you know, loosened up. The grappa finally removed the stick from his ass. The more he drank, the more he talked. No one could believe it, but they all thought it was great to see this big man let down his walls. And then he said something that stopped the party instantly.

"He'd suddenly grown somber, his laughter dying in his throat. When they asked him what was wrong, he said he had lied. He hadn't immigrated to Italy. Sydney told him it was okay, sometimes people lied because they didn't want to let others in. Then Otto got a strange look on his face. He wiped away his tears and smiled a smile that made Sydney uneasy. He had not been captured by the Germans."

Here Ashley paused again, casting her eyes around the room. *What is she looking for?* Todd thought.

"Otto told them, this entirely Jewish staff, that he'd been a prison guard at the Stutthof concentration camp in this small town in Poland. He told them how they'd killed seventy thousand people there, almost thirty thousand of them Jews. His inhibitions collapsed and he boasted that at Stutthof, they specialized in turning human fat into soap. At some point, Sydney said it was if he'd forgotten they were in the room, and instead he was talking to a fellow Nazi, maybe someone he'd lost in the war.

"The staff flew into a rage. I mean, who would blame them? They grabbed Otto and dragged him from the kitchen. Sydney wrote that the Nazi laughed all the way to his living quarters. Once they got inside, they found all sorts of Nazi stuff, and they knew he was telling the truth for the first time that season. They might have just beaten him and then called the police, but then he said something that, I guess, sealed his fate."

Ash looked at her notes.

"He said, 'It's too bad I can't wash my hands of you. Dirty hands call for dirty Jews.' According to Sydney's confession, all of them, men and women, started punching and kicking him. They beat his face until he was unrecognizable. He fell onto the floor and still laughed. Someone found the blade from a bayonet, something he'd kept from the war. They tied him up and again dragged him out. This time, they took him to the back of the ice rink and dug a hole. He cursed them as they dug, telling them how much fun he had putting shit and piss in the food of the Jews who came to eat at the Hayden.

"By this point, everyone on the kitchen staff was blind with rage. Martin, one of the dishwashers who had lost his parents to the camps, picked up the bayonet and stabbed Otto in the stomach. The Nazi was probably too drunk to feel it, so he kept on laughing and mocking them. Martin handed the blade to the next person and she stabbed him again. They each took turns, Sydney being the last. He said he was pretty sure Otto had been dead by the time he put the bayonet into him, but he wanted to, needed to punish the Nazi.

"When they were done, they pushed him in the hole, dumped his war mementos on top of him and covered him up. Sydney said he never slept better than he did that night. But as the years went on, guilt started to haunt him. In his mind, they were no better than the Nazis, dealing out punishment without a proper trial, even though Otto more than deserved what he'd gotten. But he kept quiet, afraid that he would end up in prison. They'd made a pact the morning after the murder to never speak of that night again and he would honor it until he died. One of the staff members who'd taken part in Otto's murder, a sous chef, was elected sheriff in 1965. He was the acting sheriff when the Hayden burned down. I asked Phil how

Sydney's story was connected with the fire that destroyed the resort."

Todd felt sick to his stomach. Why hadn't she told him all this that day when he'd driven them up to the Catskills? Ashley and her mysteries. She'd uncovered one and was going to set it free into the ether.

She grew very serious, again giving a furtive look over the camera. "Phil was sure his boss was doing more than making sure Otto's murder was never revealed. Once you start investigating one thing, anything else can follow. But Phil overheard the sheriff talking to his wife on the phone one day. It seems he was more worried that Otto had been the man that murdered the staff before setting their bodies on fire."

"How the hell would that even be possible?" Bill said. "They not only stabbed the guy, they buried him!"

Todd paused the video.

"Maybe they didn't kill him. I saw a guy that was stabbed twenty times who lived," Jerry said.

"What about being buried under all that dirt?" Sharon said.

"They were in a rush. They weren't thinking clearly. They made the grave too shallow," Jerry said. "It happens more than you think."

"That's a little far-fetched," Sharon said.

"Maybe not," Heather said. "Who knows if Otto had family here? It says that he didn't talk much and hid behind a lie."

"Let's let Ash finish," Todd said. He knew they were coming to the end of the recording but he never wanted it to stop. As terrifying and awful as the story was, it was still Ash talking to him.

Ash continued. "Phil thought that his boss had maybe suffered some mental break because he wasn't able to process what he'd done that night. But with the resort closed, Phil couldn't afford to lose his job. He kept his mouth shut and the Hayden was deserted. The only problem was, the strangeness didn't stop there. It's kept on going, year after year."

CHAPTER SEVENTEEN

Todd felt pressure on his shoulders. Heather and Vince were holding onto him as they watched Ash go from the practical to the fantastic. The back of his neck prickled and the feeling that they weren't the only ones in the remains of the Hayden intensified.

Death lived here. And they were all about to find out that it had consumed more lives than on the nights of the fire and the massacre.

"Since the Hayden burned down, the local police have discovered seven bodies on the grounds. Most of them were runaways and drifters, so it was easy to just cover it up. Phil was sure other people have gone missing in here, but their remains have never been found. I asked him if there have been any recent disappearances. He hasn't been on the force for a long time, but he stays in touch. He had a police scanner on low just behind him. According to him, all has been quiet, especially since the old sheriff died of lung cancer about ten years ago. Which makes me wonder if the sheriff was the one doing the killings. I can almost see him taking out the staff he'd once worked with if they'd threatened to tell the truth. He then set fire to the resort to cover his tracks and was in a position to cover it up. The other murders that happened after that confuse me, though. Maybe he got a taste for killing and couldn't stop. I don't know. Unfortunately, there's no way to substantiate Phil's claims because everything after the blaze was kept from the public. I'll bet any records have been conveniently destroyed. To say this place and everything around it is a total mystery is a huge understatement."

And you loved it, Todd thought. No wonder she'd been so attracted to the place. Anyone else hearing about a slew of murders taking place in a specific location would have stayed the hell away. Ash probably would have if there hadn't been the irresistible element of a grand, unsolved mystery.

Maybe Jerry was right and the place was bad. It turned men

into murderers. Maybe not good men, but anyone who had more darkness than light in their souls.

"I got back to Otto and asked Phil if he remembered where they'd buried the body and if he'd ever gone there to see for himself. He got really weird and I thought he was going to throw me out of the station. When he settled down, he said he had no reason to go in there, other than with a body bag. He said it wasn't like Sydney Thomas had drawn a treasure map. It was simply somewhere around the ice rink. I thanked Phil for the coffee and the story, and before I left, I asked him why he chose to tell me."

Yet again, Ash stopped and worriedly looked around the dark, deserted lobby. Todd couldn't help doing the same. "He just said, 'Because you asked.' When we came up here last week to do some recon, the gas station was closed with a for sale sign in the window. I checked the local paper and saw Phil's obituary. After tonight, I'm going to find out if he died of natural causes or if he took his own life. Something is telling me he killed himself. There was a strange, sad kind of look he gave me as I left that kinda freaked me out.

"Anyway, the first spot we visited tonight was naturally the ice rink. This is where it gets really weird. We didn't have plans to go digging for bodies. Believe me. I don't know what we were thinking. It's not like the kitchen staff would put a grave marker where they'd hidden their crime. Except there was one. Well, kinda. Fred was the one who found it. His walking stick hit into something hard and he looked down. It was lying right there, just a few feet from the back of the rink, by the double doors. This is what he found."

Ash held up a tarnished iron cross. As the camera auto-zoomed, Todd was able to make out the swastika in the center of the cross.

"Is it Otto's? Did Phil leave it here before he died? Or are there some white supremacists that hang out here? I just think it's really strange that Fred found it right where Otto is possibly buried. Maybe the staff that murdered Otto buried his Nazi paraphernalia with him, the way they wanted to bury the Nazi past."

"Fucking-A right, that's strange," Jerry said.

"Right after he found it, Addie tripped on something and twisted her ankle. She's been walking, but she says it's starting to swell. We may have to call it an early night. Even if we do, it's been pretty incredible. Some mysteries aren't meant to be solved, but at least in this case, we have some of the pieces. This is a tragic place. It didn't start out that way, but being here, now, I get the strong feeling that the Hayden wants its secrets hidden from the world. So I'm going to leave this recording here. If someone finds it, maybe that's a sign that I was wrong and the truth demands to be brought to the light."

Todd heard heavy footsteps and Sheri came back into the shot. "You done yet?"

"Yeah. Can you bring that clock over?"

"Got it."

"So, I guess this is goodbye to the Hayden. I hope the spirits that have lost their lives here are in a better place. Truthfully, I get the sense that some are still lingering. I hope it's the ones that had a great time here and just want to visit."

Ash's hand reached for the camera and the picture cut to black.

Todd bit hard on his lower lip.

"That was intense," Bill said.

"Rewind it back to my sister," Sharon said. Todd handed her the camera. He walked away from them on numb legs.

"Todd, you all right?" Vince said.

"I just need a few minutes."

"If what she found out was right, we need to stop the demolition," Jerry said.

"Why's that?" Bill asked.

"Because it's a fucking crime scene. Who knows what the hell has been going on here? What if the former sheriff was a serial killer? Just because he's dead doesn't mean we should ignore it. Todd, this could end up being the biggest murder investigation in the state. I mean, if you have fifty years of murders in one place, it's unprecedented. And we're talking multiple killers." He counted off on his fingers. "You have the staff doing some vigilante justice on a Nazi. Then you have that same group of people burned up and maybe murdered before the fire was set. Then you have, what did Ash say, at least seven more bodies show up on the property over the years, all capped off with...." He looked over at Sharon, who had taken her eyes off the camera screen as if daring him to say what had happened to her sister aloud. "It's insane. Something big is going on here."

Todd shook his head, feeling like he was going to collapse. "I need some air."

Sharon waved her hand across the room. "Dude, all the windows are broken. There's nothing but air in here."

He opened his mouth to say something but had no clue what. Instead, he ran.

"Todd, where are you going?" Vince called after him.

His foot grazed something hard and unyielding and he almost took a tumble. Regaining his stride, he bolted out of the hotel and stopped by the fountain beyond the portico. He bent over with his hands on his knees, trying to regulate his breath. The fountain was filled with dark shapes. He assumed it was refuse from the hotel that had been tossed into it by bored teens.

Pounding feet sounded behind him. It was Heather and Vince.

"It's okay," Heather said soothingly. "We're all more than a little stunned right now."

It took him a few moments to get his wind to speak. "What the hell did she walk into?"

"I don't know," Vince said. "My brain is still trying to process everything."

"What if that old man was telling the truth? She should never have come here. Goddamn you, Ash and your fucking puzzles!"

He grabbed a shattered brick and launched it into the dark. It thumped impotently in the distance. He wasn't done. He shrugged away from Vince, grabbed anything he could find and threw it at the hotel. Why couldn't there be at least one pane of glass left? Hearing it shatter would have been the most satisfying thing he'd experienced in months.

"Whoa, are you trying to kill me?" Jerry said from somewhere in the pitch. Todd could only make out his flashlight beam as he approached them.

"Let him blow off some steam," Vince whispered.

"I got no problem with that. Just blow it in another direction. Here." Jerry plucked a hunk of rebar from the ground. "Give that a whack." He aimed his light at the decorative centerpiece in the fountain. Vandals or the passage of the years had transformed the sculpture into an unrecognizable lump.

Jerry patted his shoulder and slipped away.

Todd snapped on his light and saw the shallow pool was crammed with bricks and bottles and cans. He took the rebar from Jerry, stepped over the lip and was battering the fountain after two strides. Chips of cement pelted his face as he hammered it over and over. Heather implored him to be careful, but he was beyond caring about his personal safety at the moment.

For the first time since Ash's suicide, Todd was angry. Her recklessness had destroyed so many lives. He loved her and hated her in equal measure. And he hated himself for hating her.

Tears streaked down his face as he let it all out. What remained of the statue split in half. He kicked it over, striking the pieces with the rebar, the metal reverberating until he could no longer feel his hands. Rough hands eventually pulled him away, lifting him out of the pool. The rebar clanged as it hit something metallic.

Vince held onto him, not saying a word.

Heather looked on, the tips of her fingers against her lips. She was crying as well.

As Todd settled down, one overriding thought consumed him. "You shouldn't have come here."

"We couldn't leave you to do this alone, bud," Vince said.

"We're all in danger," Todd said. "It's why I lied to you. I begged the Wraith to come get me. For all we know, he's here now. I haven't felt alone since I stepped onto the property."

"I doubt this guy listens to podcasts. You gave your freaking address. It would have been easier for him to get you at home than hope that you turned up here one day."

Heather took hold of his hands. "We're going to be fine. Jerry's a cop and he's armed. We found what you wanted to find. We can go now. Okay?" She cocked her head and looked into his eyes. "Okay?"

The anger bled from him in a rush. He sagged against Vince. "Yeah. Let's get the hell outta here." He looked around. "Where's Jerry?"

"Back in there," Vince said, his thumb jerking toward the hotel. "He went to get Bill and Sharon."

"I can't find them."

None of them had heard Jerry approach.

"What do you mean you can't find them?" Vince said.

"It means they're not in the hotel. I even checked that elevator shaft to make sure they didn't fall in."

"Where on earth would they go?" Heather said.

Todd looked over to the ruined Cosmos Theater. It had once been attached to the hotel via an underground tunnel and been the centerpiece for entertainment at the resort. The fire had ravaged the theater, devouring most of the walls and ceiling. No, they wouldn't be in there.

The foursome shined their lights around, the onyx night swallowing them whole.

CHAPTER EIGHTEEN

"Where the hell is that idiot?" Jerry grumbled.

"I'm sure right behind Sharon," Vince said. Heather called out for Sharon and Bill, but not so loud that she could be heard beyond the fence.

Todd remained at the rear, worried about Bill and Sharon but also watching their backs. After listening to Ashley talk about the dark, hidden history of the Hayden, he no longer felt safe in this far from empty wasteland.

"Bill said he'd seen her before," Jerry said. They were walking down a once-paved road that wound around the east end of the resort. Bungalows with collapsed roofs, their windows and doors long gone, the facades resembling wide, vacant faces, were on their left. They passed by one that smelled like years of accumulated excrement. Heather waved her hand in front of her nose.

"Where did he see her?" Vince said.

"At Ruffles. He's pretty sure he got a lap dance from her. He was pretty drunk at the time so he's not one hundred percent sure."

"I saw you drooling a little yourself," Heather said.

"Of course I was. She's hot."

"More like a hot mess," Vince said. Heather pierced him with a look. He stammered and said, "I m-mean, who wouldn't be?"

Todd was glad none of them stopped to look back at him, the man who might be the king of hot messes.

"I should have known not to let her out of my sight," Heather said.

"We'll find them," Jerry said. "They have to turn up if they want a ride home."

"The rink is just over there," Todd said, pointing through the trees. Their lights illuminated the exterior of the outdoor ice rink. That was where things had gone very, very wrong for Ash and her friends. And, according to Phil, Otto. Todd hoped it wouldn't happen again. His only consolation was that they were not walking in blind, and thanks to Jerry, they were armed.

As they made their way through the trees, he couldn't help but cast a small wish to the heavens that the Wraith was somewhere in here, waiting for them. Jerry was an expert marksman. Nothing would make Todd happier than to see his friend take the Wraith dead center in the chest.

"Jesus, I'm a mess," he said too softly for them to hear. His thoughts and emotions were all over the place. He felt like a compass hovering over a wildly fluctuating electromagnetic field.

"You there, Bill?" Jerry called out.

Nothing.

The four of them emerged from the trees. "That's seen better days," Vince said.

The roof of the ice rink had collapsed long ago. The center of the rink looked like a bonfire heap of timber just waiting for a match. Todd was surprised someone hadn't set the whole thing blazing.

Back in its day, the rink looked like a long oblong gazebo. There had been benches outside for people to sit down and put on their skates or just kick back and watch everyone glide or stumble by. The benches were long gone. The counter where you would get your skates was also gone. Wooden slots in the wall were empty, save for a bird's nest here and there.

Vince leaned against the wall, the top edge coming to his waist. "Doesn't look like they came this way."

"But they will," Todd said.

"Why do you think that?" Heather asked.

"Because aside from Ash talking about this being where Otto was buried and where Fred found the iron cross, it was also detailed in the police reports that this is one of the places where the Wraith attacked them. Sharon wants to try to make peace with everything, walk where Sheri walked, this is where she'll go. Trust me, I understand why."

"Well, they better get here soon. It's colder than a witch's tit out here," Vince said, blowing into his cupped hands.

"Why do guys say that?" Heather asked. She craned her neck

to look into the clouds, maybe with the hope of finding a sliver of moonlight to chase away the gloom.

"Say what?"

"Colder than a witch's tit. It makes no sense. Why would a witch have cold tits?"

"You got me," her husband said. "It's just a thing people say."

"That doesn't mean it makes any sense." Heather stamped her feet, her breath looking like dragon's smoke.

"I rescind my earlier statement. It's colder than a well digger's ass. How's that?"

Heather nodded.

"I'm gonna kick Bill's ass if he doesn't get here soon," Jerry said. "I need to get out of here and think about what I'm going to do next."

Todd, who had been staring across the rink into the pitch, said, "You really going to report this and stop the demolition?"

Jerry massaged the back of his neck. "Man, I have to. This isn't even just a crime scene. It's multiple crime *scenes*. Not to mention we have a corrupt police department in Topperville."

"Had," Todd reminded him.

Jerry picked up a shard of wood, possibly once part of the roof, and chucked it onto the pile. "Either way, this can't go ignored. Not anymore."

Todd thrust his tingling hands deep into his pockets. "Maybe it's better off leveling the entire place. Destroy whatever it is here that attracted all the bad."

Jerry huffed. "That's new age stuff that has no real-life application. I don't give a shit about bad juju. This is stone-cold homicide and corruption. Ash may have just given us what we need to put some very worried family members at ease, or at the very least, end their years of not knowing what happened to their loved ones."

Todd didn't even know where to begin arguing with him. He was right. They couldn't just gloss over the fact that many more people had lost their lives here than the world thought. "Maybe Phil was crazy, or lying."

"There is that possibility. But we have to find out if he was, in fact, not crazy and telling the truth first."

"He's right," Vince said. "As much as it hurts you to see this place still standing, Ash could end up a hero."

"She already is to all those final girl people," Todd said, shining his light in a circle, searching. He couldn't find the double doors that Ash had mentioned in her video. That would be near where Otto had been buried.

He nearly dropped his flashlight at the sound of splintering wood. Vince cried out. Heather shrieked.

Todd swung his beam around to find Vince was gone.

"Vince!" Heather shouted, her voice echoing throughout the vast, empty acreage of the Hayden.

"Holy crap, man, are you all right?" Jerry leaped over the collapsed wall. Vince was on his back, gasping for air. Heather was close behind. She got down and angled herself so she could cradle her husband's head in her lap.

"Just take it slow and steady," Todd said. "Don't panic. Your breath will come back to you. That's it. Relax."

After a quick inspection, they were all relieved to see Vince hadn't been stabbed by the splintered wood or been turned into a human pincushion by the rusty nails that were everywhere. His jacket was ripped in several places and the back pocket of his jeans tore off when he was helped to his feet.

"Note to self," Vince said, dusting himself off. "Do not lean on anything in this place. It was like falling through cardboard. The termites must have been feasting on the wall."

"Them and everything else," Jerry said.

"Guys, is that you?"

Bill and Sharon came trotting over.

"Where the hell did you guys go?" Jerry said.

"We came here and then we went back looking for you," Sharon defiantly replied. "What happened to him?"

"He just fell through the rink's wall. He's fine," Heather said.

Bill was out of breath. Todd couldn't remember the last time he'd seen his friend run. "You'll never believe what we found."

"It doesn't matter," Todd said. "We're getting out of here."

Sharon hefted his video camera. "Fine. But you're making me a copy of that recording. And I'm keeping this."

She opened up her hand to show them the iron cross in her palm. It looked exactly like the one in the video.

"How is that even possible?" Todd said.

"It was back there," Bill said, pointing to the other side of the rink. "Looks like Fred really did put it back."

"Or Otto's ghost did," Vince said, much to Jerry's consternation.

"Don't even go there," Jerry said. "That's dumb, even for you, Vince."

"I'm not serious, douchebag," Vince said. Sharon let him hold the cross. "I feel wrong even touching it. Suppose it really did belong to Otto? He would have worn this while ordering hundreds of people to be killed." He quickly handed it back to Sharon.

"Might be worth something," she said.

"Or it could be a cursed talisman or something," Bill added. "There's no telling what those Nazis were into and capable of."

Jerry threw up his hands. "Ghosts. Talismans. Do you guys hear yourselves? I can't believe I'm saying this, but the stripper is the only one making any sense. I'm sure some skinhead freak will pay a lot for it on eBay."

"Keep calling me a stripper," Sharon said, pointing a sharp end of the cross at him.

"Can you at least try not to be a schmuck and call her a dancer?" Heather said sharply. Jerry waved her off.

Bill's eyes were fixed on the dirt-encrusted cross. "The Nazis, at least those in the upper ranks, were into all kinds of magic. Who knows. Maybe the cross is cursed. It sure didn't bring any luck to the people who killed Otto."

Todd felt as if his head were going to split in half. "This is crazy. My car is parked in an abandoned garage way over that way. Where is yours?"

"Found a spot between a pair of dumpsters over there," Jerry said, pointing in the opposite direction. "Heather and Vince should go with you. I don't want anyone wandering around in the dark alone."

"Maybe it belongs to the Wraith, who found it by Otto's grave," Sharon said, oblivious to everyone else. "Or the Wraith could be Otto's son. He could have had a kid who was, thanks to some fucked-up genes, equally psycho."

Bill's hand covered his mouth. "Holy shit, you may be right."

"Or one hundred percent wrong," Jerry said. "In lieu of any real evidence."

"There's no point staying here and debating whose iron cross it is," Todd said. "I got what I came for. Is there anything else you need from this place?" He looked at Sharon.

She licked her full lips and cast her eyes around the woods that had sprung from the untended grounds. "Sheri's not here. Call me crazy, but I thought if I came here, I'd feel her, you know? But I don't. This place is just wrong. Sheri would never hang around here if she didn't have to. Maybe this little hunk of Nazi bullshit will help us find who killed her." She pocketed the Nazi cross. "Maybe not."

"Fine. Let's go."

They were about to leave, breaking into two groups, when something cracked in the trees behind them.

Todd's first thought was, *The police heard us!* They pointed their flashlights in the direction of the sound, but the trees in that area were tightly packed and impenetrable.

Leaves crunched. Someone was definitely walking toward them.

"Douse your lights," Jerry whispered.

"Why?" Sharon asked.

"So whoever is out there doesn't have an advantage on us. Just sit tight and we'll see if he keeps on walking."

Crunch, crunch, snap, crunch, crunch.

Whoever it was wasn't trying to hide.

Vince took Heather by the arm and pulled her behind him.

A hulking shadow emerged from the tree line.

Todd snapped his light on. The shadow darted away before he could see who it was. He assumed it was a man because of his size. The man ran, but *to* them rather than away from them. Todd's heart clogged his throat.

"Stand down," Jerry ordered. "Police!"

The man kept coming. Every time they shined their light, he managed to dodge out of the way.

"I'm outta here," Bill said. He was off and running before they could stop him.

"Bill, get back here," Vince blurted.

The man in the dark skirted around them, heading now in Bill's direction.

"Motherfucker," Jerry hissed and set off running. The rest were right behind him.

"Bill!" Heather shouted.

Bill wasn't answering. Todd was sure Bill didn't have the ability to talk and run at the same time. If he paused to answer her, he wouldn't be able to get going again. The shadow man was between them and their retreating friend.

"I said stop!" Jerry barked.

The shadow man kept running.

Bill let out a strangled gasp. The sound of his body hitting the ground was impossible to miss.

The shadow man would be on top of him in seconds.

Jerry's legs pumped as fast as they could go.

The clouds parted, the dull yellow haze of the moon piercing through the clouds and bathing the grounds in eerie, jaundiced light. Bill was on his back, scrambling like a beached crab to find cover.

Sharon overtook Jerry for the lead, her long muscular legs traversing the uneven terrain like a gazelle. Her right hand went into her pocket.

Pop!

The hard thwack was immediately followed by the shadow man collapsing face-first onto the ground. Jerry, Todd, Heather and Vince caught up to her. She used both hands to hold the gun, pointing it at the prone man. Bill had stopped moving, staring wide-eyed at the fallen man.

"What the hell did you do?" Jerry howled at her.

Her reply was colder than a reptile's gaze. "Hopefully, I just killed the Wraith."

CHAPTER NINETEEN

"Give me the goddamn gun," Jerry roared. He went for the gun. Sharon jerked her arms away, stepping around him and keeping its sights on the prone man.

"No!"

"You just shot a man in the back."

Sharon sneered. "What are you gonna do, arrest me?" The gun wavered slightly in Jerry's direction.

Todd's friend didn't back down. "Actually, I am. I'll bet my life you don't have a license for it either."

"Just keep back," Sharon ordered all of them. Vince and Heather took a few uneven backward steps. Todd was too shocked to move. He stared at the man on the ground, keeping his beam on his back, hoping to see it rise and fall.

"I think he's dead," Todd said.

"Jesus," Bill yipped. He still hadn't gotten up and his feet were inches from the man's outstretched hands. He scooted farther away, tucking his legs close to his body.

Heather said, "Sharon, honey, just give Jerry the gun."

"Not until I know he's dead," Sharon snapped.

"We don't even know who the hell he is," Jerry said.

Sharon pulled the hammer back on the .38. "We all know who it is."

"No, we don't," Jerry said. "Take a look around you. People have been coming here for years, drinking, fucking and spray-painting every bare piece of concrete and wood."

Her lips pulled back in a snarl. "I know it's him."

"You can't know," Heather said, her soothing tone in direct contrast to Jerry's caustic demeanor.

"He came right for us," Sharon said. She kicked the man's shoulder. His upper body shifted, but that was all.

"I...I don't know about that," Vince said. "It looked to me like he was running away from something. We just happened to be in the way."

Sharon's eyes grew wide, "What are you saying, Vince?"

"If he's the Wraith, what was he running from?"

Jerry held his hands up so she could see he didn't have his service revolver. "Just let me check him out. Can you do that?"

Sharon shifted, leaves crunching under her feet. She was at a loss for words, and that scared Todd even more. They heard a shifting in the grass back from where they'd come. Sharon jerked her arm away from the man, aiming the gun into the darkness.

No one spoke or moved for an interminable beat of time. The sound didn't repeat itself.

"I think I just heard him trying to breathe," Bill said.

With Sharon distracted, Jerry moved in. Todd rushed to the man as well. He heard Heather shout, "Don't!"

When he looked up, Sharon had the gun trained on him and Jerry.

"Help me get him on his back," Jerry said.

Todd fumbled for the man's pant leg and belt loop. Together, they turned him over. Bill, who was now on his knees, shined his light on the man's face.

"He's just a kid," Vince said.

Todd wanted to scream.

Judging by the baby fat on the man-child's cheeks, and blooming acne, Todd figured he was sixteen, seventeen at most. His long bangs slid to the side of his forehead. Blood bubbled on his lips.

Jerry dipped his head to the boy's mouth, his ear close to his lips. "He's still breathing."

Todd watched helplessly as Jerry unzipped the boy's coat. Blood was everywhere. He was wearing a black final girl T-shirt, Ash's face rendered in a cartoon, the silhouette of the Hayden behind her.

"What the fuck did you do?" Todd said to Sharon.

She still held the gun but her hand was shaking. "I thought...."

"If he was the Wraith, that would mean he would have been, what, ten goddamn years old when he killed your sister?" Todd leaped to his feet and snatched the gun out of her hands. Sharon spun away, emitting a strangled gasp. Heather ran to grab onto her.

"Dammit! I'm losing him," Jerry said. He shrugged out of his coat and tossed it to Todd. "Hold this." Todd saw Jerry's gun secured in the shoulder holster. He noted that Sharon saw it too.

"Don't even think of it," Todd warned her.

She buried her head in Heather's shoulder.

Jerry administered CPR. Todd helped Bill to his feet.

"What the hell are we gonna do?" Vince said.

"We have to call for an ambulance," Bill said. He took his phone out of his pocket, but he was so nervous, it slipped from his fingers.

"I'll call," Todd said. He handed Jerry's coat to Vince and went to his back pocket. His other hand held Sharon's gun that was getting heavier by the second. He tapped his phone's screen with his thumb, lighting it up. "Shit. I've got no bars." He tried anyway, tapping 911. Nothing happened.

"Wait, I have a different carrier," Vince said. "With the money I pay those assholes, it better work out here."

Todd and Bill watched Vince try his phone, frown, and try again. "I've got no signal."

"Come on, kid, breathe!" Jerry said, moving to chest compressions. With each push of his hands, more blood frothed from the kid's open mouth.

Heather was crying, telling Sharon not to look. Todd couldn't help noticing that Sharon hadn't shed a single tear. She watched Jerry try to revive the boy with cold, narrow eyes.

Jerry kept at it for several minutes. The boy emitted a wet gurgle and that was all. Jerry rocked back on his heels, his sweat steaming on his flesh, and wiped his brow with his forearm. "He's gone."

Heather wailed with a fresh burst of tears. She held onto Sharon for dear life. Sheri's sister said, "Are you sure?"

With unmasked fury, Jerry said, "What the fuck do you think? If I had cuffs on me now, you'd be on the ground eating dirt."

"I never saw a dead body before," Bill said.

"Haven't you ever been to a wake?" Vince asked.

Bill shook his head. "I can't handle shit like this." He turned from the boy and walked away, running his hands through his hair in silent agony.

"When's the ambulance coming?" Jerry asked.

"We can't get through," Todd said. "Where's your phone? I'll give it another shot."

"Inside breast pocket."

Jerry's phone was almost the size of a tablet. Todd turned it on but got the same results. "Now what do we do?"

"You all get out of here and find the police or a signal, whichever comes first. I'll stay here."

"You shouldn't be alone," Vince said.

"I won't be," Jerry said. He got up, unbuckled his belt and snapped it off. Prying Sharon away from Heather, he spun Sharon around and pinned her arms behind her back. When she tried to break free, he jabbed the back of her knee with his knee and brought her down. Seconds later, her hands were bound at her back. "I can't trust her trying to get away if I let her go with you guys."

"You don't have to be so rough with her," Heather blurted.

"I can get rough if I need to," he replied coolly.

"I bet that's the only way you can get off," Sharon snarled.

"If I want to hear wisdom from a murdering stripper, I'll ask you."

"Stop it, Jerry," Heather implored him. Sharon was her friend and she saw Sheri's sister in a much different light. In a way, Todd couldn't blame her. But Sharon had just shot a teenager in cold blood and had apparently zero remorse.

"Heather, go with Vince and Todd and Bill and get help. Please."

"I don't want to leave her with him," Heather said to Vince.

"Heath, what do you think he's gonna do? She just killed someone. He's a cop. He knows exactly what he's doing."

Vince took hold of her hand and squeezed. Fat tears rolled down Heather's cheeks.

"Come on, Bill," Todd said. "We need to get out of here as fast as we can."

Bill didn't move.

Todd looked to Jerry. "How the hell are we going to explain this? Will you get in trouble?"

Jerry exhaled, the long plume of fog misting before Todd's face. "I'm fucked, Todd. Trespassing and allowing someone to murder a child. There's no way out of that."

For a split second, Todd almost suggested they leave the Hayden and not tell a soul what had happened. He stopped himself, realizing the sheer stupidity and foolishness of such an idea. You couldn't simply walk away from murder. Not when it was witnessed by six people, one of them being a lawman.

A child. Sharon had killed a poor, misguided child.

How misguided had *they* been? Six adults should have known better than to come here. Todd should have known his friends would follow him once he'd told them his plan. He had an excuse. He was broken. He wanted, no, he needed every last bit of Ash he could find.

He couldn't help feeling Ash's disappointment. Sharon said she didn't feel Sheri here. Ash was a part of the Hayden, just as real as the SD card she'd left behind. She was here, watching them. He knew it. And he felt ashamed.

"I'll take the gun," Jerry said.

Todd looked down at his hand, jolting as if finding he was holding a rattlesnake. "Oh. Here."

"Better let him hold onto it," Sharon said.

"I said shut up," Jerry snapped.

Heather was about to pipe up but Vince guided her away, whispering something in her ear.

"Bill, let's go," Todd said, his brain calculating how long it would take to get to his car and find the police station.

"You see that?" Bill said.

"See what?" Todd asked.

"I don't think the kid was alone."

"Are you kidding me?" Jerry jerked Sharon to her feet, keeping his hand on the belt. It looked painful, but Sharon didn't so much as grunt.

"See? Over there."

The pall of sickly moonlight barely lit up the fallow fields of the Hayden. Todd had to squint into the gloom to see.

"Right there," Bill said. Todd followed his outstretched finger.

Sure enough, there was another figure enshrouded in darkness, making its way to them, but slowly. Jerry pointed his flashlight at the figure, but the light fell far short.

"Follow my light," he called out.

The person started to run.

They waved their flashlights as a beacon.

"What are they gonna say when they see their friend is dead?" Bill asked.

"We'll deal with that when it happens," Jerry said. He turned to Todd. "Looks like you'll have one more."

"That's fine."

"You shouldn't be drawing him to us," Sharon said. Jerry yanked on the belt.

"Why?" Heather asked, sniffing back the remnants of her tears.

"Vince said it before. Who was the kid running from that he was so desperate to get away?"

"Jerry said he was the police. He was trespassing. Naturally he'd run," Heather said.

"That's one way to look at it."

"I said to shut your freaking mouth," Jerry said.

The running figure was getting closer but still out of the reach of their lights. Todd silently urged them to hurry up so he could get out of the Hayden. He never wanted to see this place again.

"It's a girl," Vince said, his light catching a shock of bright pink hair. A few seconds later, they could see the mascara running down her face.

"Taylor!" she shouted.

Todd looked back at the dead boy. Now that he had a name, it somehow made everything even worse.

The girl pulled up ten feet from them, shielding her eyes from their flashlight beams. "Have you seen my friend Taylor?" She was dressed all in black with laced-up jackboots. Todd knew a final girl fan when he saw one. She saw Jerry holding on to a trussed-up Sharon and gasped, backpedaling away.

"No, please don't hurt me."

Heather muscled her way forward. "It's okay. It's okay. We're not going to hurt you."

What would she think when she saw Taylor's body? Todd was dizzy from the surreal turn of events.

When Heather reached out for her, the girl swatted her hands away. "Don't touch me!"

That's when Todd saw the big tear in the upper sleeve of her jacket. He shined his light on her arm. Was that blood beneath the tear?

"What happened to you?" he asked.

"Just get away from me," she said, oblivious to him. "Taylor! Taylor! Where are you?"

Todd nudged Jerry. "Look."

"She might have snagged it getting over the fence." Then he said to the girl, "Look, I'm a cop. I'm not here to arrest you. I just need you to calm down."

The girl stopped but she had a feral look in her eyes. The slightest wrong move would send her running again.

"Are you hurt?" Todd asked. It was too difficult to see properly in the dark and with her jittering back and forth. Maybe the jacket had always been torn. That was the big style with teens.

She absently touched her arm along the tear but didn't answer him.

"Have you seen my friend?" she asked. "I…I thought I heard a gunshot or something. We got separated back there. I just want to find him and get out of here."

"What's your name?" Jerry asked calmly. She looked at Sharon in his grasp and her bottom lip trembled.

"Why do you have her tied up if you're a cop?"

"Because unlike you, she's under arrest and this is the best I can do at the moment."

The girl's eyes roamed from person to person, as if deciding whether she would answer or take off running again. When she settled on Heather, she said, "Kaitlin."

"Okay, Kaitlin, what were you and your friend Taylor doing here?" Jerry asked.

"We…we just wanted to see it before it was all torn down."

Todd said, "Are you one of the final girl followers?"

She turned to him with wet eyes. "Yeah. I know it was stupid but Taylor had his mind set. We didn't go very far when I said I wanted to leave. It just felt, I don't know, wrong to be here. But Taylor wanted to see more. He said we'd just go see the pool and then we could go back."

"And did you?" Vince said.

"What?"

"Go to the pool?"

Kaitlin took a shaky breath. If Taylor was seventeen, she was fifteen tops. As much as Todd wanted to hate her for being a final girl follower, he couldn't help wanting to hold her and protect her from what was about to come. Should they even tell her that Taylor was dead? It might make getting her to come with them exceedingly difficult.

"Yeah, we did. We weren't in there long when we heard something crash. We couldn't see what it was. The whole building looks like it's ready to fall down. So I ran. Taylor ran after me. But then, like, we came to the trees and I ran into a branch or something." She looked over at her torn jacket, her fingers prodding within, and winced. "At least I think I did. We got turned around in the trees and we heard something breaking and there was shouting. We kinda freaked out. We both took off, but I lost him in the trees."

Todd looked at Vince. They must have heard his friend falling through the rotted rink wall.

"Please, can you tell me if you saw my friend?" Kaitlin asked. She hopped in place. "This place is freaking me out and I just wanna go home." More tears came, another coat of her thick mascara trailing down her face like lava.

"We'll take you home," Heather said. "We just need you to stay with us."

Kaitlin shook her head. "Not without Taylor. I'm not leaving him here. Maybe you can help me find him."

Todd and his friends looked to each other. There was no hiding the fact that they weren't telling her everything and she knew it.

"What?" Kaitlin asked.

"Look, Kaitlin," Heather began.

"What did you do to Taylor?" Her eyes focused on Sharon and Jerry. "You're not a cop, are you?"

"Trust me, I am. My badge is in my jacket. I can show you. Vince, can you show her?"

"I knew we weren't the only ones here," Kaitlin said. "Were you tracking us? I kept telling Taylor we were being followed."

"We weren't following you," Todd said. "As far as we knew, we were the only ones here."

"I don't believe you."

"How about this?" Vince found Jerry's badge in his coat and flipped it open, shining his light on it.

"How do I know it's even real?"

Todd watched her feet. She was getting ready to run.

Kaitlin said, "Just let me go and I won't tell anyone I saw you, okay?"

Vince and Heather angled themselves so Kaitlin couldn't see Taylor's body behind them.

"It's best if we stick together," Heather said. "But we're not going to make you do something you don't want to do."

"Who the fuck is that?" Sharon said.

"What are you talking about?" Jerry said.

Todd turned to where Sharon was staring. In the distance, perhaps more than a hundred yards out, another person was making their way toward them. Kaitlin turned around and shouted, "Taylor!"

The person stopped, and then began to run as if anxious to reunite with Kaitlin.

"If that's Taylor, who's *he*?" Todd whispered to Vince, casting a quick glance at the body behind them.

"What's he doing?" Sharon said.

Todd tuned back around.

The running figure arced his arm back and swung it forward like a quarterback on the run after the pocket had collapsed.

"Taylor!" Kaitlin shouted, waving her arms and running away from them.

There was a loud pop, followed by what sounded like a bundle of sticks being snapped over someone's knee.

Todd saw Kaitlin's head whip back so far, it bounced off the space between her shoulder blades. Her arms flopped to her sides but she kept running, her dead eyes staring at him as her head bobbed against her back.

CHAPTER TWENTY

Todd wasn't sure which one of them screamed first.

Jerry caught Kaitlin's still-moving body in his light. Todd saw the small spear of rebar protruding from her forehead a moment before her legs finally collapsed. She hit the ground hard, but her body still jittered.

"What the fuck? What the fuck? What the fuck?" Bill blurted, his fingers tearing at his hair.

Jerry let Sharon go and pulled his gun from his holster.

"Get down on the ground now," he shouted in a voice that could have been heard two counties over. Todd had never heard his full 'cop voice' before and he almost inched toward the ground himself.

The man stopped about seventy yards shy of their position.

"I said get down, motherfucker!"

No one made a move toward Kaitlin. Her left leg vibrated like a fish on land.

Todd's hand flexed on the gun.

How could someone that far away throw a hunk of rebar and not only hit the target, but hit it so hard it went through her skull and snapped her neck in half?

They couldn't. Plain and simple.

Todd raised the gun. He had no idea if he could hit the broadside of a barn at the moment or if the gun had enough range to reach the still figure.

"You hear me?" Jerry yelled. "I said get...the...fuck...down! Now!"

They watched as the figure reached for something in his pocket. It was too hard to make out what he extracted, but there was definitely something in his hand.

Jerry went into action, rushing forward with both hands on his gun, barking over and over for the man to put the weapon down.

When the man didn't, Jerry pulled the trigger.

There was no way to tell if the shot hit the man, though he stood his ground and didn't appear the least bit hurt.

"Last time, asshole," Jerry warned, still advancing.

"Shoot him," Sharon implored.

Todd was going to tell her to be quiet, that two dead people was enough, when he saw that she'd gotten her hands free and was making a beeline for him and the gun. He tensed up, waiting for the inevitable collision. She reached for his arm but he spun away. When she regained her footing and went to go for the gun again, Vince wrapped her up from behind.

"Get the hell off me!"

"Holy shit!" Bill exclaimed. "Look at him go."

Even Sharon stopped her struggling to watch the man take off for the nearest tree line. He moved so fast, he was just a blur. One second he was there, the next he was swallowed up by the young forest.

"H-h-how?" Heather choked.

"You ever see anything like that?" Bill said to Jerry.

He still had his gun out, his head cocked, listening for sounds of the running man. It was as if he'd simply disappeared. There were dead crunchy leaves and detritus everywhere. It was almost impossible to run without making a sound.

After waiting several beats, Jerry holstered his gun and got on one knee to check on Kaitlin. He didn't need to check her pulse to know she was dead. Her face was smashed into the earth even though she'd collapsed on her back. Mercifully, her body had finally gone still.

"Toss me my jacket," he said.

Todd scooped it off the ground and brought it over. Jerry took out his gloves and touched the rebar. It looked as if it had been snapped off on both ends so they came to jagged but sharp points.

"How the hell did he do this?" Jerry said.

"Are we sure it's a he?" Todd said.

"You see the size of him? And that cannon for an arm? Has to be a guy."

"How was he able to run so fast?" Todd asked.

A howling wind roared through the Hayden, bringing Todd's hackles to attention.

"Must be high on something," Jerry said. "But what I have no clue."

Sharon jerked herself free from Vince's locked arms. "Are you guys stupid or what? That was the Wraith."

"Oh, just like that kid over there was the Wraith," Jerry said.

"At least now we know who they were running from," she said.

Steam rose from the hole in Kaitlin's head. Todd moved away, horrified by the thought of those vapors touching his skin or getting in his nose.

"Now what do we do?" Bill said.

"You're still getting out of here and getting help," Jerry said.

"Unh-uh," Bill said. "I'm not going anywhere knowing that guy is still around."

"Okay, then you can wait with me and Sharon," Jerry said.

Bill spun in a tight circle. "Fuck me."

"Maybe Bill's right," Vince said. "We should find a place to hole up until daylight. Walking around in the dark, even if we have a gun, it's too risky. Whoever is out there he's strong and fast and I'll bet knows this place a hell of a lot better than we do."

Jerry looked to Todd. "We have him outnumbered, even if we split up."

Todd couldn't help feeling that Sharon was right. The coincidence that there just happened to be another murderer in the Hayden on the night before its demise – or maybe not after they revealed what had been happening here – was too vast to seriously consider. And if that was the Wraith, he was adept at killing, not to mention in possession of incredible speed and strength. Todd wasn't sure how much good Sharon's .38 would do against him, if they could even hit him.

"We could try one of the bungalows," Heather said. They were in shambles and poor protection, but at least they were in the opposite direction from where the man had slipped away.

"At least we'll have a wall at our backs," Bill said. "The odds of getting out of here increase a hell of a lot if we're not out in the open."

"What kind of odds are we talking?" Todd asked. He knew that if he engaged Bill with his favorite topic – gambling – it might help to keep him focused.

"At least three-to-one," he replied.

"I like those odds."

"Fine, we'll hide out in one of the bungalows," Jerry said.

"What do we do about them?" Todd asked, nodding toward the bodies. "Should we bring them with us?"

"No fucking way," Sharon objected.

"No one's asking you," Jerry said. "We have to leave them here. I've screwed up enough tonight as it is. I'm not going to destroy a crime scene."

"I'm not going to lie and say I'm not relieved," Heather said. "I don't think I could stay in one of those tiny bungalows right next to two dead people."

Vince said, "We better get going before he shows up again. Something tells me your gun won't scare him away for long."

Todd saw the shrouded bungalows two hundred yards to the north. Between them and shelter was a lot of wide-open space. "Of course there are trees everywhere but here," he said.

"You guys start running," Jerry said. "I'll watch your backs."

Sharon held out her hands. "What, you don't want to tie me up?"

"You'll need them free for balance when you run," he said. "I want you alive so I can book you. If you feel like separating from us, I'm sure our friend out there will be more than happy to meet up with you."

She snorted at him with disgust and went to Heather.

"I can hang back with you," Todd said.

Jerry patted him on the shoulder. "You take the lead. You have a gun."

"I'm sorry I got you all mixed up in this."

"Don't be. There's no way we could have known it would all go tits up."

"Actually, there was."

He thought about Ash and her friends and the sheer terror they must have felt. Was this the same man that had taken them down one by one five years ago? Had he never left the grounds? Or had he heard Todd's entreaty and was only too happy to oblige? Either way, Todd wasn't sure how they would fare if they crossed paths again, even with their advantage in numbers in firepower. Just look what he'd done with a rusted section of rebar. Todd couldn't believe his foolishness at baiting the madman to come get him. When wishes came true, there was always a price, some more terrible than others.

"It's a straight shot from here," Jerry said, pointing to the bungalows. "Just go into the first one that's not boarded up. Bill's right, it's smart to have a wall at our backs."

"The man knows his odds."

"That he does. Maybe we can even fortify the place a little. Then it's just a matter of sitting tight for a few hours."

Todd wondered if someone in Ash's party had said the very same thing. "Will do, cowboy. Just don't hang back too far. We need to walk out of this cursed place together."

"Just be careful. There may be other final girl kids out here. Only shoot if you know exactly who you're shooting at."

Todd tucked the gun in his pocket. "Then maybe I shouldn't shoot at all, because I have no clue what that guy looks like."

"If he's the size of a gorilla and running like a speeding car, you can assume it's him."

Todd nodded and trotted to his friends. "Everyone follow me. Just run like your ass is on fire."

Bill was already breathing heavy and he hadn't taken a step. "Normally I'd complain about all this cardio, but you don't have to worry about me holding you guys up. Fear is a great motivator."

"Sharon, please don't do anything stupid," Todd said.

"She won't," Heather answered for her. Sharon just stared ahead. Vince's head was on a swivel, looking for any signs of the return of the killer.

"Okay," Todd said. "Let's go."

He took off at a full gallop. He didn't need to check behind him to make sure they were keeping up. He could hear the pounding of their feet close behind.

As Todd ran, he shot quick glances to his left and right, wary of the killer coming for them. He wished he had night vision glasses.

The camera had limited range and it would be impossible to run and keep it close to his face and steady enough to see.

He spotted a bungalow with an open doorway. He hoped the rats were at a minimum inside.

"Right there," he shouted, veering to his right. Four sets of feet thumped close at his heels.

Todd spotted a random pile of cinder blocks a split second before he ended up tumbling over them. He leaped over the pile. Something shifted in his pocket. When he landed, there was an extra thud.

Shit. The gun!

He pulled up and turned around. Sharon and Heather jumped over the cinder blocks while Vince and Bill gave them wide berth.

"What's wrong?" Vince said.

"The gun fell out of my pocket. You all keep heading for that bungalow."

He dropped to his hands and knees, searching for the gun in the dark. He didn't want to turn on the flashlight and give their position away. Heather paused but Sharon tugged on her arm and kept her running toward the bungalow. Vince and Bill got on the ground and helped Todd.

"You guys just go," Todd ordered them with the voice he would use on the guys at work when they were goofing off too much.

"We need that gun," Bill said.

"You need to be with Heather and Sharon," he shot back. "What if he's waiting for them inside the bungalow?"

It wouldn't have been a possibility to even consider, at least until Todd had seen the killer run. He could have easily outflanked them and be sitting, waiting.

"Ah, shit," Bill said, getting up and sprinting the final thirty yards.

"You too, Vince."

His best friend kept scouring the ground. "I will. After we find the gun. You always sucked at finding things."

Todd snickered. "That was Ash's specialty. I would have been late for work at least a hundred times because I couldn't find my car keys."

"Exactly. No bloodhound in your DNA."

The grass was tall here, adding a level of difficulty they didn't need or want. Todd parted the high grass, his ice-cold fingers groping for even colder steel. From time to time, Vince and Todd lifted their heads from their tasks, nervously looking around for the killer. Todd's spine prickled, expecting the worst at any second. He came to the pile of cinder blocks.

"Dammit. It fell out of my pocket right here. How far could it have gone?"

Vince crawled about beside him. "It's heavy, so it has to be close."

Todd felt like he should personally apologize to Vince too – to all of them – but he had to concentrate.

"Come on, come on," he muttered, the fog of his breath temporarily clouding his vision every time he exhaled.

"You think they're all right?" Vince asked.

"No one's screaming. That seems to be the best way to assume things are okay in this place."

An image of Kaitlin's and Taylor's bodies flashed in his mind and a deep chill ran through his entire body. It was so powerful, he had to stop looking for the gun until it passed. This was worse than a nightmare because it was real.

Chips of cinder block stabbed into his hands, but they were too numb to register any pain. "Jesus, it's freezing."

"And we can't even light a fire," Vince said, breathing heavily.

"Even if we could, this place is so dry, it would spread like a wildfire in no time. Then again, this guy is a monster. Aren't monsters afraid of fire?"

"With our luck, we'd get the one that not only isn't afraid, but likes to chuck people into the flames."

Where the hell was the gun? The rustling of the grass was too loud for him. He felt as if it could be heard for miles in the still resort.

That was replaced by another, far more alarming sound.

Footsteps.

Very heavy footsteps.

Vince and Todd stopped searching. They saw the dark figure coming and were paralyzed.

CHAPTER TWENTY-ONE

Todd reached for his backpack, hoping to snatch the knife.

Instead, he grabbed hold of Vince's jacket sleeve and pulled him hard.

"Run!"

Todd's legs had a hard time getting started. He felt like a character in a *Scooby-Doo* cartoon where their legs spin and spin before actually propelling them forward.

We're not some meddling kids and that's not angry old man in a mask, he thought.

The toe of his boot hit into something. He looked down, astounded to see Sharon's .38. He scooped it up and kept going.

He made sure Vince got ahead of him. He knew he was responsible for all of them being here and he would do everything he could to put himself between them and the killer, no matter how terrified he felt.

With a quick backward glance, he saw that the killer was getting close. He nudged Vince in the back with his forearm. They ran straight into the bungalow, kicking rotted boards aside.

"We need to cover the door!" Vince shouted. Heather, Sharon and Bill, who had been standing by the window watching their approach, scattered around the bungalow in search of anything to plug up the empty space that seemed as tall and wide as a massive cave entrance.

"Here!" Heather said. She and Sharon had ripped a closet door off its remaining rusted hinge. Bill helped them carry it to the front. Todd and Vince grabbed one end and they all slammed it sideways against the doorframe. Vince and Todd put their backs to it.

"We need more," Todd urged them.

Bill pushed a moldy chair across the floor, sealing up the gap between the door and the floor. The back of the chair rested against the door. Bill got on the floor and positioned his feet against the chair, acting as a human doorstop.

Something heavy thumped against the door. Todd's heart leaped. He leaned harder into the door.

"Come on," he urged the ladies.

That was when he noticed the windows on either side of the door.

The empty, wide-open windows.

No sooner had he realized clogging up the door was useless than he saw a pair of legs slip through the window.

"The window!"

He and Vince let go of the door. It flipped over the back of the chair and landed on Bill. The sound of the air being punched from his lungs as the door smashed into his ribs filled the cottage.

Out of the dark, Sharon came charging wielding a thick block of wood. She slammed it against the intruder's legs.

"Aaaaaagggghhhhh!"

Todd had grabbed what might have once been a table leg and was about to leap out of the window and smash it against the killer's head when he heard, "You broke my fucking leg!"

"Jesus. It's Jerry," Todd said.

He and Vince ran out of the bungalow. Jerry writhed in agony on the ground, his hands clasped over his shin.

"What the hell did you do that for?" He looked royally pissed.

"Why didn't you freaking say something to let us know it was you?" Vince said.

Sharon came out and Jerry said, "Stay away from me. You've done enough damage."

"But I—"

Heather tugged her back inside. Bill said, "You guys need help?"

"We've got it," Vince said. "Look for more stuff to plug up the windows and door."

Bill gave him a thumbs-up.

"Can you stand?" Todd asked, his hand extended.

"Guess we'll see." Jerry took his hand and hissed loudly when he put pressure on his leg. "We better get inside fast."

"Why?" Vince asked.

Jerry jerked a thumb behind him. "I was running too hard to say anything because I thought I spotted him coming up behind me."

To Todd's horror, a large man draped in shadow was walking a straight line to them. The only saving grace was that he was walking, not running. In fact, he didn't seem to be in any rush to find them, which was even more unnerving than when he'd run like a cheetah moments earlier.

"You should fire a warning shot and get him to change his mind," Vince said.

They hobbled with Jerry between them into the bungalow.

"You see how much good that did before," Jerry said. His face was twisted with pain. His jeans had ripped where Sharon had clubbed him. Todd turned on his flashlight, careful to keep the beam focused on Jerry's leg and not light up the interior of their hideaway. "Please don't tell me you see bone."

Todd said, "No. Just a lot of blood. Heather, can you get my first aid kit out of my bag? We need some antiseptic wipes, gauze and tape." He looked at Jerry. "I have to lift your pants leg up. It's gonna hurt."

"Of course it is." When Todd pulled the cuff over the wound, Jerry pounded the ground with his fists. "Your mother's sister!"

"Is he still coming?" Todd asked Vince, who had taken sentry duty by the window.

"He stopped for a moment, but he's walking again. But real slow."

"He's out there?" Heather said worriedly as she handed Todd the first aid supplies.

"Yes, but I don't think he knows which bungalow we're in," Vince replied. The bungalows were tightly packed, but even so, the man outside would have an easy time settling on which they'd ducked into.

"Take this," Todd said, offering the gun to Vince. What they needed was to get Jerry back on his feet so he could shoot if necessary.

"Keep it down," Vince said to Bill and Sharon who had been going through the rooms and dragging broken hunks of furniture to barricade the door and windows.

"Well how are we supposed to get stuff and not make any noise?" Bill complained.

"I don't fucking know. Figure it out," Vince said in a harsh whisper.

Todd gave Heather his flashlight. "Keep it close."

She chewed on her bottom lip while he opened the antiseptic packs. They looked like wet wipes.

"You're a big boy, so you know this is gonna sting like hell," Todd said.

"Not the first time I've been cut. Not even the first time I've been cut by a stripper."

"Screw you," Sharon said.

She was instantly shushed by four people.

Todd tensed as he touched the alcohol-soaked wipes on Jerry's open wound. Jerry's mouth pulled into a grim line, but he didn't make a sound. As Todd dabbed at the blood, he kept expecting to see the yellow-white of exposed bone.

"No fracture," he said.

"It's a Hayden miracle," Jerry said.

"But you do need stitches. Heath, are there any butterfly bandages in there?"

"Let me see."

"He's still coming," Vince said.

"How far away?" Jerry asked. He shifted his body to try and peek over the windowsill, but a shock of pain set him right back down.

"I don't know. Hundred yards, maybe less."

"Whatever you do, don't pull that trigger."

"I won't."

Todd saw the way Vince was nervously hefting the gun and wasn't so sure. He knew he had to finish up with Jerry fast and get the gun back. They already had one person who had killed an innocent person. He'd be damned if he let that happen to his best friend. As long as the person approaching the bungalow was too far away to see, they had to hold their fire and assume it was another lost final girl follower.

Heather undid the wrapping on the butterfly bandages and Todd dried Jerry's skin and applied them. Blood still seeped between the bandages, but it was the best he could do. What he needed was a doctor.

"Good as old," Todd said.

Jerry was scanned the interior of the bungalow. "We can't stay here. Too many access points."

"There's a bedroom with a boarded-up window," Bill said.

Jerry thought it over for a moment. "I don't like the idea of being trapped with only one way in or out."

Vince shuffled quickly back from the window and nearly fell. "Shit, he's running and he's coming straight for us."

Todd shoved his hands under Jerry's armpits and lifted him from the floor. "Looks like we don't have a choice."

"Everyone grab something as a weapon," Jerry said. Todd helped get him into the bedroom where Bill and Sharon were waiting with a door and a dresser missing its drawers.

Vince took a cautious step back to the window. "I can almost see him." He lifted the gun.

"Vince, get in here," Todd snapped.

His friend peeled away from the window, his face masked in terror.

They clogged the doorway with everything they could find. Heather turned on the lantern she'd brought so they could see. There was no sense trying to pretend the killer hadn't spotted them. Jerry slumped into a corner and checked his gun.

Todd found a board with several bent and rusty nails poking out of it and passed it to Vince. "Trade you for the gun."

Even though Vince was scared, he seemed happy to give the gun back.

Looking around the room, Todd saw that everyone had hold of some makeshift weapon. Heather had found a shard of glass shaped like a saber. She'd torn a chair cushion and wrapped it around one end as a kind of hilt. Sharon, her flinty eyes locked on the barricade, held a pipe in each hand. Bill gripped a two-by-four, holding it over his shoulder like a batter waiting for a fastball.

"Stand over there," Todd whispered to Bill, nodding his chin to a spot beside the doorway.

"Gotcha."

The block of wood trembled in Bill's hands, but he didn't hesitate to position himself so he could give the killer – if it was the killer – a good whack if he pushed his way through.

Todd stood before the barricade with his feet spread apart and the gun raised. He made sure to keep everyone else behind him.

"What if he doesn't come?" Sharon asked.

"Then we wait in here until daylight," Todd said. It almost seemed as if Sharon wanted the killer to come for them.

And then it hit Todd.

So did he, if this was, in fact, the same man who had killed Ash's friends and destroyed her.

They heard boots scraping along the grit on the floor of the bungalow's main living space.

"He's here," Bill muttered. He lifted the two-by-four even higher.

Everyone froze, not daring to make a sound. They listened to the man walk around the bungalow, his footsteps so hard and heavy, Todd wondered if he'd end up falling through the rotted floorboards. They could only be so lucky.

Todd pulled the hammer back on Jerry's gun, the click sounding like fireworks going off.

Something was thrown against a wall.

Heather let out a startled gasp before clamping her hand over her mouth.

The person in the bungalow stopped moving.

Jerry put his finger to his lips and urged everyone to stay still.

The bungalow was as silent and still as death.

Todd's heart beat like a wild horse barreling down an open field. He had a hard time swallowing.

Come on, come on. You know we're in here. Make your move.

He wanted to pull the barricade apart and see the killer's face. Anything was better than this waiting. And what if the killer decided he wanted no part of them and walked away? Could Todd just let him walk free? This might be his one chance to avenge Ash.

Sweat dotted Bill's upper lip, despite the cold. Todd looked over at Jerry, who hadn't taken his eyes off the doorway. He could feel Heather's, Vince's and Sharon's tension at his back. It was palpable, displacing the air, as if something humongous were oozing into the room.

Any second now, there would be hands pounding on the door that had been slapped against the opening.

Todd's whole body was as rigid as a steel girder.

Was the killer just inches from the barricade, listening for them?

The question was, which side would crack first?

Jerry went to adjust the weight on his good leg and his foot scuffed against the floor just the slightest bit. The noise it made was calamitous.

There was a collective intake of breath, which seemed equally booming. Jerry shook his head, upset with himself. Todd spotted drops of blood on the dirty floor and Jerry's boots.

The waiting was driving Todd mad. He wasn't sure how much more he could take. Inaction had never been his strong suit. His thumb grazed the cocked hammer.

That was no final girl fanatic out there.

His nose itched where a bead of sweat had trickled down his face.

In the space of time it took his finger to reach his face to scratch it, wood exploded, people screamed, and darkness pulled them into its malicious embrace.

CHAPTER TWENTY-TWO

Todd stood staring at the barricaded door, his confusion paralyzing his legs and arms. The back of his neck hurt like hell. It felt as if he'd been stung by a hive of bees.

It took him a moment – a moment he couldn't spare – to realize the board that had been screwed into the window had blown apart as if it had been charged with dynamite. He spun around, his arm straight as an arrow, hand gripping the gun for dear life.

Jerry, being the closest to the window, was on the ground. So were Vince and Sharon. Heather shouted, holding onto the remaining shard of glass that had been broken by the wood shrapnel. She'd been cut, blood cascading down her wrist and dripping on the floor.

An instant before the lantern was extinguished by a well-thrown hunk of brick, Todd saw the killer, framed in the window, his hulking body heaving with each breath.

His face had been mangled so badly, it no longer resembled a human face. His nose was split in two and mashed, covering both cheekbones like a fleshy tarp. The few teeth in the ragged red hole of a mouth were a cancerous yellow and serrated. Where there should have been eyes, there were two onyx marbles, or were they just vast, empty sockets bleeding the depthless pitch of space?

Then it went dark.

Todd wanted to shoot, but he feared hitting one of his friends in the inky blackness. The moon must have been swallowed up by storm clouds as there was just barely enough light to illuminate the outline of the window.

Todd stuffed the gun in his pocket and desperately fumbled for anything that could be used to batter the deformed man before he stepped inside.

Sharon yowled and he heard her rushing toward the window.

The sound of metal crunching bone was unmistakable.

Todd's fingers touched on something thick and heavy, more splinters piercing his flesh. Ignoring the pain, he grabbed it and ran to join Sharon, hoping they didn't end up hitting each other. He bumped into her shoulder as she was in mid-downward stroke. The rebar clanged off the windowsill.

Up close, Todd saw the shadow of the deformed man but was mercifully spared the stark sight of his face. He jabbed the hunk of wood into the center of the shadow. It felt like battering a brick wall. The wood reverberated like a bat hitting a ball. This time, the pain went directly into his marrow. Todd dropped the wood, shaking his hands.

Sharon let out a piercing war cry and went to slam the rebar onto the killer again.

Except he was gone.

Todd yanked her away from the window, in case he was waiting for her to stick her head out looking for him.

"We need some light," he said.

There was no sense trying to hide anymore. They needed light not only to see the killer when he returned, but also to check on the state of their wounded friends. Sharon got the flashlight from her coat pocket and snapped it on.

Heather still stood in the center of the room, bleeding and speechless. Vince was unconscious, a swelling knot protruding from the center of his forehead. Jerry had also been knocked out by a flying section of wood. Bill swayed by the door, a hunk of two-by-four still raised, but his eyes were flat and glassy. Todd could have shouted at him, asking why he didn't help, but he was afraid his high school buddy wouldn't have even comprehended what he was saying.

First things first. He had to stop Heather's wrist from bleeding. He found his backpack that had been buried under shafts of wood and got his flashlight. The first aid kit was where Heather had left it.

"Keep an eye on the window, but don't get close," he said to Sharon.

A ragged line had been cut on her cheek and there was some blood, but physically she seemed okay.

"Did you…did you see him?" she said, her voice sounding far, far away.

"Yeah. I'm trying not to think about it at the moment. Heather, I need you to sit right there." He led her to an overturned armoire.

"I'm sorry," she said.

He slipped the first aid kit open. "Sorry for what?"

"For not helping. I...I think I'm hurt."

She hadn't looked down at her wrist yet, most likely out of self-preservation. He carefully plucked the glass hilt from her and tossed it away.

"It's okay," he said, unwrapping the last ball of gauze in the kit. "I just need you to raise your hand over your head. Can you do that for me?"

Heather nodded. When she did, blood spilled down her arm like a waterfall for a moment, and then slowed to a trickle, much to Todd's temporary relief. He quickly swiped the wrist wound with some antiseptic pads and got to work pushing the skin together and applying butterfly bandages. When he was done, he saw that he was out of them now too. He wrapped gauze around her wrist and applied pressure. She stayed oddly silent the entire time, not even asking about her husband.

"Bill, move Jerry away from the window," Todd said.

Bill shook himself free from his immobility and dropped the two-by-four. "Uh, yeah, yeah, I got him."

Jerry woke up when Bill started to slide him away from the window.

"Wuh tha fu?" Jerry slurred.

Todd was positive he'd find the side of Jerry's head giving birth to a sizeable lump. He just had to pray he wasn't concussed.

"You think you can keep your hand on your wrist and press it like I am?" he asked Heather.

When she started to drop her hand, he took hold of it and put it back above her head. "You have to keep it just like this. Okay?"

"Okay."

"Great. I have to check on Vince."

Hearing her husband's name brought an instant shiver of realization through her body. "Oh God, Vince."

Todd flicked through the first aid kit and found the capsules of smelling salts. He cracked one open under Vince's nose, hoping the heady ammonia smell would wake him up. If not, they were in even deeper shit.

Vince's face puckered and his eyes fluttered open. Before Todd could move the open capsule away, Vince sat up and slapped his hand.

"What are you trying to do, kill me?" he said groggily.

Todd's rocked back on his heels, relieved. "Just the opposite, buddy." He looked over at Sharon. "You see him?"

"No, but that doesn't mean he's not close."

Against his better judgment, he gave Sharon her gun back. "This will do better than some old rebar."

"Thank you." Her hand lingered on his for a moment. She was as petrified as the rest of them, but she wasn't going to let it overwhelm her. He assumed in her line of work, she'd seen some pretty rough stuff. Nothing could prepare a person for this, but it must be helping keep her shit together.

"Jerry, you think Bill could take your gun?"

Jerry pinched his eyes. "Are you kidding me? I wouldn't trust Bill with a BB gun."

"Gee, thanks," Bill said.

"Are you able to keep watch on the door then?" Todd asked.

"I can, just not from a standing position. What the hell happened?"

"While we were all looking at the door, he busted in through the window."

Jerry lifted his good leg and rested his gun hand on his knee. "I take it he got away?"

Todd hesitated, then said, "If you can call it a he."

"It was a chick?" Jerry said, one eyebrow arched high.

"No. Definitely not a woman." And definitely not a final girl kid. He prayed there were no others out there now, looking for a piece of the Hayden Massacre to take home. If there were, they would never make it home. Of that he was certain.

Heather's strength was faltering. Her upraised arm quavered. "Bill, hold Heather's arm up, will you?"

Bill seemed happy to do whatever Todd asked him to do, as if making up for freezing earlier.

"Why does my head hurt so much?" Vince asked, his fingertips finding the bulging knot on his forehead. "What hit me?"

"A hunk of thick board," Todd said. "You feel like you can stand?"

"A headache never kept me from walking and chewing bubblegum at the same time." He helped Vince to his feet. Vince finally noticed Heather, saw the blood on her arm and rushed over to her. Todd let them talk. He crept to the window and stood beside Sharon.

"I don't hear anything," she said.

"He didn't make a single sound when he walked out of the bungalow before either. Don't let your guard down."

She flashed him an incredulous look with her nearly black eyes. "After what I just saw? Not a chance. He shows up again, I'm emptying this gun in him."

"Take the gun away from her," Jerry said. "Have you lost your mind?"

"It's all right," Todd said.

"Hell no, it's not all right. She's a murderer. And you just gave her back her goddamn weapon."

Todd knelt in front of Jerry. "You didn't see him."

"So what? That doesn't mean you should weaponize the woman I have to take to jail."

"You have to trust me on this. You didn't see him, so you don't know. I'd give her a freaking bazooka to cover us if I had to."

"You're not making any sense."

"Nothing about tonight is." To keep his mind off the horrifying images of the man in the window, Todd checked the bandaging on Jerry's leg. It seemed to be holding up. The true test would be when Jerry tried to put any pressure on it. "I think you'll live."

"I hope you can say that for all of us now that you gave Bonnie Parker her gun."

Sharon glanced at them and shook her head.

"I'm pretty sure she's not going to shoot us," Todd said.

"I may not, but I'm not going to jail either," she said.

Jerry gave Todd an *I told you* so look.

"Sharon, you're not making things any easier."

"She's right," Bill said. "She's not going to jail. No one's going anywhere. There's no way we're ever getting out of here."

"What happened to everyone while I was out for a few seconds?" Jerry demanded.

Bill licked his dry lips, his eyes swinging between the open window and barricaded door. "He didn't have eyes."

Vince, who had taken over holding Heather's arm up, said, "What do you mean, he had no eyes?"

"Just what I said. He…had…no…eyes. Heather, you saw him. Tell him."

Heather had gone frighteningly pale. "I didn't see him. Everything happened so fast. The board exploded and I felt something hot on my wrist. I…I kind of blanked out for a bit."

Bill found his two-by-four and held it with both hands. "Half of us saw him. It looked like his face had been hit by a wrecking ball. He had no eyes, but it was like he could see perfectly. I looked into where his eyes should be and…and I felt him looking back at me!"

"You mean to tell me you're all freaking out over a blind guy?"

"He's not blind," Bill insisted.

"Look, buddy, if he has no eyes, he's blind. A five-year-old could tell you that."

"Maybe we're mistaken," Todd said, looking to defuse the situation. "It was only for a moment anyway before he destroyed the lantern. I saw something that looked like eyes. They were black, but it's dark. Maybe he's wearing some weird kind of contacts or something."

"Whatever," Jerry said. "We're going to need a medical chopper to get us out of here if this keeps up."

"Sharon got him pretty good," Todd said.

Sheri's sister nodded. "I think I nailed him in the shoulder. It hurt *me,* and I was the one holding the rebar."

"I got a poke at him in the gut, but man, he didn't even react," Todd added.

"It must have done something," Sharon said. "Because he took off right after."

"Oh honey, sit," Heather said.

Vince wobbled on his feet, his hands holding his head. "Just a little dizzy. It'll pass."

"Guess we're not going anywhere for a while," Jerry said.

"Not without some stretchers," Todd replied. They might have been surrounded by four walls, but he felt entirely exposed. And now half of them were seriously wounded. There was no *running* out of here, that was for sure.

"How many hours till dawn?" Bill asked.

Sharon answered, "About four and a half."

"You think we can wait it out in here?" Heather said.

Todd took a quick peek outside. The moon was hiding behind the clouds and the Hayden still looked as if it had been swallowed in black ink. "I don't think we have a choice."

Jerry tried to get to his feet and failed, never taking the gun off the barricade. "Well, you know what they say."

"What's that?" Vince asked as he slowly lowered himself to the ground.

Jerry scratched the side of his nose with the barrel of the gun. "Remember the Alamo."

CHAPTER TWENTY-THREE

Time passed interminably.

In the prolonged silence, crickets had resumed their night song. The temperature dropped to below freezing. Everyone but Jerry and Sharon had their arms wrapped around themselves. The pair of opposites were too busy keeping their guns aimed at the ports of entry to seek the illusion of warmth. Todd thought of asking Sharon for the gun, but she looked like she was far more capable than he was. There was a cooling body outside to attest to it.

Heather's teeth chattered.

"I don't think I've ever been so cold."

"Unzip your jacket," Todd said.

She looked at him as if he'd asked her to dance on her head. "That's the last thing I want to do."

He shook her off. "Vince, you do the same. Basically, hug each other and wrap your coats around yourselves. You need some collective body heat."

Vince unzipped his coat. "Since when did you become a nurse?"

Todd eyed the open first aid kit. Jerry's and Heather's bleeding had stopped and he'd treated the cut on Sharon's cheek, even though she protested the entire time.

"I took a bunch of classes for work. There's a lot of potential for accidents in construction. Someone has to know how to keep a guy alive until the pros arrive. Plus, I watch a lot of those dude-in-the-woods-alone survival shows. It's television. It can't be wrong."

Vince huddled next to his wife. He'd complained about being nauseated a few minutes earlier. Todd wasn't sure if it was nerves – they were all scared to death – or a concussion. He hoped for the former.

"So you only play a doctor who plays a doctor on TV," Vince joked. His laugh was cut short by a wince of pain.

"That sounds about right."

They'd given up whispering. The killer knew exactly where they were. They kept one flashlight on so they could see one another, and spot the maniac if and when he showed up again.

No one spoke for a while. The only sound was the chattering of teeth.

Sharon broke the stillness and said, "You know that was Otto, right?"

"Oh yeah, he's definitely a Nazi cook who was killed forty fucking years ago," Jerry retorted. "I mean, who else would it be?"

Sharon curled her full lip at him. "You didn't see his face, man. I'm telling you, it was Otto. Now I know who killed my sister. I'm not leaving until that asshole is worm food."

Heather gingerly touched her bandaged wrist. "He's right, Sharon. It can't be him. The staff not only killed him, they buried him, probably alive too. And even if it was Otto, he'd be like a hundred by now. The person out there is not some feeble old man."

Sharon shifted over toward Todd and tapped his backpack – Ash's lucky backpack – with her boot. "Watch the video again. Ash said the old man told her they beat Otto until his face was all smashed in. Don't you think it's odd that a man matching that same description is out there?"

Vince cupped his wife's face in his hand. "Seeing him or not seeing him, it's kind of impossible to think that man out there is an old, supposedly dead Nazi."

Bill, who hadn't said a word in a long while, leaned against the wall, exhausted. "So you're saying we're talking out of our asses?"

Vince turned to Todd. "Help me out here."

Todd didn't know what to say. Either way, he was going to piss off one of his friends. He took a while before answering, "Vince, his face was all messed up. I'm not saying he didn't have any eyes. But his nose had definitely been broken...bad. His mouth and teeth were a mess, like they'd been kicked in."

"Did he look like a hundred-year-old man who'd clawed his way out of a grave years before we were born?" Vince asked pointedly.

Todd chucked a pebble into the barricade. The air was frigid and sharper than a switchblade. It hurt to breathe. What he wanted to do right now was make a fire, not debate whether or not the lunatic outside was Otto or not. In the end, it didn't matter. No matter who was out there, they were still wounded and trapped.

"I don't know," he said.

"I do," Sharon said.

Jerry pushed his back against the wall with his good leg and used it to leverage himself until he was standing. Todd couldn't help staring at his friend's leg, waiting for the bandages to break and the blood to start flowing again.

"Otto the dead hundred-year-old Nazi line cook is not our problem," Jerry said. "Because that guy sure ain't him."

"You can be as blind ignorant as you want," Sharon said. "That kind of thinking might get you killed."

"You'd like that, wouldn't you? Then you can just skip on out of here and not take your punishment for killing that kid."

"I didn't know he was a kid," Sharon said. Todd could hear her wall cracking just a bit. He saw the regret in her eyes.

"Doesn't matter. You still smoked him," Jerry said. He swiveled toward Todd. "And why does she still have the damn gun?"

"Sharon's not the enemy here," Todd protested.

"Tell that to that kid's parents."

Sharon raised her hands in disgust and for a scary moment leveled the gun at Jerry. "Would you lay the fuck off me?" She looked down at her hand and realized what she'd done and was quick to shift the barrel away. "I promise, you can make my life hell when we get out of here. Will that make you happy?" Nothing about her tone implied that she meant it.

Jerry edged toward the window and looked outside. "Oh, well now that you say it that way, by all means, keep your murder weapon."

"Guys, stop it," Todd said. He stepped between the two. "Jerry, will you chill the hell out if I took the gun?"

"It would be a start."

He turned to Sharon and held out his hand. "Please. We can't afford to be distracted by fighting."

Sharon pulled away.

"Please," Todd said.

When she exhaled, the plume of fog nearly blinded him. "Fine. I was tired of keeping watch anyway."

Todd took the gun, the grip warm from Sharon's hand, and joined Jerry at the window. "You think he's close?"

"A guy who can run like that, he doesn't need to be. We're not out of his sight, I can tell you that."

"What if there are other people out there? He could be on the other side of the resort now. We could make a run for it."

"Let's hope not," Jerry said. "I don't want to think of any other kids getting in his crosshairs. You should check the phones again."

"I've got it," Bill volunteered. He powered up each of their phones, the verdict the same for each. "No go."

"Is nighttime always this long?" Vince said.

"Try spending graveyard shifts in a squad car waiting for someone to speed past you. Night goes on forever," Jerry replied.

Sharon found her rebar and positioned herself on the other side of the barricade. She looked like she was hoping the killer would break through at any moment. Revenge kept her hard and ready.

Lowering his voice, Jerry said, "You don't really think that's Otto out there, do you?"

Todd considered his words. "I honestly don't know. That man. He didn't look human. Not entirely. And we all saw how he ran. And how he threw that rebar all the way through that girl's head. If he's not Otto, what the hell is he?"

"And I'm the one that was hit in the head."

"You're a cop. Consider the evidence."

"I know enough to discount eyewitness testimony."

"Then just go by what you've seen, man."

Bill crept toward them. "There is a way this could be possible."

Jerry said, "Oh yeah? How's that?"

"This Otto guy. If he was a Nazi officer, he had access to stuff the regular foot soldiers didn't."

"You mean meth?" Vince interjected.

"That was for Hitler and his inner circle," Bill said.

"How the hell do you even know this?" Vince said. He and Heather had stopped shivering.

"I love Nazis," Bill said.

When everyone gave him a look, he backtracked. "I'm fascinated by them. I read and watch anything I can about Hitler and his followers, even the crazy shit about them having bases beneath Antarctica and the moon."

Todd shook his head. "Dude, your father is Jewish. Why the hell would you give two shits about the Nazis?"

Bill wagged a finger. "Know thy enemy. Trust me, no one is more intrigued by the Nazis and the Third Reich than the Jews. It's so we know the signs and make sure it never happens again."

Jerry was visibly weary of Bill's fascination. "Bill, that guy out there is not some Nazi, so whatever Hitler fetish you have doesn't matter."

"You don't get it," Bill said. "The Nazis weren't just into world domination. When it came to the upper ranks, they were obsessed with the occult and the paranormal. Hitler and maniacs like Rudolf Hess and Joseph Goebbels were always looking for ways to justify the Aryan race and find any way, even if it meant calling on Satan, to give them control of not just the world, but the future."

"Come on, Bill," Jerry said.

"I'm not making this up. They scoured the planet for mythical relics and supposed magical places. They may have been stoned and crazy and desperate, but maybe, just maybe, they actually found something."

"Something like what?" Sharon asked with unguarded irritation.

"How the hell do I know? Something that makes it so this Otto guy can't die."

Todd had had enough. "Nazi zombies? Really, Bill?"

Bill shrugged. "You find a better explanation, I'm happy to hear it."

"Give me ten seconds, I'll give you fifty," Jerry said. "Look, we just need to keep our cool and wait this fucker out. For all we know, Sharon and Todd bashed him good and he's dead or licking his wounds somewhere. As soon as it's light, we'll get help and I'll personally lead a search team to find this asshole."

No one had anything left to say. Todd hated that a part of him was falling for Bill's line about magic and Nazis and zombies. It was ludicrous.

But Bill had seen the man's face, just like Todd. He wasn't sure Jerry would be so dismissive if he had as well.

He checked his phone. Less than four hours until dawn.

If you can hear me, Ash, I think we're going to need your help. You've been through this. Let me know what to do.

Something crackled in the dark outside the bungalow.

Whup!

"What was that?" Sharon said, instantly on the alert.

The stench of sulfur wafted into the room.

It was followed by the distinctive snap and pop of flames.

Tendrils of smoke snaked through the window.

"Goddammit," Jerry hissed, sticking his head out of the window for a second before pulling it back in. "He set the roof on fire."

They all looked up. They could hear the dry, rotted timber embrace the flame. It wouldn't take long for the entire place to be engulfed.

"Looks like he got tired of waiting," Todd said.

Jerry's eyes darted around the room. "Which means we have to exit in the direction he least expects."

"Just like how he caught us off guard by coming through the window," Sharon said.

"Exactly. Problem is, I don't know how this psycho thinks."

Todd's gaze pinged between the window and the doorway. They had a 50-50 chance of making the correct choice. But either way, they would be too slow to gain any ground on him. He wasn't even sure if Jerry could walk or if Vince could go far before getting dizzy and falling.

He looked across the room. A faded painting of a bucolic park with a lake hung crookedly on the wall. The roof groaned, embers slipping through the cracks. If they didn't get out of here soon, they would be burned alive.

Todd put his hand to the wall, his fingers nearly pushing through the ancient drywall.

He backed up, lifted his right boot and smashed it into the wall. The rotted structure gave way, nearly opening all the way to the outside.

"Start tearing the barricade down," he ordered Bill and Sharon.

"Make as much noise as you can." When Bill tossed the door aside, Todd timed his next kick to mask the sound. His foot went completely through the wall. Vince saw what he was doing and left Heather to help. He had to put an arm over Todd's shoulders to steady himself. After a half dozen blows each, there was a sizeable hole in the wall.

Todd dropped to his hands and knees and eyeballed the opening. There was no one out there waiting for them.

A flaming board fell through the ceiling, nearly braining Heather. Black smoke poured into the room. They were running out of time.

"Heather, Sharon, start screaming. I'll go out first. If I survive, follow me."

Every particle of Todd's being recoiled at the thought of being the first outside. For all he knew, the second he stepped through the hole, the killer would be there waiting for him.

The gun was little reassurance, but it was better than nothing.

"We have to get the fuck outta here," Jerry said, hobbling across the room, his gun swinging between the window and the now-empty doorway.

Another board collapsed. The flames touched the threadbare rug, followed by a jarring *whup!*

Todd leaped through the ragged hole. The back of his jacket caught on a shard of lathing. Half of him was outside in the mercifully empty cold. He struggled to pull himself out. If he asked for help – and in his panic he was moments away from screaming – he would give his position away.

If he didn't extricate himself soon, his friends would be burned alive.

He had to set the gun aside so his fingers could find purchase in the dead weeds and dirt. He dug the toes of his boots in and pushed and pulled at the same time.

His efforts gave him an extra four inches of freedom.

Todd felt hands on his legs and butt. They gave a great push. The lathing dug into his back. He was sure it had shredded his coat and shirts and punctured his skin. The pain was instant. It sprinted up his spine and locked his jaw.

Still they pushed. He wanted to cry out in pain, to tell them to stop, but he couldn't let one syllable escape.

Something snapped and he was finally able to scrabble out. Hurt and panicked, he grabbed the gun and checked the area behind the burning bungalow. Jerry had been right. The killer was expecting them to run out the front door.

A dull thud almost made him pull the trigger. He looked down and saw they'd tossed his backpack through the hole. Heather came next, followed by Sharon and Bill.

"Oh my God, Todd," Heather whispered. She put a steadying hand on his shoulder. He hadn't a clue what she was so concerned about.

"Don't move," Bill said.

"Why?"

Todd followed Bill's gaze to his back. The lathing stuck from his lower back like a stake through a vampire's chest. Seeing it made the pain suddenly worse.

"I don't think it's in too deep," Heather said so softly, Todd could barely hear her. He turned his head to see Vince crawling out.

Heather ripped off her coat and stuck the sleeve in Todd's mouth. "It will help."

She yanked the lathing out before he could tell her to remove it carefully. Hot blood ran down his back, soaking his ass and the back of his thighs. His teeth clamped down on Heather's coat. His throat sealed up, preventing the yowl of agony that rocketed from deep in his core.

"Stay still so I can see what we're dealing with."

Todd said, "There's no time. Where's Jerry?"

The damaged bungalow groaned like a giant awaking from a long slumber. Flames had devoured it to the point where its brightness hurt his eyes. Half of the roof on the living room side completely collapsed.

Bending down hurt like blue blazes. Todd stuck his hand through the hole, hoping to come in contact with his friend as he tried to get out.

He touched nothing but boiling air.

Getting down even farther, he looked into the bungalow.

Jerry lay facedown on the floor, overcome by the smoke and heat.

He had to get him out of there...and fast.

CHAPTER TWENTY-FOUR

"I have to go in and get him," Todd said, somehow managing to keep his voice down despite his rising panic.

As if in answer, the bungalow's foundation moaned. Now the sides of the house were caving in as well as the ceiling.

"The rest of you run and find a safe place to hide."

"We're not leaving you," Vince said.

There was no time to argue. Todd tossed the gun to Vince. It was a careless and stupid thing to do, but he didn't have time for caution. With his back wailing in torment, Todd plunged through the hole. A chunk of wood, engulfed in flame, fell toward him. He put up his arm just in time to deflect it before it hit him in the face.

The smoke roiled, filling the room. He could only find Jerry by getting on his belly. Each breath felt like hot needles in his lungs and ended with violent coughs. He crawled his way to Jerry and pounded on his shoulder.

"Jerry. Jerry!"

Shouting in here wasn't a problem. The cacophony of the flames drowned out his voice.

His friend didn't respond.

Through the smoke, Todd saw tiny flames on the back of Jerry's jacket. He slapped them down, hoping that would wake Jerry. It didn't.

Wood and flame cracked above and around him. Todd couldn't see a thing. In fact, he couldn't even find the hole in the wall.

He grabbed Jerry's shoulders and tugged, careful to keep his head down. If he lifted it just an inch too high, he was going to draw in a breath of that thick, black smoke and it was goodbye forever after that. Drawing Jerry toward him while he was on his belly wasn't easy. Every muscle in his arms felt as if they were on the breaking point.

Todd backed out slowly, in constant fear of being buried under burning timber any second. The bottoms of his feet touched a wall.

Dammit! If he'd somehow gotten turned around, he wouldn't have enough time to find the makeshift exit.

A coughing fit hit him violently. He saw bright sparks all around him. He couldn't tell if that was his brain firing off warning shots that he wasn't getting enough oxygen or actual sparks from all of the falling timber.

He looked behind him.

Smoke was billowing through the hole just a few feet to his left.

Making the adjustment was difficult, Jerry's dead weight – he prayed it wasn't, in fact, *dead weight* – almost too much for him.

The roof fell in just inches from Jerry's boots.

Todd buried his mouth in his shirt, took a deep breath and got to his knees. Using the last surge of his flagging strength, he tugged Jerry close and backed out of the hole.

Cold night air suffused with acrid smoke was little relief.

No one else was around to help Todd drag Jerry ten feet from the collapsing bungalow. Once he felt he was safe enough away, he scooted to grab his backpack and collapsed next to his friend, his back feeling as if it were going to break from the savage coughs that made it nearly impossible to breathe.

He propped himself up on his elbows and watched the bungalow implode. The fire licked high into the sky. The heat was overwhelming.

Rolling over, he checked Jerry's neck for a pulse. At first, his heart sank when he couldn't find it. That was because he had his fingers on the wrong spot on Jerry's neck. On the second try, he found it.

"We gotta get moving, buddy," he said.

His back popped and his lungs felt as if they were going to flop out of his mouth as he stood and took hold of Jerry's hands to drag him even farther away.

Once they were far enough that he no longer felt as if he were getting a massive sunburn, he fell down again.

If the killer was close by, Todd and Jerry would make easy pickings. Todd wasn't even sure if Jerry had holstered his gun or if it was underneath the burning wreckage.

Neither could run.

They were sitting ducks.

Todd didn't have the strength to worry about it.

He couldn't stop coughing, hacking up huge wads of what he was sure was black phlegm, letting it drop from his mouth into the tall, dry grass.

The only thing that gave him pause was hearing Jerry cough.

"Oh thank God," Todd said. "I didn't have it in me to give you CPR."

Jerry winced, opening one watery eye toward him. "Where are... we?"

"Not being roasted to death, that's where." Todd took a tremulous breath of clean air but coughed it all back up instantly. The edges of his vision got all fuzzy.

They sounded like patients at an old-time tuberculosis ward for several minutes, neither drawing enough air to speak in full sentences.

Once they settled down, Jerry fumbled for his holster and heaved a sigh of relief. He slipped his gun out and showed it to Todd. "Silver lining."

"Tarnished."

"Where is everybody?"

"I told them not to wait for me. Hell, I didn't even think I was getting us out of there alive."

Jerry shifted to his side, his weight on his bad leg. "Man, that hurts. I'm getting my ass handed to me by this place." He managed to get to his feet. "Looks like they went that way."

Todd saw the tamped-down grass, heading toward the main hotel.

"Why would they go back there?"

Jerry took a pen light from his pocket and scanned the ground. "I was afraid of that."

Even though Todd's body wanted nothing to do with being upright and mobile, he forced himself to stand. He stumbled toward Jerry, looking down at what the small cone of light was illuminating.

"Is that blood?"

Jerry grunted loudly as he bent to touch his fingers to it. His fingertips came back red. "Yep." He looked around the area, several times looking like he was about to fall. "The only good thing is, there's not much of it."

"It could have been Heather's bandaging coming loose," Todd said, now worried that he hadn't done a good enough job to keep her from bleeding out.

"Don't you find it strange how we've been sitting out here lit up by the fire and that maniac hasn't come around?"

Todd wiped his forehead and stared at the smudge of gray on his palm. "To tell you the truth, I've been too damn tired to care. But now that you say it...."

"Which means he's not here. He doesn't seem like the type that would pass up a free kill. You get my drift?"

They looked to the hotel in the dark distance. Todd listened for any shouting or screaming, but the snapping flames dominated the night.

"Guess where we're going," Jerry said.

"At least Vince has the gun."

"I just hope he doesn't shoot himself."

They limped away from the burning bungalow. Todd said, "We should be hearing sirens soon. The fire may have nearly killed us, but it'll bring the cavalry."

Jerry grabbed Todd's shoulder and leaned into him as they walked. "They better haul ass. The less time we're here, the better."

★   ★   ★

Todd wondered if Ash had walked this same path, dazed and battered, praying, like he was, that she would make it out alive. There had once been a winding paved road beneath their feet. It was now cracked gravel and sprouting weeds. Walking was treacherous, but it was far from the tree line where the killer could be waiting.

The sirens got louder and Todd saw flashing lights in the distance. The only sight and sound that would have been sweeter was the rumble of the army coming to their rescue.

"Your people are here," he said to Jerry.

"Good. We need lots of 'em."

"Maybe we should split up. I'll look for Vince and the gang, you go meet the cops and firefighters at the bungalow."

The foot of Jerry's bad leg scraped along the shattered drive. He hissed loudly. "Oh yeah, because splitting up always works so well in the movies."

"This isn't a movie."

"Exactly. Which is why I'm doubling down on our staying together."

The hotel loomed ahead of them.

Todd said, "You think he got to them?"

Jerry sucked on his teeth and spit. "If he did, it was while we were in there," he said, jerking his thumb behind them. "We would have heard them screaming by now. If they're lucky, he might have spotted them but they got away. If they're smart, and they are, they're hiding, but someplace where they can't get trapped in a corner and too big to burn down so fast."

They came to the fountain in front of the hotel.

"It can't be Otto, right?" Todd said.

"No. It can't. So get that out of your head, dude. This is a real flesh and blood lunatic."

Todd couldn't deny that he was flesh and blood. But was he resurrected flesh and blood? It was ridiculous, but his Lutheran upbringing had laid a foundation for the possibility of people rising from the dead. Aside from Jesus and Lazarus, there were many other cases of people being brought back to life. He remembered one of the books of the Bible talking about scores of people rising from their graves the moment Jesus perished on the cross. They appeared all throughout Jerusalem. It must have been one hell of a terrifying mindfuck to the living.

Very much like here, thousands of years later.

But the revived dead in the Bible had been, to a man and woman, good people. The good might have died young, but they got second chances. Not so with the bad. Why would God breathe life into the wasted corpse of a Nazi deviant?

"What did they discover?" he whispered.

"What's that?" Jerry asked, pausing at the now glassless revolving door.

"Just thinking about what Bill said about Nazis."

"Yeah, well, think about finding Bill so he can live to gamble another day. I wonder what odds he'd give on us getting out of here alive."

The corner of Todd's mouth curled up. "I'd say they just increased dramatically once he heard those sirens."

"What's the surefire odds he always says to avoid because there's no payout? One-to-nine?"

"Yep. 'You can't make cheddar on chalk'. The man is full of wisdom."

"Oh, he's full of something all right."

They were about to step into the hotel lobby when the sirens suddenly cut off. Todd whirled around. The red, blue and white strobing lights that had been painting the grounds a good distance from them disappeared.

"Did they just leave?" Todd said.

The fire still raged. It looked like it had started to devour the bungalow next to it.

"No way. They wouldn't let the place burn, even if it is scheduled to be demolished."

A dark suspicion picked at the back of Todd's brain with a pointed talon. His body prickled with goose bumps. "We better hurry up and find them."

Todd took a breath to call out for their friends when Jerry put an arm across his chest and shook his head. "We go in smart."

Jerry carefully picked his way through the debris so as not to make any noise. He turned on his small flashlight, but cupped his hand over the bulb. "Take this."

Todd kept the light doused. Jerry's gun led the way.

The lobby felt sinister, haunted, since they'd been inside it just hours earlier.

"Keep the light low and sweep the lobby," Jerry whispered.

Todd scanned the ground, the light petering out to a dull film just a dozen feet from them. He saw a splash of blood glinting off pearls of broken glass, and pointed.

"They definitely came here," Todd said.

"Let's hope they stayed. Look for more and we'll follow it."

Todd searched for more blood, both hoping and not hoping to find it. There was a trail, with long breaks between markers. It wound through the lobby, leading them to the breezeway that led to the dining room. Something flitted overhead. Jerry jerked his arm to the ceiling, ready to pull the trigger. The flap of wings whooshed over their heads. Todd pulled his cap on tighter.

"I'm not a fan of bats."

Jerry took a few calming breaths. "So I guess that means you won't be pissed if I shoot one?"

"I will if it drives...." He fumbled for the correct name to use. *Killer* was too generic and *Otto* was not allowed to be on the table. "If it drives the Wraith toward us."

"Tell the wildlife not to dive-bomb me when I'm tense as a motherfucker."

"Duly noted."

They walked quietly, but it was impossible to be silent. Between the noise and the subdued light, Vince, Heather, Bill and Sharon would have detected them by now if they were near.

Todd looked at a gilt frame, a torn menu still inside it. One of the appetizers was beet soup. It didn't sound very appetizing.

The dining room was crammed with broken tables and chairs. It reeked of mold and animal urine. Todd stepped in something that squelched. He looked down expecting to see a puddle of blood. Instead, his foot was almost through the wet, rotten floor. Casting his eyes upward, he saw huge rents in the ceiling.

He pointed the flashlight to the far wall and clicked it twice.

No response.

Jerry shifted hard to the right as his foot sank into the wood. Todd grabbed his arm and pulled him away before it got worse.

"I don't think they're here," Todd said.

There was a hole in the dining room floor about fifteen yards ahead of them. A rusted chair clung to the edge of the hole, one of the legs snarled in the rotting carpet.

"If they were, they're in the basement now. Try to back out the same way we came in."

There was a clatter to their left.

A shadow darted past a window, the board probably having decomposed and crumbled away ages ago.

"Christ, is that a raccoon?" Jerry said.

"I think so." Todd's breath caught in his throat. "Big sucker."

The raccoon trundled along the windowsill before dropping out of sight. It looked like it hadn't missed a meal for quite some time. At least it was smarter than the humans and knew enough not to walk on the floor.

"Okay, where to next?" Todd said.

They had lost the trail of blood in the hallway. It was as if his friends had been sucked up into the sky.

"I know they won't go back to one of those bungalows. You know another place that could give them space and cover?"

Todd closed his eyes and conjured up pictures and videos that he'd found on the internet. The nightclub had collapsed completely before Ash had come here. There was nowhere to hide by the rink. The ski chalet was too far for them to have reached in so little time.

"There's the pool," he said, unsure.

"Where is it?"

"In the other wing. I think you had to go down from the lobby to get to it."

Jerry rubbed his chin, the crackling of his bristles too loud for Todd's comfort. "I forgot to bring my bathing suit."

"Then you should be okay...for now." They jogged back to the lobby. "The skinny dippers always bite it in slasher flicks."

"I'll remember not to show you my ass then. Be careful."

Todd almost tripped over a baby carriage. It was an old-time pram with a frayed hood. Its presence in the middle of this place of death and rot was more than a little unnerving.

They bypassed the elevators and hit the door to the stairwell. The handle came off in Todd's hand. He nudged it open with his shoulder while Jerry kept it open with a brick encased in jagged mortar.

The stairs had survived the ravages of time because they were made of metal. They were rusty, but a few test steps proved them to be sturdy enough to support their weight. Their movement was causing a storm of dust particles to swirl around their flashlight's beam.

"Never thought the best I could hope for on a night out with my buddies was asbestos poisoning," Jerry said.

"I have masks in my backpack."

Jerry coughed into the crook of his arm. "I'll live. Let's go."

Because he had the light and the stairs were narrow and littered with junk, Todd had to take point. His feet pushed away soiled clothes, construction debris and crushed beer cans. That was, until he noticed someone had already made a clear path down the stairs, hugging close to the rail.

"Could be a good sign," Todd said, his breath curling over his head and blasting Jerry in the face.

"Or we could be walking a Wraith game trail. Just keep your eyes and ears open."

Todd couldn't help doing anything less. He was worried the Wraith would be able to hear the pounding of his heart.

They came to the basement level and a gray metal door that once had a window with wire mesh at the top. Now, all that remained was the mesh.

"Open the door slowly," Jerry said, leaning into Todd. As Todd pulled the handle, Jerry inched the gun into the widening crack.

Stepping up to what was once the pool reception desk, Todd spied a pinball machine that had been left behind. Someone had decided to smash it to splinters. One of the silver pinballs had been either thrown or pushed into the drywall. Back in the day, there were kids playing games and running around, parents lining up for soft white towels, the smell of chlorine and the sounds of laughter and people having fun in the pool.

Now, it was black and dusty and ominous. It was difficult to picture this ever being a place people would willingly go.

Unless they had to find their friends before a crazed killer did.

There, just before the crooked doors to the pool area, Todd's light fell upon more blood. If Heather had lost this much blood, he worried if she'd even be able to walk now.

"They're in there," Todd whispered.

Jerry took the flashlight from him and slowly panned it across the walls. Like everywhere else, graffiti covered just about every inch. Except down here where the air seemed thinner and the pressure was so thick that Todd yawned to make his ears pop, the spray-painted tags and murals seemed far more sinister. Everywhere they looked, there were upside-down pentagrams, 666, satanic faces and foreboding quotes like *Welcome to the fiend's lair* and *Blessed are the destroyers of false hope, for they are the true Messiahs.*

Someone had painted a very realistic mural of a woman copulating with a goat while it was being cut in half by a saber. A naked man wearing a red mask with large black eyes wielded the saber. His erect penis sported curled horns.

"What the fuck drugs do the kids up here take?" Jerry said.

Beside what had once looked to be a snack counter, the flashlight shined on a wall emblazoned with swastikas of every size and color.

"Maybe more locals knew about Otto than we think," Todd said. The swastikas, more than the juvenile attempts at scaring people with satanic scrawls, gave him chills.

"Moron kids love to paint that shit because they know it upsets people. Let's just find everyone and get the hell out of here."

There was nowhere to hide in the game room, so it was on to the pool.

The ground was gritty with broken glass. Their boots crunched through it as they navigated their way through the doors that barely hung onto their top hinges. All of the window boards were still in place, but there was still an opening that led from the indoor part of the pool to the outdoor side. Swimmers would have to hold their breath and glide under it, popping up into the fresh air rather than the nose burning of confined chlorine.

There was a flash of light and a simultaneous boom. Something pelted Todd in the back of his neck and he found himself facedown on the filthy ground, writhing in pain.

CHAPTER TWENTY-FIVE

The back of Todd's neck was wet. Pebbles of concrete or tile were embedded in his flesh.

"Stop shooting!" Jerry wailed. "It's us!"

"Are you crazy? You could have killed them," Todd heard Bill shout.

He looked up and saw three figures emerging from the empty pool. Jerry angled his light so it blinded their friends for a moment. Vince shielded his eyes, saying, "I told her it was you guys. Are you hurt?"

Todd's next to worst nightmare stared at him from fifteen feet away.

Sharon was holding the gun.

Jerry went into a rage.

"Put the gun down, you psycho bitch, or I'll drop you right here."

She looked over at Todd, though not with much concern. It seemed to him as if she were only trying to gauge whether or not she'd killed her second person of the night with cool passivity.

"I thought you were him," she said, not relinquishing the gun.

"I'm sure you did. Put the gun down now."

When she didn't obey him immediately, Jerry fired a warning shot into the ceiling. Debris cascaded between them, just missing all of their heads.

"Are you crazy?" Vince said. "You want that maniac to find us?"

"I'm pretty sure he's not deaf. He already heard the stripper nearly kill us."

Sharon lowered the gun but her fingers were still curled around the grip. "Stop calling me that."

Jerry snickered. "What a shock. A stripper who doesn't have pride in her work. Last chance. Drop the gun or I drop you. Your choice. Vince, Bill, I need you to step away from her real quick."

Bill took a half step from Sharon. Vince, on the other hand, grabbed her by the waist and jerked the gun from her hand. He let her go, pushing her away so he had a moment to jam it in his pocket. "There. Problem solved."

"Not by a long shot," Jerry said, advancing on Sharon.

Todd cast aside the burning pain on the back of his neck and got hold of Jerry. His friend was angrier than he'd ever seen him, and Todd was honestly afraid of what he'd do to Sharon. "Not now. We have to get out of here quick before the Wraith finds us." Sharon massaged her hand, shaking out her fingers. Todd asked Vince, "Where's Heather?"

Vince nodded his head toward the pool. "She's too weak, man. While we were waiting for you guys to come out of the bungalow, Bill spotted *him* coming around the corner. I'm sorry, but we started running. Heather fell on her hands and knees right away and her bandages came loose. There's no more of those butterfly bandages in your kit, are there?"

Vince was on the verge of tears.

"Let me see her," Todd said.

He heard Jerry say to Vince, "How the fuck did she get the gun?"

"We're in the goddamn dark and I have other things to worry about, Jer. Lay the hell off me."

Todd found the shallow end of the pool and jumped. Desiccated bushes had grown through the broken pool bottom. It was like leaping into a greenhouse of the dead. He found Heather, ashen-faced, leaning against a broken diving board that had been propped up against the side of the pool. Her bloody wrist and hand lay on her equally bloodied thigh.

The first thing he did was elevate her hand. Her eyes fluttered open and started to tear up. "Oh my God. You're alive."

"Bet you didn't know I'm flame-retardant."

Her head lolled and he thought she was going to pass out. "There's so...so many things I could say to that."

"Yeah, well save your breath for now. Let me see what I can do about this wrist." He undid his belt and used it as a tourniquet around her upper arm. If he couldn't stop the flow of blood to that deep cut in her wrist, she would bleed out before they got to the Hayden's entrance.

The entrance where the first responder vehicles had mysteriously gone dark. If they weren't there, he wasn't so sure Heather would make it to their car and then hold on for the drive to the hospital.

One thing was for sure, she wasn't walking out of here on her own. They would have to carry her. It was a good thing she was so petite.

Vince startled him. Todd hadn't heard him come up behind him. "Is she going to be all right?"

He clasped his best friend's shoulder and lied. "Yes. Jerry and I saw police and fire arrive before we came in here."

Heather was out again. Vince cradled her head against his chest. "We heard the sirens and were about to make a run for it when we heard what we thought was that lunatic walking around. Heather fainted dead away in my arms and Sharon grabbed the gun from my coat pocket. I couldn't have stopped her."

Todd plucked pebbles out of his neck, trying hard not to wince in front of his friend. "I know, buddy. I know. You okay to carry her? I can barely carry myself at this point. My lungs feel wrecked."

"I've got her. You go up first. We'll be right behind you."

Todd slung Ash's backpack over his shoulder and pulled himself the short distance to the pool's edge. He lay on his back for a moment to catch his breath, and then rolled away to make room for Vince and Heather. "He's going to need help getting Heather up."

Bill hustled over, reaching down to take Heather. Jerry and Sharon were in a staring contest.

"Sharon," Todd said.

She flicked her eyes to him. "What?"

"Help Bill. Please."

When he tried to stand up, a fresh round of coughing locked his spine. He spit foul-tasting sputum. Once he settled down, he shot her a look that sent her into action.

Jerry helped him to his feet.

"Heather's in bad shape," Todd said. "We don't have time to waste."

"That we don't." Jerry cast a worried glance at the pool doors. "Maybe we go out through the pool instead. I don't like the idea of being trapped in those stairs with us carrying someone."

"Hold up," Todd said to Vince, Bill and Sharon. "Jerry says we should get to the outside through the pool."

"That would be easy if it wasn't filled with all kinds of heavy shit," Bill said. "Looks like they've been dumping huge chunks of mortar and stuff in there."

Todd and Jerry noticed for the first time all of the debris clogging the far end of the pool.

"Is there any way we can get through it?" Jerry asked.

Bill shrugged his shoulders. "There might be. We didn't give it a thorough check in the dark, you know what I mean?"

Jerry holstered his gun. "Then we better give it a look. You want to lay odds on my finding a way out, Bill?"

"I don't like to think of the odds in this place."

Todd didn't blame him. Every minute they were still down here, he felt their chances of getting past the Wraith and Heather to medical help slipping away.

Vince cradled Heather in his arms and backed away so Jerry could jump down.

"You first," Jerry said to Sharon.

"Why me first?" Her arms were folded defiantly across her chest.

"Because I don't want you at my back for even a second. And because I'm a cop and you're a murderer and I said so. Capisce?"

She gave him the finger.

"You're not helping," Todd said to her.

"You're not the one being threatened by this asshole and dragged to jail."

Todd stepped close to her, so close he could smell her hairspray. "If you keep wasting time, none of us are going anywhere. That man out there doesn't give a shit about your pain and how angry you are. He'll kill you, and us, just the same. Now go."

He stopped short of pushing her to the edge. She had nearly shot him and Jerry was right.

"Bunch of candy asses," she said. She made the small jump and kicked something away from her. "You see him, you shoot him."

"You see how well that worked before," Jerry said. He landed right beside her.

"Should we wait up here in case that's a no-go?" Bill said.

"Probably a good idea. Vince, give Todd the gun," Jerry said.

Todd bent down and took the gun from Vince's outstretched hand. This .38 had been passed around like a hot potato all night. Having his prints on a murder weapon was slightly disconcerting.

He saw Jerry's light dance toward the pool divider, knowing Sharon was a few paces ahead of him.

"Did Heather wake up?" he called down to Vince.

"No. She's really out."

All for the better, Todd thought. The last thing she needed was stress and anxiety, something they were all experiencing in abundance.

Bill said, "I swear, once we make it out of this, I'm giving up gambling. I never want another adrenaline rush for the rest of my life."

"And you'll have enough money for the therapy you'll need to wipe this night out of your head," Todd replied, feeling sorry all over again that his big mouth had brought them all here.

Bill had a hard time standing still. "Not enough money in the world to make that happen."

Todd turned back to ask Vince to see if Heather's wrist was still bleeding when he heard Bill let out a gurgled gasp. He spun around to find Bill struggling against a child-sized life preserver wrapped around his neck.

"What the hell?"

Bill's hands frantically clutched the edges of the preserver. He stumbled backward and lost his grip. Todd saw the rope attached to the preserver vibrate as it was yanked hard. This time, Bill lost his footing and hit the ground with a dull snap. He gasped for air and was dragged away, his legs thrashing in futility.

CHAPTER TWENTY-SIX

"Somebody help me!" Todd shouted.

He lunged for Bill, just missing his feet as he was pulled farther away. Todd's flashlight went out when it cracked against the tile floor.

Bill's choking became more frantic.

Todd reached out for him again and wrapped his arms around his friend's legs. They were both dragged as if they were made of feathers. He crawled up Bill's body and felt for the preserver. Lifting it off him proved impossible. Bill gasped, splashing Todd's hands with hot spittle.

There was only one way to get Bill free.

As he went for his gun, Bill's body was given a hard tug, flipping Todd off him. The scraping sound of Bill's body being rapidly dragged into the pitch black made it impossible for Todd's hands to work properly. For the life of him, he couldn't get his finger around the trigger.

Bill let out a final cry and went sickeningly still.

Todd couldn't see a damn thing in the dark without his flashlight.

"Bill! Bill! Where are you?"

He heard the rush of feet coming up behind him, saw the flickering of their lights against the floor and walls.

One of the beams brushed across Bill.

Todd's mouth dropped open.

In the flash his friend became visible, he saw that Bill's feet were well off the ground. The preserver held him aloft, his neck at an angle that told Todd it had been snapped.

A rushing image of Ash hanging in their basement, her head tilted to the same side, nearly dropped him.

"Todd! Bill!" Jerry shouted behind him.

And then he saw him. Or at least the shadowy outline of the man who had hanged Bill.

Without hesitation, Todd lifted the gun and fired. The shadow jerked back as one...two...three bullets punched home.

"In here," Todd screamed. "I shot him! I shot him!"

He was on the verge of collapse.

I just killed a man.

The fact that he'd shot a monster who had just strung up his friend didn't soften the razor-blade realization that he had taken a human life. At least not yet.

Sharon was the first to reach him. She saw Bill and said, "Holy shit."

"Give me your light," Todd said, ripping the flashlight from her hand before she could pass it to him.

They both gasped in horror when the beam painted the back of the man. He was tall with broad shoulders and a back that could double as a billboard. His head was bald and chalk-white, the left side of his cranium appearing as if it had been caved in at some point.

Todd was too stunned to shoot again.

I know I hit him. Three times. How is he standing?

He might have been on some drug and didn't feel it. Todd shook the fog from his brain and aimed. Before he could pull the trigger, the giant man took off running.

"Shoot him," Sharon screeched. He took off after him. Just like when they'd first seen him, the man proved to be unnaturally fast, especially for someone so large and wounded. Todd knew there was no way he could keep up with him.

However, sooner or later, the man, the Wraith, would come to a dead end. Todd knew he wouldn't hesitate to finish him off. With Sharon beside him, he pushed his exhausted legs to the limit. They passed the game room and down a corridor. Jerry called after them, but he was too far behind for them to wait for him.

The hulking Wraith bashed through a door, the sound of it breaking from its hinges like cannon fire. Sharon had a hand on Todd's back, urging him to move faster. They had to leap over scattered bits of furniture to keep from falling. The Wraith merely plowed through them like a cattle catcher on a steaming locomotive.

Todd fired wildly, the bullet ricocheting off the wall. He instinctively ducked, almost losing sight of the Wraith.

"There! There!" Sharon shouted, pushing him to the left. They spilled into what looked to have been an employee lounge. Round tables, most of them on their sides, and plastic chairs filled the room. There were empty counters, though one was supporting a family of squirming rats, alarmed by the sudden intrusion.

I've got you now, fucker, Todd thought when he saw where the room ended.

Keeping his back to them, the Wraith dipped to his left. Todd aimed the flashlight to see where or what he was up to. He lighted upon the double doors of a service elevator.

"Take this," he said, handing the flashlight to Sharon.

He wanted these shots to count.

"It's out of service," Todd said, pulling the trigger. The gun kicked and his shot went high, bringing dust onto the Wraith's head.

The Wraith dug his fingers into the crack between the doors and slammed them open in one mighty shove. He leaped into the shaft.

Todd and Sharon ran to the open elevator.

Perfect. He was even more trapped now.

Sharon shined the light above, catching sight of the Wraith hauling himself up the cables, one hand over the other. He scaled the cables as if he were lighter than air. The speed he was ascending was remarkable. Todd didn't have time to waste.

He stuck his arm in the shaft and emptied the .38, the single shot making his ears ring.

Any second, he expected to see the Wraith's body plummeting down the elevator shaft.

Instead, the crunch of metal echoed down to them. They looked up in time to catch the final glimpse of the Wraith extricating himself from the shaft, jumping out several floors above. His footsteps thundered for a few seconds and like the sirens outside the resort, simply stopped.

"How is that possible?" Todd said.

"Did you see how fast he went up there?" Sharon said, hugging herself. For the first time that night, she seemed afraid.

"Yeah."

They stood there, looking up through the empty shaft, in stunned silence. Only Jerry's arrival was able to break the spell.

"Did you get him?" He was limping badly and his face was coated in sweat.

"I...I thought I did." Todd let the gun tap against his thigh and felt the burn of the sizzling barrel but didn't react.

"You must be the world's worst shot," Sharon said, her words as defiant as ever but her tone sounding as if she was far, far off.

"I know I hit him back there. I saw his body fly backward. And there's no way I missed him in the elevator. He's so big, he almost took up the entire space."

Jerry took the gun from Todd and checked the cylinder. "Well, you definitely didn't leave any behind. Where did he go?"

Sharon said, "I think the third or fourth floor. But you had to see him." She tried tugging one of the doors closed. The rusted elevator door wouldn't budge. "He made opening this look like it was on greased tracks. And, and he pulled himself up those cables like he was fucking Spider-Man."

Jerry looked up the shaft. "I know it seems that way when your blood is running high and you're chasing a perp. Everything kinda speeds up."

Todd shook his head violently. "No. You don't understand. This guy, he took at least three bullets and moved around here like...like...like he wasn't even human."

"I have to go up and find him," Jerry said. He didn't look like he could take another step, much less hobble his way up the rotted stairs.

"What about Bill?" Todd asked. Saying his friend's name aloud made his chest hurt. Bill had never hurt anyone in his life. When they were kids and a fight broke out, Bill always found a way to extricate himself. Some kids called him a coward. He would respond that self-preservation was a virtue, showing bravery in the face of the worst of all childhood indignities – losing face.

Jerry bit his lower lip. "He's gone, Todd. There's nothing we can do for him now except kill the fucker that did that to him."

"We have to at least cut him down," Todd said.

"There'll be time for that later. Stay down here and get everyone outside. Maybe I'll still have a career if I catch the Wraith." He took two stuttering steps and had to lean against the wall for a moment. "Probably not. But if I'm going to have to hand in my badge and my gun, I want to make sure I hand it in empty."

He left the room at an unsteady trot. Todd wanted desperately to go with him, but he refused to leave Bill hanging and he had to help Vince get Heather to help.

He tugged on Sharon's sleeve. "Come on."

They left the room, but not without a lot of backward glances, each expecting to see the Wraith erupt from the elevator shaft.

As they walked down the narrow corridor, she said, "I'm real sorry about your friend. No one should ever have to die that way."

He thought of her sister Sheri and how she'd been mangled almost beyond recognition. That night had forever altered the course of Sharon's life, bringing her right back here, wounded and damaged, faced with the possibility of suffering a similar fate.

"No. No they shouldn't."

Todd found it near-impossible to look at Bill. His body slowly turned in the makeshift noose.

"How are we gonna get him down?" Sharon said.

There was no delicate way to go about it. They had to find something to cut the rope. Bill's dead weight would most likely be more than either of them could manage.

He shined his light around until he found where the rope had been tied off around a beam. He picked up a jagged hunk of rock and gave it to Sharon. "Use this to saw through the rope. I'll hold onto Bill."

She took the rock and waited for him to get a grip on Bill.

As Todd got closer, he smelled that Bill had shit himself as he died. His body was physically repulsed at the mere thought of having to get this close, but his mind rode herd over his atavistic response. Wrapping around his arms around Bill's waist, he said, "Okay."

The rope vibrated as Sharon hacked away. Todd tried breathing through his mouth, the side of his face mashed against Bill's belly.

"I've got you, buddy. I've got you."

It felt like it was taking forever for Sharon to cut him down. Not that she had the best tool to work with. Like the Wraith, they had to use what the Hayden provided.

The final fiber of rope finally snapped and Bill's weight came crashing down on Todd. He fell on his back, Bill mashing him down like a wrestler going for the pin. Todd was completely winded, his arms and legs scrabbling feebly to free him from the oppressive weight.

He didn't hear Sharon run over and loose a savage grunt as she tilted Bill's body to the side. Todd jerked up, gasping. His flesh crawled and his mind reverberated with a trapped scream. Sharon's hand was on his back making soothing circles.

It took him a good minute to get his breath back so he could talk. He looked over at Bill with tears in his eyes. "I'm so sorry."

Sharon disappeared, returning with a stained, crinkling swath of plastic. She placed it over Bill.

Todd knew there was no way he was going to be able to carry Bill out of the Hayden. Even if he wasn't hurt and exhausted, he wouldn't have been able to bear the weight. It pained him to leave him, facedown on the filthy floor where rat and other feces peppered the bare concrete.

"We have to go help Heather," Sharon urged him. He looked at her as if she'd appeared out of thin air and nodded.

"Yeah. Yeah. Help me up."

Heading back to the pool, he kept an ear out for Jerry and the Wraith. In the silence of the dying resort, he thought he'd be able to hear them moving about with clarion clarity. The utter stillness ratcheted up his unease.

"Where's Jerry. Is Bill okay?" Vince said. Heather was in his lap, still unconscious.

Todd jumped into the pool, the pain rocketing through his legs and settling in his hips. He took a deep, steadying breath. "Bill's gone."

"What do you mean Bill's gone?"

"He...he hanged him. Broke his neck."

"Oh my God." Vince hugged Heather tighter.

"I shot him." Sharon landed next to him. "I know I shot him. But...but he kept on going. Jerry went after him. We have to get Heather out of here. There has to be someone who can help her. I'll come back for Jerry."

"I'll see if there's a way out," Sharon said, taking a flashlight to the refuse piled up at the end of the pool. There was a lot of clanging and crashing as she tossed things aside, seeking a clear path outside.

Vince rocked Heather. "I can't believe it. How can Bill be dead? How is any of this happening?"

Todd checked Heather's bandage. Once again, the bleeding had stopped, but for how long? If the wound opened up again, she might not have enough left to keep her alive.

"I don't know," Todd said, hugging Vince. "The Wraith must have followed me here. I never should have opened my mouth on that goddamn podcast, but I was so angry. And I never should told you guys about this."

Vince's silence cut deep.

What bothered Todd even more was the creeping assumption that the almost superhuman man the world had called the Wraith was, in fact, Otto. As impossible as the concept of a supposed-dead Nazi coming back to wreak havoc on anyone who dared to enter the Hayden's forbidden ground seemed, there was something about the killer that defied the absurd.

He'd shot the son of a bitch practically point-blank. There was no way a man could get shot like that and proceed to run and climb his way to freedom.

But there was one way to know.

"You making any progress, Sharon?" he called over.

"I think I see a way out. Just need a few minutes."

He patted Vince on the shoulder. "I'll be right back. Mind if I take Heather's flashlight?"

"Where the hell do you think you're going?"

"I...I have to check something before we leave. Trust me, it's important."

"You still have the gun, right?"

Todd showed him the weapon. "Sure do."

"Good. Don't take long."

"I won't."

Todd lifted himself to the pool's edge. It was better to let Vince think the gun was more than just a paperweight. Something told Todd he wouldn't have the need to use it now even if it was loaded.

The Wraith...or Otto...was out there, waiting for them, but just as he'd done to Ash's friends, he would take them one by one, always one step ahead.

CHAPTER TWENTY-SEVEN

Todd had to pause when he found Bill's body. The plastic sheet was splattered with splashes of paint and filth. It was a horrible thing to cover him with, but it was all that was available.

Where were you when I shot you?

It was hard to get his bearings in the dark confines of the pool and rec area. With everything in ruin, it all looked the same. Todd searched for any marker that would seem familiar.

Glass and grit crunched under his boots. He kept the light trained on the ground, sweeping the floor.

It has to be here somewhere.

If he'd done what he thought he had, it would be hard to miss.

His attention was caught by skittering paws to his left. His boot squelched into a puddle on the floor. He shined the light down.

Black ichor fanned out on the floor, some of it pooling into thick ringlets of gore. In the corner of his eye, he spied a rat scampering away from Bill's body.

"Must be the light," he said, crouching down to run his finger through the substance. He brought his finger into the flashlight's narrow beam.

The runny liquid was ice-cold to the touch. It was gritty. And it wasn't red. It was black – as black as the gloom in the unlit corridors and corners of the Hayden. Todd looked around the room. Yes, this was where the Wraith had been standing when Todd shot him.

But this couldn't be blood. What in the name of all that was holy could it be?

Whatever it was, there was a lot of it.

Had he hit the Wraith, or had the Wraith been carrying something, a bag of old oil perhaps? Had he been planning on using it to set the hotel on fire?

Todd sniffed the liquid on his finger.

It didn't smell anything like oil. Between his construction job and working in an auto repair shop in his teens, he knew oil when he smelled it.

This reeked of earth and mold and tangy minerals and something gone foul.

"How the fuck?"

He frantically wiped it off on his pants, nauseated by the thought he'd even touched it.

There was more to be found, a trail of it leading to the lounge.

He had his answer, and it only gave birth to more questions.

He ran back to the pool. Vince was on his feet with Heather in his arms. "You find what you were looking for?"

"I think. Did Sharon find a way out?"

Vince nodded. "She's waiting for us."

Todd found a hollow metal pipe and picked it up. Vince gave him a wondering look, as if asking why Todd would need a pipe when he had a gun. Todd said, "We better hurry."

Sharon stood at the entrance to the tunnel she'd cleared. "I'm not sure how sturdy it is or how long it'll hold, so you all better haul ass."

Vince went first, and Todd told Sharon to follow. The uneven detritus above and around them made disturbing shifting noises. It felt and sounded like it could topple onto them at any second. Sharon practically pushed Vince forward.

"Just a little farther," she said.

A blunt object clipped Todd in the head as the ceiling of debris tilted. He dropped to a walking crouch, massaging his head. "Hurry!"

The rumbling started at his back.

Crap!

It was all coming down.

The crash of wreckage sent his heart into overdrive. The thought of being buried alive under all of this waste nearly had him running over Sharon. Dust floated through the cracks, stabbing into his already tender lungs.

"I see it!" Vince exclaimed.

"Run!" Sharon barked.

They hustled through the mass of debris, shoulders and legs clipping on exposed brick, sticks of furniture and ceiling tile.

A gust of wind propelled Todd forward as the tunnel collapsed a few feet behind him. Something sharp pelted his legs. Dust roiled like smoke, blinding them.

Todd lost his footing and fell.

The tunnel groaned, the ceiling dropping lower, ready to break.

Hands grabbed his wrists and pulled. His belly slid along the littered pool floor. His shoulders ached, the bones feeling like they were about to pop free from their sockets.

He felt the impact of everything crashing down in his marrow, heard the deafening roar of destruction. Todd knew he was dead. It all happened so fast, he didn't have time to lament the snuffing of his life.

And then he was coughing. Someone rolled him onto his side. He took a sharp breath, his lungs recoiling from the bitter cold air that felt like sharpened icicles.

He looked up and saw the pool's edge. A ladder was still affixed to the wall.

"You see your life flash before your eyes?"

Todd blinked away the dirt and confusion.

"Huh?"

Sharon dusted him off. "You know. The whole near-death thing."

He got on his hands and knees, and with her help, managed to stand. "Um, no, I didn't see anything. I was too busy being blinded and waiting to be crushed to death."

Sharon twisted her lip. "Huh.."

"Maybe this wasn't really a near-death experience then." Todd's legs felt like rubber. He couldn't imagine climbing the ladder to get out. "I mean, don't you have to die to have a near death experience?"

"Not necessarily. A brush with death can dig up all kinds of things. I was caught in the middle of a drive-by one night when I left this club I was working down in Charlotte. A bullet just missed my head by like two inches. I saw a lot of shit about myself I'd rather not relive in that second between the sound of the gun and the bullet whizzing by my head. It should have changed me, but it didn't."

Todd's head hurt from trying to follow the conversation. Who the hell cared about near-death visions? They had much bigger fish to fry. And he'd lost the pipe he'd found for protection. No matter.

There were enough sharp, heavy and dangerous things scattered everywhere to use for defense or offense, if needed.

"Who knows," he said, weaving his way to the ladder. "Are Vince and Heather up there?"

"I sure hope so."

He looked back at the tremendous mass of garbage that had almost squashed them. It was still settling, the noise echoing in the silent night.

"How did you do that?"

"Do what?" she asked.

"Pull me out. I'm not exactly light."

"I can hold my body completely perpendicular from a pole. Weak bitches can't hack what I do."

"Never thought stripper muscles would save my life."

"They're dancer muscles, not stripper muscles. Tell your friend, Jerry."

He motioned for her to climb up ahead of him. She bumped into him as she slipped her hands and feet into the rungs. "It's a fucked-up world, isn't it?"

There was no arguing that.

Vince was sitting on the ground waiting for them. "I thought you were dead."

"Not yet," Todd said.

But for how much longer? he thought.

Heather hadn't woken up despite the crazy scramble to get out of the pool and the ensuing carnage. That was a very bad sign. Todd checked her pulse again. It was soft and thready. There was no time to waste.

"Okay, if we go that way, we'll come to the main drive that leads to the front gate. That's where Jerry and I saw the lights before."

The lights that were still nowhere to be seen. He looked to the west and caught the last burning embers of the bungalows. The fire had made quick work of two of them, stopping short of gorging on the rest. If the fire department had made it inside, he would have seen the shadows of bodies against the flames, working to put them out. Something had happened to them. He felt it down in the marrow of his bones. No one emerged from the Hayden unscathed when the Wraith was around. The only way to survive was to save yourself. Now able to fully grasp Ash's nightmare, his eyes started to tear. He wiped them roughly. Ash hadn't given up and neither would he.

Todd wanted to run like hell, but his legs could barely stumble. Thankfully, Vince was in better shape than him, trotting with Heather tight in his arms. They turned the corner, coming to the front of the hotel.

They were about to skirt the fountain when they were stopped by the *whup, whup, whup* of gunfire within the hotel.

"Jerry!" Todd shouted.

He couldn't tell where the shots had come from within the rotting edifice. There was movement inside, footsteps pounding on the weak floorboards.

"Why the hell aren't the cops and fireman coming in here?" Vince asked. "I mean, we've been shooting up the place and nothing."

"I don't think you'll like to hear what I'm thinking," Sharon said.

Todd had been wondering that too, and he was sure he and Sharon were in synch. He couldn't shake the feeling that despite their brief elation at the sights and sounds of the first responder vehicles, they were out here on their own, trapped with a maniac.

"The rest of you go," Todd said. "I have to find Jerry."

"But shouldn't we stick together?" Sharon said.

"We're already split up. Go." Before they could take a step, one of the boarded windows on the third floor burst apart. A man came flying through the open window.

Oh no!

Instead of splattering on the pavement below, the man landed on his feet. Todd expected to hear the snap and crunch of Jerry's legs and hips shattering on impact. He forced his weary legs to run to his friend.

Someone snatched the collar of his coat.

"Don't. Look!"

The man, who was enveloped in shadow, turned his head to them and ran. Todd realized he was much too big to have been Jerry. He ran like a cheetah, heading toward the front gate, as if knowing that was their plan as well, daring them to try to leave.

Todd looked into the vacant window. He cupped his hands around his mouth and called for Jerry.

Jerry cautiously popped his head out the window, his fingers wrapping around the frame. "Where is he?"

Todd pointed to the resort's entrance. "He went that way."

"How the fuck is that even possible?" Jerry couldn't take his eyes from the spot on the ground where the Wraith should be lying, bleeding and broken.

"He just took off running," Sharon said.

"That can't be," Jerry said.

"I don't know how he did it either," Todd said.

Now Jerry looked to him. "No. I shot him in the chest. When he kept coming, I shot him in the goddamn face. He was only about two feet away. I may as well have been pelting him with rocks."

He shot him in the face.

Todd stared into the shadows of the night.

What the hell had they fallen into?

CHAPTER TWENTY-EIGHT

While they waited for Jerry to make his way down, Todd pulled Sharon aside and asked, "You have any more bullets?"

"Nope. I didn't think I'd need more than one or two."

And why would she?

By Todd's estimation, the Wraith had taken at least a half dozen bullets. They hadn't slowed him down one bit. If he tried to puzzle out the how and why, he'd be too distracted to stay alive.

For now, he had to accept that the Wraith was something more than a man – a giant possessing tremendous strength, speed and agility who might not be able to be killed. If he was impervious to brute force, they would have to find a way to outsmart him.

And there was Heather to consider. How much time did she have until they passed the critical juncture? How the hell could they strategize if they had no time?

Sharon went inside the hotel to see if Jerry needed any help. It was dangerous in there, even without the Wraith lurking about. She was the most physically capable of them all at this point, so he didn't stop her.

"I believe Jerry shot him," Vince said.

Their heads swiveled back and forth between the hotel's facade and the deep darkness at their backs.

"Yeah. I shot him before too. He just kept going. I know I hit him though. I went back and found something. I thought it was blood, but it was thick and black. At first, I wondered if it was some kind of chemical he'd been carrying and hoped to use to burn us out. Now, I know what it was. It was blood. His blood, or what passes for blood in his veins. It's cold too. Cold as death."

"What the hell, Todd? Is this what Ash went through?"

"She was stronger than I even thought before."

What Vince didn't need to say was that it was a miracle she'd held on for as long as she had. How could anyone cope with coming across a supernatural monster? It was no wonder her brain had willfully buried it all too deep for her to find. This was beyond witnessing a series of murders. It was coming face to face with the unthinkable.

"If we can't shoot him, how the hell do we stop him?" Vince asked. He brushed the hair from Heather's pale forehead.

"I'm thinking, Vince. I'm thinking."

"I know, buddy. I'm just scared. And not for me."

They looked down at Heather. Her face was so soft and serene. In the end, Todd considered, she might be the luckiest of them all.

"One thing I've realized," Todd said, "is that he doesn't like it when you come at him. He's a hunter. Hunters don't know what the hell to do when the prey turns on them. He's used to stalking his victims and scaring them to the point where they can't even think straight."

"If you're telling me not to be afraid of a…a thing like that, it's not going to happen. Just thinking about him makes me want to shit myself."

Todd clapped his best friend on the shoulder and started walking toward the entrance when he heard footsteps. "You and me both."

Jerry and Sharon emerged from the shadows. Jerry was limping worse than before. His hair was gray from dust and dirt.

"You believe I shot him now?" Todd said.

"Unfortunately, yes."

"You have any more rounds for your gun?" Sharon asked.

Jerry patted his coat pocket. "I do, not that it seems to make much of a difference."

"It won't stop him, but it does get him running in the other direction," Todd said. "Even if it just buys us a little time, it's good to know we're not out of ammo yet."

"So where do we go now?" Sharon said.

"Exactly where we need to go," Todd replied, giving a quick nod to the resort entrance in the distance.

Sharon kicked a crushed can into the dilapidated carport. "But he's probably there now, waiting for us."

"I may be wrong, but I think that's what he wants us to believe so we try to get out someplace else. *That's* where he'll be waiting."

"And how will he know where we'll go?"

Todd found another pipe, this one thicker and heavier. His boot pushed around the rocks and construction debris until he found a shard that was closely shaped like an arrowhead. He pushed the rock into one end of the pipe. "Huh. Perfect fit." He looked to Jerry and Sharon. "He doesn't have to know. He'll find a way to lead us to him."

Jerry loaded his gun. "So your big plan is that we zig when he wants us to zag?"

"That and if he confronts us, we don't run. We take it to him and make *him* run."

"I'm not gonna lie, it sounds like a suicide mission," Jerry said.

"We're dead if we do what's been done before." Sharon caught his eye and looked away. He didn't want to sound insensitive, but there was no time to worry about feelings being hurt. "Forensics showed that when he came upon Ash and her friends, they scattered. He spent the rest of the night hunting them down. We can't let that happen to us. We stand our ground and we stay together."

Vince had laid Heather on the ground, using Ash's backpack to cradle her head. Todd hadn't heard him approach. "And what if the Wraith doesn't run the next time? Are you going to take him down with your fake spear?"

Todd shrugged. "I'll sure as hell try. At that point, what's there to lose?"

"How about our lives?" Vince said irritably.

"We're already dead," Sharon said. She angled her face into the cold wind that swept through the barren resort. It carried the pungent scent of burning wood. "Maybe that is Otto out there. Hate and anger are a powerful combination. Maybe with enough of both, you can come back. If that's the case, I'm not going anywhere anytime soon."

★　★　★

They found the winding driveway choked with waist-high weeds as brittle as ancient skeletons. Todd kept hoping to see the return of the flashing red and blue lights, but so far, the pitch of night still reigned.

"It's fucking freezing," Jerry said. He was shivering, which, Todd knew, wouldn't make for a good shot if he needed to take one.

Every breath hurt Todd's lungs, but it was better than the alternative.

"We could have always stayed by the fire, toasted some marshmallows."

"Right now, I'll take a warm hospital bed with a hot nurse checking my vitals."

"Among other things," Todd said.

"Naturally."

"Pig," Sharon muttered.

Jerry stumbled for a second, and then righted himself. "Hey, maybe a lap dance will warm me up. You know, one last dance before lockup."

"You couldn't afford me."

"Lay off her," Todd said.

Sharon quickened her pace to get ahead of them, but not before giving Jerry a look that could slay thousands.

"Nothing sexier than an angry stripper," Jerry said.

"We don't need this shit now."

"Yeah, Jer, knock it off," Vince said. Todd could tell his friend was struggling by the steady clouds of air he was exhaling.

"You want me to take Heather?" Todd asked.

"I've got her. You look like you couldn't carry my boots."

Todd had no doubt he looked like forty shades of hell. If he looked half as bad as he felt, he'd make a great Halloween mask.

"You guys want to bang Sharon?" Jerry said after a stretch of silence.

Vince turned on him. "Have you lost your mind?"

"Just wondering why you think you need to come to the aid of a pole dancer who killed a kid."

"She saved my life back there," Todd said. "She may have accidentally killed that boy, but she's not a bad person. I mean, remember the last time we saw her when we picked Sheri up at the house? She was doing her homework at the kitchen table and had a Hello Kitty backpack. She was a straight-A student, a total geek. Set your anger aside and remember that girl. That's who she really is."

Their flashlights swung in every direction as they were all on the lookout for the Wraith. With the way the man could run, they would have very little warning before he was literally on top of them.

"That's who she *was*," Jerry said. "She's a murderer now."

Todd was about to say something but closed his mouth. It was going to be a lost cause. What even Vince didn't know was that Jerry's heart had been dragged over a bed of nails by an exotic dancer he'd met in a diner one very late night a year ago. Their relationship had been hot and heavy but brief. Jerry hadn't told anyone but Todd that she worked the Satin and Lace club over in New Jersey. For Jerry, it was better she worked on that side of the Hudson where dancers had to wear pasties. It helped lessen his jealousy, but not by much. She'd left him for a middle-aged slime ball who just so happened to be her biggest tipper.

Sharon called out, "Hold up."

"What is it?" Todd asked, edging toward her.

Sharon's light was locked on something on the ground.

"Oh Jesus!" Todd took a step back, bumping into Jerry.

The severed head of a man stared up at them. His eyes had been hollowed out, rivers of blood drying on his face. His mouth was wide open, and it looked like his tongue had been ripped out. There was very little blood on the ground around the head, which meant he'd been killed elsewhere, the head left on the driveway for them to find.

Jerry was able to get into a half crouch to get a closer look. "You son of a bitch." He pointed at the ragged flaps of skin on the neck. "You guys see that?"

Vince had turned away. "More than I've ever wanted to see."

"I'm no medical examiner, but I'll swear that his head wasn't cut off. It looks like it was ripped right off his neck."

"How is that even possible?" Todd said. He felt like he was going to throw up. Like Vince, he had to look away.

"You've all seen him," Sharon said. "The Wraith isn't human. Or not what we consider human."

No one, not even Jerry, contested it.

Sharon stepped around the man's head, swinging her flashlight back and forth. "Looks like he's been busy too."

Now Todd did empty his stomach.

Before them lay more than a dozen scattered heads. Two of them still wore their fire helmets. Some looked like their noses had been bitten or torn off. Others were missing their lower jaws, front teeth or ears. There were men and women, all presumably first responders. Todd drew in a quick breath when he spotted the head of Officer Landers, the cop with the tattoos. His eyes were gray-white, a splash of black ink visible on the flap of flesh that had been his neck.

Now they knew why the lights and sirens had suddenly stopped.

"What the fuck?" Jerry said, his breath curling into the air.

"Maybe he knows…the end is coming," Todd said, gasping and spitting up the remnants of his bile.

"If we can't even slow him down by shooting him, what will he care about some bulldozers knocking the place down?" Sharon asked. Instead of horrified, she sounded even angrier than before.

"Could be he's tied to this place. If the Wraith is Otto, maybe being buried in the Hayden's grounds has tethered him here. Without it, he won't exist."

"Stop with that Otto shit," Jerry said.

"Stop being willfully blind to what's happening," Todd said, whirling on his friend. "You want to explain how bullets can't stop him? How he can bust through a boarded window from three stories up, land on his feet and run faster than my car can drive? How he was able to murder all of these people? Christ, we didn't even hear them scream. Sharon's right. He's not human. I don't think he qualified as a human when he was alive, doing God knows what in a concentration camp. He's a fucking monster, man. When those workers took justice into their own hands, something happened. Don't ask me what could bring a man back from the dead. I don't even care how it happened. He's here, and he's fucking with us now."

There were so many heads in the driveway, they'd have to get off the cracked and pebbled road and wade through the high weeds to circumvent them.

Todd's stomach couldn't stop cramping. He'd never seen such

carnage. All of those lives lost, just because they were doing their job to stop a fire in a place that should be set ablaze and left to burn to the ground.

Jerry kept his light on each severed head for a few moments, studying them, making angry grunts. "Okay, what's he trying to get us to do now?"

Todd looked into the darkened sky, wishing for some breaks in the clouds so they'd have some semblance of light. It was as if Otto even had control of nature itself. "He definitely doesn't want us to keep going forward. I'll bet he figured we'd be running scared by now."

"Which we aren't," Sharon said.

"Which we aren't." *Yet*, he thought. "We have to keep going, and fast, before he figures out we're not acting according to plan and makes a course correction."

Vince stepped into the weeds with Heather, jogging as fast as he could. "Course correction. You mean running into us to kill us."

"I have an idea. You'll have to follow me."

Todd slipped ahead of Vince, along with Sharon. Jerry kept watch at the rear. All Todd wanted to do was sprint as fast as his aching legs would allow. The ground cover was so wild and dead, each footfall crunched loud enough to cause a responding echo. Stealth was not on their side. Unless Otto was deaf, he could easily find them.

They hustled until they could see the front gates up ahead. It was too far to make out any police cars or fire engines. But Todd knew they were up there, dark and silent and, if they had any shred of luck tonight, with keys still in the ignitions.

Todd peeled off to the left of the gates.

"What the hell are you doing?" Vince hissed. He was panting hard, running out of steam. The sight of freedom was the only thing keeping him going, and Todd was taking that away from him.

They traipsed farther from the exit. Todd felt Vince's bedeviled glare burning into the back of his neck. If Todd was right, Otto would assume by now that the obstacle of severed heads hadn't deterred them. Their ultimate destination would be those front gates, where the undead Nazi, even with a skull squirming with maggots, would know enough to intercept them. There was a break in the fence about two hundred yards from the front gates. Todd remembered it from his recon. It was right around where the shuffleboard court used to be.

All they needed now was to get to it before Otto.

CHAPTER TWENTY-NINE

Todd only realized they were at the shuffleboard courts when his foot smashed into a hidden lip of concrete and went sprawling.

"Todd!" Sharon gasped, reaching out in vain to stop his fall.

He landed on his chest in the grass and frozen earth that was as hard as stone. Grateful he hadn't heard a rib crack, he rolled with the momentum and picked himself up quickly. "I'm all right."

He was back running, barely missing a step. They were so close. And so far, there'd been no sign of Otto.

Todd deliberately thought of the killer solely as Otto now. The Wraith had been a mysterious, homicidal man. To think of the maniac as simply that made them weaker. "It should be right there," he said between hurried breaths, pointing ahead.

"What should be right there?" Sharon asked. She was in full stride, barely breaking a sweat.

"There's a...there's a part of the gate we can crawl under."

"You know all of our cars are in the opposite direction, right?"

"We just need to get the hell out of here. We'll bang on every door of every house and get some help."

He heard two heavy thumps and spun around.

Jerry, Vince and Heather were on the ground.

"Godammit, my leg," Jerry wheezed. He clutched his wounded leg, rocking back and forth. Vince was on his knees, barely able to keep Heather off the ground. "Sorry I hit into you, bro."

Todd waved them on. "We're almost there. I just need you to push it a little further."

"You want us to hide in the trees?" Vince said.

A long cluster of trees had grown along the edge of the property, hiding the fence line.

"We can get out through the fence," Todd replied. "It's just past the trees."

"I don't think I can get up," Vince said, struggling to lift his unconscious wife. Todd and Sharon each took a side and lifted him.

"Here," Sharon said. "I'll take her."

Vince's protest died on his lips as Sharon easily transferred Heather from his arms to hers.

Todd reached down for Jerry.

His friend snapped on his light to inspect his leg. Fresh blood seeped through the bandages. "I'm fucked, man. You guys go. I'll slow him down if he tries to follow you."

"You're fucked if you stay here," Todd said. "You're coming with us."

"My leg is on fire. I stopped feeling my foot about five minutes ago. I couldn't walk if my ass was on fire."

Todd almost laughed. "Your ass almost was on fire before. We'll just have to potato sack it."

"What the hell are you talking about?"

"Come on. We were the potato sack race kings every field day."

Jerry batted his hand away. "That was grammar school. And we don't have a potato sack."

Todd grabbed him by the lapels and lifted him with a measure of strength he didn't know he still possessed. "You'll just have to pretend. Now, arm around my shoulder."

"I still can't move my leg."

Todd snapped his fingers at Vince. "Let me have your belt."

Vince was confused but didn't hesitate to pull it out of his pants loops.

"You guys wanna hurry up? Heather's not getting any lighter," Sharon said.

"One sec," Todd said. He looped the belt around his leg and Jerry's damaged leg. "This way, I'll pull your leg along."

"Are you insane? He'll kill the both of us with you tied to me like this."

Todd squeezed Jerry's shoulder. "You still have the gun. I'll take our odds."

Jerry tilted his head to the ground and snorted. "Fucking Bill."

"He'd be calling long shots about now."

"No chalk for us."

204 • HUNTER SHEA

"Nope. No chalk. Come on."

Walking tied to one another was awkward at first. But after a dozen or so feet, they started to get their rhythm. A hard gust of bitter wind punched them in the chests, nearly stopping them in their tracks. Todd hoped Jerry couldn't feel his foot because of the cold and not blood loss.

You know you're in trouble when you pray for frostbite, he thought.

Pulling Jerry along wasn't easy, and now his own leg was crying out for relief. The wound on his back got wetter from the friction of Jerry holding onto him. He kept swallowing to cut off the coughing fit that threatened to overtake him. There was no way he was going to vocalize his struggle. That would only get Jerry to insist they leave him.

The tree line was just a few feet ahead when a shrill scream erupted.

Sharon dropped to the ground and Vince tumbled over her.

Heather hit the floor and popped back up, frantically batting at the air. She was screaming at the top of her lungs, looking at her husband and friend as if they were out to kill her.

She started to run, though unevenly at first, fear and adrenaline making for an awkward dash into the darkness

"Heather! Stop!" Todd yelled.

With Jerry tied to him, he couldn't run after her. She bolted toward the trees, then seemed to think better of it, and circled back. She skirted around Sharon and Vince and headed his way.

Vince was quick to get back on his feet. "Heather. It's me, honey. You're all right. Calm down."

Todd took Jerry's flashlight and turned it on so it shined directly on his face. Heather was about to pivot away from him and Jerry when she paused in her all-out panic to look at him.

"T-T-Todd?"

Vince nearly tackled her from behind, wrapping his arms around her midsection. Sharon stepped in front of Heather, cupping her face in her hands. Heather's mouth opened to scream once more, but Sharon's slap across her cheek stopped her.

"Heather!" Sharon barked in her face.

Heather's eyes softened as clarity settled in.

"Sharon?"

Sharon smiled and kissed Heather on the tip of her nose. "The one and only."

Heather turned around, saw Vince and started to cry. She slipped her arms around his neck. "I was so scared. I...I didn't know who you were."

Vince and Heather swayed as he rubbed her back. "It's okay. It's okay. You've been out for a while. I'm just happy that you're back. I'm sorry we scared you."

Heather's shoulders hitched with sobs.

Todd scanned the emptiness behind them. He felt precious seconds slipping away.

"Heather, you think you'll be able to walk the rest of the way out of here?" Todd said.

She stepped away from her husband and wiped her eyes with the back of her hand. She still looked pale as death but being awake and ghostly was a huge improvement. How long it would last was anyone guess. Todd knew her sudden alertness was a result of a chemical rush, and not an actual improvement in her physical state.

"We're...we're getting out of here?"

He pointed over her shoulder. "Just through those trees."

Her eyes flitted around. "Wait, where's Bill?"

Vince massaged her upper arms. "I'll tell you along the way. Come."

She resisted his slight tug. "We're not leaving him here, are we? Why would we do that?"

Jerry said, "He's dead, Heath."

"What do you mean he's dead?"

"I know it sounds impossible, crazy even, and I know what you're feeling right now." Jerry nudged Todd so they could approach her. "We all loved Bill and it hurts like hell to leave him behind, but we have to get out of here now. You understand me?"

Her eyes were glassy with tears. When she nodded, they spilled down her face.

"How?" she asked, taking her first stumbling step toward the trees.

"I'll tell you everything...later," Jerry said. "Right now, we have to save ourselves."

She looked at Todd's and Jerry's legs tied together and there were many more questions dancing in her eyes, but the answers would have to wait.

"Bill," she muttered over and over. Vince kept his arm around her, whispering in her ear. Todd wanted to scream at them to run, but Heather was in too fragile a state. Sharon had to pause every few steps for the rest of them to catch up with her. She stamped her feet as if trying to keep her blood flowing, but Todd thought it was more out of anxious frustration.

"Sorry if I sounded a little harsh there," Jerry said to Todd, keeping his voice low enough so Heather couldn't hear him. "I learned long ago it's better to deliver the news quickly and clearly. If you don't, it's like a slow death of a thousand cuts, you know?"

"No, I get it. How many times have you had to break news like that to someone?"

"More times than I would ever want. I'm just glad she didn't pass out again when I told her. That happens a lot."

"She's up and moving and that's more than I thought I could ask for."

They limped along after their friend, Jerry with his gun at the ready and constantly checking their backs. The tight space between the trees was blacker than the night and felt alive. It seemed to whisper, "*Step inside so I can swallow you whole.*" Todd thought of fairy tales and lost babes in the woods and how in the real stories, the endings were never good. Otto could be in there right now, his preternatural senses tracking their every move, waiting for them. There was no way he hadn't heard Heather's screams, or their clumsy march to freedom.

It was almost as if the woods of the Hayden were working with Otto, keeping them lost, wearing them down, offering them up to the Nazi.

He was close.

Todd didn't know how he could be so sure, but he had no doubt that Otto was tracking them, biding his time.

It wasn't a matter of if.

It was just a matter of when.

CHAPTER THIRTY

Cri-crack!

A heavy branch snapped overhead. Jerry raised his gun, the sudden jerking of his arm unbalancing the connected tandem. Todd flailed his arms, finding a nearby tree trunk to keep from falling. Four flashlight beams danced among the trees like twirling spotlights.

"You see anything?" Sharon said. She had a pipe held high, ready to strike.

The few dead leaves that still clung to the gnarled, twisted branches weren't enough to provide any cover for Otto. There was nothing they could see, but it was little relief.

"Might have just been a dry branch starting to break," Vince said.

The second they'd stepped under the trees, it felt as if the temperature had plummeted even further. Todd thought if trees could shiver, they would break apart in the punishing cold. His own joints were aching from the constant shuddering. Like so much that had happened over the past few hours, even the air itself felt imbued with the supernatural. The cold, dead heart of the Hayden was somehow connected to the resurrected killer who cleansed the grounds of the living.

"Probably a bird," Todd said.

"How much farther until we get to the fence?" Heather asked.

"Not far," Todd said, but he wasn't so sure. The trees were so tightly packed here, he worried that they'd been turned around. They were definitely taking a circuitous route to the property's edge. Again, it was as if the woods were alive, working with the killer, keeping them trapped.

"That was one heavy-ass bird," Jerry said.

"You ever see how big owls can get?" Todd said.

"How the heck would I ever see an owl where we live?"

They resumed walking.

"You never watched a nature show?"

Jerry exhaled loudly when they stepped in a divot and their legs twisted. "Why would I watch nature shows when I have like a hundred other *cool* things on my watch list? You finish watching *Californication* yet?"

"Can't say that I have." In fact, despite Jerry's constant insistence, he'd yet to start. He couldn't get into the idea of watching a show about a boozing, philandering writer. It reminded him too much of his father – everything except the writing.

"You're missing out on a lot of boobs, man. So many boobs."

"Is that all you think about?" Todd asked.

"Yeah. Well, that and getting the fuck outta here."

Such frivolous talk seemed ridiculous in the face of what they were experiencing, but it was also strangely comforting. It helped take Todd's mind off his increasing anxiety that they were lost. He was sure the break in the fence had been right here. How had he missed it?

Being in pitch dark, hurt and afraid could have something to do with that.

"How you holding up, Heath?" Todd asked.

"Still standing," she replied, a huge vapor cloud enveloping her head.

They kept walking, each of them clipping their shoulders into a tree or tripping on exposed roots. It was far from easy going, and the longer they roamed within the trees, the surer Todd was that they would end up a bewildering distance from where he'd intended.

There was more rustling overhead.

"Definitely a bird," Todd said.

Jerry made them stop, his light and gun sweeping the trees again. "Tell those fucking birds to cut the shit before I pop one."

"I will, as soon as I learn to speak bird."

"Forget the damn birds," Sharon said. "Todd, you don't know where we are, do you?"

He was tempted to say he couldn't see the fence for the trees. He was beginning to wonder if they should just stay here, hidden in the trees, the dry vegetation giving them ample warning if and when Otto approached. Once dawn broke, it would be easy to find the way out, even if it was a cloudy morning. On the other hand, there was a real concern that they might freeze to death.

"To be honest, no," Todd said.

"We should just set this all on fire," Jerry said. "I'm so cold, my ass is numb. Plus, it'll light the way."

"I say we do it," Sharon said without a moment's hesitation.

"That's crazy," Vince said.

"Who cares about a few trees? We have a lunatic that wants to kill us," Sharon snapped. She searched her pockets. "Dammit, I didn't bring my lighter."

"You don't smoke," Heather said, her voice sounding as if she weren't completely with them in the moment. All this walking was taxing her and it would only get worse.

"No, but other people do. I like to be prepared."

Jerry showed her the Zippo lighter he had in his jacket pocket. "A Girl Scout stripper. Do you get a badge for bedazzling your G-string?"

"Screw you."

"Sorry, I don't have any cash on me." He flicked open the Zippo and thumbed the striker wheel. The tiny flame danced in the wisps of wind wending through the trees but didn't go out.

"We're really gonna do this?" Todd said. He ran through his mental files, trying to picture where the nearest houses were. If they started a wildfire, would any of them be in danger, especially with the local F.D. decapitated in the resort?

"It's either this or we wander for the next forty years," Sharon said. "And I don't feel like the chosen people right about now." She nodded at Jerry. "Do it."

"Wait!" Todd said.

Jerry didn't touch the flame to the nearest tree, but he didn't shut the lighter. "What?"

"You saw what *he* did when the first responders came to the fire before. Who's to say the same thing won't happen again? You think you can live knowing you got more people killed?"

Sharon waved him off. "As long as I'm alive, I'll be fine."

Jerry sighed and snapped the Zippo lid down. "Shit."

"Are you crazy?" Sharon said, striding toward them as if she were about to rip the lighter from Jerry's hands. He must have sensed it too, because he quickly pocketed it.

Heather tugged on Sharon's arm. "No, Todd's right. It's wrong to put other people in danger just to save ourselves." Vince put his arms around his wife in solidarity.

Sharon threw up her hands and stepped away. "Unlike the rest of you, I'm not cool about joining Bill." She rummaged through her pockets, searching for her own lighter.

"We need to keep moving," Todd said. He touched the tip of his nose and found he couldn't feel it at all. The air within the trees was as cold as a meat locker. He thought his eyeballs would freeze. His toes were tingling, which, for now, was a good sign. When he stopped feeling them at all, it would be time to worry. "Come on, Sharon."

"You don't know where the fuck you're even going," she snapped at him. "Who appointed you leader anyway?"

Vince stepped in. "Todd and I looked this whole place over last week. I admit he was paying a lot more attention than I was. He's the only one of us who knows the layout."

"It sure doesn't seem like it." She pulled one of her pockets inside out. Loose change hit the ground.

"Sharon, cut it out," Heather said. "Fighting isn't going to help."

"No, but fire is. And since you're all too chickenshit to save yourselves, I'll have to do it myself." She ripped off her coat and threw it on the ground in frustration. She got on her knees and thoroughly checked each pocket. When that was done, she rocketed back up and went through her jeans pockets, shivering so hard, Todd worried her teeth would chip from clacking together. "Where the fuck is it?"

Jerry started walking, dragging Todd with him. "You're free to keep looking, but you'll have to do it while you walk," he said to Sharon.

She emitted a cross between a grunt and a growl, slipping into her coat and picking up the pipe while still searching her pockets with her free hand.

"I'm glad you didn't just ditch her," Todd whispered to Jerry.

"I can't," he said, hissing between his clenched teeth when they had to step over a fallen tree. "I'm bringing her ass in no matter what."

They continued in silence except for the crunching of leaves and expelling of labored breath. They definitely should have come to the fence by now. Todd looked behind them and could see absolutely nothing. It was as if the world ceased to exist, the heavy nothing always one step from their heels.

"We are so lost," Vince said. He had his arms wrapped around Heather because, with her blood loss, she was probably the coldest of them all. It made for cumbersome progress, but Todd and Jerry, who weren't walking so well themselves, kept the couple in front right where they could keep an eye on them.

"No shit, Sherlock," Sharon said.

Jerry flipped the Zippo lid open and closed, each click almost as loud as the chattering of their teeth.

Everyone froze at the crash of something coming up fast behind them.

"Jesus, no," Vince said.

Jerry drew his gun as he and Todd spun around.

"Give me light," Jerry barked.

They spun their lights into the pitch. Whatever was out there was just beyond the reach of the light, though from the sound of it, they wouldn't have long to wait.

CHAPTER THIRTY-ONE

Todd braced for the inevitable. If he was right, Jerry's shots would send Otto racing in the other direction and buy them some time. The only problem was, he had no idea where to go from here.

The flashlight beams jittered as nervous hands did their best to find the source of the fast-approaching steps. Todd's shoulders bunched up so tightly, it felt like the veins in his neck were going to burst.

"I can't see anything," Sharon said, swinging her light from left to right, catching nothing but tree trunks and dead leaves.

"Over there," Vince said, pointing with his light.

"No, I think it's coming from there," Todd said, swinging his flashlight in the other direction.

Sound was distorted in the tightly packed trees. Todd recalled summer days in the yard reading the paper and drinking his beer, listening to the sound of jet engines overhead. He'd look up, searching for the plane and more times than most, cast his eyes in the wrong direction. The big difference was, not knowing where the plane was coming from couldn't get him killed.

"Where the fuck is he?" Jerry said. He sounded more angry than worried. Todd was sure he wanted to put a bullet in Otto's brain as payback for what he'd done to Bill. If Otto had a brain in the traditional sense. His blood was definitely not the same as theirs.

"I see something!" Sharon shouted. Her light wavered on a spot a little to their right. Todd thought he saw something dart between a pair of trees about forty feet away, but couldn't be sure.

"Shoot him," Heather pleaded.

"I can't shoot him if I can't see him," Jerry said calmly.

Todd and Vince joined Sharon's beam. There was definitely something there. The splash of light gave it pause, but only for a moment.

"Here he comes," Vince said.

Jerry murmured, "That's right, you ugly bastard. Follow the light. There are people here to kill."

Their light fell dead center on a shape emerging from the tangle of trees. Jerry pulled the trigger three times. There was a loud, night-splitting cry, followed by a heavy thump.

"Did he get him?" Heather asked, her view blocked by Todd and Jerry.

The deer lay on its side, gasping. There was a bullet hole in its neck, one in its side, and one of its eyes had been obliterated.

"Crap," Jerry blurted. Todd knew he was more upset about wasting ammo than felling the deer.

The doe made a wailing, gurgling sound that made Todd's balls shrivel.

"You have to put it out of its misery," Todd said.

"It'll die soon enough. I'm not wasting another bullet."

"I got it," Sharon said, striding past them. She drove the pipe into its shattered eye socket. Its back legs kicked wildly for a moment, and then it went mercifully still. Todd's beam lit upon the blood that had splashed on her jeans. Sharon didn't seem to notice – or care.

"I couldn't just leave it like that," she said.

"We know," Todd said, though he was taken aback by how quickly and easily she'd dispatched the fallen creature.

He was about to ask Heather if she was all right when there was an explosion of leaves behind them. He'd been lying in wait for them all along, concealed underneath a pile of dead leaves.

Otto burst from his hiding place in the forest.

The Nazi lunatic that shouldn't exist wrapped a massive arm around Heather. When Vince went to pry her away, the burly killer kicked him in the gut, folding him in half. Todd and Sharon tried to capture him in their light, but he was too quick. Heather yowled in pain and startled fear. Her cries ended in a pained *ooofff* as Otto tightened his arm hold on her, cutting off her air.

Jerry aimed his gun at Otto, but he couldn't take the shot, not with Heather pulled in front of him like a shield. Heather fought feebly, her limp arms slapping against the killer's arm.

Otto started to run.

Sharon threw the pipe at him. It got tangled in his feet and he went down, using Heather to cushion the blow. As he turned to them, scrambling to his feet, Todd saw his face in full and immediately wished he hadn't.

Otto's flesh was pale as moonlight and hairless as a newborn's cheeks. His skull was uneven, half of it sunken in. His cheekbones were equally shattered, leaving the placement of his eyes uneven, unnatural, with a nose that was mashed flat. His lips were split in several places and what teeth he had in his awful mouth were cracked and jagged. He wore the black-and-white checkered pants of a chef, but his torso was wrapped in a moth-eaten gray coat. A tattered red-and-white armband with a swastika was on his left bicep.

He hissed at them like a wild animal.

Heather screamed like a woman gone mad. Her eyes rolled into her head and her body shook as if she were having a seizure.

Otto was on his feet, keeping Heather in front of him.

Vince had also regained his footing. "Put her the fuck down!" He balled his fists and lunged for the Nazi.

Todd could have sworn that Otto smiled. Otto grabbed Heather by the chin and pulled. He yanked her head back until her neck snapped. Sharp bones tore through her flesh until the raw and red inner meat of her neck was exposed, steaming in the cold air. Blood shot from the neck wound, dousing Vince with his wife's precious fluid. He slipped in the blood and fell on his back.

Jerry pulled the trigger. The shot punched through Heather's lifeless body, making it flinch as it left her meat and flesh and buried into Otto's stomach.

Otto twisted her head until it came free and threw it at Jerry and Todd. It hit Jerry in the chest and they both went down.

As he was falling, Todd saw Otto sprint away, not letting go of Heather's body, while Sharon ran after him, cursing him with every step. They disappeared into the darkness, the echo of their flight dying in the wilds of the Hayden.

Todd undid the belt around his and Jerry's legs so he could get to Vince quickly.

"Heather! Heather!"

Todd had to tackle Vince to keep him from running after Otto.

"Get the fuck off me!" Vince said, squirming to get free.

"I can't let you go," Todd said, his throat raw and eyes burning with tears. "She's gone, Vince. I can't let you go."

"You don't know that!" Vince raged.

"Yes, I do."

"No!"

Jerry limped to them and helped Todd keep Vince down.

"*You* killed her," Vince said, whirling on Todd. "This is all your fault! First you killed Bill, now Heather!"

"Todd didn't kill anyone and you know that," Jerry said.

"We wouldn't be here if it wasn't for him." He almost made it out of their grasp. "Heather!"

Vince's body shuddered with deep, moaning sobs. Todd was inches away from breaking down himself. He loved Heather to no end. No one had been a more steadying hand for him and Ash than Heather.

And Vince was right. He repaid her love and kindness by luring her to the very same place that had wasted Ash and her friends. It was happening again, all because he wanted that one last bit of Ash, no matter the cost.

Todd said, "Look, Vince—"

"Don't fucking talk to me! Don't you dare," Vince blurted between his pained blubbering.

"I'm sorry."

"Fuck your sorry."

There was nothing Todd or Jerry could say or do to ease their friend's suffering. Todd swept his flashlight over the copious amount of blood on the leaf-littered ground. He wondered how long the trail would last before there was nothing left in her body. And how long would Otto allow himself to be chased by Sharon before he decided to do the same to her?

Once Vince no longer felt like he was going to fight them, Todd and Jerry gave him some space. Every time he tried to get up, he dropped to his knees again, overwhelmed by his grief.

"What do we do now?" Todd asked Jerry. He had some of Heather's blood on his hands and jacket sleeves.

"I'm not leaving here without my wife," Vince said.

Todd felt his gorge rocket up his throat when he spied Heather's head on the ground. Her mouth was closed tightly, but her eyes bulged to the very edge of their sockets. He stepped to the side to hide it from Vince. He didn't need to see that now...if ever.

"Then we stay," Todd said.

He expected some pushback from Jerry, but his friend nodded instead. "We're not going anywhere without her, buddy," he said to Vince.

Todd tugged Jerry's jacket and motioned toward Heather's head. "Do we take it with us?" he said, soft enough so as not to be heard above Vince's sobs.

"With what? It's too cold to take our jackets off and wrap it up."

A quick glance at Heather's face had Todd tasting hot bile as it splashed onto his tongue. He covered his mouth with his cold fist.

"We can't just leave her here," Todd said, careful to say *her* and not *it*. "If Vince isn't leaving until he has her body, he sure as hell isn't going anywhere without...without all of her."

"No, I won't," Vince said, surprising them by being back on his feet. He sniffed back a wave of tears and took off his coat.

"Vince, you'll freeze to death," Jerry said.

Vince slid a look their way that stopped them from moving or speaking. He unbuttoned his flannel shirt, let that fall to the ground, and pulled a gray thermal shirt over his head. Wearing just an undershirt, he knelt beside his wife's head and averted his eyes, hands fumbling until he was able to roll it into his shirt. He tied the sleeves, carried it to where he'd left his shirt and coat and put them back on. Without saying a word, he turned away from them and started walking in the direction Otto and Sharon had left.

Todd grabbed the belt.

"No tying ourselves up again," Jerry said. "I'll walk."

They followed Vince deeper into the woods, Heather's wrapped head occasionally bouncing off the side of her husband's leg.

CHAPTER THIRTY-TWO

There was blood everywhere in the beginning, but just as Todd feared, it began to peter out. Still, there was enough to know they were on the right path, if there was such a thing as a right path in the damned resort.

Vince hadn't once turned around to make sure they were still with him. Todd couldn't blame him. He knew that hollowed-out feeling all too well. Anger was the only thing animating Vince at the moment.

Jerry limped badly, but he kept the pace.

"I'd have thought we'd hear Sharon by now," Todd said.

"That's assuming she's alive."

At the moment, that seemed too much to assume.

So many families destroyed by Otto. By the Hayden. Maybe the escaped Nazi was always meant to be here. There was something to this place that must have called out to him, was keeping him alive, or undead, he wasn't clear what Otto was. He sure as hell wasn't a zombie, at least not like any he'd ever seen in movies. Even fast zombies didn't move like that. Otto was a pure killing machine.

"She has to be," Todd said.

"Just like this Otto guy has to be dead, but he sure as hell ain't."

The dwindling blood trail led them out of the trees. They came to the bottom of the bunny ski slope. The gondola had been torn down long ago, but there was still a chalet at the top of the hill. Vince stopped walking, his head bent, light fixed on something on the ground. Todd and Jerry pulled up alongside him.

"Whatcha got there?" Jerry asked.

Vince bent down and lifted a leather bracelet from the grass. Todd knew it was Heather's. He'd been with them at the Jersey Shore the day Vince had bought it for her. Heather had never been a fan of jewelry. The only thing she ever wore was her wedding ring. But for some reason, she loved that bracelet, the small leather strips braided together.

The bracelet was still tied. Todd's stomach plummeted.

"How did this fall off?" Vince asked the night wind.

They looked at the chalet at the top of the hill.

Vince crushed the bracelet in his fist and shoved it in his pocket.

Jerry was the first to find the hand. It was just a few paces back from where Vince had found the bracelet. The wristbone and flesh looked mangled. Todd pictured Otto twisting and ripping it free, like unscrewing a bottle top.

The question was, why?

Heather was already dead. Why mutilate her body?

"Breadcrumbs," Jerry said.

Todd's head was spinning too much to concentrate. "Huh?"

"He's just about bled her out, so he has to leave something for us to follow."

Vince stared at his wife's hand. "That sick German pig fucker." He gracefully placed the bundle holding Heather's head on the bare ground. Slowly untying the sleeves, he put the hand next to her head and sealed it back up, his calm unsettling to watch.

"He's waiting for us," Vince said.

"Which is why we need to take a moment and think of the best way to proceed," Todd said.

Vince spun on him. "You said we need to take it to him. That's exactly what I'm going to do. I really don't care what you do."

Todd dared to grab Vince's arms. He waited for a punch, but Vince merely stiffened. "You saw him. What are you gonna do when you find him?"

"I...I...."

"We have to think this through."

"Jerry, give me your gun," Vince said.

Jerry backed away. "No can do. Odds are, you'll shoot yourself before you clip Otto."

Vince pointed at Jerry's ruined leg. "You sure as shit aren't going to make it up that hill. I'm fine with shooting myself."

"Yeah, but I'm not."

"Just give me the gun."

"No."

Todd scanned the bunny slope. He looked for signs of life in the chalet, but it was too far and too dark to make out anything. At the very least, he hoped to hear Sharon, even if she was crying out in pain. At least that would mean she was still alive.

He said to Jerry, "I think you should give him the gun."

"Have you lost your mind?"

"Yes. I definitely have. Vince, I'll go up with you, but I think, and I hate to say this, we need to split up."

"I don't want you with me," Vince grumbled.

"You want Heather back?"

Vince balled his fist.

"Then you'll have to do what I say."

"See how far that's gotten us," Vince snapped.

Todd was close to reminding Vince that he'd ditched them to come up here alone, that it was their decision to follow him. But in the end, it was his fault for bringing it up in the first place. They were worried about him, and they wouldn't allow him to walk this place of nightmares alone.

"If he's up there, we may be able to push him out. Once we're on top of the hill, we'll have a perfect view of how to get the hell out of here, and we'll have Heather," Todd said, quietly hoping they'd find Sharon as well. "The gun, Jerry."

"And what the hell am I supposed to do?" Jerry said in protest, still holding onto his weapon.

"Hide. Hide as best you can. You're too injured to run and without the gun, I don't want you grappling with this Nazi motherfucker." Jerry opened his mouth and Todd silenced him. "I know it's against your nature to take a back seat, but you're going to have to swallow your pride on this one. Besides, we need you to explain all this to the cops when we make it out."

"If I tell them the truth, we'll all end up in the nut house."

"Three hots and a cot, right?" Todd said.

"And all the zombie meds you'd ever need," Jerry said, his stance softening.

Vince held out his hand. "Please. Let me avenge Heather."

Jerry's sigh created a wall of dragon's breath that clouded his face. He put the gun in Vince's hand. "You know how to use it?"

"Any idiot can shoot. You forget I was in the army."

Jerry said, "The safety is already off. You don't have to pull the trigger so much as you squeeze it. And always aim for the center mass. Don't try to be fancy and go for a head shot. You'll miss."

"Hit or miss, it doesn't make a difference," Vince reminded him. "I just need him to get away from Heather."

Todd looked for a place for Jerry to hunker down. He found a boulder with two trees sprouting from either side. It wasn't ideal, but it was the best they were going to get. "Jerry, you lay low over there. If this works, we're going to lead Otto this way. I need you to stay out of sight, no matter what. If he sees you, we're not going to be able to help."

Jerry spit and wiped his mouth. "I feel like a goddamn coward."

"It takes a hero to just survive this place, man," Todd said.

They looked at one another for a moment, and Jerry finally clapped them on the arms. "Go. I'll hobble my ass over there and keep a low profile. Vince, you're going to get Heather back."

Vince's eyes clouded over and he nodded quickly.

"I'll go with you halfway," Todd said. "Then I'm going over there." He pointed to a cleft in the hillside. It looked like the ground had sunken or something had been removed. He could slip into the cleft and be invisible to anyone – or in Otto's case, anything – looking down from the chalet. What he'd spotted were coiled ropes of what looked to be cable wire.

"You hide while I go in the chalet?" Vince said, his tone mocking Todd's perceived cowardice.

He told Vince his plan.

His best friend who now hated him listened and said, "It's never going to work."

"That's the thing, the Hayden doesn't believe in never. We just need time, and if this works, it'll give us just that. "

Vince looked down at the shirt in his hand. "I love her so much. I don't know what's going to happen to me after tonight."

"We'll burn that bridge when we get to it. Until then, let's fuck Otto up and make him regret what he did to Heather. You with me?"

Vince gave a resigned nod. Todd knew if they lived to make it out of the Hayden, he and Vince would never be the same. He'd already lost him. They just needed to be on the same page this one last time.

"Good luck," Todd said.

Vince's eyes were cold and flat. "I don't need luck. I just need my wife."

They trudged up the hill, Todd feeling the dead Nazi's gaze lingering on them.

As they came to the cleft, Todd peeled off as fast as he could. Vince forged ahead without so much as flicking a quick glance his way. Todd made it to the cleft and pushed his back against the dirt lean-to. He nearly wept when he saw that there were steel cables and not frayed rope. Lifting the smallest coil was no easy feat. The bitter cold steel burned his palms and was heavy as hell. He hoisted it onto his shoulder and stayed in a crouch, barely popping his head over the lip of the cleft to see where Vince was in his ascent.

He should be at the chalet in a less than a minute. Todd would have to run as if the devil were stabbing at his thighs with a pitchfork if he was going to make it to the chalet in time. Right now, his legs felt like overcooked spaghetti.

Ash, if you can hear me, I need your strength. Only you were bold enough to make it out of here, and I honestly don't know how you did it. I'm not asking you to save me. Just help me help Vince. Help us get Heather away from him. It's strange how I feel so close to you here. I keep expecting to see you behind every tree and broken building. If something happens to me, I know you'll be here to take me with you. I actually can't wait for that moment. But I need this one thing to happen before it does. Show me how to beat this monster, Ash. Please...show me.

Vince stepped under the awning over the chalet door.

Todd looked at the onyx sky, hefted the heavy cable, and ran for his life.

★   ★   ★

"No. No. Nonononononononononono!"

Vince's keening nearly stopped Todd, the weight of his sorrow like a gut punch.

But Todd had to keep running. He had to make it to the chalet. Every second was crucial and he had none to spare.

He scrabbled up the hillside, his heart thudding in his ears, each frenetic breath stinging like needles.

To the right of the chalet, under the big bay window that faced the slope, was a metal pole sticking from the frozen ground. It looked like it might have been the base of a flagpole.

Vince continued to wail inside the chalet, freezing Todd's blood. Todd made it to the pole and looped the cable over it. Numb hands gripping the ends of the cable, he scooted under the window, careful not to be seen.

"What did you do? What did you do to her?"

Todd planted his ass on the ground and pulled the cable tight.

"Why? Why?"

His spirits, which weren't high to begin with, flagged as he began to suspect that Otto wasn't in the chalet. If he was, wouldn't he have approached Vince by now? Todd desperately wanted to peek inside the window, but if Otto was inside, he couldn't risk being seen and ruin the whole thing.

More than anything, he wanted to be beside his friend, who sounded like he was on the brink of a complete mental and emotional breakdown.

Grasping the cable felt like holding liquid nitrogen. Todd's gloves were in his pocket, but he didn't trust his ability to feel for them and get them on in time.

He heard Vince stomping around the chalet. Any second now, he would call out to him and tell him to come inside, that his great plan had failed.

Todd tried to steady his breath. He pulled back tighter on the cable to keep blood flowing to the muscles in his arms and back.

And then it came.

"You! You motherfucker!"

Todd eyed the window.

"You sick son of a bitch. Go back to hell!"

Gunfire erupted in the chalet. The whine of a bullet punching through the wall zinged over Todd's head. He reflexively ducked, loosening his hold on the cable.

The remaining glass in the window exploded, raining down on him like sleet.

Todd pulled the cable as hard as he could.

The shadow of a man burst from the window and hit the ground. Todd knew in an instant it was Otto just by the sheer size. The dead Nazi went to take a step to his left, but his ankle smashed into the taut cable. Otto flipped over the cable, hitting the slope hard. For a brief moment, it looked as if he was going to keep his balance. Todd tossed his heavy backpack, hitting him in the center of his chest. Otto's arms flailed and he went tumbling end over end down the hill. Todd watched him spin out of sight, heading in a direction that would deposit him on the opposite side of where Jerry was hiding. His backpack, another piece of Ash, rolled away and out of sight, down where Otto had slipped from view.

Todd dropped the cable. His frozen knees protested mightily when he jumped to his feet and ran into the chalet. It was like slamming into a cement wall. Vince was sitting on the ground with the gun in his lap and his flashlight pointing toward the ceiling. Todd struggled for air.

"Sweet Jesus...no!"

CHAPTER THIRTY-THREE

"Vince."

Todd remained in the open doorway, unable to step inside the chalet. What had once been a place where happy people gathered to warm up, maybe drink some hot chocolate before hitting the slopes, was now a charnel house.

Bits of Heather were everywhere. It looked as if Otto had torn her to pieces with his bare hands. Flesh was ripped, bones snapped, her innards looped around beams or stuck to exposed nails in the walls. She'd been dismantled into hundreds of pieces.

Todd had to look away.

On the chalet's doorstep was the shirt that held her head and hand.

"Vince."

He had to get Vince out of there, but his body was openly rebelling against his brain and refusing to let him enter the chalet.

His friend stared at the wall where ragged hunks of flesh and splintered bone had been dumped in a pile.

"Vince!"

The stench permeating the chalet was too much. Todd stepped away, bent over, his hands grasping his knees. He let his spit fall from his mouth in a long, ropy line, his stomach clenching and unclenching.

When he looked up, he saw past the Hayden's perimeter to the town below. He knew exactly where they needed to go to get out of this hell on earth.

But would he be able to get Vince to leave?

He had to go inside.

Steeling himself, Todd locked his eyes on Vince, trying hard not to look at Otto's version of modern art, and strode into the center of the chalet.

"Vince. Can you hear me?"

Without taking his eyes off the grisly tableau in front of him, Vince replied, "Leave me alone."

"Come on. We have to get out of here." When he bent to touch Vince's shoulder, he was met with the barrel of Jerry's gun. Vince still wouldn't look at him, but the gun was aimed straight at his heart.

"I never wanted to come here," Vince said. "But Heather, she convinced all of us that you shouldn't – no, *couldn't* – be alone. She worried about you, about Ash, all the time."

"Vince, I—"

"Say one word and I'll kill you." A line of drool clung to Vince's lower lip. "I told her not to come. At the very least, it should have been my job to follow you up here. And I didn't want to. You understand? The last place I wanted to be was here. But she loved you, and she wouldn't change her mind."

The words hit Todd harder than the horrid smell of death.

What came next was even worse.

Vince finally turned to him with eyes as red as raw steak. "Why does everyone who loves you have to die?"

Todd's jaw locked while his head swam. Vince's bitter question washed over him, leaving a cancerous caul that enveloped Todd's body and soul.

"I know you hate me," he said, his mouth filled with sand. "And you should hate me. I hate myself." Todd pointed out the broken window. "But I hate that *thing* more than anything that's ever walked the earth. And I'm not going to let it kill anyone else *I* love. That means you. Jerry's down there right now. We have to get him and get the fuck out of here. You can come outside and see for yourself that the fence isn't far from here. Please, Vince."

His friend slid his eyes away from him and back to Heather's remains. "How can I leave her?"

"We're coming back for her. And for Bill. But we need help. We're in no condition to fight him."

Vince stood up so suddenly, Todd backpedaled a bit.

"No one can fight him. Todd, I did just what Jerry said. I shot him right in the center of the chest. The gunshots didn't knock him

226 • HUNTER SHEA

out that window. He did that all on his own, as if I'd been hitting him with peanuts. He can't be killed."

Todd took a chance and grabbed hold of Vince's arm. "At least in the light of day, he can't take us by surprise. For some reason, I don't think he likes the daylight."

"Are you saying he's a vampire?"

"No. But maybe there have been others like him that people base the vampire myth on. I don't know. When Ash got away, they estimated that she made it out just as dawn broke. He'd stopped chasing her by then. It's not much to go on, but it's all I've got at the moment."

A hard gust of wind rattled the chalet's rotted walls, swirling the fetid odor trapped within. Todd covered his mouth and burped acid.

"I can't get Jerry out of here alone."

Vince looked around the room with tears in his eyes. "Okay," he said, the single word barely making it past his lips.

They stepped outside and Todd pointed out the closest exit point to the east of the slope.

"Where's Otto?" Vince asked, looking down the hill.

"Hopefully far enough away for us to grab Jerry and go."

The inexorable pull of gravity made getting down the hillside much easier than plodding up, but they had to be careful not to lose their footing and tumble down it as Otto had.

As they made it to the bottom, Todd kept expecting to see a black blur motoring their way. Otto wouldn't go far. And he could make up lost ground lightning fast.

Bill's odds of their making it out alive would be depressingly small right about now. That didn't mean that Todd should stop trying.

"Jerry," he whispered when they got close to the hiding spot.

When there was no reply, his stomach dropped.

Vince brushed past Todd and hustled behind the rock and trees. His head popped up in an instant and he waved Todd over.

At first, Todd thought Jerry was dead. His mouth hung open, his pale face shining through the darkness. Todd's hands were numb. There was no way he could feel for a pulse. He was about to press his ear against Jerry's chest when a small puff of vapor curled from Jerry's mouth.

"He just passed out," Todd said. He shook Jerry lightly by the shoulders. "Hey buddy, wake up."

Jerry's mouth closed and opened again, his eyes sealed shut.

If Jerry didn't wake up, they would have to carry him out. Todd wasn't sure if either of them were physically capable of doing it at this point.

He slapped the side of Jerry's face. "Come on. Jerry, we need to get up and out of here."

His eyelids fluttered.

"Like this," Vince said, giving Jerry a hard slap.

This time, Jerry came wide awake, his eyes narrowing at Vince. "Who the fuck hit me?" He rubbed his jaw.

"We thought you were dead," Vince said.

"You make a habit of slapping dead people?"

Todd was already hooking his arms under Jerry's armpits and lifting him. "I know the way out. We need to haul ass."

"Where's Otto?"

"I don't know. But he's not here at the moment, so we better take advantage of it."

They followed Todd, skirting around the base of the bunny slope, heading east. Vince handed Jerry's gun back to him.

"I did just what you told me to. All direct hits."

Jerry puffed hard, gritting through the pain. "You got him in the chest?"

Vince nodded. "Not that it did much good."

Jerry kept the gun in his hand, rather than securing it in his holster. "If I'd known, I would have brought a goddamn cannon."

It was slow going, which had Todd more anxious than a cat at a dog kennel. They avoided the trees skirting the eastern edge of the slope. He knew it would be far too easy to get lost again if they slipped between them. Without any cover, they were too exposed for Todd's liking. It would have been better if they could run, but the best they could do was a steady plod.

"You guys see any sign of Sharon?" Jerry asked.

Neither Todd nor Vince answered. How could they describe what they saw in the chalet? Sharon might have been in there. It was impossible to tell, and paralyzing to even think about.

Jerry got the hint, for once not pressing them for more.

They had to stop when Jerry said, "I'm crying uncle."

The fence line was nowhere in sight, but Todd had burned it into his brain when he was at the top of the hill. They still had a lot of ground to cover. Jerry settled onto the frozen earth, hissing in pain.

"Just leave me be and get the hell out of here," he said.

"No," Vince replied fiercely. "So don't even fucking ask again. You hear me?"

Jerry held up his hands. "I got you, Vince. I got you. I'm just trying to make it easier for you guys."

"Nothing will ever make it easy for us," Vince said. His eyes searched all around them. There might not have been anyplace to hide for a bit, but at least if Otto came at them again, they'd be able to see him.

Jerry turned his head to Todd. "Is it weird that my leg doesn't hurt anymore? Now, all the pain is in my back, all the way to my shoulders, and it's even worse than before."

"No, that's normal," Todd said, not knowing if it was or not. "It's like when we played tackle football in the street and that time Bobby Wager drove me into Mr. Abernathy's Caddy. I thought he broke my shoulder."

"And man, did you whine like a bitch about it," Jerry said, smirking.

"At least until you stomped on my foot and said, 'See, now your shoulder doesn't hurt so much.'"

"Trade one pain for another."

"Exactly."

"Except this pain is even making it hard to breathe."

"We have to go now," Vince said.

"Then run," Jerry said, not making a move to get up.

Vince chewed on one of his knuckles. "You don't understand." He pointed behind them. "He's coming."

CHAPTER THIRTY-FOUR

Jerry checked his gun and spun around.

Sure enough, the hulking shape of Otto was running toward them. Todd, Vince and Jerry had nowhere to go. They were going to have to face him head-on with very little to defend themselves.

Todd should have known it was foolish to think they could just walk out of the Hayden. Even if they weren't hurt and on motorcycles, Otto would have found a way to stop them. They'd made the fatal error of traipsing on his killing ground.

"Shitshitshitshitshit," Vince muttered.

Otto had been shot in the face and the chest and God knows where else. Nothing had even slowed him down. Jerry might be able to divert him for a little while, but it would never be enough for them to limp to freedom.

Not that they could ever be free.

Ash had lived with the memory of Otto, even if it was hidden, bleeding into her nightmares. In the end, she knew Otto couldn't die, and as long as he existed, so did the threat of his finding her and cleaning up his unfinished business. Now Todd knew the true, soul-shattering terror she'd been living with. And he understood why she'd taken matters into her own hands and beaten Otto to the punch. After what he'd seen the Nazi do to Heather, he knew that even if he somehow survived this night, he'd never be able to free himself from the knowledge of what Otto was capable of. How long would it be before Todd found himself at the end of a rope? Would he be able to live with the memories of this night, the surety that Otto was still out there, as long as she had?

It looked like those were questions that had no answers.

Otto was going to end them, here and now.

"Just stay behind me," Jerry said. His hands trembled, not from fear, but from pain and exhaustion.

Otto kept running in a straight line, right for them. It wouldn't be long before he reached them.

Todd heard the pounding of footsteps behind them.

Are there two of them?

He spun around and saw someone approaching from behind a bend in the hill. She was carrying something long in both hands.

It could only be Sharon.

The spitfire ran like a pole-vaulter, the ends of the pipe dipping up and down with each hurried step.

A shot rang out and Todd flinched. Otto had gotten close enough for Jerry to shoot him. It didn't slow him down.

"He's still coming!" Vince wailed.

He and Jerry hadn't noticed Sharon yet. Todd wanted to scream at her to stop, to drop the pole and run the other way. He'd no sooner drawn a breath than she was rushing past him. Instead, he had to yell to Jerry, "Don't shoot!"

Sharon's hair cascaded behind her like wild snakes writhing in the wind. He thought he heard her growl as she sped past them. The pipe she was holding like a lance looked like it had been pulled from the plumbing works somewhere in the resort.

She darted into Jerry's line of fire and his arm jerked skyward just as he pulled the trigger. The bullet sailed above them and into the night sky.

Otto and Sharon were on a collision course.

"Sharon, no!" Todd yelped.

At the last second before impact, Sharon drove the back end of the pipe into the hard ground. She pointed the front end at Otto's stomach. His incredible forward momentum prevented him from slowing down or veering away. Instead, he impaled himself on the pipe. The furious impact of the supernatural force hammered the back end of the pole deeper into the earth. Sharon leaped away, allowing room for Otto's body to slide farther and farther along the pipe. Otto's shoulders and arms slumped lifelessly, his body frozen at a forty-five-degree angle, knees bent and touching the ground. A clump of something dark and ropy hung off the end of the pole.

"Bam!" Sharon shouted, arms flailing in victory. "Take that, you ugly motherfucker!"

"Don't get close to him," Jerry warned her. She looked like she wanted to get in Otto's face and taunt him. She circled his motionless body, steam coming off her in trailing wisps.

"Come on," she taunted. "Let's see you walk away from this." She hocked up a load of phlegm and spit on his back. "Don't mess with a bitch who knows what to do with a pole." Her eyes bordered between gleeful and manic.

Todd swung his light to get a better look at Otto's face. The second the light touched upon it, he wished he hadn't.

There was a deep furrow in Otto's cheek where Jerry's bullet had buried itself in his massive head. The flesh looked like a clump of clay, after someone had pushed their finger deep inside. There was no sign of blood, no surrounding destruction from the bullet's entry. Half his face should have been obliterated. But there was only the small, deep hole.

Otto's eyes were deep-set and open and gray as death. Todd couldn't detect a pupil or iris. Otto's lower jaw hung open, his teeth blunted and brown, his tongue the mottled black and purple of a tumor.

Sharon leaned in to get a better look, just inches from Otto's face.

"I mean it, Sharon," Jerry said. "Back the hell up."

She sneered at him. "You can tell me what to do when you parade me into jail. Right now, I'm not hearing you."

"He's right," Todd said. "We don't know if he's really dead."

Todd and Vince cautiously approached the impaled body. "He was always dead," Vince said. "The question is, what level of dead is he now?"

"He was not always dead," Jerry said. He stayed where he was, his gun locked on Otto, just in case.

Vince gave a wide berth to the body. He examined the clump of innards hanging from the pipe's end like a flag on a windless day. "What the hell is this?"

Todd came over and they spotlighted it with their flashlights. The formless black substance looked a lot like a clod of wet dirt. Sharon reached over and touched it.

"It's cold. Like dry ice cold."

"I'm gonna take your word for it," Vince said.

She sniffed her finger and her nose crinkled. "Smells like, I don't know, the ground by a septic tank that's overfilled."

Todd looked at her. "That's very specific."

She shrugged. "It happened once at my uncle's place. It's the kind of stench you never forget. Here, give it a whiff." She jammed her finger under Todd's nose. He snapped his head back, but not before latching onto the vile scent. He'd never experienced what she had at her uncle's house, but he thought that was a perfect assessment of the rank odor on her finger.

Without warning, Vince kicked Otto in the back. His heavy body slid farther down the pipe.

"Fuck you!" He kicked the corpse again and Otto inched closer to the ground. Vince slammed the back of the Nazi's head with his flashlight, over and over until the light sputtered out and the entire thing cracked in half, batteries spilling out. Vince cried as he bashed Otto. Todd wrapped him up in his arms and swung him away. He held Vince as his body shuddered, hot tears coating Todd's cold neck. "I want to do to him what he did to Heather," Vince choked. "I want to tear him into pieces so small, I can feed them to the rats."

"I know, buddy. I know."

He saw Sharon wipe her finger off on Otto's moldy jacket. It looked like it had fused with his skin. He could only imagine what horrors lay beneath that filthy fabric.

Otto looked human in the sense that he had a torso, arms, legs and a head, no matter how misshapen. But being this close to his corpse, every hair on Todd's body stood on end as he began to realize the resurrected Nazi was far less, or perhaps greater, than a flesh and blood person. As tempted as he was to touch Otto's face and feel that flesh, he just couldn't bring himself to do it. He wasn't as bold – or was it reckless – as Sharon.

"I say we light him up," Sharon said.

"What?" Jerry said.

"Let's set the asshole on fire." Unlike Todd, she had no issues with touching Otto. She patted his clothes, flicked her fingers through his hair. "It's freezing out here. At least he'll be good for something. He'll go up like dry kindling. Jerry, let me have your lighter."

"I'm not warming myself by a burning man," Vince said. "Fire will only make him smell worse."

When Jerry hesitated, she said, "Don't make us the assholes who don't finish the killer off when they had the chance."

Jerry put his gun down and said, "Screw it." He tossed his Zippo to Sharon. She then held it out to Vince.

"You should do the honors. I nailed him like a diseased butterfly for Sheri. Now do this for Heather." A river of tears ran down her cheeks.

Vince accepted the lighter with a shaky hand. Todd stepped in front of him to block the wind. It took Vince several tries before he got a flame. He looked into Todd's eyes.

"For all of them," Vince said.

"Yeah," Todd said, barely above a whisper because his throat felt tighter than a drumhead. "For all of them."

Vince touched the flame to Otto's coat. The fire jumped from the Zippo like a returning wartime soldier seeing his love at the end of the reception line. There followed a loud whoosh of air and Otto's body was engulfed in flames quicker than it would have been if he'd been doused in gasoline. They had to step back quickly before they got burned.

"Damn," Sharon murmured. The reflected flames danced in her wide, wild eyes.

Thick coils of black smoke rolled off Otto's burning corpse.

Jerry covered his mouth and gagged. "Jesus, that's rotten."

The heady stench of Otto's roasting flesh smelled like burning garbage. Todd's eyes watered and his guts twisted. He buried his mouth and nose in the crook of his elbow.

Vince and Sharon didn't seem to notice the smell. They were mesmerized by the burning monster.

Jerry hobbled to Todd's side. "That's not burning meat." He spit over and over onto the cold, dry grass.

"What do you mean?" Todd said.

"I've smelled a dude that was on fire. He got in his car one night after a blowup with his wife and poof, set himself on fire. I'm not sure whether it was to get away from her or teach her a lesson. Probably both. Anyway, I know what a person on fire smells like." He pointed

234 • HUNTER SHEA

at Otto, his body slipping farther down the pipe like a roast on a spit. "And that ain't it. Makes you wonder what he really was."

It did, but not enough for Todd to care.

Otto – the Wraith – was finally dead. Todd hoped Ash, Heather, Bill, Sheri and everyone who had ever spent their last terrified moments in Otto's wicked presence could see this now. It might not give them rest, but maybe it would bring them pleasure.

As inviting as the warmth coming off the fire was, Todd had to step back and turn his head. Otto's foul redolence was a physical force pushing him away. Even Vince and Sharon had backed up by a few paces, keeping upwind.

"We should get going," Jerry said.

Todd held him back. "No. We stay until there's nothing left."

Vince and Sharon didn't have to say a word for him to know they were in full agreement. Todd had watched Ash slowly fall apart and die over five years. He would savor however long it took to see Otto reduced to fetid embers.

There came a loud pop, as if a pocket of liquid under Otto's flesh came to a boil and exploded, followed by the crackling of fireworks. Everyone but Jerry leaped back.

The flames around Otto turned as blue as the budding fire on a gas stovetop.

And then Otto's crisping body began to twitch.

CHAPTER THIRTY-FIVE

At first, Todd thought it was Otto's muscles retracting as they tightened and curled from the heat. He'd read that corpses will raise their arms during a cremation, as if imploring a higher power to set them free from the burning flames.

Otto's legs tensed and his body tipped forward just slightly.

Jerry was quick to point his gun at the impaled corpse.

"It's all right," Todd said. "Just his body breaking down."

"No it's not," Jerry said. "Get out of the way."

Todd spun on his heels and saw Otto's arms go rigid, then jerk forward so his hands could grab hold of the pipe. In the span between Todd's worried breaths, Otto had pulled the pipe free from the ground and gotten off his knees.

"No!" Sharon screamed.

Otto, coated in blue fire, stood before them with the long pipe jutting from his midsection, chest heaving with a life that shouldn't be.

In a night of horror and impossibilities, Todd couldn't believe what he was seeing. "Oh my fucking God."

The Nazi turned his burning head to Todd and sprang into action.

Jerry fired into Otto's chest. The bullets didn't stop him. He tried to yank Todd out of Otto's fiery path, but his fingers slipped on his jacket and he fell onto his side instead.

Todd couldn't move.

Otto ran at him, the pipe dangling like the tip of a lance.

Only one word filled Todd's bewildered mind – Ash.

Something crashed heavily into his side. Todd pirouetted, arms flailing, trying not to fall.

The pipe slipped through Vince with a tearing sound that echoed off the nearby slope.

Vince!

236 • HUNTER SHEA

Otto rammed forward until he and Vince were as close as conjoined twins, Vince's face bouncing off the giant's neck. The strange flames engulfed Vince as quickly as they had Otto.

Vince's cries were an icy dagger in Todd's chest.

Otto, even encumbered with a long pipe through his body and Vince's added weight, picked up speed. Vince's screams reached a ragged crescendo and suddenly stopped.

Todd watched with impotent rage as the Nazi sprinted away from them with Vince's lifeless feet dangling inches from the ground. He made the turn around the wide base of the slope and disappeared. All that remained was the acrid stench left in his wake, along with something else that Todd knew with dread was the smell of his friend broiling.

"What...what the hell just happened?" Jerry said from his position on the ground. He looked like he'd not only just seen a ghost, but had been mauled by one while walking down a long, dark hallway. Sharon was too stunned to speak, the literal fire in her eyes from earlier gone flat and dull.

Before he knew it, Todd was on his knees.

"Why did you do that, Vince?"

He knew he should be screaming, hands balled into fists, or even crying at the loss of his best friend.

Instead, he was as numb inside as he'd gone outside.

No one spoke. There was nothing to say. No language had developed the words that could properly convey what they had just witnessed, nor what they were feeling.

Todd remained with his knees on the hard ground until the pain pushed its way through the shocked miasma that gripped his brain. It hurt just as much to unlock his damaged knees and stand.

"I'm not leaving," Todd said, staring inward, seeing nothing before him.

Jerry had managed to get up on his own. "If you stay here, you'll die, just like everyone else."

Todd shuffled in the direction Otto had gone. "I know."

"I'm with Todd," Sharon said, sniffing back tears. "We either kill this fucker or we die trying."

Jerry holstered his gun, craned his head back with a loud crack as far as it would go and closed his eyes. "Well, I can't leave without your help. So it looks like I'm staying too. The only problem is, how the hell do we kill...that? The son of a bitch can't be shot, impaled or burned."

Todd kept walking ahead of Jerry and Sharon in slow, purposeless steps.

"Because that's how you kill a *person*," he said.

He heard the shuffling and foot-dragging behind him and turned to find Sharon supporting Jerry as they followed.

"What does that mean?" Jerry said, grimacing.

Todd stopped. "It means Otto isn't human. You saw his face. Sharon, you even felt it. Does that look like a living, breathing person to you?"

Sharon shook her head. "He was cold. It was like touching ice. And his skin, it didn't feel right."

"What did it feel like?" Todd asked.

"I don't know. I never felt anything like it before."

"I'll bet you have, but you just can't square how he felt with what we think he should be. Think."

Otto was a true mystery, but so far, they'd survived long enough to gather some clues. It was all a matter of putting them together now. Todd needed Ash more than ever. He could only hope to be a conduit for her questioning spirit and try to open his mind wide enough for an answer to come.

"Seriously, it was weird," she said, exasperation straining her face.

"What the hell isn't weird here?" Jerry interjected. "Just say the first things that come to mind."

Todd was pleasantly surprised that his friend had ceased mocking and baiting Sharon.

"Cold," she said.

"You said that before," Jerry said. "Keep going."

"His face was kinda hard, almost like when you touch butter that you took out of the freezer and it's starting to thaw."

"Good. Was it greasy like butter?"

She looked at the hand that had touched Otto. "No. The opposite. It was dry, like...like..."

"Dirt?" Todd said.

Her eyes widened. "Yes! Like dirt. Really hard packed."

"His face felt like dirt?" Jerry said incredulously.

"Not exactly, but it's the closest I can come up with. I know it sounds crazy. I also know I don't need you mouthing off to me."

"Cool your G-string. I'm just trying to process this."

Todd stormed back to where Sharon had impaled the Nazi. A clump of near-frozen dirt was at his feet, having been unearthed when Otto ripped the pipe free. He reached down and palmed it, his fingers tracing its uneven contours. "Sharon, come here."

It took her a bit since Jerry came with her, latched onto her arm.

"Feel this," he said, holding the dirt out to her.

"Okay. So?"

He took the lump of earth back and dropped it. Then he went over to the strange stuff that had come out of Otto when Sharon drove the pipe through his body. It still reeked. This time, he did more than touch it; he scooped it into his hands. Jerry's face pinched as if he'd just bitten into a lemon. Sharon had to turn her head away for a moment to catch a breath of unfouled air.

"Now feel this."

She tried to push his hand away. "No thank you. I did enough of that before."

He shoved it back at her. "Feel it."

The frigid stuff sent a chill that settled into the marrow of his hands. The smell was frightful, but he did his best to ignore it.

Sharon pushed a tentative finger into the mess and gasped.

"That's it."

"What?" Jerry said. "You say the stuff that came out of him feels just like his face?"

"Close enough," she replied, freely exploring the exposed innards. When she pinched them between her thumb and index finger, what looked like a section of some kind of black organ mushed flat. As she rubbed her thumb and finger back and forth, it began to crumble, little flakes raining onto the ground. Breaking it down made the smell even worse. Todd let the rest fall from his hand and then took several steps away, nausea hitting him so hard, he got dizzy.

After dry heaving, Sharon said, "It's like he's made of dirt."

"Or fresh shit from a sick animal," Jerry said, covering his nose with his forearm. Todd bent down and wiped the remains from his hand in the dead grass. If he could have cut his hand off and tossed it far away, he would have.

"I told you, Jer, he's not human." Todd kept his hand away from his face.

"He's human enough to run around and kill people. Are you saying he's some kind of mud man? If that's the case, let's just douse him with water and call in a bunch of kids to make mud pies out of him."

"You're joking, but you may be right."

Jerry rolled his eyes. "Of all the times I've been right and you didn't admit it, this isn't the time to jump on my bandwagon. There's no such thing as people made of mud and shit."

Sharon ran her clean hand through her curls. "Actually, there is."

"What?"

She sat heavily on the ground. "I learned a little about them in this class I took."

"You went to college?" Jerry asked incredulously.

She didn't bother shooting daggers his way. "I took continuing education classes at night. Just the ones I thought were interesting. There was this one on theology taught by a Lutheran pastor. Or maybe he was a former pastor. I forget. He made religion seem cool. I don't believe in God, but that doesn't mean I don't like a good story. He told us this one about a thing called the golem that really stuck with me."

"A golem?" Todd said. "What is it?"

"It's basically a man that's molded from stuff like clay and whatever else its maker can find. It comes from the Jewish mystic tradition. There was something about a rabbi making a golem. People used magic incantations to bring these things to life. Some of them even looked perfectly normal with human feelings and desires. There was even some story about a golem falling in love with a woman."

"And why would anyone need a golem?" Jerry asked.

"To do their bidding. To make a kind of slave. I think most of the time, it was to create a being to do their dirty work. Like, you need to get back at somebody, you order the golem to kill them. Once the deed is done, you destroy the golem and it returns to the earth, leaving no evidence behind."

The gears in Todd's brain went into overdrive. "How did they destroy it?"

She shrugged her shoulders. "I...I can't remember. If it's magic, I guess you do the reverse of whatever it took to manifest it in the first place. Or was there something that had to be removed from its mouth or head. I forget."

Jerry threw up his hands. "Well, we're a little late finding Jewish mystics in this place. Maybe we can find a time machine and put out a call for one during dinner. 'Is there a golem-making mystic in the house?'"

Sharon said, "But why is he trying to kill *us*? Is it because of our ties with Sheri and Ash? I mean, it's obvious there are lots of people that come out here. If he killed them all, there'd be no way to hide it."

Todd thought for a moment. She was right. The graffiti alone was proof that the Hayden was busier than it should be. "Maybe it's because when the others come here, they come to desecrate the Hayden. Otto has no beef with people who defile things. In fact, he probably hopes they come around and screw and break things. But can a golem rationalize something like that?"

"If some can perfectly imitate people, then I'd say yes," Sharon replied softly.

"Of course you would," Jerry said, but they both ignored him.

Todd chewed on the insides of his cheeks, the pain helping to keep him focused. While they debated the nature of the killer, Otto could be close by, listening and waiting to pluck them off.

"Even if Otto is a golem, why would someone create him in the first place? He was a murderer of Jews. What Jewish person would wish to bring him back in any form, much less this one?" Todd blew into his hands, but it did little to warm them up.

Sharon snapped her fingers. "Unless he was a golem in the first place! Bill said the Nazis were into some strange shit, right? Maybe they forced a rabbi to create him. They could have threatened to kill his family in front of him if he didn't do what they said. How was he to know they'd kill them all anyway? It worked, and Otto managed to escape the war and make his way here."

"That's a pretty big leap," Todd said.

"No way," Jerry said. "We all saw him. That's not the kinda face that flies under the radar."

"Maybe he didn't always look like that. Maybe, when he was quote, unquote, *killed*, and then buried, his being under all that dirt, and made of dirt, kind of broke down the human mask. The longer he was down there, the more he started to return to his natural state. For all we know, golems have a shelf life, and he could be close to the end of his."

"Well, I hope I can move like that when I'm nearing the end," Jerry said, closing his mouth and shaking his head, realizing the end might only be minutes, or seconds, into their future. "No matter what, we're still no closer to figuring out how to stop him."

Todd gaped at the last place he'd seen Otto and Vince. He wondered if Otto was busy tearing Vince to shreds as he'd done to Heather, or if he had a more horrific debauchery in mind.

"You said something about removing a thing from a golem's mouth to stop it. You know what it would be?"

"No clue. Normally, I'd just look it up, but that's not going to happen out here."

Pinching the bridge of his nose, Todd said, "No matter. You know how in movies you have to shoot the zombie in the head?"

"Yeah," Jerry said with a heavy note of trepidation.

"In this case, when we get the chance, we're gonna have to aim a little bit lower."

CHAPTER THIRTY-SIX

The first thing they decided to do was the exact opposite of what anyone else would do. Mainly, instead of trying to get out, they would plunge back into the center of the Hayden. Otto, if he had the capacity of forethought – and all signs pointed to yes – would expect them to try for the fence. Possessing supernatural speed meant he could quickly make up for being wrong.

Their chess move would buy them some time, but not a lot. Todd and Sharon kept Jerry between them, his arms crooked over their shoulders.

"Okay, Custer, where do we make our stand?" Jerry asked. His lips were starting to go as pale as his face, and his breathing was becoming more labored. As the pain escalated, so did his chances of going into shock.

Todd pointed to a half-standing structure to the right of the main hotel. "I think that was the Cosmos Theater. They used to show all kinds of acts in there, and then movies sometime in the early sixties."

"Great," Jerry said with a hissing wince. "Maybe the spirits of the borscht belt comics will come to our rescue."

"Doesn't seem so far-fetched right about now, does it?" Sharon quipped. Todd could tell she was bearing the brunt of Jerry's burden. He was both grateful and ashamed. But truth be told, he wasn't sure how he was managing to stay upright himself.

What wore Todd out more than anything was the mounting tension. He knew Otto was going to come for them. The only question was when. He felt a little easier when they had to navigate their way through a plot of trees. Once they were out and again utterly exposed, his anxiety ratcheted up exponentially. Giant, looming, golem-Otto could be running his earthen ass off at this very moment, just seconds away from cutting them off from their destination. Jerry kept insisting that the moment Otto returned, they were to take his gun and leave him as either a distraction or an impediment to the killer's forward progress. Todd was getting tired of telling his stubborn friend to stuff it. "Martyrdom doesn't become you," he'd said to finally shut him up.

To his shock and brief-lived delight, they made it to the old theater without any unpleasant interruptions.

The Cosmos Theater, like everything in the Hayden, had seen better days. It looked as if a cleaver had descended from the heavens and lopped off the front half of the building. Its guts were left exposed to decades of baking sun and drenching storms, bitter cold and heavy snow. The stage was still there, though there were great holes in the floorboards, the backdrop where a movie screen once hung now a blighted and mildewed mess. Hundreds of rusted seats were still affixed to the floor, their fabric and stuffing long since removed as nesting for the local birds. There was evidence of a fire by the left wing, the wall black with soot, a lone theater box somehow defying gravity and decay. Todd spied the gnarled rigging of stage lights lying in a heap in the center of the stage.

"Okay," Sharon said, shrugging off Jerry's arm and leaning him against the frame of a seat. It was a miracle it held him. "Why here?"

"I'm hoping there's just enough left to bury him again," Todd said. He cautiously approached the stage, put his palms flat on the cold, cold wood and pressed down. It replied with a slight crack and heavier groan. He swiveled onto the precarious stage.

"Sounds sturdy," Jerry said. His arms were wrapped around his chest and he was shivering.

"Hopefully," Todd said, pulling himself onto the stage, "it's just sturdy enough."

"Todd, be careful," Sharon said. She jogged to the stage, holding out her arms for him.

Todd tested his weight. "I'm all right. For the moment at least." He took a tentative step, adding his weight bit by bit until he was confident the floor would hold. Then he took another, and another, his eyes on the stage, wary of holes great and small. He got as far as the dead center of the stage and stopped.

"If you start to tell old jokes, I may shoot you," Jerry said through chattering teeth.

"Sharon, would you say Otto is at least fifty pounds heavier than me?"

"I'd guess from the size of him," she said. "But he's not made out of the same stuff as us. He could be even heavier. Or lighter."

With his hands on his hips, Todd looked around him. "I'm going to bet on heavier. I'm pretty damn sure the wood on this stage can't support his weight." He clicked on his flashlight, aiming the beam into one of the holes. It was about a four-foot drop into rotted boards and rusty nails. "Good thing I've had my tetanus shot."

"What are you gonna do? Invite him to go up and sing a duet with you?" Jerry said.

Todd arched an eyebrow. "In a manner of speaking, yes. Except I'm not the one who will be singing along with him."

"I'm assuming this guy will be," Jerry said, pointing at his chest.

"Only because you're incapacitated. Sharon and I will have other things to do."

"I finally get to make my stage debut, and it's as bait for a murdering Nazi golem." Jerry paused and scratched his head, looking confused. "Now there's a sentence I never dreamed I'd say."

"We can't stick him up there and hope we get to Otto before he gets to Jerry," Sharon protested. "You've seen how fast he is."

"Your concern for me is making me all warm inside, honey," Jerry said.

Sharon looked at him and rolled her eyes to Todd. "On second thought, what's the rest of the plan?"

"See those lights?"

"I do."

"If we sit Jerry right here, Otto should find himself falling through the stage right about here." He pointed at a weak spot five feet before where they would sit his friend. A few fist-sized holes had rotted through the wood. When Todd touched the tip of his boot to the area, it felt like stepping on wet cardboard. "Once Otto is momentarily incapacitated, we pin him down by dropping the lights on him. I'll go down there and get whatever may be in his mouth and rip it out."

Jerry pulled himself up by the back of the chair in front of him. "Whoa, whoa, whoa. Your whole plan falls apart if he's not a golem.

And I think it's fair to say the odds of Sharon being right are pretty goddamn slim."

She flipped him the middle finger.

"Likewise," Jerry responded. "Once you're down there, you're trapped with him. And if you're wrong, he's going to get up and he's going to do some pretty unpleasant shit to you."

"I'm willing to take that chance," Todd said.

"I'm not," Jerry said. "I don't mind being bait, but not so my buddy can commit suicide. I say once we have him down there, we dump everything we can on him. Then we get to one of the fire engines or cars outside the front gate and drive the hell out of here."

"I'm not leaving until I know Otto is dead," Todd said, his voice rising with each word.

"If he's a golem, he already is dead. Or was never alive. Shit, I don't know."

A steady wind howled across the Hayden. It pushed at the bill of Todd's ball cap, threatening to flip it off his head.

"Vince was the last one," Todd said. "No more. You're with me on that, right, Sharon?"

"I am. Even if it means going in there with you and tearing him apart so we can scatter the pieces everywhere. I want to give Sheri something to smile about."

Jerry limped to the stage. Todd and Sharon pulled him up.

Todd said, "You know we can't let him kill anyone else."

"Here." Jerry slipped his gun in Todd's pocket. "I have a few rounds left. Before you go playing dentist in that fucker's mouth, you shoot it at point-blank range. If there's some kind of magical whatever in there, maybe you can blast it out."

Todd clapped him on the back. "Thanks. You ready for your lines?"

A shiver shook Jerry from head to toe. "No. But tell me them anyway."

★   ★   ★

For the first time since Otto had killed the two kids out for a bit of Hayden Massacre ghoulish road tripping, Todd worried about dawn coming too soon. They had to get Otto before the sun came up. He didn't know if golems had a whole light of day aversion, but he did know that someone would discover the abandoned cop and fire vehicles and it would be near impossible to sneak back in to finish the job. There was also the strong possibility that they would be thrown in jail as suspects for all of the murders if they were here when more help arrived.

He crouched next to Sharon in the dark corner of the stage. The only thing visible of them on the stage itself was their breath, but there was nothing they could do about that. He didn't know how long he'd be able to draw a breath and was hyper aware of how wonderful the usually automatic act was.

Jerry sat fifteen feet away, clutching his leg and wailing. Todd was pretty sure his friend didn't have to fake the pain he was in.

"Jesus, it hurts!" he bleated. "Todd! Sharon! Where the hell are you?"

Sharon whispered in Todd's ear, "You sure this is going to work?"

He swallowed hard and replied, "Not at all."

"Thanks for the confidence boost."

"No problem."

Jerry made sure not to cast even the quickest glance their way. It was vital he not tip Otto off that they were waiting in the wings.

"What if Otto doesn't fall for it?" Sharon asked. "It looks kind of obvious."

"I'm betting that a man made out of mulch isn't a deep thinker."

"I wish I'd paid more attention in class," Sharon said, rubbing her hands together to warm them.

"You and me both."

Jerry continued to rock back and forth, appearing to be getting angrier that he was left on his own. Todd tightened and loosened his grip on the ice-cold framework for the heavy lights. He and Sharon had tested pushing the rigging before slipping out of sight, just to make sure they could actually move it.

"I have a confession to make," Sharon said.

"I'm not a priest."

"You're gonna hear me out anyway. You know, there's a reason I never reached out to you after...well, you know."

"You were a kid. I should have been the one to check in on you."

"That's not it. When I was younger, I didn't like Ash very much."

He slowly turned his head to her.

Sharon continued. "I thought she was a bitch. I worshipped Sheri, and when Ash was around, I didn't exist. I blamed it all on Ash. And when Sheri died, doing something that was Ash's idea, and Ash lived, I grew to hate her."

"I don't need to hear any more," Todd said. No matter Sharon's feelings, Ash was the love of his life. The last thing he wanted was to listen to Sheri's damaged sister speak ill of her.

"Hear me out. I realize now I was jealous. When I look back, Ash was always nice to me. It's just that she and Sheri were older and had totally different lives than a kid in grade school. But I couldn't make all that hate go away. She never forced Sheri to come here. I know that. Doesn't make it any easier to tear down the thing that you've built yourself upon. And I'm sorry for that."

Todd wasn't sure to do with Sharon's strange apology. On the one hand, he couldn't blame her for feeling the way she had. On the other, he was too preoccupied to care.

He said, "Does that mean when we get out of here, you're going to have to reevaluate everything you think you knew? Maybe get out of stripping, get back to school?"

She shook her head. "Hell no. You know how much money I make in the clubs? I don't do drugs or drink, so I'll have enough money to retire, especially if I invest it right, by the time I'm thirty."

Todd was about to ask her how much she made when he saw movement down by the seats. He put his finger to his lips and used that same finger to show Sharon that Otto had arrived.

Jerry stopped his complaining for a beat. He'd seen him too.

Todd's heart went into overdrive. He licked his painfully cracked lips. It hurt to swallow.

The shadow of the hulking golem was brought to light by a sliver of moon as it peered out from the clouds. Otto's pale flesh, or whatever it was, had been charred black as the night. His white eyes were in stark relief, like boiled eggs, against his charcoal face.

"No!" Jerry said, his eyes locking on Otto. He pushed back on the stage, but not too far. They'd tested the section where he'd been set up and were confident he had some wiggle room, but not much.

Otto held something in his right hand.

He raised it into the moonlight.

Todd nearly cried out.

It was Vince's arm, still covered in the sleeve of his gray coat.

Jerry shouted, "Stay the fuck away from me! You want to get shot in the face again?"

In response, Otto kicked the seat in front of him. It came unmoored from the floor and flew a good forty feet into the lip of the stage. Jerry recoiled, holding his arm over his face as if it would protect him from a rocketing metal chair.

Don't look over here, Todd thought. *Keep him coming.*

Otto stepped into the space he'd made.

"Stay back!" Jerry reached into his pocket.

Otto kicked another chair. This one sailed to the left and clanged against the stage. At this rate, he wouldn't need to make it to the stage to kill Jerry. The seats were like missiles and Jerry had nothing to defend himself with.

"I said stay back!" Jerry kept his hand in his pocket. Todd wondered if Otto considered the possibility that he had a gun in there. Even if he did, it didn't look like he cared.

More chairs were launched, one of them just missing Jerry's head by inches. Otto cleared a path through the rusting seats like a thresher in a wheat field.

"This isn't gonna work," Sharon said.

A seat sailed over the stage and onto the sheared roof. This time, Jerry did turn his head their way, but only for an instant. Todd saw real fear there. He couldn't just sit here and wait to spring a trap that had no chance of being sprung.

Sharon was thinking the same thing. She whispered, "You think you can move this all by yourself?"

Todd was honest when he replied, "I don't know."

"Well, you're gonna have to."

Before he could stop her, Sharon had crawled out of their hiding spot and slipped off the stage, out of Otto's sight line. Running in a crouch, she popped up between two of the rows of seats to the stage's left. "Oh God! Jerry!" she shrieked.

Otto turned his entire body toward her.

Sharon stepped into the aisle.

"Sharon, get out of here. Run!" Jerry blurted.

She didn't move.

Otto plowed through the chairs in his way, heading for the aisle.

CHAPTER THIRTY-SEVEN

"Come at me, motherfucker," Sharon spat.

Otto was only twenty feet away.

Todd dug his heels in, ready to shove the light rigging across the stage.

Jerry got to his feet, bouncing on his good leg, ready to leap off the stage and get Sharon out of Otto's path. Todd stopped short of shouting at Jerry to stay where he was.

The Nazi golem started striding down the empty aisle.

Sharon yelped and turned toward the stage.

She'd almost made it to the stage when Otto threw Vince's arm at her. It spun through the air like a rogue helicopter blade. Sharon had her back to the monster and didn't see it coming. The arm whacked her in the back of her head and she went down.

Otto paused to admire his work, his head cocking to the side.

There was no stopping Jerry now. He bounded across the stage on one leg, dropping to his ass at its edge and jumping down beside her prone body.

Todd unleashed a slew of curses under his breath. There was no point hiding anymore. He burst from the shadows and leaped off the stage. He looked up in time to see Otto running toward them.

While Jerry struggled to get Sharon into a sitting position, Todd ripped the gun from his pocket.

Otto was upon them in seconds.

Todd opened fire.

The first shot hit the golem in the shoulder, his body jerking to the right.

Todd adjusted. The next pull of the trigger produced a deep furrow in Otto's head.

Lower, dammit, lower!

Otto's hands swiped at the air, just missing them.

Not knowing if he had any ammo left, Todd pulled the trigger again. This time, the bullet punched through Otto's mouth. The golem staggered backward, hands at his ruined face. It was hard to believe this monstrosity once passed for a human being. If he was a golem, he was one that had come undone, his mask rotting off his face while he'd moldered in his grave.

Todd rose up, ready to shoot the golem again. He squeezed the trigger, but nothing happened. His ankle rolled and he nearly fell. He looked down and saw he was standing on Vince's severed arm.

Otto fell to his knees, his disfigured head turned away from them. The last shot had bought them the time they needed.

"Come on," Todd said. He grabbed Sharon and hoisted her over his shoulder. He handled her weight easier than he thought he could. She moaned close to his ear. He helped pull Jerry onto the stage.

With a sharp glance, he noted that Otto was still turned away from them, nursing his wounded mouth.

"We still doing this?" Jerry said breathlessly.

"I don't think that'll keep him down for long."

"You can't move that shit by yourself," Jerry said, eyeing the tangle of lights and metal. "Hope Sharon won't mind being my bait understudy."

Todd didn't like the idea of leaving a semiconscious Sharon on the stage for Otto, but Jerry was right. While Jerry hustled into the dark wing, Todd laid Sharon down. "We've got you, Sharon. You're going to be all right." He smoothed back the hair from her face, looked over at Otto who still hadn't recovered, and dashed to his friend.

He'd just settled into position when Jerry said, "Looks like tall, dark and ugly is back in the game."

Otto faced the stage. His mouth was a shattered ruin. It looked like he'd tried to mash his malleable flesh back into place. The result was a lower face that had no mouth, just a solid, misshapen lump.

If something was in Otto's mouth that would need to be extracted to stop him, it would be very hard to remove it, if not impossible.

Otto's head jerked when he spotted Sharon.

With his superhuman speed, he sprinted down the aisle and bounded onto the stage. The old flooring cracked and shivered, but held steady.

Jerry nudged Todd with his shoulder. They flexed their grips on the rigging.

Otto didn't waste time going for Sharon. He took two quick strides. His third step found him plummeting through the stage.

"Now!" Todd shouted.

He and Jerry put all of their weight into the rigging. For a terrifying moment, it didn't budge. Letting loose with a primal scream he didn't know he had in him, Todd painfully ground his molars and shoved. The rigging began to move, and then it slid across the stage, wood curling up as the sharp edges cleaved a path. It teetered on the edge of the hole and Todd almost didn't let go in time. At the last second, he pulled his hands away and watched it flip over the edge. It landed with a thunderous crash.

Jerry flashed his light and shouted, "Yeah baby!"

Todd scrambled to the hole's edge and looked down.

"Holy crap, it worked."

Otto lay on his back, the heavy rigging over his chest, tackling him down. He lay there, eyes closed, motionless. His arms were spread wide, the heavy steel bars of the light rig keeping them pinned.

"Is he down there?"

Sharon was sitting up, massaging the back of her head. Jerry wiggled the light over Otto to show her. "He's down."

"But not out," Todd said. He wasn't going to be fooled into thinking Otto was completely incapacitated. He also knew that rigging wouldn't hold him down for long, not after the way he'd witnessed Otto laying waste to the theater seats as if they were made of cheap plastic.

"Shit, what happened to his mouth?" Sharon said.

"Todd got him right in the pie hole. That's Otto's attempt at fixing his face."

Sharon scooted away from the hole. "Or protecting the one thing that can hurt him."

Todd still wasn't fully convinced that Otto was a golem. It wasn't as if any of them were experts on the matter. He could be jumping into that hole to his death if they were wrong.

Then again, he was going to die tonight anyway if they didn't stop Otto.

Jerry swung his legs so they hung into the hole. Todd pulled him away.

"What the hell do you think you're doing?"

"You're not going down there. You're too hurt to get back up if anything goes wrong. I'm going," Todd said.

"Dude, no—"

Todd jumped down, his feet landing on a landslide of debris. His ankle twisted but held and he managed not to fall on top of Otto.

"You okay?" Sharon said.

Todd waved his hand over his head.

As he stared down at the Nazi golem, Todd's flesh wanted to crawl off his bones. Otto was a hideous sight to behold, his face and head resembling a child's failed attempt at sculpture. Todd searched for signs of life, not sure if Otto even needed to breathe to exist and kill.

Every second that passed was a second lost.

Todd dropped down and grabbed hold of the monster's lower jaw. It was like plunging his hand in the waters of a frozen lake. The vile odor coming off the giant in such close quarters had a physical weight to it. It felt like trying to press through a wall of thick, cold molasses to even get close to him.

Holding his breath, Todd plunged his fingers through the solid clay of Otto's mouth. His fingertips brushed against something hard an inch deep.

Teeth.

Otto's teeth were clamped shut.

He tried digging around them, but no matter which way he went, he was eventually met with something hard and unforgiving, as if there were some sort of makeshift bone structure beneath the fetid loam that comprised the killer.

The harder it was to break through, the more he thought Sharon was right. There must be something precious in there for the golem to protect it so well.

"You feel anything?" Jerry called down.

"You don't wanna know," Todd said, turning away from Otto so he could expel his held breath and take another. His eyes watered and his resolve was beginning to flag. Prodding farther and deeper, he desperately sought a way in. The wet, squelching sounds his ministrations made didn't make things any easier.

"Did you find it?" Sharon asked nervously. Her dark hair hung in loose strands around her face as she leaned down to see what he was doing. He worried the wood might give way and send her tumbling.

"I don't even know what I'm supposed to be looking for," he said. His fingers grazed Otto's back molars. He pressed on, hoping to find a jaw hinge. Maybe he could find a way to break it and unlock Otto's mouth.

He wasn't so lucky.

"They teach you anything about golem anatomy?" Todd asked her. As flippant as it sounded, he was looking for anything that could help. He felt like he was running out of time. His head swam from the funk as much as his fraying nerves.

"Let me help you," she said.

"No, stay there. I have an idea."

He pulled his hand out and looked at Otto's face. It was even more of a disaster, thanks to Todd's rooting around.

There has to be a weak spot, he thought. He pictured Ash standing beside him, puzzling out the best way to gain entry in the golem's vault-like mouth.

Otto's neck was thick as a bridge cable. His head was tilted back slightly, the ruin of his chin pointing up.

Go under.

It was as if Ash had whispered in his ear.

Todd angled Otto's head as far back as it would go, exposing his neck and the soft spot under his chin.

A flash of the movie *The Great Escape* – one of his mother's favorites because she loved Charles Bronson – flashed through his mind. Just like Bronson, Todd was going to dig.

Gritting his teeth, he steepled his fingers into a point and jammed both hands in as far as they would go.

To his shock, they pushed easily through the icy matter of the golem's lower jaw. The Nazi had an Achille's throat!

His hands separated within the muck. The fingers of his left hand brushed against something that didn't feel like anything else he'd touched so far.

Otto's eyes opened.

The twin charcoal orbs locked onto Todd. There was no way not to feel the pure animus radiating from that stare.

Todd's left hand punched through the back of the golem's teeth and his mouth sprang open.

Struggling to reclaim the thing his left hand had touched, Todd wasn't fast enough to pull his right hand out before Otto clamped his jaw shut.

The pain skyrocketed up Todd's arm as he watched the tips of two of his fingers roll down the side of Otto's hideous face.

CHAPTER THIRTY-EIGHT

Todd yanked his hand free from Otto's mouth with a loud slurp. His blood splattered over the golem's face. Otto, in turn, opened his mouth wide. Todd wasn't sure whether it was to try for his hand again or drink his blood.

"Get the fuck outta there!" Jerry shouted. He reached down for Todd.

Otto was trying to wriggle free, his eyes a conflagration of hate.

Todd cupped his bloody hand.

My fingers!

He reached down to grab the severed tips but they rolled off Otto's twisting face, hitting the floor and rolling under his head.

"You son of a bitch!" Todd slammed the heel of his boot into Otto's face. For a terrifying moment, he thought he wouldn't be able to pull his foot free. It was like stepping in quicksand. He twisted his leg and it slid out of the newly formed crater.

"Come on, come on!" Sharon screamed. Four hands flailed above him.

Todd's original plan was to pull himself back up, but with only one hand now, it would be too difficult. He reached up for Jerry with his good hand.

"I've got you, buddy," Jerry said, his voice strained as he pulled.

Sharon blurted, "Faster!" She grabbed hold of Todd's bad hand, the pressure opening the floodgates for the pain. The wound on his back from earlier felt as if it had opened, fresh blood warming his flesh. Todd raised a cry that shredded his throat as they attempted to pull him up. Sharon freaked out and let him go. His body sank a few inches back toward the floor.

When he looked down, he saw Otto shedding the light rigging off his body.

"Don't let go of me," Todd said to Jerry.

Jerry was too busy straining to speak. He shot a quick look at Sharon and she recovered, this time getting her hands on the collar of Todd's coat.

Todd heard the clang of metal beneath him. Otto would be rising to his feet so he could rip Todd from their hands. After that, Todd didn't want to contemplate what would happen.

Something hit his feet. Todd kicked furiously.

"Ease up," Jerry said. "I'm losing my grip."

How the hell could he ease up when an undead monster was inches from breaking him in half and tearing him to pieces?

Todd's collar cinched around his neck so tight, it was hard to breathe.

His eyes flicked upward to see Sharon on her feet and in a squat. He ascended rapidly as she tugged on his jacket, and he landed on his stomach on the stage. Suddenly, he felt himself being dragged across the floor. He had to turn his head to avoid having his face shredded from the splintered wood. Jerry and Sharon pulled him off the stage. They landed in an unceremonious lump on the hard ground.

The trio lay in a heap intertwined with one another, panting desperately.

There was no time to recover.

Otto burst from the stage, sending planks of jagged wood in every direction.

A hunk of timber clipped Sharon's shoulder, knocking her down so her face bounced off the ground. Todd covered her with his body while the rest cascaded around them.

A fist punched his back.

"Get her and fucking run!" Jerry said. He was on his knees, facing Otto across the stage.

Todd tried to help Sharon up but his hand slipped free, leaving a swath of fresh blood on her coat. He looked down at his hand and got woozy.

"You're coming with us," Todd said.

Jerry shook his head. "We both know I can't run. Now get out of here while you still can. I'll do what I can to hold him off." He plucked a metal seat leg from the ground. It wouldn't be enough to fend off an angry dog, much less Otto.

"We'll help you," Sharon said. Her eyes were on Otto. Blood trickled from her nose. The freed golem glared at them but didn't move. It was as if Otto was feeding on their terror, reveling in their pleas to save Jerry's life.

Jerry moaned in pain as he got to his feet. "Todd, I love you, brother."

Todd blinked away tears. "Please."

"You're one tough bitch," Jerry said to Sharon. "You take care of my boy and get his ass home." Sharon sucked in her lower lip and nodded. "Now go!"

Sharon jerked Todd's arm. Jerry turned away from them. He said to Otto, "Just you and me, you fugly lump of toe jam. Let's see how you do when you take on someone who's not afraid of you."

Todd's legs stumbled away from Jerry at Sharon's insistence. He kept looking back, his friend in a stare-down with the golem.

Otto hadn't looked their way. His full attention was on Jerry.

"Shalom, you kraut piece of shit!" Jerry taunted. "Fuck the führer!" He gave a Nazi salute, followed by flipping him the bird with both hands.

The stage rumbled as Otto extricated himself from the hole. His intense weight made the wood sag.

"Jerry! No!"

Jerry looked back at Todd and winked.

"We need to run," Sharon hissed.

But Todd couldn't turn away from his friend. He awkwardly walked backward, expecting Sharon to leave him. And he wouldn't blame her.

Otto stomped across the stage. Todd saw what was left of the structure begin to quake.

"Let's go, you Nazi pussy!" Jerry urged him on. The whole thing was about to collapse on top of Otto.

But only if the golem remained on the stage.

Todd cupped his hands around his mouth and yelled, "Stop, Jerry! Stop!"

Jerry spun around. Todd pointed at the swaying walls and ceiling.

Otto came to the lip of the stage.

Jerry threw the hunk of metal at the golem. It plinked off Otto's chest. The crumbling foundation of the theater wailed.

Before Otto could jump off the stage, Jerry started running toward him, his limp momentarily gone. Otto spread his arms wide, waiting to gobble him up and crush him to death. Jerry stepped onto the seat closest to the stage, using it to propel himself right into those arms. His weight knocked Otto backward. They tumbled onto the stage. Todd heard Jerry cry out, and then there was a loud snap that might have been his spine or the cracking of the walls and ceiling.

Todd stared open-mouthed and numb as the remains of the Cosmos Theater rocked to the left, raining dust and debris, before collapsing on top of Jerry and Otto. A cloud of detritus engulfed the ruined mess, boiling across the empty, rusted seats, heading toward Sharon and Todd.

"Get down," Sharon said, pulling him down. They lay on the ground, covering their faces as the cloud of dust washed over them like an incoming wave. The sound of the collapsing theater reminded Todd of old monster movies he loved as a kid, an atomized or prehistoric beast roaring as it fell down a steep valley.

After waiting for the choking dust to pass, Todd picked himself up, coughing into his fist. His eyes stung and his nostrils burned. For all he knew, they were breathing in tiny shredded bits of asbestos and other toxic chemicals that were commonly used in construction back when the Hayden was first built.

"Sweet Jesus."

All the remained upright of the Cosmos Theater was a single jagged shaft of the left wall. It looked like an enormous stalagmite, pointing at the heavens. It was as if a bomb had landed in the center of the stage. The mound of rubble, or what he could make of it behind the dust and darkness, resembled the earthworks seen in an active quarry.

Underneath it all was Jerry.

Todd felt the ground slip out from underneath his feet. He was about to fall when Sharon grabbed hold of his arm and his belt.

"I'm so sorry," she said.

Todd wiped the grit from his eyes.

"We have to go," Sharon said. "Otto's not coming back from that."

"I've lost...everyone."

She stepped in front of him so they were eye to eye. "Yes, but you're still here. And I'm here. And that murdering thing is buried for good. It's not going to bring any of them back, but at least they'll be the last. That has to count for something."

A lone tear sprang from Sharon's eye.

She said, "Ash and Sheri would be proud of us."

Todd pulled Sharon close and hugged her, his cheek resting on the top of her head, but his eyes were on Otto's burial mound.

CHAPTER THIRTY-NINE

They stood there for a while, holding one another, watching the pile of debris shift and settle. The wind picked up, biting through their clothes and stabbing their marrow, but they were too exhausted to even shiver.

"Everyone in town had to hear that," Sharon said.

"I know."

"They'll be coming soon."

"I know."

"Do we meet them at the gate?"

Todd stepped away and brushed the dirt off Sharon's shoulders. "No. You go find my car and get home." He handed her his keys. "I'll take it from here."

"You want me to just walk away?"

The wind blew her hair into her face.

"You have to. There's going to be a lot of questions after this. Whoever's left behind will be a suspect. Those are my friends out there. Even if I went with you, it would all point back to me. I might as well face the music now."

Sharon stuffed her hands in her coat pockets. "But what will you say to them?" She took out a glove. "Give me your hand."

Through it all, Todd had forgotten about his missing fingertips. His hand throbbed, but the sharp pain had ebbed. She wrapped her glove around the two fingers, the white fabric instantly reddening.

Todd shrugged. "I don't know. The truth? That would land me in the nut house for sure. Not that it would be such a bad thing." He tried to think of his future and could only see darkness and regret. Maybe a life on Thorazine would help him forget.

Forget it all.

But not Ash! I wouldn't want to live if I couldn't have my memories of Ash.

He cupped Sharon's face. "I'll think of something."

"You're in no condition to spell your name right now."

"True. Maybe I'll just give them the shocked silent treatment until I come up with a story that doesn't sound like science fiction. Honestly, I'm too damn tired to talk, so that won't be so hard."

Dawn would be breaking very soon. Something cold and wet landed on his cheek. He would have ignored it if it wasn't followed by more on his head, face and neck. He shone his flashlight into the sky.

"Snow," he said. "Winter was always Ash's favorite season. We used to talk about moving to Vermont someday. She really wanted to learn how to ski."

Fat flakes lazily drifted from the clouds.

Sharon pulled up her collar. "My sister was a total beach bum. She wouldn't even wear sunscreen in the summer, like she thought just because she was black, she couldn't get skin cancer. I remember learning about skin cancer in sixth grade health class and crying my eyes out when Sheri refused to protect herself."

Todd tilted his face into the snow. "That's the problem with loving someone. Sooner or later, you realize that no matter what you do, you can't protect them. Not all the time. And it only takes that one time to tear your heart in two."

He told her how to get to his car, but she only seemed to be half listening. Part of him knew that Sharon was right in that he should be waiting at the front gate for the next round of responders to arrive. But he couldn't bring himself to walk through that field of severed heads. So they would just have to come to him. It was better that way. He wasn't sure if he could depend on his weary legs to get him anywhere at this point. Maybe, if he was lucky, there'd be enough time to simply sit down and freeze to death, like Nicholson in *The Shining*. There were far worse ways to go. Otto had shown him that in horrifying Technicolor.

"I really don't think I should leave you," Sharon said. "If you have to try to explain this alone, they're not going to buy it."

"I'll tell them the Wraith came back. Or he never left. It isn't the first time he's killed."

She grabbed onto his upper arms and shook him. "Yes, but what if they decide you were the Wraith all along? You did know everyone that's been murdered here five years ago and tonight. Pinning the blame on you will be a lot easier than digging up Otto and trying to explain that."

An electric shock ran down Todd's spine. "They can't dig him up."

"So you're just going to leave Jerry down there? Otto will either be in pieces or squashed flat. Todd, he's not coming back from that. I promise."

He took a few tentative steps toward the remains of the theater. "But we didn't get that thing from his mouth."

"In a head that's flatter than a dollar bill. Not to mention, we don't know if I was talking out of my ass."

"I felt something in there. I think you were right."

Jerry's sarcastic voice floated through his brain, several comebacks about strippers and dollar bills on his ethereal lips. It almost made Todd smile.

"But we don't really know that, do we? I mean, we can't be sure at all."

Sharon was about to respond, but then closed her mouth and thought for a bit. "After everything we've seen tonight, we'd be foolish to think that the normal rules apply here. I'll give you that. But my money is on that Nazi fucker never getting out of there. And someday, he'll be carted up with the rest of the trash and thrown in a landfill or sent out to sea where he belongs. With or without the thing that was placed in his mouth and gave him life. You know what I'm saying?"

Logically, he fully understood her.

But logic had no place in the Hayden.

"I have to know."

He headed for the mound.

"Are you crazy? Todd, get back here!"

"I have to know. Just go!"

Reinforcements should be there soon. He wondered how much time he'd have to dig for Otto's remains. Of course, they would be preoccupied with the slain cops and firemen at the entrance. That would buy him some time. This whole night seemed to be about buying time – time that was never properly given to them. As he got closer to the still-smoking heap, he realized there might never be enough time to get through the giant pile with nothing but his bare hands.

Not that it would stop him from trying.

If he walked away without knowing, it would be like Ash setting aside a crossword without finishing it. The mystery would still be unsolved. They might never know Otto's origins, but Todd would settle for knowing the golem would never have a future, other than living in his and Sharon's tortured memories.

He scrabbled up the small mountain of detritus, grabbed hold of a hunk of wood and tossed it over his shoulder.

"Hey, you almost hit me!"

"I thought I told you to leave."

Sharon crossed her arms over her chest. "Do I come across as someone who takes orders from anyone?"

Todd sighed and shook his head. "What little strength I have left I need to dig. I don't have it in me to fight you."

She carefully climbed through the uneven debris, her arms outstretched to keep her balance. "Good. Because I'm not in the mood to fight."

There were a thousand things he could have said, *should* have said, but it wouldn't have mattered. They were in this together. They had been for over five years and just hadn't realized it.

"If they're anywhere, I think it's here," Todd said, surveying the damage. He couldn't stop coughing. His lungs felt like they were filled with tiny tacks.

Sharon kicked a hunk of brick. "I hope you're right." She worked at the spot by her feet with her boot, her heel coming in contact with a board that had been sheared in half. "Looks like this is the closest thing we'll have to a shovel."

Todd hunkered down to his knees. The mound shifted and he worried it would open up like a sinkhole and drag them under. "You use that. I've got these." He flashed his hands. "Don't want you to break a nail."

She jammed the board into the scrap and chucked it down the side of the mound. "Honey, it'll take months to get these nails back in shape. Good thing people don't pay to see my hands."

They worked with their backs to one another. Todd scooped the refuse with both hands and lobbed it under his legs and away from them. At first, his wounded fingers would feel like they'd touched live wires, but eventually everything went numb. Fresh cuts opened on both hands like red, hungry mouths. He kept on digging, despite knowing it was like finding a needle in a haystack.

What if he found Jerry first? Would the sight of his friend's broken body be the point of no return for him? He liked to think he wasn't inured to death. Even the toughest, most jaded people had their limits.

"You know this is crazy, right?" Sharon said, huffing and coughing. "Normal people would already be on the road by now, heading home to a bottle of whatever will make the pain go away so they can sleep."

"I don't think we can ever call ourselves normal people again."

"Not sure I did consider myself normal. At least since Sheri died." She used the wood to scrape away the top layer, working her way down. "You think they know?"

Todd coughed and spit over his shoulder. "Who?"

"Sheri and Ash. You think they can see what we did tonight?"

His chest seized and he had to stop for a moment. "I really...I really don't know. I'm not a religious person, so I don't go for all that heaven and hell nonsense. But I like to think a part of us lives on." More so since Ash's death. Hope that she might be somewhere waiting for him was what kept him going.

"I used to. Believe, I mean. The year after Sheri died, I went to church every single day. I was so worried about her soul being trapped here, I prayed to God that he would take her under his wing. I know it sounds corny."

Todd found a piece of rebar and pulled. A puff of dust exploded in his face as a hunk of drywall came up. He whipped his head away so as not to breathe it all in. "Actually, I think it's kinda beautiful."

Sharon hacked away with the wood. "I was all in for it. That's until I found out a couple of my regulars were so-called men of the cloth."

"Maybe they were there to convert you. Save your soul."

Todd thought he detected sirens in the far distance. They'd made so little progress. It made him sick to think he'd be carted out of the Hayden without being able to confirm that Otto had been destroyed.

"The only thing they converted was dollars into dances." Sharon made a half grin. Todd couldn't help smiling back.

"The world's a fucked-up place," he said. "After tonight, I don't think we'll ever need further proof of that."

"Amen, brother."

The raw ends of his severed fingers scraped against something sharp and jagged. The pain cut through his deadened nerves, forcing him to dig with one hand, the other tucked under his armpit until it recovered.

Sharon stopped shoveling. "You hear that?"

"They'll be here any minute."

They stared down at the giant burial mound, looked at one another, and doubled up their efforts. The snow intensified, making it harder to grip things. It was getting harder to see their progress, any cleared gap filled by slick powder. Todd's blood peppered the freshly fallen snow.

All sense of time was lost. Neither noticed the lightening of the skies, nor did they hear the sirens as they pulled up to the Hayden's main gate. Todd didn't realize he'd been crying until the salt of his tears slipped into his mouth. The despair that he wasn't going to find Otto amidst the ruins nearly locked his muscles. He fought through it, but it was getting harder to stand on his own two feet.

He wanted to tell Sharon that yes, Ash and Sheri were with them at this very moment, giving them strength, just as he and Sharon had given them closure. Did closure matter to the dead? Or was it just a construct for the living, something to strive for when nothing made sense?

"Stop and put your hands above your head!"

Thinking the voice was something he imagined, Todd kept on digging. He heard the *plunk* of wood next to him, but didn't turn around.

"I'm talking to you, asshole! Stop right now and do what I tell you!"

"Todd," Sharon said.

He paused, looking over at her. Sharon's eyes were fixed on something behind him, at the base of the mound.

He was shocked that he could see the pair of cops with their guns drawn. The snow beat at their faces, but they didn't so much as blink. They looked mad enough to chew through a steel girder.

"Your hands up, now!" the other cop shouted with spittle flying out of his mouth.

"Better do what they say," Sharon said. Her hands were held up as high as they could go over her head. "They look like they're more than happy to have an excuse to shoot."

Todd's head slumped into his chest. Of course they would be. They had to have seen the bodies. Now here were two prime suspects, one of them appearing not to give a shit. He raised his arms, the muscles in his shoulders on fire.

"Now come down to us, slowly."

Todd went first. If one of them got trigger-happy, he wanted to keep in front of Sharon.

"That's it. Slower."

Todd's heel stepped on something that gave way and he fell, sliding most of the way down. The way the cops reacted, he thought for sure they were going to empty their guns in him. One of the cops rushed over, grabbed him by the collar and yanked him forward until his face was in the snow and a knee was in his back. He heard Sharon's short squeal and knew the other one had done the same to her.

"Man, I really wish you'd tried to run," the cop hissed in Todd's ear. It was hard to breathe with the cop's full weight on his back. His arms were jerked back and he yowled in agony as the cop tried to grab his wrist and got his wounded fingers instead. "Looks like someone got a piece of this one," he said to his partner.

"Yeah, but not nearly enough."

"We didn't do it," Sharon protested. Todd heard the rush of air expelled from her lungs as she was either punched or had the cop press her farther into the ground.

"Save it for your lawyer. Hope you can't afford a good one and get some greenie right outta law school."

Todd didn't say anything because he knew there was nothing he could say that they would believe. Not that he could draw enough air to speak.

Handcuffs clinked behind him, the cold metal wrapping around his right wrist, cinching so tight he thought his bones might break.

With his face numb in the snow, lungs so constricted he was close to passing out, all he could think was, *I'm sorry I failed, Ash. I'm so sorry.*

He thought he could hear the unearthly rumble of Otto's laughter from deep in the mound behind them.

CHAPTER FORTY

"You're making a mistake," Sharon bleated. "Ow. You're hurting me."

"You're lucky that's all I'm doing."

Todd drew what breath he could and shouted, "Leave her alone. It's me you want."

A punch to the back of his head was his only reply. The cop fought for control of Todd's left arm. Todd's vision swam. Sharon sounded like she was putting up a struggle.

Something shifted behind them. Todd felt it in his chest that was pressed to the snowy ground more than he heard it.

Dear God, no!

He tried to shift to his side and throw the cop off his back. It was like trying to move a mountain with a teaspoon. The cop hit him with a sharp jab to his ribs.

"You don't understand," Todd gasped.

"I think I do," the cop said, wrestling with Todd's free arm. "It's you and your girlfriend who don't have a fucking clue."

"We didn't kill them."

"Which is what every killer has said to every cop when they got busted. Now shut the fuck up and stay still." More pressure was applied to the small of Todd's back and arm. It felt as if his shoulder was going to slip out of its socket.

"Gungh!"

Hot rain showered the back of Todd's neck.

The heavy weight on his back instantly went away.

Todd looked at the snow around his head. It was red as Sunday gravy.

He managed to spin around, sit up and scrabble backward at the same time. A shard of wood poked out of the cop's neck. Bloody froth bubbled from his lips as he gurgled his last, his hands prodding at the thick splinter protruding from his throat. He fell forward, the impact nearly driving the wood out the back of his neck.

Otto stood over Todd, his clothes in tatters, the general shape of him bent into impossible dents and angles. He defied the laws of physics just being able to stand, much less kill a man.

The other cop sprang off Sharon. He shot the golem.

Otto twisted around, his bent and broken arms swinging at his sides.

"What the fuck?" the cop muttered. He backed away from Sharon, firing round after round into Otto's chest. The bullets were absorbed into his earthen flesh with no effect.

Sharon crawled out of Otto's path as he lashed out at the cop, clipping his jaw and sending him reeling. His gun fell into the snow. Sharon grabbed it and ran to Todd.

Todd could barely stand. Fear was the only thing keeping him upright. Fear and a last chance to end Otto's reign of terror.

"Get away from me," the cop wailed.

Otto plucked two cinder blocks from the snow. The cop turned to run. Otto smashed his head between the blocks. His skull crunched and his brains exploded skyward. Todd and Sharon watched the cop's body take several uneven steps before it collapsed, headless, into the blood and brain-soaked snow.

"The gun," Sharon said, nodding toward the cop who had tried to cuff Todd. He unsnapped the holster and drew out the weapon.

Otto tossed the cinder blocks aside, turned and stared at them. No matter how misshapen his head, his facial features mashed and blurred, those onyx eyes still drove daggers of ice into their hearts. They were eyes colder than the grave.

Sharon also slipped the cop's nightstick out.

"You know what to do," Todd said, so close to Sharon, their shoulders touched.

"And I'm dying to do it."

They pulled their triggers simultaneously. Otto's head reared back, the bullets catching him square in the face. Twin runnels ran deep into the area where his mouth should be.

Otto's shoulders heaved. He started to run toward them.

They opened fire again. Otto fell to his knees with his face in his hands.

"Don't stop," Todd said, stepping forward and shooting Otto's hand, hoping the bullet passed through and buried itself in his face. Sharon did the same. Otto's hands fell to his sides. This time, they had a clear shot at his mouth, and were only five feet away. Todd squeezed the trigger over and over. Sharon's gun emptied first. Todd grew emboldened as chunks of Otto's face blew away, revealing his horrid, yellow teeth, the top row shattering and his lower jaw coming unhinged.

Todd saw it first.

A tan slip of paper was jammed in the ruined mess of Otto's mouth.

He pointed.

Sharon flew into the wounded golem, bashing at him with the nightstick. A step behind, Todd lunged at him as well, wrapping his arms around his foul-smelling midsection.

Using the nightstick as a tongue depressor, Sharon jammed it as far as it would go in the golem's mouth. She reached in, fingers slipping in the muddy grime, the paper seeming to sink farther inside, like a vampire retracting from the sun.

Todd felt Otto's weakening body stiffen. The golem's arm lashed out, finding a curved wedge of metal, presumably a part of one of the destroyed theater seats. Otto drove the metal into Sharon's side. She screamed in a mix of rage and agony, reaching deeper into his mouth.

Leaping to the other side of the golem, Todd grabbed hold of his arm, preventing him from driving the metal any deeper. Blood spurted from Sharon's pierced side. Still, she fought, using both hands to tear at his face, the nightstick lodged firmly in his mouth.

"Give...it...to...me!" Sharon screeched.

Otto's head suddenly reared back. He emitted a sound that was unlike anything Todd had ever heard. It was like the collective sound of every animal in a zoo being tortured at the same time.

Sharon fell backward, her hands steaming. Todd caught her before she hit the ground. The end of the metal shaft in her side pricked the raw stumps of his fingers.

Otto's horrendous wailing stopped suddenly. His head craned

forward, his evil eyes on them. Todd cradled Sharon in his lap. There was no way he could get her safely away from the unstoppable beast. The best he could do was wrap his arms around her chest and let her know she wouldn't die alone.

The golem tried to stand and failed.

Sharon chuckled at the sight.

Todd said to her, "I won't leave you."

She looked up at him, her eyes glassing over. "That's good."

When she raised her hand to him, she smiled. Her fingers unfurled. The folded slip of paper, encrusted with dirt and other filth, sat in the palm of her hand. In her other was the Nazi iron cross. "Maybe Bill was right. The cross is cursed. Wherever it goes, so does Otto. We...we need to get rid of it. Throw it in the goddamn ocean." It slipped from her fingers. When Todd picked up the cross, the tips of his fingers tingled. Was it just his imagination, or did it feel as if the hunk of metal was being drawn to the stunned golem?

They watched Otto begin to crumble apart. His head caved in, his chest breaking into pieces. When his neck exploded outward, Otto's head fell into the disintegrating cavity that was his chest. His arms became worthless clods of dirt, his legs two lines of fetid soil.

It only took seconds for the Nazi beast to deteriorate entirely. When it was done, all that was left were the few scraps of clothing that had clung to his frame, the fabric disappearing in the squall of snow.

Sharon rested her head on Todd's chest. Her breathing was wet and labored.

"Looks like you can give Ash a break now," she said, her voice weak and thin.

He leaned over her to keep the snow from her face.

"What do you mean?"

She reached up and touched his chin, her fingers colder than icicles. "Looks like you're the final guy now."

Her eyes fluttered and closed.

Footsteps crunched in the snow behind them. Todd saw the police approaching. There were five in all, their guns at the ready. They saw their dead brothers first, and then Sharon. Todd laid her gently down and raised his hands. He didn't have time to get to his feet before they opened fire.

A bullet hit the iron cross in his hand, sending it spinning into the darkness where it plowed into the newly fallen snow and was quickly covered up.

Todd's world went from white to black an instant later.

EPILOGUE

No matter how many times she came here, she was always nervous. She couldn't sleep the night before, tossing and turning until she decided to throw in the towel around three in the morning. She tried reading a book but couldn't get past the first page, having to reread it so often she eventually tossed it aside. Everything on television was either an infomercial or a movie she'd seen a dozen times.

She passed the time until sunup rearranging her kitchen cabinets, pulling everything out, looking at expiration dates on the canned food and boxes of pasta and rice. She washed every glass and dish, tossing out a dusty mug she'd picked up on a trip to Cape May during the summer of her high school graduation. The radio was on low the entire time, more white noise than a needed distraction or entertainment.

By six she was in the shower, doing such a terrible job at shaving her legs she worried she might bleed to death. Her fingers lingered on the old scar on her side, slipping over the raised ridge of flesh. She refused to look at it in the mirror. Touching it was bad enough. Sometimes she caught its reflection in the mirror by accident – black, puckered and angry. Plastic surgery would make most of it disappear, but she wasn't a Beverly Hills housewife with money to toss around on cosmetic procedures. It wasn't a thing of life or death. It was simply something she preferred not to see. And it wasn't as if she was going to give anyone else a chance to see it, anyway.

It was also a reminder.

When things felt like they were going to spiral out of control, or worry about bills and breaking cars and what her future would be would threaten to paralyze her, all she would have to do was reach under her shirt and feel it. The scar grounded her. It kept her sane.

She hit the road early, opting for the scenic route and bypassing the parkway. There was a diner that she would stop at from time to time and today she was hungry. The special was a short stack of pancakes, two links of sausage and eggs any way you liked them. It felt good to eat. To really eat. The days of starving herself to stop the march of cellulite or the slightest puffing of her belly were all behind her now. She tucked into the hot pancakes, drizzling them with soft butter and warm maple syrup. She dipped the sausages in her over easy eggs, washing it all down with strong black coffee.

Back in the car, she listened to talk radio because music didn't seem appropriate. The day was chilly, the skies gray as slate, low clouds making the world seem so much smaller.

There was no hurry. She'd get there in time. She always did.

As she passed by the big green sign to the exit, her heart thundered. This was where it always got worse.

Her friends told her to stop doing this to herself. What was the point? In their eyes, she was only hurting herself, and there had been enough hurt in her twenty-four years to last two lifetimes.

They couldn't understand and she would never try to make them. Life was too short to linger on the impossible.

She pulled up to the front gates and swallowed hard, her bowels loosening just a bit, as they always did. Gripping the wheel until her knuckles whitened, she pressed the brake pedal all the way to the floor, the tension in her leg turning it to stone.

"Here we go."

She drove through, winding up the hill, the wind buffeting the car, the old shocks groaning.

God, she hated this bleak gray place.

Getting out of the car didn't come without effort. She locked the door, turned her collar up against the biting wind.

Today was worse than the other times because....

Because it felt just like that night.

She looked up at the newly erected sign, wondering why it was even necessary. Everyone knew what this was the moment they laid eyes upon it.

FISHKILL CORRECTIONAL FACILITY

"I'll be back soon," she said to the mangy black cat in the carrier she'd belted into the passenger seat. Elvira, curled in a ball within the soft blanket, opened one eye and blinked. It was as good an acknowledgment as she was going to get. She opened the front cage door and ruffled between the cat's ears. Elvira purred and closed her eyes and went back to sleep.

Sharon Viola went through the usual questions and indignities that came with visiting anyone in the maximum-security wing. This was where the fluttering nerves turned to anger. She was much more comfortable with anger.

She was shown to a seat within a small cubicle, webbing of steel in the glass before her.

Minutes later, Todd came shuffling in. He was pale, drawn, having lost almost half his body weight since the multiple surgeries to save his life. The gunshots had left him with a bad limp, bent over like an old man, his left arm close to useless and his speech, which he had to relearn to do, slurred and wandering.

A guard guided him into the chair, lifted the phone and put it in his good hand, the hand missing his fingertips. When he saw her, the cloud of fog and death in his eyes cleared.

"Sssharon."

It broke her heart every time. Todd had officially died that night, and had been revived, his soul deposited in this broken vessel.

A bit of Sharon died each time she saw him, and came back to life when she saw that flicker in his eyes. He'd promised he'd never leave her when he thought Otto was going to kill them. Now it was her turn to never leave him.

Sharon smiled and put her hand to the glass. She had the Hebrew letters for *aleph, mem* and *tav* tattooed on her palm. They were the letters written on the paper in the golem's mouth.

"Todd."

He let the phone slip from his ear and put his palm to hers.

They wept as they smiled.

* ★ *

Tabitha hated living at the Dunwoody. The luxury living community had way too many rules.

Don't ride your bike on the sidewalk.
You can't draw with chalk on the ground.
No diving in the pool.
You can't leave your scooter anywhere but in the assigned bike/scooter rack by the front of the property.
No kids under fourteen allowed in the game room unless they have an adult with them.
No bouncing a ball or running in the apartment after eight pm.
No-no-no-no-no!

It was so much better when they had their own house in Saugerties. Back home, there were woods to play in, pools to hop and so many places to ride her bike with her friends. They had the run of the neighborhood. She could stomp all night long with her friends if she wanted to because the only thing below them was the furnace, and not that crab-ass Mrs. Detweiler.

Her parents had never adequately explained why they had to move here to this cramped apartment. She knew it was because they thought she was too young to fully understand. Just because she was young didn't mean she was stupid.

She'd just been kicked out of the pool by the property manager because she was caught running. What was she supposed to do when that ugly Bill Weaver was chasing her with a live worm?

Pissed at Bill and the manager, she'd stormed home and hatched a plan.

Kids – and adults – weren't allowed to dig holes anywhere on the property.

Grabbing her mother's gardening spade (you could have potted plants on your patio), she set out for the tucked-away corner behind building eight. She was going to dig a hole where no one could see her. And she wouldn't fill it up either. Let them find the hole and send out another one of their stupid emails reminding people of their stupid rules.

She tucked her hair behind her ears, dropped to her knees, looked around to make sure no adults were nearby, and got to work.

Now, she knew you couldn't dig a hole to China, but she wished she could tunnel her way to her house in Saugerties.

But this wasn't about escape. It was about rebellion.

She dug and dug, her sweat dripping off the tip of her nose and into the widening hole.

The pointed end of the spade hit something soft and squishy. The ensuing smell made her jump away from the hole.

"Eeeeewww! That's nasty."

Had dogs been digging here and hiding their poo? It sure smelled like it.

Tabitha pinched her nose shut and crept back toward the open maw of the hole. The smell was so bad it painted her tongue and slipped down her throat and into her stomach.

What the heck was down there?

Never one to contain her curiosity, Tabitha reached into the hole. The tips of her fingers slipped into dirt that was colder than the inside of her freezer.

Weird, but cool.

She touched on something hard and oddly shaped. It definitely wasn't a rock or a root. Pinching it between her thumb and forefinger, she pried it out of the mushy ground.

"Oh wow!"

It was jewelry. From the looks of it, some kind of antique. Tabitha rubbed the dirt off with the edge of her shirt. It was a cross. And a big one too. Not like the little crucifix her mother wore on the thin chain around her neck when they went to church. This cross didn't have a battered Jesus on it, which made it so much cooler. The last thing Tabitha ever needed to see was a naked man impaled on two blocks of wood, even if he was the son of God. That didn't make it any less creepy. She wasn't allowed to watch scary movies, but she was forced to stare at a dying Jesus above the altar every Sunday. She couldn't tell a big person the meaning of the word *hypocrite*, but she intrinsically knew the concept.

"Maybe there's more."

Setting the cross into the grass, she pushed her hand farther into the muck, twisting her head to the side so she could breathe through her mouth and not puke.

Something shifted under her hand.

Tabitha's hand was swallowed up to her wrist.

She yelped and tried to pull her hand back.

What felt like sharp stones nipped at her fingers. The tears came before the pitiable wail.

No matter how hard she tried, the frozen earth wouldn't let her go.

FLAME TREE PRESS
FICTION WITHOUT FRONTIERS
Award-Winning Authors & Original Voices

Flame Tree Press is the trade fiction imprint of Flame Tree Publishing, focusing on excellent writing in horror and the supernatural, crime and mystery, science fiction and fantasy. Our aim is to explore beyond the boundaries of the everyday, with tales from both award-winning authors and original voices.

·

Other titles by Hunter Shea:
Creature
Ghost Mine

Other horror titles available include:
Thirteen Days by Sunset Beach by Ramsey Campbell
Think Yourself Lucky by Ramsey Campbell
The Hungry Moon by Ramsey Campbell
The Influence by Ramsey Campbell
The Haunting of Henderson Close by Catherine Cavendish
The House by the Cemetery by John Everson
The Devil's Equinox by John Everson
The Toy Thief by D.W. Gillespie
One By One by D.W. Gillespie
Black Wings by Megan Hart
The Playing Card Killer by Russell James
The Siren and the Specter by Jonathan Janz
The Sorrows by Jonathan Janz
Castle of Sorrows by Jonathan Janz
The Dark Game by Jonathan Janz
House of Skin by Jonathan Janz
Dust Devils by Jonathan Janz
The Darkest Lullaby by Jonathan Janz
Will Haunt You by Brian Kirk
Hearthstone Cottage by Frazer Lee
Those Who Came Before by J.H. Moncrieff
Stoker's Wilde by Steven Hopstaken & Melissa Prusi
The Mouth of the Dark by Tim Waggoner
They Kill by Tim Waggoner

·

Join our mailing list for free short stories, new release details, news about our authors and special promotions:

flametreepress.com